Bessie
Lost & Found

Jody Overend

♣

Illustration by: Patrizia Morena Di Sciascio

Published by:

FriesenPress

Suite 300 - 852 Fort Street
Victoria, BC, Canada V8W 1H8

www.friesenpress.com

Distributed to the trade by The Ingram Book Company

Dedication

For our beautiful Nancy Ann, now shopping at the Seventh Heaven Mall. Nonnie, our sister bond is alive and well.

My Heartfelt Thank Yous

Without you, Joanne Sicard, I would never have received the messages I needed to hear from the Other Side, guiding me through this process. You once told me that you were only the messenger. But without the messenger, there is no message. Visit Joanne at: www.mediumsoulchoice.com

If a picture is worth a thousand words, then Patti, your illustration of Bessie is worth an infinity. To connect with this gifted artist, visit: www.pattidisciascio.com or email: pattidee@rogers.com.

Charlie Tessaro, not only are you my wonderful, seafaring husband but my anchor. And thank you, nephew Peter, for your very fine photo.

"Row, row, row your boat,
Gently down the stream,
Merrily, merrily, merrily, merrily,
Life is but a dream."

Children's song, author unknown

CHAPTER 1: HEAVEN

At fifteen years and one month, Bessie MacIntyre isn't what you would call pretty. She's far too interesting for that. Lying back on the grassy hillside peppered with wildflowers, she pillows her head on her arms. Her eyes close, dream-like. A warm breeze lifts her pale red bangs, revealing an inch-long scar over her left eyebrow in the shape of a small bird. From somewhere behind her, a fluttery voice materializes. "Bess, where'd you go? Bess!"

Bessie turns her head to catch the familiar lilt. Hunching up on her elbows, she looks back up the hill from where she has just been. In the distance a school bell rings. She ignores it, starting to giggle.

"Bess? You over here?" The girly-girl voice is attached, finally, to a stunning beauty of mixed heritage. Lean as a stick, her poodley hair flowers six inches from her movie starlet makeup glowing on a copper complexion. She stumbles over the hilltop in one lime green platform, carrying the other. Plopping down beside Bessie, she tosses the broken footwear on the grass. "Stupid ass shoe, anyway."

"Ash, focus. How many deaths will there be this flight from, say, traffic accidents?" Bessie picks up a blade of grass to chew. "Guess how many accidents, not how many dead people."

Ash leans back, her elegant hands displaying a remarkable color of lemon-orange nail polish, complete with rhinestones. "Just this next flight coming? Okay, I say thirty-forty car wrecks, maybe three trucks ... Does a bicycle count as a vehicle? One bus and ... my feet hurt."

The school bell rings again with neither girl acknowledging it, evidently a time-honored tradition. Ash leans forward to rub the toes of her left foot before stretching her leg back out. Pulling two cans of Hector's Nectar from her giant shoulder bag, she snaps the tabs, handing one to Bessie. "Then there's the suicides. Murders, of course."

"Don't forget the obvious." Bessie takes a long gulp, turning to her friend, smiling. They stare into each other's eyes and chime in unison, "War."

The girls, still slurping their sodas, gaze out over the lush hillsides spreading out around the airport in the valley below. The word "airport" is somewhat of a misnomer. The building resembles more of an open-air platform. Without walls, the pine-beamed floor on four corner posts boasts a cedar shingled, peaked roof. At the rear, away from the girls, a crystal door suspends in mid-air, glowing with a colorless aura. On the roof peak, an impressive crystal tower houses a magnificent golden bell. In front, a carved plaque on chains above an arched doorway modestly announces: HEAVEN INTERPORTAL.

Gardens of extraordinary beauty surround the platform like a flowery hug. Winding away from the front and sides, small flagstone walkways bordered in stout hedges, thread through the valley up into the surrounding hills.

As the girls creep towards their usual hiding place behind a particular hedge running horizontally about halfway down, clusters of spirit people stream along the walkways to join an excited crowd gathering at the front of the airport. They look very much like their former Earthly selves, except for their air of weightlessness and ageless incandescence. And like Bessie and Ash, they cast no shadows.

Angels materialize amongst the crowd, some in their spiffy, powder blue Air Heaven uniforms, and others in regular street clothes. Unlike all other beings in Heaven, angels are distinguished by their glitter-like, silvery auras that sparkle and glow in any light.

Still moving in a crouched position, Bessie hisses at Ash behind her. "News flash. Over there to your left. Angel Mel."

Huge and bald, dressed in jeans, sandals, and his constant Hawaiian shirt over a rotund belly, Angel Mel clasps a half-inch wad of typed paper held precariously together with two brass fasteners top and bottom. Talking full-blast on his cell, his voice booms so loudly, it carries up to the girls. "Yeah, so I'm gonna channel it tomorrow to Goldie Hawn during her yoga session. She'll love it, I tell ya. Lo-vah it."

He listens for a bit. "What's that? Oh, I call it *A Bouquet of Reincarnations*, ha ha. Get it? Pretty on-the-pulse, if I do say so myself. Which I just did ha ha."

"Such a goof." Bessie pushes her hair out of her eyes as she searches for their special spot, a little space they carved out inside the hedge. She lifts a branch to hold it up for Ash to squeeze in first.

The bell in the steeple begins to swing in slow motion, ringing seven distinct times. As the spectators watch, a huge, white, jet-like cloud moves swiftly across the sky towards the rear of the airport, as the massive crystal door slowly opens wide.

"Gotta run," Angel Mel shouts into his phone. "For whom the bell tolls ha ha." He shoves it into his pocket and turns his attention to the docking plane.

The jet-cloud hovers in place overhead while a hatch at the front of the aircraft swings open, spilling out a white staircase which attaches to the sacred opening of the crystal door.

A pilot angel emerges from the plane first, spectacularly handsome in his white and gold Air Heaven uniform. "Last stop, Heaven!" He announces cheerfully. Under his breath, he murmurs, "And you can thank the good Lord for that."

He ducks back inside, allowing a frail, elderly woman to step onto the staircase. She shakes the hand of an unseen flight attendant inside the plane before making her way smartly down the steps, clutching her purse to her chest.

As she steps through the entrance onto the platform, a ground crew angel - his name-tag identifies him as Angel Stewart - approaches her. "Linda, welcome home. Long time, no see." He tucks her arm through his and together they stroll towards the waiting crowds. Before releasing her, he gives her a warm hug, creating a rosy glow that envelops them both. She now looks the essence of healthy, ageless radiance.

"Thank you, Stewart, dear." Linda grins fondly as she holds his hands in both of hers, facing him. "Let's see, it's been, what ... ninety-six years and five days!" She looks around. "Where's Howard?"

From behind the hedge, Ash whispers, "Natural causes?"

Bessie nods. "Agreed. Died in her sleep."

Meanwhile Angel Stewart directs Linda's attention to a tall, bow-legged man waving a bouquet of yellow roses wildly in the air outside the front arch. "There he is. Can't wait to see you. How long has it been?"

"Thirty-three years and fifteen days since he walked in front of that ice-cream truck, the big, stupid dummy." She gives Angel Stewart a farewell peck and walks briskly out the floral arch into the waiting arms of Howard. He hugs and kisses her like he'll never let her go. At last he takes her hand as they begin to stroll along an uphill pathway, mumbling, "I know, I know. Should of been more careful. I know, I know."

She stops for a moment to punch him in the shoulder. "I've missed you all these years, for what? A banana split."

"Ouwww!" Howard rubs his arm. "Strawberry sundae." He grins at her, flirting like a schoolboy. "Hey, Lindy, know what else I've missed?"

As more transitioning souls descend the staircase to enter Heaven Interportal, Ash and Bessie focus silently on the parade of newly dead humanity. They appear in all ages and nationalities, all manners of death. Some look peaceful, others highly agitated.

A grouping of dark-skinned children, emaciated beyond imagining, huddle near the base of the staircase, shuffling their feet, their arms clutched around their torsos, fearful of what the next moment will bring. Several angels rush towards them with open palms. A slight hope flickers on the children's faces. Anything is better than where they've been.

Outside a man of impressive height and equally dark skin rushes to the front of the milling crowd, shouting, "Milata, Gibral! Daddy is here! Mama is here! All your families is here!"

One by one the angels envelop the little ones in healing hugs. Once released, the children, newly restored to glowing health, race through the archway to be scooped up by their joyful family members.

Tears dribble down Bessie's cheeks as she turns away. "I miss my …"

Ash lays her arm around her friend's shoulder, mascara dripping in lines of navy blue. "Me, too."

A commotion draws their attention back to the Arrivals area. A group of soldiers, dazed and confused, riddled with bullet holes and missing limbs, crowd together, staring at another group of soldiers across the platform. It's evident by their mode of dress they're from opposite sides of the same conflict.

Ash and Bessie turn to share a look. Bessie pipes up, "You guess first."

Ash gives her an eye roll. "Middle East. Where else?"

As they watch, angels greet each soldier, giving them hugs. In the rosy glow created, the warriors return to their youthful, pre-death images. The two groups stare at each other, reality sinking in.

A few feet away, an Air Heaven angel with a checklist outside the airport turns to her companion. "War *is* hell. When on Earth are they going to figure that out?"

Back behind the hedge, Bessie absentmindedly rubs her forehead scar, staring at the spectacle. "Hey Ash? How come we can't remember how we died?"

Ash twists a curl around a fingernail as she turns to look at Bessie for a moment, her eyes sad. Then her short attention span is drawn back to the airport. "Look."

A straggling passenger stumbles down the staircase. His bellowing accent is cranky Cockney. With his tee-shirt half in, half out of his jeans, his tattooed arms flail in the air. Eye makeup smears his pitted features. "Where in the freakin' hell's me limo driver? I say, is this freakin' LAX or what? Concert's in 'alf an 'our for fucksakes!"

A stunning blonde angel rushes over as he bangs and batters his way through the sacred crystal entrance.

"Got no time for groupies now, dearie! Need me freakin' driver! Where in the 'ell is me limo?"

The angelic beauty glows rosy. The late arrival shrinks back in fear, almost toppling over. "Bloody 'ell!"

The girls giggle inside their leafy shelter, all thoughts of sadness over. Barely containing themselves, they snicker and spit out at the same time, "Drug overdose."

Bessie jumps up, brushing herself off. Fifty feet below them, the staircase is folding back into the plane. A stocky male angel has joined the blonde to help her deal with the still protesting rock star. The engine of the jet-cloud begins to hum as the plane vanishes into the sky. Slowly the crowd drifts away from the airport, strolling up and along the pathways.

"Show's over." The words are barely out of Bessie's mouth when someone catches her eye.

One last passenger, a tall, fair youth about seventeen, all limbs and sticking-out hair, steps out from behind a corner post to stand alone on the platform, his pale eyes filled with unbearable pain. He watches listlessly while an angel approaches, glowing rosy to encircle him in her gentle embrace. Afterwards his image returns to a healthier, although still skinny, version of himself. They walk quietly arm-in-arm to the exit arch.

As he steps off the platform, a man of similar build, wearing a flannel shirt and jeans, walks up to the young man. They hug shyly. No words are spoken. The older one leads his younger counterpart along a path, gesturing upwards. Then, without warning, the young man stops in his tracks and spins around. He stares up the opposite hillside. Directly at Bessie.

Gasping for breath, the young girl reaches up to touch her scar, her fingers trembling. Ash stares at the scene below. "What's *he* doing here? I thought he … never mind."

Soon the girls' attention is diverted by something far more important. A woman marches smartly towards their hiding place - a petite, middle-aged angel in a severe power suit. The silver chains on her reading glasses dance back and forth; her features scowl.

Bessie's eyes widen. "Oh oh."

Ash hisses, "Angel Rachel."

As the two girls disappear over the hilltop, the manicured hand of Angel Rachel reaches down to pick up a lime green shoe. She holds it away from her as though it were a dead fish, shaking her head. "One of these days they'll be the death of me, those two." She smirks at her own joke.

CHAPTER 2: HEAVEN

Bessie and Ash stand outside a modern glass and steel structure known as the Seventh Heaven mall which is sprawled in a field surrounded by a parking lot. Vehicles come and go in all shapes and sizes, similar to the Earth dimension, but with one major difference - no engines, no fuel. No need, as they run on universal energy.

They head towards the far end of the mall where the Past Lives movie theatre is located. Looking up at the marquee, they see what is currently playing - ARTHUR BESTER, ACCOUNTANT WITH A SECRET FILE. The next one - AZIZADINE VELLANI, TERRORIST OR PHILOSOPHER? YOU DECIDE. And finally - MARIA HELENA, FROM CASTLE TO CRACKHEAD.

"Did you see that one about Princess Maria?" Bessie comments. "She had seventeen lovers, some of them priests even, before she was run over by a donkey cart."

"I know, that was wild. Loved that one."

They turn to walk back to the central mall entrance. Inside, hallways travel in each direction filled with shops boasting Heaven-ware fashions and accessories, the latest foot gear, bags, reincarnation book stores, cosmetics, and small eateries. In other words, an awful lot like malls on Earth.

Ash starts walking left. "Shall we, my dear?" She speaks in an exaggerated British accent.

Snickering, they soon enter the tiny crowded shop of Bodysuits Boutique. A nervous Nelly angel peers out at them over her glasses from behind the counter. She stands all of four-foot-seven. On her flowered dress the word SOULSLADY is elaborately lettered on a ceramic rectangle. At the sight of the girls, she pushes her glasses up her nose and squares her scrawny shoulders.

All around them, neat rows of body shells seem to float on hangers like mystical Halloween costumes. There must be thousands of them, all organized beneath various signs like: SLIGHTLY USED, GO RETRO, UPPER CRUST, WHAT'S YOUR FAVORITE CENTURY? And, JUST IN, THE NEW FALL COLLECTION.

An elderly gent lifts down the body suit of Frank Sinatra as he tiptoes towards the changing room, humming *New York New York*.

"Anything in particular today, ladies?" Soulslady spits out every syllable.

Ash smiles warmly and insincerely. "Just browsing."

Soulslady sniffs as she turns to walk away. "As per the usual."

Ash mimics the woman under her breath. "As per the usual."

The store clerk stops for a moment before being distracted by a young nerdy type making a mess out of the Go Retro selections.

Ash and Bessie eavesdrop as the nerd asks politely, "Got Jim Morrison?"

She points him to a crowded rack. "Used & Abused. But it's probably out. Everybody wants to wear Jim Morrison, for some weird reason."

The girls smile at Nerd Boy as they finger-walk through the hangers in the Slightly Used section. Ash pulls out the John Kennedy Jr. shell to hold it up to her. "Only, like, the most beautiful, sexy man in the entire universe." She sighs.

Soon Bessie is standing beside her, holding up the Carolyn Bessette Kennedy version. They check themselves in the full-length mirror.

"So sad," says Bessie. "A love story gone terribly wrong."

"If only they'd driven instead of flown," Ash adds. "I mean, like, how long can it be, New York to…Where were they going anyhow? Long Island?"

"Martha's Vineyard, I think," Bessie corrects her. "For some cousin's wedding. What a waste. And her sister, Lauren, too."

Sensing Soulslady's glare, the girls smile brightly as they hang up the shells in the wrong places. The woman stomps over in her quick little annoying steps, just as Ash and Bessie rush over to the Used & Abused section and yank out the bodysuits of Janis Joplin and John Belushi. Smirking, they rush into the change room before she can catch them.

Lifting the bodysuits from their hangers, they tug them over their heads, smoothing them down around themselves, admiring each other for a moment. The images of Ash and Bessie are nowhere to be seen. Only those of Janis and John. It's a game they never tire of in the endless time of Heaven.

Ash pulls back the changing room curtain, dancing out into the tiny shop, pulling Bessie by her hand. In a perfect sixties jive, they sing at the top of their lungs, or rather moan loudly about why can't they drive a decent car like a Mercedez Benz.

Other customers join in, clapping their hands to Janis' immortal song, whining about how they've worked so hard all their lives and don't they deserve an expensive ride?

"O-kay, ladies, that's it. Quite e-nough fun for one day." Furiously, Soulslady drags them by their arms towards the change room.

Their voices continue to screech into the poor woman's ears. Doesn't she realize the Lord owes them a Mercedez? Apparently not. But there is definitely something else she thinks they deserve.

Back outside in the parking lot, Ash and Bessie notice a guy on a spindly ladder who is painstakingly changing the names of the movies on the Past Lives marquee, letter by letter. Down come the titles of Maria Helena, Arthur, and Arazadin. Up go this week's first offering - EDNA SNERD, THE TALE OF A SMALL TOWN NURSE WITH A TWIST. Then, UDAY AND GUSAY HUSSEIN, CAN YOU TELL THE DIFFERENCE?

"Wish they'd have a movie star for a change." As more letters go up, Ash's face breaks into a smile. The man climbs down his ladder while the girls gaze up in awe. KATHRYN HEPBURN - FROM HOLLYWOOD TO HEAVENWOOD.

"Next life? I'm gonna be a famous actress, too." Ash sighs deeply. In a surprisingly good Hepburn imitation, she enunciates, "Don't be such a bloody nincompoop, Spencah. Of coursah we ah dead."

"Someday we'll be hanging up in Bodysuits, after we reincarnate, that is." Bessie muses. "What category I wonder?"

Ash stops to brush a speck of dust from the toe of her purple flip-flop. Her voice is tinged with sadness. "Slightly Used. What else?"

"Hey, wait up!" Bessie breaks into a run towards a rather tall, older woman, busy jabbing at the kickstand of a rickety bicycle with her toe. As Bessie gets closer, she sees the bike's basket is overflowing with cleaning supplies - polishes and soaps, a replacement mop head, dust rags, and a new whisk. "Grandma, wait up!"

The older woman turns, flicking back a grey ponytail over her shoulder before kicking the stand back down and holding out strong arms.

As Ash wobbles across the parking lot, Bessie is swallowed into her grandmother's warm, hearty hug before the older woman pulls back to take a good look at her. As always her grandma is sporting shapeless pants and a loose shirt. On the left side of her chest, a gaudy green shamrock broach perches haphazardly. Her skin is bronzed and freckled from so much time outdoors. When she speaks, her voice is thick with Irish lilting. "Well, how in the blazes are you two rascals? Heard you played hookie and went to the airport again." She winks at Bessie, her rough hands on the younger woman's shoulders. "Good for you, sugar plum. Good for you."

"How's grandpa?" Bessie manages to ask before Ash dives in for her hug.

"Well, hello, Ashley dear. Oh, you know. Still working on that still in the orchard, bless his old alchie heart. Making hooch out of nectarines this time. Pretty good batch, I must say."

Bessie pokes around in the basket. "Need to talk to you about something, grandma. Hey, how come you bought all this cleaning stuff, anyways. Expecting company?"

Grandma Millie shoos her hands away. "None of your beeswax, missy. Not yet, anyway. Well ..." Her eyes fill with kindness. "So what's on your mind? Trouble in paradise?"

Ash pipes up. "We saw Jason yesterday."

The older woman's facial wrinkles tighten into hard lines.

"Just arrived on the nine o'clock flight." Bessie's fingers rub her scar.

"You sure it was him?" Her grandmother touches Bessie's chin with her fingertips to tilt her face towards her. "Positive? Lots of skinny lads crashing up their cars on the Earth roads these days. God only knows."

"Oh, it was him alright, Millie. I'd swear it was him." Ash puts her hands on her hips in a supermodel pose.

Grandma Millie glances back and forth between them. "Well, in that case, you both better come and visit soon. We'll have a nice long chat. Decide what to do. Bessie?" Old blue eyes pour love into young blue ones. "You'll come soon?"

"Sure, grandma." Bessie smiles finally. "It's not as if we're going to school or anything."

"That's my girl." Millie kisses the top of her granddaughter's head. Turning away, she grabs hold of her handlebars, kicking up the stand before climbing onto her bike. "Can't leave the old fart alone too long. You know how he is." She mimes pouring and tossing back a generous slug of whiskey.

Riding off down the road, she yells back over her shoulder. "Soon then. Very soon. Now you two keep in trouble, you hear?" Her giggle fades as she gets further and further from sight.

"Wanna go watch the cows recycle?" Ash sticks a pink jawbreaker into her mouth, chewing vigorously for a moment. Blowing out a huge bubble, she sucks the air back in, expertly popping it with a loud smack.

"No can do." Bessie's fingers are back on her scar again.

CHAPTER 3: HEAVEN

Bessie slumps in an armchair positioned front and center of a spacious office decorated in movie posters and memorabilia, mostly from the Fifties and Sixties. Windows face out onto magnificent formal gardens. She's alone until Angel Mel materializes out of thin air, binoculars in hand. With his back to her, he focuses outside on the manicured lawns laced with winding pathways.

"About time," Bessie snaps.

He ignores her rudeness. "Movie ran late. You've seen it yet? About that nurse, Edna Snerd? Or should I say, nurse slash serial killer. Emphasis on the slash. Too bad for her men friends, she collected all those hunting knives, ha ha. Okay, where were we? Trying to recall your death. Any luck?"

Bessie stares at his peony-shirted back. His shoulders are pit bull wide. "I try. But the harder I try, the less I can remember. Grandma remembers hers, clear as a bell. Drifted off on a deck chair at the cottage reading an Agatha Christie murder mystery."

She changes positions in the chair, flicking her coppery bob to get her bangs out of her eyes. "And even grandpa remembers his. Fell out of a tree celebrating his eightieth birthday with a bottle of Irish whiskey."

Angel Mel turns and smiles. He's got the face of everybody's favorite uncle. "Maybe you should stop trying so hard. Let it flow. Like a breeze." He sets down the binoculars on top of a messy pile of paper on his desk. His hands flutter back and forth in front of his portly figure like a caricature of a hula dancer. "Let the breeze catch your memories and bring them to you." He turns back to the window. "When it's time."

Bessie's in no mood. "And when will that be, Mel? When hell freezes over?"

"What am I, God? The time will be when the time will be." He leans down to her level, touching her shoulder. "You need to heal first."

"Heal from what, Mel?" Her eyes accuse him. "And you know. And I know you know."

He stares back for a long moment. His lips wobble in and out of a smile. Distracted by something or someone outside the window, he grabs his binoculars to rush over. In the distance a stout man in formal attire, complete with black bowler, walks with a cane in the gardens.

Angel Mel dances with excitement. "Why, I'll be darned. I do believe that's Alfred Hitchcock over there! Always wanted to ask him what he thought of that dreadful remake of his brilliant *Psycho*. More like *Fiasco,* if you ask me."

Bessie jumps up to join him. Together they watch the man make his way slowly and deliberately towards the rose gardens. She mumbles, "So how long have I been here, can you answer me that, at least?"

"There is no time here, Bessie. No beginning, no middle, no end. Just timelessness." She gives no reaction so he barrels on. "You know when you go to the movies? You're all excited to see the latest rom-com or whatever?" He waits for her to nod. "So, let's review. First you go in and sit down and start munching on your popcorn you just bought, with lots of butter, real butter, mind you, not that artificial crap, and parmesan cheese if they have it—"

"Cut to the chase, Mel?"

He gives her a look. "Well, the point is, grumpy face, and there is a point. You don't know what the plot is going to be, unless you cheat, of course, and read the reviews that reveal everything but what cereal they eat for break—"

"Point?" Bessie rolls her eyes.

He picks up his binoculars, looking into the gardens. It appears that Hitchcock is now chatting up an hourglass platinum blonde in a skin-tight silver evening gown. "Well, I'll be a … Carole Lombard!" He pauses for what seems like forever. "So the story's all there before you arrive at the theatre. All written, shot, edited, and ready to unfold before your very eyes." He lowers his binoculars, turning towards her, waiting until their eyes meet. "All you have to do is … sit tight and enjoy. But the point is, my little mushroom, the story already exists." He steals a quick glance outside. "They're meeting someone, I can feel it."

Bessie stares at the bald spot on the back of Angel Mel's head. She picks up the top screenplay from the pile on his desk.

"Yep, it's Clark Gable. Clark Gable, as I live and breathe." He turns to grin at Bessie. "Metaphorically speaking, of course."

She's busy reading the title of the screenplay. "*Mel's Angels*?"

"What? Oh, just a little something I'm working on."

She sets it back down, wandering over to the window. "What are you going to do with it when you're finished?"

His binoculars are tracking the trio outside as they chat and admire the yellow tea roses. "Channel it to Clint Eastwood."

"Maybe I died from some mysterious, yet-to-be-discovered virus."

Angel Mel lets his binoculars dangle from one hand. He turns to look at her intently. "Maybe."

"Maybe ... Jason did something."

The angel's right eyebrow shoots up. "Jason? Tall and skinny? Sad eyes? Arrived yesterday on the nine o'clock? And that hair!"

"That's the one." Bessie takes his binoculars from him, adjusting the focus.

"Wasn't he your boyfriend?"

"Was. *Was* my boyfriend. Past tense. Followed me everywhere. And I mean, everywhere."

From somewhere Angel Mel has found himself another pair of binoculars. He swings around to stare at Bessie, staring at him. "Apparently so."

"Oh, big ha ha. Very amusing."

She tosses the binoculars on his desk, slumping back onto the armchair. "So what else have you channeled?"

"*Waterworld.* To Kevin Costner. Seemed like a great setting at the time."

"Better luck with *Mel's Angels*."

He gives her a sunny smile. "Hope springs eternal."

CHAPTER 4: EARTH

In the small town of Ravenspond in rural Pennsylvania, Bessie's eleven-year-old sister, Leila, lays under a sheet in her single bed, the spread being folded down due to the warm night. The most prominent piece of furniture in her room is a massive bookcase where her collection is neatly lined up in alphabetical order by author.

A slight girl, Leila wears an over-sized, navy tee-shirt emblazoned with a picture of the singer Chris Lisack. Her straight brown hair is pulled back into a messy pony-tail. Leaning on one elbow, she pushes up blue-rimmed glasses on her nose from time to time as she reads by a small gooseneck lamp on her bedside table. At the end of her bed, an old golden retriever sleeps on the spread.

As she turns the pages, the cover reveals the source of her absorption - *The Secret Window of Death* by Ruth Reynolds. Her bedroom door opens and she looks up as her mother, Heather, a pretty, redheaded woman in a fluffy bathrobe, comes and sits on the edge of her bed.

"Wish you wouldn't read those things. You're far too young. Why can't you read normal kids' stories like Harry Potter or ...." The woman pats the bed fretfully.

"Nancy Drew?" Leila would have sneered had it been anyone but her sweet mother. And in their current circumstances and all.

"Where do you think they are, Lee?"

"Well, you know Bess like I do, mom. One minute she's madly in love with Jason. The next she wants to sing with Chris Lisack."

Her mother sips on a small glass of red wine. "Tomorrow we're meeting with Ash's parents at the police station."

Leila reaches out to touch her mother's arm. "I'm sure they're alright. I mean ..." She gazes intently into Heather's eyes. "It's summertime. And it's not like they haven't run away before. Remember two years ago?"

An embroidered hankie appears from her mother's pocket. She dabs at her eyes. "When they went to Cleveland to see …" Her voice wanders off.

"Ash wanted to meet Paris Hilton. She was supposed to be at that club and, of course, she had all her facts wrong. As usual."

Heather smiles weakly. "I'll let you go to sleep." She leans in to kiss her daughter's forehead before reaching over to pat the dog's paw. "Nite-nite, Mouser." At the doorway she stops, walking back over to flick off the light. "I'm sure they'll turn up soon."

"They always do, mom. They always do. With some lame-ass excuse."

"'Nite, sweetheart."

"'Nite, mom." She waits until her mother is gone to retrieve a mini-reading light from her bedside table. Attaching it to her book, she begins to search with one finger for her place.

The dog lifts his head for a moment to observe and she returns his glance. "Where in the hell did they run off to this time, Mouser?"

CHAPTER 5: HEAVEN

Bessie sits cross-legged in pajamas on a small blue mat in a sea of small blue mats, each with a teenage girl on it. Facing her, Ash also sits in lotus position. All but two are earnestly meditating, eyes closed.

Ash pulls out two mini-packs of NecNac Snaks from her lap, taking some before leaning over to hand the other bag to Bessie. She talks through her fingers, munching and whispering. "So this guy? He tells me the reincarnating souls? They, like, go back to Earth at exactly four A.M." A loud crunch echoes in the meditation room as she stuffs another chip in her mouth with her rhinestone-encrusted fingernails. "Our version of time, that is."

Bessie stops mid-chip, stuffing the bag under the edge of her mat. "Angel alert."

Reassuming lotus positions, they poise their hands upwards on their knees with thumbs touching their middle fingers. Too loudly, they hum, "Ommmmm … ommmmm …"

Footfalls of a slim angel in yoga pants approach. She stops beside Ash and Bessie, looking suspiciously from one to the other and back again before moving on down the hardwood floor.

When she's finally far enough away, the girls relax, pulling out their squished NecNac Snaks. Bessie leans forward. "For sure? Four A.M.? Ommmmm. That's what the guy said? Ommmmm."

Ash brushes lint from one of the golden snacks. "On the button. It's the midpoint of night or something, when, like, this layer between life and death, or Earth and Heaven is the thinnest. Ommmmm. Or so he tells me. Ommmmm."

"Oh, really?" A small smile creeps over Bessie's face.

Ash stares at her garish timepiece sparkling in a circle of zircons. "You thinking what I think you're thinking?"

"Set your watch for three-thirty."

—

The night sky is extraordinary with stars glistening and glowing with unearthly radiance. Bessie and Ash stroll down an empty road winding through lush countryside. The air is thick with the scent of summer lilac and wild roses. Frogs croak in unseen ponds. An owl hoot-hoots from the branch of an elm. A host of night birds swoop in the sky.

Bessie breaks the silence. "Remember that song we used to sing at camp when we were kids?" She begins, wistfully at first. "Row, row, row your boat …"

Ash joins in, in traditional round style, just as they did around the campfire long ago. "Row, row, row your boat …"

Now Bessie sings, "Gently down the stream …"

Ash jumps in, "Gently down the stream …"

Bessie with more gusto, "Merrily, merrily, merrily, merrily …"

Followed by Ash's version, "Merrily, merrily, merrily, merrily …"

Stopping in the middle of the road, they stare at each other. Together they sing the last line, very softly, very slowly, "Life is but a dream …."

They walk in silence for a while before Ash pipes up, "What's that mean, anyway? Life is but a dream." She waves around her arms, jingling her many bracelets. "Life is but a dream. I mean, like, if life is but a dream, then what's reality? Heaven?"

They stand as still as statues, barely breathing. Craning their necks to stare at the magnificence of the night sky, the stars seem to be communicating with them, the way they twinkle and dip, as the truth sinks in.

Ash whispers, "Holy moly."

—

"You sure that guy said four?" Bessie feels her legs cramping in her scrunched down position. They are in their usual hiding place inside the hedge outside of Heaven Interportal Airport.

Ash peers through the leaves. "Swear that's what he said." The area is as deserted as a beach in winter. Then, "Bess, Bess!" She bangs on her friend's arm.

"What?" Bessie looks up from stretching out her left foot. "Oh!"

Out of thin air, a long, wooden table materializes, set with elegant silver candlesticks. The table grows in length until the end is invisible. Air Heaven personnel begin to appear, very crisp in their powder blue uniforms with tiny embroidered gold wings embossed over their chest pockets. Everyone seems to be in a party mood, chatting away.

"Over there!" It's Bessie's turn to bang on Ash's shoulder.

On the far hillside, a long slow line of heavenly residents, dressed in flowing white gowns, drift down the pathways towards the airport. Each is carrying a white candle burning brightly in the night sky. Alongside, an occasional Ground Crew angel supervises.

"The reincarnating souls," Bessie whispers.

"Oh … I … it's so…wow, like … totally …" Ash, for once, is lost for words. Then, "Hey, Bess, there's Miss Tight Ass."

Sure enough, Soulslady from Bodysuits Boutique appears simultaneously with an impossibly huge clothes rack, jam-packed with empty hangers. She stands, holding her hands in front of her, watching the approaching candlelit parade of souls about to return to the Earth dimension.

Soon the lines reach the gardens outside the airport, each participant nervously holding their candles high. They shuffle about, apprehensive and excited at the same time, as Air Heaven angels calm and soothe.

One angel who seems to be the leader, carries a large white box laying on her open palms. Her voice has the quality of maple syrup. "Are you ready for your big new adventure, everyone? You remember your instructions?"

Heads bob up and down. They start to approach the wooden table all at once.

"One at a time, people. One at a time." Head Angel speaks with infinite patience.

The first gowned passenger heads to the table to set his candle into a candlestick. Soon the remainder flows in a rhythmic hum, putting their candles into silver holders before returning to their places in line.

Ash and Bessie gawk with jaws slack, eyes like owls.

"Oh wow. I … I can hardly …" Bessie's voice stumbles. "Look, there's Lady Diana! And she's with that—"

"Dodi Al Fayed, her fateful lover."

They watch in awe as Diana and Dodi take their turns putting their candles into candlesticks. Bessie wonders out loud, "Do you think they were really ever gonna get married?"

Ash's voice is tinged with sadness. "She's so beautiful. You know, she always said she'd never be the Queen of England. And then that terrible crash. Was it an accident…or was it …?"

"Shsh. Something's happening."

Head Angel now stands before the table glowing in candlelight. "You're about to say goodbye to your old images and prepare for your next lives. Remember what we practiced, everyone? Are you ready?" She treats her audience to her camp counselor grin.

Voices titter nervously. Diana looks over at Dodi with a shy smile. He leans in to give her a light kiss.

Head Angel's voice rings out. "Okay, then. In orderly fashion, please."

A flutter of white gowns head for the Soulslady and her rack of empty hangers. One by one they stand forward, reaching up to the crowns of their heads to tug off their images by small silver threads. All that remains is a shimmering outline the size of an infant, in an aura of rainbow shades.

Soulslady efficiently takes their old images, neatly hanging them on hangers before putting them on the rack.

"This is, like, so totally. Totally." Ash babbles like the valley girl she always wants to be.

"Like awesome?" Bessie teases. "Say goodbye to the Princess."

Diana and Dodi now stand together before Soulslady, smiling into each other's eyes one last time. Giggling, they tug off their images in unison and hand them over. Two sparkling little auras race back into line.

When all the discarded images are safely stored onto the rack, Soulslady and her new stock for her boutique vanish into thin air.

Head Angel walks from aura to aura, handing out ivory envelopes from the box she's carrying, addressed in intricate gold script. One aura fumbles and drops his, scrambling to pick it up again. The angel addresses the gathering, "And for the love of God, don't lose them on your flight."

A humming sound begins overhead. In the distance, an Air Heaven jet-cloud approaches rapidly until it hovers over the back of the airport.

The massive bell in the glass steeple begins to toll - one, two, three times. The crystal door swings wide open. The staircase spills out of the jet-cloud, attaching to the Sacred Portal. A commanding female pilot steps out proudly and stands at the top of the stairs, smiling.

Swiftly, the line of shimmering auras files through the front arch of flowers across the platform, their envelopes swinging back and forth. Head Angel calls out, "Good luck, everyone. Live the life you're dreaming of!"

From their hideout, Ash and Bessie watch the baby-like auras float through the open-air platform, out the sacred exit, up the staircase and into the aircraft. It appears each one is receiving a hug by the attendant at the door who is crouched down on his knees.

Finally all passengers are on board and the door closes. The jet-cloud disappears into the night sky. Even the angels vanish. All is still except for two teenage girls collapsing backwards onto the ground, worn out from all the excitement.

"Too bad we can't go back. Yet."

"Not until we figure out our old lives, or so sayeth the Angel Mel."

A twig breaks, startling them into upright positions.

"Who's there?" Bessie demands of the darkness.

Out of a nearby stand of trees, a shape creeps towards them. Sensing Bessie's gaze, the shape stops in its tracks before taking another step out into the moonlight.

Jason.

Bessie jumps to her feet, the color draining from her features. Words won't form in her mouth. She yanks on Ash's shirtsleeve. Finally, "He's ... he's ..."

"Who?" Ash untangles her lanky limbs to get on her feet. "Someone's here? Who?"

Holding hands, they peer into the blackened stand of trees. No one is there. Only a branch moves ever so slightly. "Oh, you're just imagining things, Bess. Maybe you just, like, thought—"

"Let's go." Bessie tears off uphill and down towards the road, trailed by a stumbling and complaining Ash.

Jason walks over to the spot where the girls had been hiding inside the bushes. In a lower branch, he spies a piece of Bessie's tee-shirt torn off in her haste to leave. With long bony fingers he carefully removes it, holding it to his cheek and sniffing it. He stands there in the moonlight, his sandy hair tufting in a million directions. His body is so tall and lean, it seems to waver in the slight breeze like a blade of marsh grass.

CHAPTER 6: HEAVEN

"Ah, my sweet, delinquent lassies, just in time for lunch." Grandma Millie sweeps the flagstone path of her cottage with vigorous strokes. An orange cat meows in protest as the edge of the broom catches it mid-nap. "If you want to see your grandpa, he's out back building a new secret still. The angels found his old one. Silly fool."

Ash leans down to stroke the feline as it resettles on a warm stone already swept, and consequently safe from the broom. This is not an easy task for a girl in a micro-mini and hot pink platforms on legs so long they seem to reach her armpits. Finally she steps out of her shoes and flops on the grass. "Hi, Peach," she addresses the cat.

"Gram, I just wanted to ask you about ..." Bessie's thoughts are distracted when she notices all the furniture airing on the lawn. A quilt hangs between two chairs. On the clothesline running between maple trees at the side of the yard, she can see area rugs and curtains waving in the breeze alongside the regular laundry. "What's all this?"

Either Millie doesn't hear her granddaughter, or she's ignoring her question as she tosses her broom aside and heads into her cottage.

"She's up to something." Bessie runs her hand over the old quilt fashioned from worn-out shirts, grandpa's ancient wool suit, a plaid hiking jacket, and a flowered dress. Funny, she knows where every patch comes from. But she can't remember how she died.

A rustling from the orchard announces the arrival of Grandpa Will, all five-foot-five of him. He wears the same thing he does every day - jeans and a long-sleeved white shirt with the sleeves rolled up - as he swings a clay jug from one hand. "Well, bless my soul. How's my sweet lovelies?' He calls out as Bessie and Ash dash over for hugs. "My best batch yet." He sets the jug on a side table. I'll let you have a wee taste test after our picnic but don't tell your grandma."

"Picnic?"

"Millie's gone and torn up the kitchen something fierce, so we'll be eating outside for a bit."

The woman in question reemerges with a wicker tray of sandwiches and cupcakes with chocolate sprinkles. "Here we go." She sets it on the picnic table. They all dig in, swishing it down with glasses of nectarade, her secret recipe.

A lazy hour of laughter later, Ash wanders off with Grandpa Will to inspect the new still. Bessie gets up to help her grandmother retrieve laundry from the line.

The older woman stops, holding a pillowcase in her hands, staring intently at her granddaughter. "So what's on your mind, sweet pea?"

Bessie mumbles, "I told you, Jason's here."

Millie methodically folds the cotton. "Jason? Wasn't he your—"

"*Was*. Emphasis on *was*. Past tense. Finito. *Was* my boyfriend. I think he—"

"You think he what." The older woman tosses the folded pillowcase into the basket at her feet, as Bessie looks away. She watches her intently before turning back to her clothes line. "You still can't remember, dear?"

Her granddaughter reaches up to unsnap clothes pegs from a sheer, pale-green negligee. "Neither can Ash."

"Well, what does Angel Mel have to say?"

"Oh, he just keeps going on about how it takes time. Even though there's no time in Heaven. Tells me to relax. Go watch some more movies." The young girl tosses the fancy lingerie into the basket, mimicking Angel Mel doing his little hula dance, her arms waving in the air. "Let your memories flow to you … like the breeze."

Millie chuckles, handing her granddaughter one end of a sheet.

"Do you remember me from then?" Bessie folds her two corners together in rhythm with the older woman.

"Of course I remember you. Here." She waltzes towards Bessie with her corners of cotton, taking her granddaughter's from her fingers. In a single motion, she flips the sheet in half, then half again, and once more before tossing it into the basket.

Bessie smiles as she pops off the pegs from a racy red bra on the line.

"Be careful with that. It's Will's favorite." Millie takes down a matching pantie. "You will remember all the details, lovey. When it's—"

"Time. I know." Bessie wanders off a few steps, staring at Peach washing his front paws, first the left one, then the right. He stretches out his hind left leg to chew at the fur between his toes. "Hey, grandma?"

"Hmm?" Millie stares at Bessie's back as the young girl reaches down to pick up a blade of grass to chew on before she speaks. "Ever been to the Hall of Akashic Records?"

"You know about that?" Millie drops her clothes peg. Her fingers reach up to fiddle with her shamrock broach, twinkling in the sunshine on her shirt.

"You didn't answer my question."

"It's forbidden." Millie stoops to retrieve the peg, playing for time. "And extremely dangerous."

Bessie watches her pick up the loaded basket before spinning around to head into the cottage. She yells after her, "Dangerous how?"

Millie stops in her tracks, turning to stare directly into her granddaughter's eyes. "Listen to me, entering the Hall of Akashic Records is forbidden by the highest angels. Trust me, you don't want to cross them, or you could end up setting your soul's journey back a thousand years." She holds her stern gaze and repeats, "A thousand years!"

~

The late afternoon sun beats down. Both girls are still full from the picnic feast. Bessie sprawls in a field, deserted except for twittering birds, her grandparents' cottage far below. Ash hops about in her platforms, picking buttercups.

"Do you think I could find nail polish this color?" Ash sticks a buttercup petal over one fingernail.

Out of nowhere, Bessie hears a crackling sound. Her neck stretches upright; her eyes dart here and there. "You hear that?"

"That what?" Ash spits on the petal she's attempting to glue to her nail.

The crackling sound repeats itself. "That." Bessie jumps upright. She spots something or someone heading out of the distant forest.

Jason, with a shred of her cotton tee-shirt dangling from his fingers.

Ash scrambles to her feet, all thoughts of buttercup nail polish forgotten. Tearing down the road, the terrified girls don't stop until they reach Girls Dorm. Panting and sweating, they lean against the exterior wall, darting glances at each other.

Bessie whispers. "Ash. Do you … think …?" She brushes wet bangs from her forehead, revealing her scar. "Can someone kill us … twice?"

CHAPTER 7: HEAVEN

Outside Boys Dorm, six or seven teenage youths toss a football around on the back lawn while Jason sits alone on the porch steps. His hands play with the piece of Bessie's torn shirt like Grecian worry beads. Instead of watching the game, his eyes stare off into some distant land of inner consciousness. He's unaware that one of the boys, stocky and Latin handsome, and who he knows as Miguelito, stops in mid-tracks some twenty feet away, facing him, football in hand.

"Hey, farm boy, let's see your stuff." Miguelito whips the ball at the startled Jason who jumps up to catch it instinctively.

Angry, Jason tosses it back as fast as he received it. He collapses back onto the step, playing with the tee-shirt again, ignoring the sturdy lad in front of him.

Miguelito whips the ball right back at him, showing off his white teeth in a mischievous grin. "Hey, farm boy. Heard you were college material."

Apart from them, the other lads are getting impatient. One of them, Rameen, yells over. "Aw, leave him alone. He never wants to play, anyhow."

Jason pitches the ball back, swift and hard, aiming at the Latin boy's head, praying he'll be left alone. But Miguelito catches it handily, sending it right back, his grin widening.

Jason's stormy features suddenly transform into a small smile. For the first time since he's been in Heaven, he actually chuckles. Ball under his arm, he strolls over to Miguelito, hands it over and gets in the game.

CHAPTER 8: HEAVEN

On a spectacular cliff far above a canyon on a late afternoon, Bessie and Ash tiptoe up behind a plump, seated female. Her glittery silver aura identifies her as an angel as she sits cross-legged on the grass, strumming a flower-painted guitar on her lap. As they get closer to her, they can see the daisies on her flowing dress, ropes of multi-colored beads around her neck, and various blossoms braided into her waist-length hair.

A nearby sleeping St. Bernard yawns as he stretches out his paws and resettles his head on them, while his angelic companion attempts the classic hippie anthem about going to San Francisco and wearing flowers in one's hair. The problem is Angel Rainbow Sunshine couldn't hit a note in tune if her wings depended on it.

Ash snickers. Bessie puts a finger to her pal's lips to shush her. They continue on tiptoe until they reach a small stone pedestal about thirty feet away from the wannabe musician. On it, a modest telescope stands, surrounded by silver rope. Hanging from it are various hand-made signs: SACRED TELESCOPE; RESTRICTED AREA; FOR ANGELS ONLY. And, BY ORDER OF THE ANGEL COURT. Not to forget the girls' particular favorite: SURVEILLANCE 24/7.

As they make their way to the forbidden Sacred Telescope, Bessie can't resist commenting, "So who do you think is smarter? Angel Rainbow Sunshine or that goofy dog of hers?"

Deftly they slide under the rope to climb up onto the pedestal. Ash stands on guard as Bessie removes the lens cap, allowing it to dangle from its chain. She leans forward to peer in. Milky swirls fill the lens then clear.

An aerial view of Ravenspond, Pennsylvania, zooms onto a suburban street, closer, closer, then onto a modest bungalow where a Navy blue Honda and a rusty green Chevy Impala are parked in the driveway. A girl's bike lays in the front yard, with multi-colored streamers sprouting from the handlebars. Pansies, marigolds, and rose bushes dot the flowerbeds.

The lens zooms into the interior of the house, refocusing to reveal Bessie's sister, Leila, lounging on her bedspread. It appears she is totally absorbed by a Ruth Reynolds' novel, A Mind for Mischief. *Her window is wide open, allowing the slight breeze to enter and stir the sheer curtains on this warm night. Somehow she manages to nibble on a ChocOnut bar while she reads, tearing back the paper in tiny pieces.*

Without warning, her hand stops in mid-air. Quietly she sets the candy bar on the bedspread. Her eyes lift from the page. Her neck elongates as if she senses she is being watched. Sitting up, she looks around her darkened room. Mouser at the end of her bed lifts his head for a moment, sniffing the air before he resettles.

Slowly closing her novel with a bookmark, Leila climbs out of bed to walk to the open window and crouch on her knees. Her solemn gaze turns skyward as she stares directly into Bessie's eyes.

In Heaven, Bessie jumps back from the Sacred Telescope, her eyes widening in shock. What just happened? Could it be? Her expression turns to one of dreamy delight. Could her dear sister, Leila, in her bedroom at home, actually sense she was watching her all the way from Heaven? Missing her? Longing for her? Is it possible? Or did she imagine it?

No, the truth is as clear as Angel Mel's twinkle. Leila had definitely turned to gaze up at her sister into the night at the same time Bessie was staring at her through the lens. *She knew she was there.* Somehow Leila knew.

All her life, Bessie had known that they shared a very special connection, a bond that defied logic, and the differences in their ages and personalities. And now, here she is in Heaven, and the bond between them is still alive!

Bessie's features beam with hope as she jumps down from the pedestal to allow Ash her turn.

CHAPTER 9: HEAVEN

Hours later that same day, in the bedroom in Girls Dorm she shares with Ash, along with two other roommates, Bessie sits up in her twin bed, intertwining her fingers this way and that. Staring up at the wall clock, she sees it is 3:30 A.M. She glances over at her best friend, sound asleep with an open copy of *Angel* magazine on her lap.

Bessie tiptoes over. "Wake up, Ash. Ash." She shakes her shoulder. "Ash."

Ash bolts upright, scattering her magazine. "Awake. I'm awake."

"You still game?"

"Like I'm gonna let you have all the fun."

Shoes in hand, they scamper out their bedroom door, past the dozing angel at the front desk.

Soon they're back in their favorite hiding place - the bushes outside Air Heaven Interportal Airport. Peering out, they observe the last of the reincarnating souls in white gowns lining up to hand over their old images to Soulslady. Efficiently she drops them onto hangers, snapping them into place on her wardrobe rack.

"That one over there. Is he really Kurt Cobain?" Ash pokes Bessie.

"Where?"

"Right in front of Miss Snippy Pants. Too late. You missed it. He's undressed already."

A glowing aura shuffles back into the line-up where envelopes are being handed out. The humming jet-cloud hovers over the rear of the airport. The crystal door slowly swings open. The staircase unfolds to await the boarding passengers.

"Get ready, Ash."

The bell tolls - one, two, three. The enfant-sized auras swiftly drift through the flowered arch, across the platform, out the Sacred Portal, and up the staircase.

"Wait for it, wait for it." Every muscle in Bessie's body tightens like a cat's.

"But Bess, how are we gonna get—"

"Go!" Bessie springs to her feet and takes off in full gallop, Ash close behind.

The staircase is folding up into the plane as they tear across the platform, a blur of astonished angel faces spinning around to look.

Bessie runs through the Sacred Portal accompanied by a whooshing sound. She grabs the edge of the bottom rung, swinging herself neatly up moments before the staircase begins to disappear into the plane. "Come on, come on!" She yells behind her.

Ash whooshes through the portal, reaching up for the edge of the rung. She almost gets it, but stumbles at the last minute. As she jumps again, she loses her new scarlet-striped sandal. Turning away, she leans down to grab it. Too late she realizes her mistake. The staircase folds back into place with a snap, and the door of the plane swings closed with Bessie inside.

Back on the ground, a frantic Ash glares up the plane, her shoe in hand, before catching sight of three Air Heaven personnel marching swiftly towards her. Just in time she makes it back to the shelter of the hedge and flops on the grass. Tossing her footwear aside, she stares longingly after the plane as it vanishes into the night sky like a mirage.

—

By a huge stroke of luck, in the chaos of boarding auras jamming the aisles, Bessie manages to stuff herself into a near empty cupboard in the mid-section of the plane. She squishes herself amongst the dishes, glasses, and napkins. Soon she can hear the muffled voices of two flight attendants outside her hiding place, chatting while they arrange drinks on trays.

"Big crowd today, Gloria. Must be repopulating after that tsunami. Who's got the NecNac Snaks?"

"Think I saw Tom carrying them."

"Tom with the magnificent butt?"

Laughter. "That would be the one."

Inside the cupboard Bessie makes herself as comfortable as she can. Her breathing finally returns to normal.

From beyond the door, a voice pipes up, "Where are those extra cups? In here?"

In a panic Bessie crams herself as far left as she possibly can while the door partially opens. A searching, well-manicured hand reaches around.

The other voice replies, "No, think they're under the sink."

The hand leaves, the door shuts, and Bessie lets out a huge intake of breath. For now she appears to be safe from detection. A murmur of chirpy voices reaches her, offering passengers NecNac Snaks, Hector's Nectar, and words of encouragement to the reincarnating passengers. Eventually she drifts off to sleep in her tiny hiding place.

It could have been minutes or hours when she awakens to more clattering of dishes and utensils. Two voices, one now familiar, and a new one with mellow male tones, begin a conversation outside the cupboard.

"So you working the return flight?"

"The Newly Dead? Yeah. You?"

"Yep, that's mine. When's it leave again?"

"Four twenty A.M. Tom, you want to grab a nectar latte after we land?"

"Sure, why not? We've got time."

Inside the cupboard, Bessie grows alarmed, pushing the button on her watch to light up the face, mumbling, "Four twenty? I've only got twenty minutes?"

CHAPTER 10: EARTH

A jolt shakes the Air Heaven plane as it comes in for an Earth landing. The peace on board is quickly replaced with motion and chaos. Bessie can hear the main door opening, the staircase unfolding. Voices chatter from nervous auras and soothing attendants.

A commanding masculine voice booms out, "Thank you for flying Air Heaven. See you again when you're ready to return. Remember, live with love and courage."

Bessie creaks open the cupboard door to peek out. As best she can, she attempts to blend into the rushing crowd, scrambling along the aisles to exit the door, down the stairs, and across the simple pine flooring of a platform very similar to the one at Air Heaven Interportal.

With relief she spies a huge oak tree about twenty feet away and scrambles off the platform to hide behind the shelter of its trunk. Gazing around the rough bark, she spies a wooden plaque bearing the simple words: EARTH PORTAL, dangling from chains from the shingled roof.

Earth Portal swarms with frantic auras clutching envelopes, waving them in the air, trying to be the first to hand them over to waiting angels, dressed in Earth-friendly, street clothes.

"Calm down, everybody. Just calm down." The in-charge angel, his arms spread sideways, pats the air with his palms. His outfit of choice is business-casual. "All is well. Now listen up, please. We know you're all excited to be back on Earth, and we wish you all a warm welcome." The other angels concur, nodding heads and smiling. "Let me make some introductions first. We are your guardian angels for this incarnation. Your tour guides, as it were. So just relax. All will be revealed. Form lines, if you would, along the platform and facing this way."

Shuffling about, the baby-sized auras get into the requested formation. As Bessie observes, the angels move to stand one-on-one in front of the trembling auras as they extend their envelopes in front of them. Swiftly the angels retrieve them and pull out embossed white cards that resemble elegant invitations, then read them aloud.

Bessie cranes her neck to catch snippets of the announcements, such as -

"Mr. and Mrs. Juan Santana, Puerto Vallarta, México. Good choice."

"Mr. and Mrs. Tung Thu, Ho Chi Ming City."

"The Honorable Stanford and Mildred Mulligan, Cambridge, England."

As soon as they are read, the cards vanish. Afterwards, each guardian angel withdraws a lacy, gossamer veil from their pocket, and drapes it around their assigned aura from head to toe. As Bessie's jaw drops in awe, translucent wings materialize on the angels' backs, much larger than the beings themselves. Wrapping their arms securely around their now veiled charges, the angels, one by one, fly off into the star-studded sky.

On the platform, an angel reads to his little charge, "Ricardo Fernandez and Susan Einstein, Morocco."

Another one speaks in soft tones, "Miss Natalie Delaney, San Francisco, California. Hmm. Single mother." The angel pauses for a moment to add, "Be extra kind to her."

One more reveals, "George Samson and Henry Washington via their surrogate Maria Laluna. Now, that's a first for me. Gay parents." She addresses her little one. "You're in for a very interesting life, my dear. Make the most of it."

Now there is only one tiny aura left, sniffling loudly. The last remaining angel, a motherly sort, leans down to take his trembling envelope. Her voice fills with love and concern. "What is it, dear heart?" Swiftly she reads the contents of the card silently before she speaks. "Why, you're going to a lovely new home in the South of France. A villa, no less. Seventeenth century updated with swimming pool, movie theatre, gym, and a brand new Goldendoodle puppy, just for you." She leans down to touch the weeping aura. "What on Earth is wrong?"

His words tumble out around his sobs. "I … I … I've changed my mind. I …. I … don't want to be re … reborn. I want to … to stay in Heaven."

She crouches down to his level. "Sweet one, I know you love Heaven. Goodness, everyone does. What's not to like? But now it's time for you to live a little. Experience a brand new adventure. Learn new things. Expand your horizons." Stroking his head ever so lightly, she continues, "I am Angel Serena, your guardian angel. And I promise you, I will stay with you every moment of your new life." She holds him back so he will look up into her smiling face. "I will be your little piece of Heaven on Earth."

The sniffling stops for a moment. "You … you promise? You'll stay with me? All the way?"

"Every precious moment." She gives him an encouraging smile. "But after you're born, you won't be able to see me like you can right now. But I'll still be there. Always. Promise. Cross my heart." She hugs him to her chest. "Hush now, little one, and I'll show you a special surprise. Close your eyes tight. Really, really tight. No peeking."

Angel Serena lets go of him and rises to her full impressive height. Her wings materialize in a glory of radiance. "Keep your peepers closed, remember."

"I promise."

The angel flutters her wings vigorously. Even Bessie from a distance can hear and sense the whirring sound. "Can you feel that? That little breeze?"

Suddenly the little aura jumps up and down. "I can feel it, I can feel it!"

Serena grins, still fluttering. "So now, listen carefully. Whenever you need me, in your whole life, you just need to close your eyes …" She flaps her wings even stronger for effect. "And you will feel that little breeze. And you will know that I am with you." For a few more moments she continues to flutter in silence. "Now open your eyes."

The aura gazes up at her in awe as the wing motion continues.

"You see? That little breeze you feel? It's me!" So whenever you feel that sensation and there's no wind around, you will know in your heart of hearts, that it's me. And I, your guardian angel, am with you. Always. Every step, every breath." She stops now, taking the silver veil from her pocket.

He shrinks back for a moment. "What's that for, Angel Serena?"

"This is the Veil of Forgetfulness. So you will forget all about your old life and focus your energies on your new one." She gently drapes the veil around the tiny aura and gathers him into her arms. "Now we've got to get you to your parents, pronto. Your poor mother's been in labor for eighteen hours already, God help her."

Bessie almost loses her balance as she stares up to catch them vanishing into the night sky. Looking back at the empty platform, she realizes she's alone. And far from home. "Home …" She calls out. "Home…home … where is home anyway? Where on Earth is home?" Her throat closes and she gulps for air. She pleads once more, "Home …"

The word itself reverberates and multiplies in the atmosphere into "home-home-home-home." Just as she's realizing it sounds strangely like "om", she vanishes from the airport.

In a blink, Bessie reappears in front of her house she had seen through the lens of the Sacred Telescope. Tears slide down her cheeks as she reaches up to touch the scar on her forehead. Knowing from endless movies how this is going to go down, she doesn't hesitate, but walks right through the door into a dimly lighted hallway.

Only a little lamp illuminates from a side table cluttered with magazines. Peering into the living room, she tiptoes in. On a worn sofa, a retriever sleeps on a blanket, a faded mouse toy inches from his paw. As Bessie stands nearby, his nose begins to twitch, his eyes open. He lifts his head to sniff the air. His tail begins to wag lazily and he barks.

"Mouser, you know me!" Bessie crouches down as if to hug him. Somehow he knows where she is and rubs up against her. She strokes him, realizing he can feel it. He picks up his mouse, dropping it on the floor and barking. An old game.

"Animals are so much more intuitive than us," she whispers in his ear.

Footfalls creak on stairs. Her ears perk up.

"Who's there?" The voice is gruff. "Where are you, you old bag of bones? Some watchdog you are. Watchdog, my ass. Does nothing but watch. Wonderful." Art MacIntyre stomps into the living room in a worn housecoat, almost tripping over his loose belt. Mouser gets up, stiff with arthritis, wandering over to get his head rubbed.

Wordlessly Bessie reaches out trembling arms to her father, to no avail. She hugs herself instead.

Roughly her father strokes the dog. "What did you bark for? Thought you heard something? Nobody here, you dumb mutt. I'll just check the back door, in case. All these damn kids running around all the damn night. You'd think their parents would ..." He disappears into the kitchen, still talking. "Care what happens. God knows what they're up to."

Bessie bites her bottom lip hard, trying to gain control of her feelings. Conflicted on whether to follow him or go upstairs, she hesitates. Glancing at her watch, she chooses the latter.

At the top of the stairs she runs to the rear of the hallway, walking into a room with wall-to-wall posters of the singer, Chris Lisack. A thirty-gallon aquarium sits on her dresser where three large goldfish swim back and forth, winding their way among various plants and the plastic head of a pirate doll. An old wooden chest, a gift from her grandma sits at the end of her bed.

"Home. Can't believe I'm home!" Joyously she flings herself backwards onto her bedspread, glancing here and there, taking in every last, precious detail. Turning to look at her desk under the window, she frowns. Something's missing.

"My laptop. Where's my laptop?" Spinning around in a semi-circle, she sees a jumble of torn bits of paper in her wire wastebasket. Getting down on the floor, she peers closer. Photos of her and Jason fill the container, dozens of them. At least they were photos before she had apparently torn them to bits. She blows at them but they don't react. "Get out of my life!" She hisses. Blowing again to no avail, she adds, "And my after life!"

Now she sits on Leila's bed. Her sister sleeps restlessly, her novel beside her out-stretched hand. Bessie strokes her arm, her eyes filling with longing, remembering the bond they share. "I wish …" She kisses her gently on the forehead. Leila stirs for a moment as if she knows Bessie's there, rolling over on her side before drifting back to sleep.

Reluctantly Bessie glances at her watch. It's 4:04. So soon! She turns to blow Leila a kiss before she disappears into the hallway.

Now she stands at the open door of her parents' bedroom, a smile playing on her face. One word, "Mom," slips from her lips as she steps forward eagerly.

Eying the room, her expectant features transform into ones of utter shock. A scene of bedlam greets her. The mattress is a mess of sheets, half on the floor. Her father's shirt and pants are strewn on the carpet along with a nest of socks and boxer shorts. His shoes rest on the rocking chair. Only the dressing table remains neat with bottles of perfume lined up alongside an antique, silver-handled brush and mirror. A plaid dog's bed lays on a rug near the window.

Where's mom?

"Mom? Mom?" Bessie cries out in anguish. "Mommy!"

She's distracted by her father entering the room, followed by the dog carrying his inevitable stuffed mouse. Art tears off his housecoat, tossing it on top of his other clothes on the floor. He climbs in, mumbling to himself. "Think those damn parents would keep a better eye on their kids. Running around all night like a pack of wolves."

The dog sits on the floor beside him, staring him down, eye-to-eye.

"What're you looking at, mutt head?"

Mouser wags his tail. Inexplicably, Art yanks back the top sheet. "Get in, you big baby." The dog jumps up and wiggles in. It's as if he's grown accustomed to the ritual.

Torn between fear and shock, Bessie yells, "Where's mom?" She runs over to her father's side of the bed, attempting to shake him to no effect. "Daddy, where's mom?"

Her eyes slip to the clock on the bedside table. It reads 4:09. The flight leaves in eleven minutes! Realizing she can't linger, she races for the doorway.

Just as she's about to disappear down the hallway, her father's voice barks out, "Got to keep a close eye on your kids these days. Real close eye."

Bessie freezes in her tracks, hoping he'll say more.

And he does. "Otherwise you'll wind up like us with our girl gone. Just like that." Silence and then: "Move your paw, you great, smelly lump."

Bessie's hand jumps to her scar.

Downstairs in a room off the back kitchen, fondly referred to by the family as the Wreck Room, Bessie's eyes dart from cluttered bookshelves to shoeboxes of recipes clipped from magazines, to hand tools, to a Singer sewing machine buried under bolts of material, to unframed photographs loaded over frames without pictures, to an old public school desk with seat attached.

"Yes, my computer!" A laptop teeters precariously on top of several dictionaries. By habit, even though she doesn't need to, she steps over old winter boots to cram herself into the tiny seat. "Mom was probably using it in here." She touches the keys before realizing she can't press them. Jumping back up, she paces the tiny room, glancing at her watch. 4:12. Tick tick tick.

Frantically she leans over to strike a key in frustration. Nothing happens. She strikes another and another. Sizzling with anxiety, she stops for a moment to remember how she got home from the Earth Portal. Taking deep breaths, she closes her eyes, her fingers poised over the keyboard. "Focus my energy. Focus. Focus."

She tries again, calmer now. "Fo-cus." She can feel the key react to the vibrations from her finger. "Fo-cus." Opening her eyes, she smiles a little. Working hard at keeping her cool, she carefully clicks on Internet Explorer and Googles her name. Up comes an article from the local *Ravenspond Review*. Concentrating, she scrolls down, skimming the words in a rushed whisper, "Two local teenag ... from Ravenspond ... Bessie MacIntyre ... Ashley Moreno ... both fifteen ... last seen July 15th when ... found missing next day ... left notes ... going to each other's homes ... friends since childhood ... police believe the pair ... missing persons report ... filed Sunday. Anyone with any informa ... contact local law enforcem ..."

Frantically she checks the time. 4:13. Finding another news story, she scrolls down. "Missing teens, Bessie Mac ... Ash Moren ... spotted yesterday ... bus station in Chicago ... man traveling from New York alleg ... saw them heading from one bus to ... carrying duffle bags."

Bessie's head snaps up from the computer, grinning. "Ash? With a duffle bag? As if." She glances at her watch again. 4:14. *Shit.*

Linking into a third story, she rushes over the words, "Two girls thought to be missing teens from ... identified as students from Montreal ... search for missing ... now going into the ... Jason!" A photo appears of a solemn-faced Jason in his high school basketball uniform. Words tumble from her lips, "Jason Wallet, Also Missing."

In her shock, her fingers have lost their power. The more she pounds the keys, the less anything happens. 4:16. Her breathing becomes ragged. Shivers scoot up and down her spine.

From behind her, she feels a shock. Leila's singsong voice, brimming with sleep, calls out, "Bess? Are you here, Bess? Bessie?"

Bessie spins around. Her sleep-walking sister peers into the Wreck Room before moving on down the hallway, her eyes open but unseeing. "Bess, you here?" She passes from view.

Bessie dashes out and up to the wandering Leila. She tries to shake her, but she can't. Her sister drifts into the kitchen, still repeating, "Bess? Bessie?"

"Lee, it's me! Lee-lee, please see me. It's Bess. I'm right here now!" She runs after her, towards her, and right through her, as the younger girl wanders back down the hallway into the Wreck Room.

"Bess? Where are you?"

Bessie sighs deeply. "If only you knew."

Leila stops suddenly to shout into the air. "We need you, Bessie! Daddy and I, we need you! Mommy ..."

Bessie freezes. *Mommy what?*

Her little sister breaks into small sobs. "First you're gone, and now mommy, she ..."

"Mommy what, Lee? Mommy what?"

Bessie's eyes dart to her watch. 4:19!

Leila's voice fills with anger. "Where are you, Bessie?"

Bessie stares at her sister, her heart aching. Reluctantly she closes her eyelids, focusing and whispering, "Earth Portal ... Earth Portal ..." The last syllable "tal-tal-tal" vibrates in the air.

As Bessie's image vanishes, Leila jerks back into consciousness. She looks around her, stunned. Something's happening. *But what?* Her eyes stray to the open laptop. Cautiously she steps over debris to take a closer look. She stares down at Jason's newspaper photo. Alert as a fox now, her eyes widen as she searches the room. Bessie? *Could it be?*

—

Bessie slumps in a window seat of an Air Heaven plane as it prepares for take-off. She gazes outside at the chaos of newly dead passengers shuffling restlessly on the Earth Portal platform. As she resembles them, no one pays her much attention.

An elderly gent sits down beside her. He leans forward to snoop through the brochures in the net basket attached to the back of the seat in front of him. After a few minutes he tries to chat her up. "Me? Sat down to watch a rerun of *Seinfeld* and boom. Slipped away during the first commercial. So, how did a little cutie petootie like you die so young, anyway?"

Bessie turns her head to look at him. Her voice is pancake flat. "Don't know."

She continues to stare intently at him for a while, as if hoping he has the answer before turning to look back out the window at the parade of transitioning humanity boarding the flight.

A way-too-perky male Air Heaven attendant comes down the aisle offering glasses of nectar and snacks. Bessie shakes her head no, turning away. The attendant looks at her for a moment, mildly curious, before moving on down the aisle. It would seem it's not the first time he's seen this sort of reaction to death.

CHAPTER 11: HEAVEN

The sound of the prepare-for-landing announcement, read over the loud speaker by a jolly flight attendant, jolts Bessie awake. Moments later, as the plane comes to a complete stop, the pilot's voice chirps, "Last stop, Heaven. Thank Heavens for that!"

As the massive bell suspended in the glass steeple atop Air Heaven Interportal tolls seven times, she swiftly leaps out of her seat to meld into the milling crowd, jostling for position in the aisles. Some passengers are smiling serenely, some weeping in confusion. Others are stoic or stunned, either not grasping their situation yet, or grasping it too late.

Gingerly Bessie scrambles down the staircase, whooshing through the Sacred Portal, rushing across the platform, while keeping to the inside of the moving chaos, eyes downward. By some miracle she manages to avoid the attention of greeting Air Heaven personnel. Slipping out the flowered arch at the front, she scrambles up the hillside to the protection of the familiar bushes.

There she waits until the airport is completely cleared. Now only slow lines of the newly arrived souls accompanied by family members drift up the pathways on the far side of the hill. So far so good.

Smiling to herself, she walks briskly, keeping to the edges of the woods alongside the road to Girls Dorm. As she passes the Boys' version, she glances up at the dark windows, unaware that one disheveled lad with sad eyes, bony elbows, and sticking-out hair, stares longingly into the night.

CHAPTER 12: EARTH

In the kitchen of the MacIntyre home, Leila squirts chocolate syrup into a mug of coffee. She stirs it, tastes it, and adds more syrup. Mouser noisily eats from his bowl on the floor, pushing it across the tiles.

Her father looks up from the newspaper, frowning. "It was a dream, Lee."

"Jason's photo on Bessie's laptop was a dream? Not." She grabs the syrup and squirts another glob.

Art rolls his eyes. Snapping his page, he goes back to reading. "Anyway, I probably left it like that yesterday."

Leila picks at the label from a ChocOnut bar, nibbling on a square of chocolate and almonds. "Like you know how to open the Internet on the computer. Not."

Art gives her one of his looks. "Nice breakfast." He turns his page. "Not."

"No comment. Not."

Suddenly a banging on the back screen door distracts them. They turn to see the fuzzy-through-the-screen image of Eric Pederssen and his Italian leather briefcase. He looks more like a Viking stockbroker than a cop.

Art jumps up from the table while Leila grabs a mug and the coffee pot from the stove.

"Eric! Come in, come in. Sit. Sit. Coffee?"

Eric takes an evidently familiar seat. Leila pours his coffee like a pro before sitting back down.

"Thanks, I need some." He treats the young girl to a gleaming, white-toothy smile.

"Got any news for us today?" Art pushes the china creamer towards him.

Eric glances over at Leila, back at Art.

"She can stay," Art reassures him. "She's smarter than all of us."

Reluctantly the policeman pulls out a series of sealed plastic bags from his case, laying them in a neat row. One type of item is pressed into each one: denim cut-offs, a white tee-shirt, dirty sneakers, green-and-pink plaid shorts with a matching sleeveless top, and a pair of neon pink flip-flops with glittery trim. In two larger bags are visible a dark green backpack and a Sacha Boutique carrier.

"Recognize them?"

Leila answers quickly, "Yes."

"A homeless woman was spotted with them in her shopping cart in the park yesterday. Said she'd found them in a corner of the gazebo under a stack of newspapers. Which ones are Bessie's?"

Art is frozen in his seat, all emotion.

Leila takes over, pointing to the bags one by one. "Bessie. Bessie. Ash. Bessie. Rest is Ash. Backpack, Bessie. Fancy shopping bag, Ash."

Eric runs manicured fingers through his buzz-cut so blonde it doesn't seem real. And maybe it isn't. "After here, I'm taking them over to the Morenos. So ..." He lets his sentence hang.

The three of them stare at the bags to avoid looking at each other.

Finally Art spits out, "What on God's green earth are those damn girls up to?"

CHAPTER 13: HEAVEN

Teenagers from various cultures slump on wooden seats in Angel Jigjag's class. It's just before lunch break in Reincarnation School. Wearing a long colorful caftan and a turban over his pitch-black curls, the angel towers well over seven feet tall. On the blackboard behind him, he writes in large, loopy letters: GET A LIFE. His deep Caribbean accent booms over the disinterested teens as he repeats the words, "Get. A. Life."

Bessie loves his eyes, a brown as rich and dark as mud after rain.

"Now, what are we here for, Carl?" He says "for" like "foh".

A chubby boy in the front row mumbles, "To choose our next life."

"Bravo!" Angel Jigjag tap-tap-taps his pointer on Carl's desk with gusto. "To choose our next life. A most honorable goal for one to attain."

Ash whispers to Bessie, sitting beside her in the very last row. "And how in the hell are we supposed to do that—"

"When we can't even remember what happened to our last ones?" Bessie finishes her thought.

"Something amusing the part-time students you wish to share with us, hmmm? And nice of you to grace our humble philosophy gathering today." Angel Jigjag's gigantic sandals begin to make their way to the back of the room.

As luck would have it, or was it predestination, the bell rings. Teens scramble to escape while he grins down at Ash and Bessie, displaying spaces between his huge teeth. "Off the hook. For the moment, ladies. For the moment."

Now outside, leaning against the outer brick wall, Bessie shares her bag of NecNac Snaks with Ash.

Her friend speaks through nibbles, "I am, like, so pissed off I missed the flight last night. So spill, girl friend. Haven't had a chance to gab since you slipped back into your bed in the wee hours. I want to know every gory little detail. Nice idea, by the way, to attend school today."

"Diversionary tactic. Think I got away with it?"

A shadow swoops overhead, blanketing the bright sunlight, accompanied by a furious whirring sound. Both girls look up to see Angel Rachel hovering overhead, the chains on her reading glasses swinging back and forth, her glittery aura almost blinding them.

Ash swallows her chip whole. "Negative."

CHAPTER 14: HEAVEN

In a small, dark courtroom, Ash sits between Angel Mel and Angel Jigjag. Bessie's grandparents sit on uncomfortable wooden benches in the spectators' section. Millie's shamrock broach is pinned to the collar of her prim blouse. Grandpa Will, squirming in a dark suit, holds a suspicious-looking, brown paper bag in his lap.

At the front, Bessie hunches alone behind the defendant's podium. She glances around, and is rewarded by a series of encouraging grins and thumbs up. All except for her grandpa who is drinking something from the brown bag. Millie gives him a swat and he hastily hides it in his vest pocket.

Facing them all, a glorious black angel in a smart grey uniform stands beside the empty judge's bench. "All rise. This Angel Court is now in session. The Honorable Judge Rachel presiding."

As everyone respectfully stands up, the petite Angel Rachel dramatically emerges from a door behind the bench in her black robes trimmed with a feminine lace collar. She takes her place in the oversized chair behind the elevated desk. The audience sits down, all except for Bessie.

The Bailiff angel continues, "The defendant has been sworn in, your Honor."

"Thank you, Boyd." Angel Rachel gives him a quick side smile. She directs her attention to the defendant, her brown eyes flashing. Not a hair is out of place in her fluff of coif. A smile that-is-not-a-smile plays across her thin lips. Makeup is meticulous on her ageless, oval face. Impressive diamonds sparkle in her tiny ears. "Now Bessie, what flimsy excuse do you have for me this time for your outrageous behavior?"

Bessie tries to speak, but can't find her voice.

"Cat got your tongue?" Angel Rachel actually looks like a smiling tabby herself. One who has just cornered a yummy mouse.

"Well, I just wanted to ... you see, I can't remember—"

"Speak up!" The cat bellows. "We can't hear you!"

"Wanted to ... thought if I could see my family, I might be able to put ... the ah ... pieces together and—"

"And what? Solve the mystery of the universe all by yourself?"

A murmur of chuckling fills the courtroom despite the gravity of the situation.

Angel Rachel leans over her desk to peer down at Bessie, the chains on her glasses shaking. "On my *worst* day, and on your *best* day, you will never. Never. I repeat, never. Be as smart as me." She leans even further. "*Capiche?*"

Bessie stares back in that unreadable way teenagers have perfected over the centuries. She mumbles something unintelligible.

Grandpa Will takes a swig out of his paper bag, ignoring his mate's elbow to the ribs.

Angel Rachel sits back to shuffle papers and adjust her glasses. She mutters under her breath to the bailiff, "They never learn, do they, Boyd. You'd think by now they would know, that for every action, there is an opposite and equal ..." She stops for effect. "Reaction!"

Boyd nods agreeably, arms cradled across his chest. "Oh, I concur, your Honor. I concur."

Now Angel Rachel stands up, leaning so far across her desk, it seems the honorable judge might topple right over. "Now listen to me, Bessie Millicent MacIntyre, and listen carefully. The airport is a sacred place. Sacred. In fact, the most sacred place in all of Heaven outside of the Hall of Akashic Records. The airport is how all those poor souls from Earth and other destinations far and wide come home. That is how ..." She leans even further. "*You* got here." She sits back down in her seat. "Get it?"

The only sound in the courtroom is the buzz of tension.

"Have you anything else to say in your defense? Anything of any remote significance? So I don't have to write you off as a complete ..." Again, that pause for effect, "Nitwit?"

Bessie strokes her forehead scar nervously. Finally she speaks in soft tones. "I was just trying to find out how I died, your Majesty, ah, I mean, your Honor." A ripple of titters pervades the atmosphere.

Angel Rachel mocks. "Boyd, she was just trying to find out how she died." She gets scary-serious again. "Your manner of death will reveal itself to you when it is time. As, no doubt, Angel Mel has explained to you. Countless times."

She glances over at the angel in question for acknowledgement. Sheepishly he puts down his cell phone he was busy texting on and nods yes.

The Honorable judge picks up the thread of her rant, "As would his colleague Angel Jigjag, if the defendant ever managed to get herself to Reincarnation School more than once to cover her tracks from her escapade the night before." She points to her own eyes with her index finger, grinning with feline delight. "You see these? They don't miss a trick. You should know that by now, if you weren't such a *moron*."

Bessie takes a quick glance backwards for support. Weak smiles and more thumbs up appear.

Now Angel Rachel is taking off her glasses, polishing the lens with a white linen cloth she removes from her breast pocket. "Entering Air Heaven Interportal Airport without permission is a very serious offence which we do not take lightly. Compounded with the even more serious and hare-brained offence of ..." She pokes a scarlet fingernail at her head. "Boarding a sacred reincarnation flight ..." She puts her glasses back in place, leering at Bessie. "Without a valid envelope!"

Bessie tries to protest. "But I just thought maybe—"

The judge's voice is calmer now. "You didn't think. That's the problem. You didn't think. You were ir-res-pon-si-ble." Angel Rachel glances sideways at Angel Boyd. "They just don't think, do they, Boyd?"

He shuffles from one foot to the other, nodding his handsome head.

Bessie swallows hard, waiting for the next blow. And here it comes.

"You were a stowaway. On a sacred reincarnation flight. A stowaway!"

This time, when Bessie glances around, her supporters are looking down at their shoes.

Angel Rachel shuffles papers again before directing her comments now to two elderly spectators. "As for you, Millicent and Will Dodd, you are the grandparents. The primary custodial grandparents, God help us all."

Startled, Grandpa Will quickly hides the brown bag he was just sipping from.

"You're supposed to be the - and I use the term loosely - adults. Setting her a shining example of responsible grown-up behavior." She waits again. "Get my drift?" She watches them nodding in her direction like bobble-heads. "Good."

Angel Rachel relaxes back into her seat, speaking in a civil tone now. "Therefore, let's see, summer barbeque season is in full swing on Earth." She looks over to the bailiff for confirmation. "What do you suggest is a proper punishment for this crime of supreme stupidity, Boyd?"

CHAPTER 15: HEAVEN

In a packed dirt yard, in what appears to be the middle of nowhere, Bessie and Ash, both in dungarees - Ash's are designer pink, naturally - stare without expression overhead. Although it's summer-sweaty hot, they wear long-sleeved shirts, rubber gloves up to their elbows, and huge brimmed straw hats with Jackie Onassis sunglasses. Nearby, a large rickety barn stands with its doors wide open.

"Well, this doesn't seem too bad so far," Bessie comments.

"Like, how hard can it be?" Ash agrees, loosening the ties of her hat so it can hang down her back.

"Shouldn't take us, what, maybe one-two hours tops?"

"Then we can catch that new Jayne Mansfield movie. Did you know she died tragically?" Ash gestures by dropping her head backwards. "By a truck?"

"Do you hear a hum?"

"Yeah, sort of like the airport hum. Personally I think she was so glam. A beautiful blonde glam queen. With big boobs." Ash looks down at her own non-existent ones under her dungarees. Pulling up a bit of material with her fingers, she attempts to create the semblance of a chesty chest. A lost cause.

The hum in question soon reveals itself to be a distant helicopter-cloud. They watch as it slowly approaches. Moments later the cloud is directly overhead as they tilt back their faces to watch. It drops to about twenty feet above the ground over the yard to hover in place. A hinged trap door in the bottom of the aircraft swings open.

"How's this gonna work, I wonder?" Ash puzzles out loud.

They soon discover. Unseen hands toss out chickens, one by one. In shock the girls reach up to catch an excited bird and set it safely on the ground. And another, and another, and another. And another-another-another.

One lands on Ash's head, pulling off her hat, allowing another bird to perch, getting his feet caught in her foot-wide mess of curls. He pecks at her scalp in a manic effort to escape. By now the ground is a mass of swirling feathers accompanied by a cacophony of cluck-cluck-cluck and peck-peck-peck.

Four hours later an exhausted and filthy Ash and Bessie flop backwards in the nearby barn on bales of straw, staring out the open doorway. They can see the helicopter-cloud mercifully vanish. The chickens are now calmly pecking on the ground for the scattered grain provided by them, yet another chore they had to complete.

Ash reaches up to pull a feather from her hair. "From this moment on, I swear. I'm, like, totally, totally, gonna be the most religious of all vegetarians."

Bessie spits something from her mouth. She doesn't know what it is and doesn't want to know. "Thanks for helping."

"Hey, what are best friends for?" She swings her head. "Do you hear that?"

Bessie's eyes widen and her head pops up. Through the doorway they spy a small white cloud with a propeller on top heading towards the yard, exuding a faint cluck-cluck-cluck. "No, no, say it isn't so," she whines as the cloud arrives overhead, the trap door opens, and the first of countless chickens drops down.

As they slowly pull themselves upright and head towards the door, Ash sniffs her armpits and almost tosses up her NecNak Snaks. She turns her head to look over at Bess. "So is this where we get to spend all of our eternity?"

CHAPTER 16: HEAVEN

A sulking, filthy Bessie is still in her dungarees and unwashed hair after the chicken episode which mercifully ended at midnight. She slouches against a tree on the cliff a short distance from the Sacred Telescope. It's sometime after three in the morning, but as Angel Mel is always telling her, time doesn't really exist here. The vague outline of Angel Rainbow Sunshine is visible by moonlight as she abuses her guitar with an almost unrecognizable rendition of *Close to You* by the Carpenters. Her faithful audience, the St. Bernard, sleeps nearby. Her ability to carry a tune is only rivaled by her fumbling for chord after chord.

In front of Bessie, Angel Mel materializes on the edge of the cliff, in a sitting position, dangling his stocky legs over the edge. He takes a noisy slurp of a Hector's Nectar before turning to glance at Bessie a few feet behind him. Wrinkling up his nose, he comments, "A shower wouldn't kill you."

The girl is uncharacteristically nasty in her tone. "How can you drink so much of that shit?"

"I'm deeply offended. This is the nectar of the gods, for God's sake. With a little added honey, lemon, and various flavor enhancers." He slurps again to make his point. "You drink it just as much as I do, grumpy guts."

She plunks herself down beside him, leaning back on her arms. "Where's my guardian angel, anyway? How come I don't have one here like they say everybody has on Earth?"

He turns to look at her. "You remember yours?"

She snaps off a long blade of grass, fashioning it between her thumbs to make a whistle. "I don't remember anything, right? I'm Miss Brain Dead. Dah." The grass screeches into an ear-shattering note.

"Lovely sound." Angel Mel sits down his empty container, leaning back to admire the view. "Well, you really don't need one here. And anyway, you've always got Angel Rachel."

"He said to coax a smile out of her." Bessie whistles again, louder this time. The shrill note shatters the air like a terrified cricket.

"Will you stop doing that just to be irritating? You've always got me and you know that."

Bessie tosses the grass whistle over the edge. "It's Jason. He keeps following me. Peeking out from behind trees like a—"

"Like a what?" Angel Mel turns to pick up his discarded Hector's Nectar can, crushing it in one hand before tucking it into his big front pocket.

"Like a ..." She stalls for time, tossing a small stone. "Like some kind of perv. I can't believe I used to be his ..." She turns to face him. "Girlfriend. Yich." She picks up a pebble, aiming it violently into the void.

"Bessie?" He waits for her to look at him. "How do you feel when you see him?"

She stares into his eyes for a long time. Turning away, she yanks out another blade of grass. "Pissed off!" Just as quickly she discards it. "And, and confused. And a little, a lot ... scared, but the ..." She looks at him again. "Then sometimes I feel guilty. Like I should know something, but I don't remember."

Angel Mel hops onto his feet with surprising agility, pulling Bessie up after him. They walk over to a nearby wire bin neatly labeled: BE AN ANGEL, TOSS IT IN. As soon as the discarded can enters the disposal unit, it vanishes.

"Come on, let's mosey." The chunky, balding angel in the Hawaiian shirt takes Bessie's hand. Together they stroll in the direction of the Sacred Telescope.

"Are you sure Jason can't hurt me again?"

"How do you know he hurt you in the first place?" He stops mid-stride, putting a stubby finger under her chin to tilt her head up. "When people on Earth are happy, they say they feel like they're in Heaven, right? Oh, isn't this a heavenly day. What a heavenly view. Oh, what a—"

She jumps into the game. "I'm in Seventh Heaven."

"I'm on Cloud Nine."

They begin walking again. Then Angel Mel stops and looks at her very seriously. "Did you know there really is a Cloud Nine?"

Bessie's not sure whether to bite or not.

He chuckles. "Metaphorically, of course."

"Mel?"

"Hmmm?"

"Where's my mother? What have you guys done with her?"

He pats her head. "Let's go visit the Telescope."

She looks up at him with a small smile. "Thought that was off-limits?"

He grins back. "Not for me, it isn't."

Giggling and bantering, they begin to stroll again, hand-in-hand, unaware that in the shadows of trees, Jason stares after them, his eyes so full of longing, they look like they might melt.

"Why do stars... no, why do stars ... no ... why do ..." Angel Rainbow Sunshine screeches as she searches for the next key, oblivious to Angel Mel as he steps onto the pedestal, removing the lens cap and adjusting the focus.

"Is she always this easy?" He directs his comment to Bessie as he glances over at his fellow angel.

"Not sure how to answer that." Bessie stretches down to pat the big dog who has wandered over to greet them, unaware he's supposed to chase them off. "Don't want to spoil a good thing."

Angel Mel peers into the lens.

"What are you watching, Mel?"

"Oprah. I love Oprah. What a gal. She's way ahead of her time, you know." After awhile he steps down, inviting Bessie up to the pedestal with a gallant swoop of his arm. "Your turn, my dear."

She steps up to peer in. The milky swirls clear to reveal her bedroom in her home on Earth.

A bored, fifteen-year-old Ashley lounges on the bedspread. Her hand props up her head as she listens to a Chris Lisack CD.

Bessie fiddles with her computer at her desk. Also lying on the bed, Leila reads Ruth Reynolds' Fear the Attic. *With the window propped wide open, the heavy, humid heat of early Pennsylvania summer weighs down the atmosphere like wet wood. A photo of Jason and Bessie, posing proudly beside a snowman, sits on the desk by the computer.*

"Want me to paint your nails, Lee? One time offer." Ash dangles a bottle of green sparkly polish from her own just-painted fingernails and toes.

Bessie chimes in, "Why don't you paint them all different colors?"

Leila considers this while she inserts her well-worn bookmark into her page. She rolls over to face Ash, extending her bare feet. "Sure, okay. One color only, though. And only my toes. So what are you guys up to tomorrow?" She turns her head to smirk at her older sister. "Bess is going to say she wants to go to her boyfriend's farm."

Ash pulls the little brush from the polish bottle. "Bess? Is that right?"

Bessie slams down the top of her laptop and jumps up. "The farm? Are you for real?"

Ash exchanges a small smile with Leila. It seems they've heard this protestation countless times before. The older girl stuffs Kleenex in and around the younger one's toes. "So you're still avoiding him then, we are to assume." Ash grins conspiratorially.

Bessie picks up a handful of photos of herself and Jason in happier times - Jason with his arm around her in the barn just after the calf was born two years ago; Jason with his arm around her at a school dance last winter; Jason with his arm around her beside a slide when they were in grade school.

She rips them to shreds. "I hate Jason. It's so over. He's such a ... " She tosses the bits into her wastebasket, picking up more photos from the pile. "A know-it-all! He's suffocating me!"

Leila calmly adds her two cents' worth. "You guys have been on and off since you were what, eight?"

Ash sits back to admire her handiwork. "I remember when they met at the skating rink. The new boy in the jacket too big for him and his uncle's skates on. We skated over, like, almost falling. Right up to him, and he says, "I'm Jason. Jason Wallet. Like the wallet.""

Leila giggles while Ash directs her. "Okay, so wiggle them around a little bit so they'll dry faster. Then I'll put on the second coat." They both look over at Bessie Googling Chris Lisack on the computer. "So if you're really not going over to Jason's farm, then what do ya want to do tomorrow?"

A sly smile streaks across Bessie's pale freckled face. "I've got a brilliant idea."

Back in Heaven, milky swirls fill the telescope lens. Bessie steps back, frowning. To Angel Mel's unspoken question, she barks, "It's all about Jason. Jason, Jason, Jason."

He looks at her with concern, knowing her memories are flowing back into her consciousness. Resting his palms on her shoulders, he speaks in soft tones, "You're safe now, Bessie. You're safe."

Looking up into his eyes, her hand instinctively rises to rub the bird-shaped scar on her forehead. She dissolves into a hug in the great angel's arms.

Still in the shadows, Jason watches, fingering the tiny piece of Bessie's tee-shirt.

CHAPTER 17: EARTH

Upstairs in the MacIntyre home in Ravenspond, a striking black woman in a orange sherbet classic suit and French manicured nails lounges on Bessie's bedspread. A wonderfully vibrant turquoise necklace sparkles around her neck. Across from her, Leila sits cross-legged in khaki shorts and a GO GREEN OR GET LOST tee-shirt. Mouser sleeps on an area rug, one eye on the visitor. The woman sips a glass of white wine. An open bottle of Pinot Grigio perches on a wooden chair beside the bed. Goldfish swim lazily in the aquarium on the dresser. In a semi-circle on the chenille bedspread, photos are lined up in chronological order.

The woman picks up an eight-and-a-half-by-eleven picture of Ashley. Her daughter is all glammed up in full movie star makeup and garish chandelier earrings. Her wild curls are glued back from her face. "I remember this, what, a few summers ago? They made their own headshots to send to Hollywood."

Leila stares at Sophia Moreno, acutely aware of her pain, not knowing what to say. In wisdom beyond her years, she says nothing.

Sophia picks up the matching shot of Bessie, almost unrecognizable with her ginger hair teased up and sprayed to within an inch of its life. Her eyebrows are painted pitch black. Navy blue eyeliner, false eyelashes, and blood red lipstick complete the look. "You think maybe they ran away to L.A.?" She takes another gulp of her wine. "Sorry, sweetie. I shouldn't be laying this on you, especially now with your mother gone."

Leila watches her for a moment before climbing off the bed to pick up the bottle of wine. She refills the exhausted woman's glass. Sophia begins to drink too quickly as the young girl sifts through more photos, one by one.

An hour passes. Sophia is quite drunk now, lying back on the bed, the bottle empty. "'Member, Leila? How they go' all dress up and preten' to be Nicole an' Paris that whole one summer? Switch outfits ever' other day?" She giggles from the effects of the alcohol. "Always fightin' o'er those damn wigs. Who got to be Paris. Who got to be Nicole."

Leila picks up a photo of Ash in the Nicole wig and hands it to her silently.

"I lef' more wine in kitchen. Please?" Sophia holds the picture close to her eyes as Leila disappears out the doorway. She giggles again. "At least she really kinda looks like Nicole." She gazes intently into the face of her daughter. "Why didna notice that before?" Suddenly she tosses the snapshot on the floor. "Those stupid wigs."

Bolting upright on the bed, she yells, "Wigs! Wigs. Lee, Leila?" She chases the girl down the stairs to the kitchen where she's uncorking a second bottle of wine, a discarded shopping bag on the counter. "Ne'er min' that. Ne'er min' that. Wigs! Where those damn wigs?"

They stare at each other in the quiet of the kitchen. Judging from the light from the screen door and windows above the sink, it's mid-afternoon on a steamy, hot day. A dog yap-yap-yaps in the distance. A lawn mower hums. A child screams delightedly, splashing in a pool, a sound that echoes across from another yard.

Sophia is beside herself. "Wigs? Where the wigs?"

Leila sets down the wine and heads back upstairs to Bessie's room, Sophia stumbling after her. Getting on her knees, the girl opens the heavy lid of a cedar trunk at the foot of her sister's bed. Sophia crouches down to hold up the top as the girl sorts through layers of sweaters, boxes, discarded dolls, and other childhood paraphernalia. She takes everything out and lays it carefully on the floor beside the trunk.

"Empty. They're not here." She looks into the smeared makeup of the frantic woman beside her.

Dead sober now, Sophia jumps to her feet to grab the phone from Bessie's side table. She dials a number she knows by heart. "Put me through to Detective Eric Pederssen, please. Urgent. Very urgent."

Mouser lifts his head to watch her intently from his position on the rug.

CHAPTER 18: HEAVEN

In a small clearing in the woods, all is quiet on this lazy afternoon except for the odd bird song. Jason sits on a rock, the piece of Bessie's tee-shirt hanging from his jeans' pocket. On a nearby rock Miguelito watches a squirrel running up a maple tree. "You gotta give it up, farm boy." He turns to look at his companion who is staring off into the distance, shaking his head. "What is up with you?"

Jason's right leg shakes rhythmically up and down, creating a tapping sound on the hard, dry ground. He cracks his bony knuckles. Spotting a small toad a few feet away, he leans down to pick it up carefully, examining it. The toad sits as still as china in his open palm. Only the creature's pulsating throat moves, and it would appear, in unison with Jason's tapping leg.

Miguelito watches him, fascinated, as Jason eventually sets the small toad gently back on the ground. The creature sits there for a moment as if unwilling to leave the human for fear he'll do something to harm himself. With a few more pulsating throat movements, he eventually hops away towards the protection of scrub brush. Jason stares after it for a while. Unwinding his body from the rock, he lopes off into the woods.

Miguelito watches him go, shaking his head. He shouts after him. "What in the hell's the matter with you, anyway? Crazy boy. *Loco*! Jason, come back!" Should he follow or leave him to his own devices? Hearing a rustling sound, he glances down to see the little toad again. Smiling, he crouches down to gently stroke his back. "What is wrong with him, *amigo*? Did he do something very bad in his past life?"

CHAPTER 19: HEAVEN

In his cluttered office Angel Mel sits behind his desk, making notes in his current screenplay effort. Bessie lounges sideways in the armchair, staring out the window at Johnny Cash strolling arm-in-arm with June Carter Cash.

She shifts positions, taking some NecNac Snaks from the bag in her lap. "So how do you know when you're dead, anyways? I mean, really dead."

He doesn't look up as he speaks. "There is no real death, Bessie. I've told you that. Everyone survives death. Just your bodies don't survive, because, well, they're like …" He closes the pages, setting it aside. "They're like suitcases to carry our souls around in. Some souls wear Gucci. Some wear Louis Vuitton or those Vuitton knock-offs. Hard to tell these days with—"

"Some of us even wear backpacks." Bessie grins mischievously.

Angel Mel rolls his eyes. "Heavens forbid!"

"You're such a snob sometimes, Mel."

"Guilty as charged. So what do you think?" He reaches for a can of Hector's Nectar and takes a long sip.

"About what." She stuffs a huge handful of the tasty chips in her mouth at once.

"The suitcase analogy. Clever, if I do say so myself."

The NecNac bag is empty. Crunching it in her hand, Bessie tosses it into Angel Mel's wire garbage container where it vanishes. "If you were human, what kind of suitcase would you wear?"

"Oh, no question. American Tourister, definitely." He gets up to grab his binoculars, turning to look out the window, smiling. "Well, what do you know. Grace Kelly." Glancing back to Bessie, he finishes his original thought. "Bruce Willis wears American Tourister."

Bessie joins him at the window. "So what's in those Akashic Records, anyways?"

"Just every moment of every life, that's what's in them. Wait." He dangles his binoculars from one hand, turning a rare, serious expression towards her. "Wait just one small second here, kiddo. You can't just go snooping around in the Akashic Records. All hell will break loose. They're the holiest of holies." He holds a good long staring contest with her, making sure the penny drops, before turning to look out the window again through his binoculars. "Reserved for angels, certain gypsies, prophets, and psychics. Authentic ones only, of course. Wow, Rock Hudson, too? I'm scoring big today!"

Blissfully happy, he observes the glamorous group chatting on a pathway. "Oh, and, of course, cats." As he watches, the group in the gardens heads towards a tall figure in a cowboy hat in the distance. "Bessie, do you see that? They're going to meet John Wayne! Jackpot! Bessie, listen to me. Visiting the Hall of Akashic Records is one of the greatest offences you can ever commit in Heaven. It might set your soul's journey back centuries. Are you paying attention, missy?"

He spins around to make sure she's got the message but she's long gone.

CHAPTER 20: EARTH

The air is as thick and heavy as a tropical evening. The navy blue Honda Civic crawls slowly along a downtown, working class neighborhood in Cleveland. The sidewalks are filled with hot, sweaty people, either trying to escape the steamy night or take advantage of it.

Art MacIntyre drives. Beside him, a stocky Latino man squirms in the passenger seat. A stack of posters is crammed in by the console. The title is clearly visible: HAVE YOU SEEN THESE TEENS? Beneath the words, Ash and Bessie smile up innocently in school photos along with a set of their glamour head shots with the cautionary words: MAY BE WEARING WIGS. Contact information fills the rest of the sheet.

Jorge Moreno picks up half a tuna submarine sandwich from waxed paper on his lap. He takes out the slice of tomato, tossing it out the window. "I hate vegetables. Hate 'em all. Except chili peppers, of course. Love chili peppers. And onions." He stares out the window at the milling mass of sweating humanity. "Which one is really a fruit?"

Art scowls at him. "One of them is always mistaken for a vegetable. Forget which one. Look at them all. Enjoying themselves. Not a care in the damn world."

Jorge takes a whale-sized bite, dripping mayonnaise. "Maybe our daughters are too, for all we know."

Without warning Art jams on the brakes, white-knuckled. He points excitedly. "There they are!"

Indeed, half a block ahead of the Honda, on a crowded sidewalk, two teenage girls stroll - one pale Caucasian with blue black hair and one of mixed heritage with bright blonde hair. They teeter in spike heels and cheap, tight outfits. Arms are interlocked as they chatter and giggle.

Art scrambles to find a place to pull over and park. He gives up, turning off the ignition in the middle of the road. Grabbing the keys, he spills out of the car, followed closely by Jorge. Despite the heat, they tear through the crowd like boys who have just stolen a purse.

The crowd fills in. The girls disappear. Art and Jorge stop to look around, frantic.

Through an opening in the throng ahead, the girls appear again. The men elbow and tear through the slow-motion mass, pushing aside a stroller, making the baby cry. They both shout into the air, "Ashley! Bessie! Stop. Wait. Bessie!"

Now they're closing in on the oblivious teenagers. The back of their heads are together, the dark complexioned girl in an obvious fake blonde wig.

"Stop! Bessie! Ash! It's dad! Daddy! Stop for the love of God!"

Now they are narrowing the gap. A small dog on a short leash barks and snaps, pissing off the owner. "Hey, youse! You just bashed into my dog, you fuckers!"

The two perspiring men are now just a few feet behind the girls. "It's your dads, please. Ash, Bessie, stop, please!"

The teenagers finally react to the shouting right behind them, spinning around. Art and Jorge's features beam with joy. Followed closely by shock and repulsion. Instead of their daughters, two sulky, hard-faced strangers glare back, smacking wads of gum. They're a gut-wrenching mockery of their beloved girls. Sex workers, more than likely.

Art's and Jorge's faces contort in pain. The girls smirk, snap their gum, shrug their shoulders and turn back around, disinterested. They teeter off, getting lost in the crowd.

The men stand silently on the sidewalk, watching the girls' backs disappear as people push by them. Finally Art turns to head back. "Tomatoes."

Jorge turns to look sideways at him. "Tomatoes?"

Slowly, painfully, the two fathers begin the sad trek back to the abandoned car where a policeman is busy writing up a ticket. Art speaks under his breath, "They're a fruit. Not a vegetable."

CHAPTER 21: HEAVEN

"I would have made a great warrior." Bessie stares at herself in the mirror in the image of the great Iroquois leader, Hiawatha, in full ceremonial gear. She shares the changing room of Bodysuits Boutique with Ash, struggling to pull on an image, tugging at the bottom bits.

"There. How do I look?" Marlene Dietrich now stands beside the indigenous hero. Her tighter-than-skin, sparkling gown is set off with diamonds. She speaks with exaggerated German inflections, "Ah vant to be ah-lun."

"We dance?" Bessie/Hiawatha requests politely in a deep voice.

Laying her dainty, white-gloved hand over the strong brown one, Ash/Marlene pulls back the curtain. "Vy, off course, mah dahlink."

Back out in the boutique, Soulslady, much to her intense dismay, is being swarmed by a pack of excited boys, evidently new clients to the store. The girls take full advantage of the situation. Bessie/Hiawatha does a spectacular rain dance with all the accompanying whoops and hollers, swinging her tomahawk around like a baton, while Ash/Marlene waltzes to the beat of her own orchestra. Together they dance their way right out of the store into the main corridor, much to the delight of onlookers.

Ten minutes go by until Ash/Marlene spots Angel Rachel deep in conversation with Angel Jigjag, exiting a nearby bookstore. "Danger-danger!" She shouts, forgetting her German accent and elbowing Bessie/Hiawatha. Hastily they rush back into the boutique where Soulslady yanks them towards the change room firmly by one ear each. "Game over, missies."

CHAPTER 22: HEAVEN

Escaping the wrath of Angel Rachel by mere moments, Bessie and Ash scoot out of the mall and head towards the cliff in the distance. When they reach the path that will take them upwards, they can hear the strains of a beautiful song sung by a clear, strong female voice.

"I think that's Patsy Cline," Ash whispers excitedly to Bessie. "My mom just loves her music. She has every single album. When she doesn't know we're around, she sings and dances to them in the living room. What a riot and a half. She would just die to hear her in person."

Bessie stops to give her friend a smirk. "That's why we can hear her, silly. We're already dead."

The second verse of the song is sung by a sweet male voice, all soft and wistful and lonely.

Now it's Bessie turn to be all excited. "Omigod, omigod, it's Ricky Nelson. Wasn't that tragic when he died in that plane crash just as he was making his big comeback? So sad. He's the hero of Chris Lisack. Who, of course, is my hero."

The hauntingly beautiful duet grows stronger as they approach the Sacred Telescope. Now they can see Patsy and Rick leaning against two trees about six feet apart from each other, singing in the edge of the forest that borders the cliff. Angel Rainbow Sunshine sits in front of them - awe-struck, cross-legged, and with her plump arms propped behind her, beaming like the sun she is named after. To say she is in Heaven, doesn't express her joy. Mercifully she is silent.

The girls stand for a while on the path listening to the rest of *The Wayward Wind* sung by the haunting voices. "Kind of reminds me of us," Ash says with bravado. "We wander like the wind, don't we, Bess. Here, there, and everywhere."

"If only we knew where it finally took us." Bessie's voice is tinged with longing. "Come on, let's go visit the Telescope while the coast is clear. You go first."

Half an hour later, after listening to Ash's oohs and aahs - she is apparently watching Paris Hilton and Nicole Richie in some reality television show - Bessie gives her friend a poke. "Okay, my turn now." Soon she's adjusting the focus. The milky swirls clear away.

Bessie sneaks down the staircase of her Ravenspond home. She is wearing denim cut-offs, dirty sneakers, and a white tee-shirt. In her hands she carries a small, stuffed backpack, with a mini-handbag slung around her shoulder. Tiptoeing down the hallway and through the kitchen, she unlocks the screen door to slip outside. The morning sky, although still dark, glows rosy with the promise of another steamy July day.

Ash sits on a rusty swing set in a green-and-pink plaid matching shorts and top set, with neon pink flip-flops decorated in rhinestones on her feet. Beside her, a full Sacha Boutique bag perches on the grass. As soon as Bessie relocks the door, the two of them head around the side of the house, down the driveway, and along the empty road.

The sky is somewhat lighter now as they reach the park in the center of town. Looking around to make sure they're alone, they head over to the old wooden gazebo located in the middle, a perfect place to change.

Snickering, they tug off their regular clothes. Ash mumbles under her breath, "I wish my mom would quit buying me all these cutesy, matchy-matchy outfits."

After a few minutes Bessie stands up in a red-striped stretch top, denim mini, wide black belt, and navy blue wedges. Ash joins her, barely recognizable in a cheap blonde wig, a hot pink top with matching micro, and rose platforms so high, it's amazing she doesn't topple over. Ash adjusts the fake hair over her thick, dark curls. "So, how old do I look?"

Bessie gives her the once-over. "Oh, eighteen, nineteen even."

Ash's confident smile quickly fades.

"No, I mean twenty-four, really." Bessie corrects herself. "Now fix my wig for me?"

Content now, Ash applies layers and layers of makeup on her friend's upturned face as she sits patiently on a wooden bench. After brushing out the long dark locks of the Nicole Ritchie wig fitted over her palm, she leans in to tug it down over Bessie's bobbed red hair. "But what are we gonna do with all our junk?" Ash points at their former gear.

"Nobody'll look here." Bessie glances around the gazebo. "We'll just stuff it into the corners under these newspapers. After all, we'll be back in a couple of days. A week, tops."

After hiding their stuff, they wobble off towards the main road. Ash slows down to adjust a spaghetti strap. "So where are we going anyways? You still haven't told me."

"Did you remember to leave that note for your parents?"

"Yeah. Said I was going camping for the weekend with your family. Mom's so busy right now with her real estate, she won't have time to fuss over it."

"Perfect. And I said I was going camping with yours. That'll keep 'em for at least overnight."

Now they lounge on the shoulder of the road, smiling at the odd passing vehicle, few and far between at this early hour. While they wait, they practice strutting their stuff, tittering like the naughty children they are.

From the east, some distance down the highway, a well-used, baby blue Buick lumbers slowly. Ash and Bessie stick out their thumbs. The big car pulls over. An elderly woman reaches over to open the passenger door. Ash climbs in the front, Bessie in the back. On the dash, a small clock is stuck with duct-tape.

The old woman mutters crossly, "You girls shouldn't be hitching rides. Too danger-ous. You from here? Help yourselves to the tin of biscuits." She gestures to an open metal container filled with homemade chocolate chip cookies separated by layers of waxed paper. "Baked them last night, so they're good and fresh." She helps herself to one before repeating, "You girls really shouldn't hitchhike with strangers. Bad things happen." As she puts the old car in gear, she takes a moment to look over at Ash nibbling on a cookie. "Lucky you gals got me."

As the Buick moves off the gravel and back onto the roadway, a rickety brown Oldsmobile sedan with a cracked windshield rounds the corner, following some distance back, but in the same direction as the disappearing vehicle. A youth with odd, sticking-up hair sits at the wheel.

Jason.

CHAPTER 23: HEAVEN

Bessie and Ash lie wide-awake in their single dorm beds. Their two roommates are sound asleep like the boring, well-behaved girls they are. Ash hisses as she reads her *Angel* magazine, "Goody two shoes."

"Shush. Don't wake 'em."

"Says here, well, it's only a rumor but, says Angel Mel is planning on staging his own musical."

"Let me guess. *Mel's Belles?*"

"Oh, did he tell you that in your session?"

One of the sleeping roommates stirs for a moment before drifting back to sleep. "Let's get a move on." Bessie slips out of bed, fully dressed right down to her sneakers, while Ash does the same. Together they tiptoe down the back stairs, leaving through a rear window this time, having been caught too many times at the front desk.

An hour later, if there was such a thing in Heaven, they walk as briskly as Ash's high-heeled sandals will allow. The only sound is the tinkling of her many bracelets and the hoot-hoot of a distant owl.

Bessie stops from time to time, checking the right side of the road every twenty paces. She picks up stones the size of a quarter to examine them, sifting them through her fingers before tossing them back.

"This is what you heard? For-sure, for-sure? Bess, is this, ah, okay, what we're doing? I mean, what if we get caught? Your grandma said it would, like, set us back a thousand years or something. I mean, that's a long time."

Bessie gives her a broad, fake smile. "We won't." She stops again, stooping down and spies a clear blue stone. When she tries to pick it up, she can't. She tries again just to make sure. It doesn't budge. Parting the tall grasses around it, she sees an obscure dirt path leading through the woods. "This is it."

As they tread carefully along the winding trail, the deciduous forest eventually gives way to a wild, tropical jungle. Ash stares at the strange trees, looking as if they want to eat her alive at any given moment. "Need I remind you I'm not outdoorsy," she whines pitifully while parrots, macaws, and cockatoos squawk and scream from somewhere unseen above them. A small monkey swoops overhead, frantic over the intruders.

A beast roars. A lion? A tiger? They rush to hide behind a tree. "I'm going back." Ash turns to run.

"Oh, don't be such a fretty cat." Bessie drags Ash's arm impatiently along the path. "Fretty cat, fretty cat," she teases, trying to lighten her own fear as well.

They continue on, now holding hands. As the exotic calls and screams swirl around, they're thankful the roar of the beast does not repeat. Nor does the beast itself appear.

Finally a bright light filters through the foliage some ways ahead of them. It appears to be a clearing of some sort. And judging by the hum of activity, it's definitely "the place".

They stop while Bessie draws two large, dark-shaded shawls out of her small backpack. Wrapping the material around themselves from head to toe, they can barely see. Bessie stuffs their current footwear into her pack, retrieving beaded slippers previously acquired at the Seventh Heaven mall several days before. Next she pulls out strings of cheap beads in gaudy colors purchased the same day. "I'll let you decide how we wear these, you being the fashion diva and all." She hands them to Ash.

The fashion diva stares at the beads for a moment before ordering Bessie to remove her shawl. "I just put it on," Bessie complains.

"Just do as I say." Ash tosses her own shawl on the path. Now she drapes the strands of beads around their necks and wrists, saving the last two. Taking one purple string in her hand, she winds it around Bessie's forehead, securing it with multiple bobby pins. Removing a large green pendant from her pocket, she arranges it on her friend's forehead. "That's where your third eye is," she informs Bessie. "According to *Angel* magazine."

"I've got another eye? Just don't blind me."

Soon Ash has performed the same task on herself, something she appears to have practiced, before wrapping the shawls back around them. "How do I look?" She shakes her head to make her purple pendant wiggle.

"Ash, I can't breathe," the muffled voice of Bessie complains. She reaches out a hand to pull the material down below her mouth. "These aren't burkas, you know, just shawls. Like gypsies wear, hopefully." She ties her backpack to a low branch of a tree with a bright red scarf brought along for the purpose. "Let's try to walk." It takes some practice, but after a few steps they seem to get the drift. "Ready?" Ash nods yes. They make their way arm-in-arm towards the clearing.

Now on the outskirts, they crouch down to peer through palm fronds into a large, well-lighted, immaculately groomed park. In the center, a stone courtyard is cordoned off with glowing beams of blue light. Inside the barrier, on a raised marble platform, a towering, three-sided monolith of pure quartz crystal stands proudly, soaring upwards like a skyscraping pyramid. The stone is elaborately carved with petro glyphs glowing with a distinct rosy aura. At the pinnacle, encircling satellite dishes spin their heads up, down, and sideways in an endless rhythmic dance, crackling with lightening-like strikes from every direction. High above, gigantic white birds with angel-style wings swoop and dive.

Wandering through the park, a motley collection of angels, monks, shamans, priests, gypsies, seers, and wee folk - like fairies, unicorns, gnomes, and leprechauns - stop to gab and greet old friends. Cats wander amongst the crowd, apparently on the same level here.

On the far side of the cobblestones, a magnificent marble building on the scale of the Taj Mahal flies a flag of no color; rather, it glows with pure energy. Guard angels in white and silver uniforms stand at full attention every ten feet. A large stone stairway leads up to an intricately carved door. Above it, embedded into the stone, are the immortal words: HALL OF AKASHIC RECORDS.

At the entrance, a seated guard checks IDs of every soul who wishes to enter. The visitors, it seems, must peer into some sort of glowing machine; it's impossible for the girls to tell at this distance.

To say Ash and Bessie are dumbstruck, is understating their awe.

"This is gonna be a challenge." Bessie watches as a leprechaun gets approved to enter the Hall.

"Let's mingle," suggests Ash. "Looks sort of like a movie set, doesn't it?" She hops to her feet, getting into the spirit of things. Adjusting her shawl, she pulls Bessie with her into the crowd.

They meander for a while, trying to blend in, and not doing so badly, either. There appears to be many others draped in similar, nondescript apparel. Slowly they make their way over to the marble platform to gaze up at the gigantic pyramid of quartz. Regardless of the antiquity of the petro glyphs, it's as if they were carved yesterday. The satellite dishes crane their necks about gracefully and continually, in the manner of some exotic dance ritual.

'Maybe that show *The Other Side* is on," Ash whispers without turning her head.

"Or Joanne Sicard is doing a reading," Bessie whispers back.

So far, so good. No one seems to be taking any particular notice of them. Keeping to the ambling speed of the other strollers, they make their way over to the Akashic Hall of Records. Ash stops to gaze up at one of the handsome guards. She can't help it. Flirting is her natural gift, as she never tires of explaining to her best friend. She smiles, widening her eyes. No reaction. She flutters her long eyelashes. Still no reaction. She flicks a curl poking out from under her shawl with a finger. Still nothing. She shakes her purple pendant dangling on her forehead. Her prey stares straight ahead without seeing her at all.

Bessie hisses at her to stop drawing attention to them, but Ash can't resist one final move. One *pièce de résistance*, as it were. She pinches his butt. His eyebrows pop up. His cheeks redden. Aha. Mission accomplished. At least, that one.

"Pay attention." Bessie yanks on Ash's arm impatiently as a holy man of some sort leans into the magical machine at the doorway. As he stares into the screen, a holograph of his image appears above it, then is immediately sucked in, no doubt for filing purposes. The angel nods, announcing, "Entrance approved." Several angels, a gypsy, and a wee person of unknown origin, go through the same process before disappearing within the great door.

"We haven't got a snowball's chance in hell," Bessie mutters.

"Leave it to me. Walk towards the door. Go."

Bessie stares at her curiously.

"Go." Ash insists. "Go-go-go."

As Bessie reaches the first step, a loud scream erupts behind her. Still walking, she twists her head just enough to see an extraordinary sight - a creature possessed! The creature writhes and twists and tears at its clothes and hair, foam spewing from its mouth, as it screams at the top of its lungs in a strange, German-mixed-with-Spanish-slash-French accent, "'Elp me! 'Elp me! Somebody 'elp *moi! Mio dio!* A demon's got *moi* ...'Elp ... *Por favor!* Someone! 'Ellllp! He's biting *moi* ... anybody! *Diablo!* Ouch! Ouchouchouch!"

Bessie laughs in pure astonishment. Ash really is going to make a fine actress one of these lives.

Angels and visitors alike, rush to the poor, tormented soul's aid. Even the guard angel at the door abandons his post, as Bessie, still smiling, slips through the entranceway.

Once inside, she soon discovers she's in an ultramodern satellite radio station, all glass and chrome. A large sign announces the call letters: H.E.V.N. Framed photos of various deejay angels abound. Bessie hides behind the front door, peering out. Ash's histrionics can still be heard, as a chaotic rush of angels and visitors race through the lobby and outside, some still with headphones on. Bessie can hear snippets of panicked conversations: "Hasn't been a major demon sighting in Heaven since, well, since Hitler!"

"There was that real pesky one a while back. Soddom ... Saddam ... Suddam something?"

"Saddam. Saddam Hussein."

"Don't forget all those serial killers like Ted Bundy."

"They're sociopaths, not demons, per se."

"Demonic behavior by a human who lost their soul. I buy that."

Finally the crowd thins out and the entranceway goes quiet. Bessie peers out. The coast is clear. She steps out tentatively.

Across the marble floor she spies a bank of seemingly endless elevators, each one labeled from the beginning of recorded time. She rushes past in a blur until she comes to the 21st Century. As she pushes the button, the elevator doors slide just wide enough for her to enter. She rushes in.

Inside, panels of gold buttons line the walls, one for each year of the century. She searches for 1992 and presses hard. At a speed beyond supersonic, the elevator flies to the designated floor, stopping as abruptly as it started.

When it opens, Bessie sees a long hallway in both directions with a series of doors labeled by months. She tears along the empty hallway until she finds June. Hesitating for a moment, her hand shaking on the knob, she wonders out loud, "Do I really want the truth?"

It's useless to speculate as she already knows the answer. She steps inside.

Bessie looks around, stunned. "That little thing? That's it?" Staring at her from a glass table, is a small gold laptop. Over the back of a modern office chair, a guard angel's jacket and cap hangs askew, evidently forgotten in their flight to see the demon outside.

She tiptoes over to the chair and sits down. Caressing the smooth gold surface with her fingers, she snaps opens the computer. On the desktop, milky swirls flow rhythmically just like in the Sacred Telescope.

"Password, password. What's the password?" Panicking, she tries the call letters, "H.E.V.N." No luck. She tries "Heaven." No luck. She tries "Akashic." Too obvious. Everything's too obvious.

Then an inspiration. "My birth date. I'll try my birth date." She types in June 14, 1987. The swirls miraculously clear.

A plastic wading pool drips water in a backyard about twenty feet from the exterior blue siding of Bessie's family home. An abandoned hose curls up on the patio outside the back door. Further out in the yard, a shiny, bright red swing set still displays a giant yellow bow with an over-sized tag: HAPPY BIRTHDAY BESSIE.

Only the grass around the frog-painted pool is still green. The rest is parched dry and yellow, by an early hot, dry spell this particular June.

Two toddlers sit in shallow water in brightly-colored bathing suits, splashing the surface with their palms and shrieking. One, the chubby one, has fair red hair cut in a bowl shape. The other is copper-skinned, with long limbs and thin as a stick. Her fuzzy dark curls bounce around her gleeful face. A puppy with a big bow around his collar runs around and around the pool, with a fake mouse in his teeth. He barks, causing him to drop his toy. He picks it up, shaking it and running around some more, barking and dropping it again.

A young Heather MacIntyre, in shorts and a sleeveless blouse, calls over from the patio she's sweeping. "Come on now, you two. Time to get out of the pool. Ashley's mommy will be here any second." She turns her head. "Oh, here she is."

Young Bessie splashes her new puppy, yelling loudly, "But I no wanna get out of my poo-wul!"

Young Ash seconds that. "We no wanna get out of da poo-wul! We no wanna get out of da poo-wul." The chorus is repeated over and over.

Heather hands Sophia a glass of white wine with ice-cubes in it. "Oooh, I needed that." Sophia, stylish in a cream linen pantsuit with chunky crimson jewelry, takes the wine glass gratefully, tipping it back.

"So how's the real estate biz on a day like this?" Heather sips her drink.

"Quiet as a graveyard. But wouldn't you know, I've got a showing after supper." She looks over at the toddlers. "Those two."

"Inseparable." Heather chuckles.

"Little devils."

The women wander over to the pool and lean over, smiling. Sophia addresses her daughter, "Okay, come on now, Ashley, dear. Time to go home for supper."

Heather adds, "You can come back tomorrow and play in the pool again."

The little girls put their hands over their eyes, snickering. Sharing a glance, the mothers lean down closer. And closer. Now they are down on their hands and knees to lean in even more.

The toddlers lift their hands partially from their eyes, just enough to see each other. In unison, they slap the water hard, soaking their pretty mothers head to toe before collapsing backwards in fits of giggles.

"Later on in my life, later on!" Bessie in the Akashic Hall of Records pleads, punching the "enter" button frantically. She listens for any signs of returning H.E.V.N. personnel. "Later, later. I need to know what happens later on in my life!"

The milky swirls clear.

A skating session is in full swing on an outdoor frozen pond somewhere in a field. Kids of all ages and some adults are skating to their hearts' content, as the clink-swish-clink sound of metal blades on ice reverberates in the crisp air. An elderly man skates beside a small child who is busy pushing a chair for support. One loud young man sails across one end of the rink on his butt, the result of losing control. His friends are chasing him, guffawing with youthful bravado. A young girl, wearing comically wrinkled-up tights and frilly skirt, practices a twirl in the center, her dreams of the Olympics shining on her serious features. The afternoon sun shines down on a clear, cold February sky.

At the far end, a group of kids around the ages of five and six skate together in large circles as their parents huddle around the edge, some with blankets around their shoulders. The Morenos and MacIntyres are passing a thermos of doctored hot chocolate back and forth.

To one side, an eight-year-old Bessie and Ash practice skating backwards. Apart from them, a tall, skinny boy about ten, skates by himself. Ash, in head-to-toe pink, looks over at him. "There's that new boy, Jason something."

"Should we go over and say hi?" Bessie, in navy blue, sticks her arms out to balance herself.

"He lives on that farm near your grandma and grandpa, doesn't he?"

"Does he? Never knew that. Okay, let's go."

Awkwardly they skate over in a rush, stopping right in front of him. The startled new boy looks as if he thinks they're going to yell at him. Ash reassures him with a sunny smile from under her angora tasseled hat. "You're new here."

Bessie loses her balance and grasps at the sleeve of the boy's coat. "I'm Bessie and she's Ash."

He looks curiously from one to the other. "I'm Jason Wallet. Like the wallet."

The girls titter from behind their mittens. "You're funny." *Bessie grins up at him, still holding onto his sleeve.* "So where'd you live before, anyways?"

"In Michigan." *His voice is soft and low.* "We moved here 'cause my uncle died. It was his farm. Peter Wallet."

The girls tee-hee some more before Ash, spying someone more interesting, skates off with a, "There's Hans," *leaving Bessie and Jason alone.*

He looks at her shyly. "I've seen you when you visit your grandma and grandpa."

"You have?" *Bessie is flabbergasted.* "I've never seen you there before."

He tugs on the earflap of his hat. "Well, that's 'cause you never knew I was there."

She nods agreeably. "That makes sense."

"I'm gonna be a farmer just like my uncle Pete."

She stares him in the eye. "I'm gonna see every square inch of the entire world."

They look away, look back at each other, and away gain, confused and intrigued.

He extends his hand tentatively. "You want to skate?" *She takes his much larger mitten in hers, and slowly they begin.*

"Bessie?" *He repeats her name again.* "Bessie, you know what?"

"What." *Her eyes dart sideways.*

"You're pretty."

You can tell by her expression, he is the first boy to ever tell her that.

The milky swirls return. In the Akashic Hall of Records, Bessie fixates on the desktop, shouting at it, "No! No!" The hum of angelic voices from downstairs gets louder. "Please, I need to know about my death!" She bangs the "enter" button over and over. "My death, how did I die? I must know!" Her eyes dart towards the window where the chaos continues in full force. Whatever Ash has done to cause it, it seems to be working, bless her little obstreperous heart. Mercifully the swirls vanish and Bessie peers at the desktop in utter fascination.

A fifteen-year-old Bessie and Ash, in trashy outfits, wigs and heels, lounge at the side of a country road across from a rickety garage, almost devoid of customers. Bessie munches on a chocolate chip cookie from a metal tin that was previously on the front side of the old lady's Buick. They both sip on cans of soda.

"Fuck, it's hot." *Ash scratches at her shiny blonde wig.*

"Grin and wear it, girl-friend." Bessie tugs at hers, too. "Hey, we can swear all we want 'cause nobody can hear us. Hear that, Lee-Lee?"

"She's, like, such a little goodie-goodie sometimes, your sister."

"Aunt Fizzy says she's the mature one, which is so funny coming from her. Fizzy is as mature as a twelve-year-old."

Ash gazes along the highway that stretches out flat for miles on end. Young cornfields bake in the sun. "How many times has Fiona been married anyways?"

"Three. Counting the one that got annulled 'cause he was already married."

"That old lady sure was nice to give us a ride. And the cookies."

"Hand me one before you eat 'em all." Bessie reaches for the small tin. "Look, here comes a car. Stick your thumb out quick." Cookies forgotten and put away, both girls stick out their thumbs. A pink Volkswagen convertible pulls over. A painted blonde woman gaily leans towards the passenger seat, smiling. "Need a ride?"

Ash looks over at Bessie who returns her glance. They can see stacks of boxes piled in the back seat. The woman notices, and chirps, "Oh those. I can put them in the trunk. They're full of my very own cosmetics, I'll have you know. In the Pink by Lorry-Lyn. Help me move them, would you?"

The stranger's cheery disposition is infectious. Without hesitation, the girls open the back seat door and unload the boxes to put into the now open trunk. In no time, they are on the road. Ash is chatting a mile a minute to the blonde woman while Bessie settles into the back seat, watching the world go by.

As the convertible pulls out, a rusty sedan appears from a side road, traveling behind at a discreet distance. Jason's junkyard Oldsmobile.

The desktop fills in with milky swirls. Seated in front of the gold computer in H.E.V.N., Bessie gasps, "Jason again!" Her attention is immediately diverted by the sound of elevator doors opening, and the chatter of excited personnel spilling into the hallway outside. Quickly she snaps the laptop shut, grabbing the angel jacket and cap from the back of the chair. Just as two angels saunter in, she tucks herself behind the open door.

"Think it was a genuine possession, the way that poor soul was writhing and foaming like that, don't you?" One angel looks curiously at the chair before sitting down. "Have you seen my jacket? I could swear I left it on the—"

"Well, I saw the demon with my very own eyes, Hildy." The other angel pulls up the Venetian blind from the window. "He was attacking her with such force I ... Who's that?"

The seated one gets up to go over to the window. "Who's who?"

"Over there. By the transmission tower."

"Don't see anyone. Maybe it's just a … Hey! Mother Teresa!"

"You serious?"

Their excitement is all encompassing as Bessie slips unnoticed past the door. Now hunched over in the angel jacket with the cap pulled low, she catches the down elevator just as the doors are closing. It reopens onto a lobby full of chaos. Easing her passage this way and that, she disappears out the main door without a hitch. The guard angel at the entrance looks at her intently before he's distracted by a gypsy wanting to identify herself.

Bessie skips down the stairs, vanishing into the hub of the milling throng that is still heady from witnessing a possession. Out of nowhere, her arm is yanked hard. Ash's voice hisses, "Over here." She tears off Bessie's angel cap while her pal wiggles out of the jacket and rearranges her shawl.

Faces down, their heads buried in material, and holding hands so as not to lose track of each other, they steer themselves towards the woods, not stopping until they come to the path. Scampering along it, they soon return to where Bessie hid the backpack in a low hanging branch. Looking around to make sure it's safe, they throw themselves on the ground, spread-eagled on their backs. A tightly-coiled Bessie tosses her H.E.V.N. jacket and cap in the air.

Ash is beside herself. "So what'd you see? What'd you see?"

Bessie turns her head to look at her friend, eyes wide. "How did you do that? They really thought there was a possession happening out there."

"I came prepared."

"I'm listening."

Ash reaches into her ever-present handbag under her shawl, pulling out a giant can and spraying something white and foamy right in Bessie's face.

"Hey! Cut that out!" Bessie licks her lips with her tongue, discovering how tasty it is. Giggling, she examines the can, reading out loud. "Angel Whip. Guaranteed to make any dull dessert heavenly. That's too funny."

They lie back, letting their breathing return to normal. After a few minutes, Bessie stands up to get back into her normal clothes. Tossing Ash's to her, she tucks both shawls and all the beads messily into her backpack.

"So," Ash begins. "Spill. What happened in there?"

Bessie sprays some more Angel Whip on her fingers, licking them off. "It was him, Ash. Jason. We went off hitchhiking somewhere and he followed us. He's the reason we're ..." She searches for a way to say it without saying it, "He's the reason we're here."

Ash watches her, waiting for more. Bessie relates all she has learned from the golden computer. "I'm sorry, Ash. He was my weird boyfriend." Bessie's eyes fill with tears. "If you hadn't gone off with me that day, maybe you'd still be—"

"Hush now." Ash gives her a big hug. "Whatever we did, whatever we do, we do together. Then, now, and always."

Bessie pulls away. "No, this was my fault. All my fault."

"Look, you don't know that. We don't even know where we were going that day. Maybe it was me wanting to run away to Hollywood and I dragged you with me. We don't know that."

"But it was my big brilliant idea."

"Maybe it was your big idea to help me become, like, a famous star." Ash raises one eyebrow. "You're always telling me to follow my dreams."

Not convinced, Bessie sits down to tie her running shoes. Ash jumps around, shaking her bracelets to the sky. "I mean, look at the way you said we were dressed. Like so glam! Doesn't that scream the next Reece Witherspoon to you?"

Bessie gives her a small smile, not really swayed, but wanting to be. "Maybe."

As the girls trot off down the path, through the tropical and deciduous forests on their long trek back to Girls Dorm, a pale, thin youth watches, a scrap of cloth clutched tightly in his fingers.

CHAPTER 24: HEAVEN

On the front porch of Girls Dorm, Angel Coretta greets the arrival of Angel Mel. "Thanks for coming on such short notice." She extends her hand out of her house-coat over a flannel nightgown.

He takes it in both of his. "So when did you first notice them missing?"

"Doing my last bed check. They're always first on my list. Always anywhere but where they're supposed to be, those two."

He gives her a quick hug. "Coretta, dear, even God couldn't keep track of Ash and Bessie." They turn simultaneously to look down the long dark road.

"May I ask you a question, Mel?"

"Shoot." He treats her to a quick grin.

"Do they *ever* go to school?"

"Let's go in and wait in your office. Maybe you could rustle up some hot nectar?"

"I'll put the kettle on."

An hour later Angel Coretta sits across from Angel Mel, her chin cupped in both palms, smiling with tolerant amusement. Her fellow angel holds a tattered screen-play in the air that is threatening to come apart at its fasteners, as he reads with great mobster-style inflections, "Harry, Harry, how many times I gotta tell ya, ya great bozo? Ya want me to spell it out for ya? Do ya? Huh? Huh? Ya big lug?"

Angel Coretta smiles politely. "Sounds all very exciting, Mel. But I just can't help wondering …" Her eyes and thoughts drift towards the darkened road outside her office window.

Angel Mel seems determined to distract both her and himself. He leans dramatically across the table, speaking now in his natural voice, "So, Harry, he's the hit-man, he says …" His voice changes to one vaguely resembling Al Pacino with asthma. "I'm no wise guy, I tell ya. I'm an accountant."

After a few moments, the silence in the room alerts Angel Coretta to the fact that her fellow angel has finished with that part of the story, whatever it was. Her neck cranes upright. She covers a yawn with her hand while stealing another look at the entrance.

Angel Mel grins. "Funny stuff, right? The guy's a hit-man and he tells her he's an accountant."

"Hilarious, Mel. Very funny, gosh." Coretta hides another yawn.

Another hour passes. Sister Coretta's head is propped up on both palms, her eyelids drifting shut as Angel Mel continues to drone on. Jumping to his feet, he shouts in his mobster voice, "Listen up, Harry, an' listen up good. 'Cause if ya don't, I'm gonna get Lenny to whack ya! Ya got dat?" He reverts to his own voice. "You see, Coretta, Harry the hit-man, who pretends to be an accountant, is about to be hit. By an accountant! Great plot twist, don't you think? The whacker is getting whacked!" He laughs to himself. "Oh, I just love that bit."

Sister Coretta's head slumps down and hits her desk.

⸺

Along the trail back from the Akashic Hall of Records to the main road, a blast of wind comes up from nowhere, whipping trees to a frenzy. Branches claw at Ash and Bessie as they tear full-tilt through the night forest. Exhausted, Ash stumbles in her heels before falling to the wet ground. Bessie collapses beside her.

The wind stops as suddenly as it started. Only their heavy breathing fills the air with sound. Now it's too quiet. Bessie stares into the dark, thickly wooded area across from her vision.

Something. Or someone. Moved. Over there. To their right. The tiger again? Couldn't be the tiger. He would make noise. There it is. Behind the tree. Omigod. "Ash, Ash!" She yanks the poor girl to her feet. "Run, run, run!" She gulps a deep breath. "Jason!"

The name rushes from her lips, just as the person attached to it, steps out of nowhere, smack in front of Bessie. Inches away. Face to face. Moving like lightening, he reaches for both her hands in his. As he holds them in an iron grip, she darts a glance down, and sees with shock, the scrap of her old tee-shirt hanging from his pocket.

His eyes burn into hers. "Listen to me! Bessie, just listen. Lis-ten."

Out of nowhere Miguelito's voice rings out. "Hey, Jason."

Startled, Jason loses his concentration, allowing Miguelito to grab him around the neck from behind with his arm. He kicks out Jason's right leg to trip the taller boy in his grasp. Together they tumble to the ground in a heap.

Bessie wiggles free, tearing off down the road, dragging Ash behind her. The sounds of Jason's voice pleading for her echoes in the night air.

Sometime later, Bessie and Ash see the outline of Girls Dorm in the near distance and begin to relax. There's no one on the road but themselves and some tree bats flitting in the branches at the side of the road.

In no time they're standing outside Angel Coretta's office, peering in. The angel's head is flopped on her desk, her arms outstretched in front of her. Pacing back and forth, a self-absorbed Angel Mel holds court, his lips flapping. His one hand gestures in the air as he reads from his screenplay. Suddenly he tosses the papers in the air, clasping his great chest with both hands, writhing about in some odd death sequence he picked up from a western, no doubt, before he disappears from sight.

"Such a goof," Bessie snickers.

"This is gonna be tricky," Ash mutters under her breath.

Turning the knob ever so slowly, Bessie finally begins to open the outer door. In the hallway they stop to listen outside Angel Coretta's office. A muffled Angel Mel's voice booms, "And then Bobby's daughter, Olivia, she was named for Olivia de Havilland, you know, the actress in *Gone with the Wind* among other great films, a classic, maybe the greatest classic of all time. Where was I? Yes, well, Olivia, she hugs her uncle Guido through the prison bars. Very emotional scene, I must say. So then after the guard drags her away, she ..."

Snickering, in spite of their need to be quiet, the girls huddle to listen.

"She's in love with the hit-man, you see, well, not really in love. She just thinks he's the key to the stash of money they stole ..."

Ash tugs at Bessie's hand. Reluctantly they begin to tiptoe down the hallway to their bedroom at the back. Slowly they open the door, pleased to note both roommates are still sound asleep. Bessie inches the door shut. They tiptoe across the room, climbing carefully under their covers, finally lying back only to see ... Angel Mel with his screenplay still in hand, at the entrance.

"Busted." He positively twinkles.

"How did you get here so fast?" Ash's mouth drops open. Her head pops up.

"Dah, I'm an angel. Hello. Have we met? I'm Angel Mel. Do you two delinquents have any idea of how much worry you've put Angel Coretta through tonight? Never mind what's going to happen when Angel Rachel finds out."

The girls cast their eyes downward. Bessie mumbles, "Angel Rachel's going to go ballistic."

"I'd say that's putting it mildly, young lady." He can see they're fighting to keep their eyelids open. "Well, we'll leave it like that, for now. Snuggle under your covers and pray for mercy." He grins wickedly before vanishing into the night air.

Ash rolls her eyes and her head flops back on her pillow. "Mercy from Angel Rachel? I doubt that."

The girls turn to face each other for a moment. Before she falls asleep, Bessie grumbles under her breath, "I really wish he'd quit doing that."

CHAPTER 25: EARTH

Detective Eric Pederssen tries to find a comfortable position in the tiny Victorian chair, taking the cup and saucer from the elderly woman's blue-veined hands.

"Use cream and sugar? Right on the coffee table, if you do." The woman sits on another chair across from the table, her teacup delicately poised in her lap. "Clotted."

"Excuse me?"

"Clotted. The cream, detective. Clotted like the English have. Born in Fishbourne in West Sussex. Lived there until I was three. But that's a long, long time ago. You've been to England?"

Eric glances around the room. "Ah, yes." Every inch of wall space is covered with a framed picture of a person, probably a relative, and judging by the style of dress and hair, long since dead. As for the middle-aged gent in the frame above the fire-place ... deceased husband? Most likely.

She rambles on. "Sorry it took me so long to call the police, but I just didn't put two and two together." She points to her head of grey perm frizz. "Not that I've slowed down upstairs, neither, just so as you know." She takes a little sip, wrinkling the skin above her lips in neat rows. "Those girls. Well, it wasn't until I saw the newspaper which I don't take regular anymore these days. And when I first saw the pictures, didn't half look like them, did they. Not like the ones I give a ride to, with all their makeup and wigs and that. Biscuits?"

Startled out of his reverie, he watches her lift a china plate of ginger snaps. "Guess you young folks call them cookies nowadays. When I grew up we called them biscuits."

"About the girls?" He helps himself to a cookie, resting his elbow on the doily on the arm of his chair. Glancing around, he tries to guess how many damn doilies there are altogether in this wallpapered room.

"Said they were secretaries at first, didn't they. On vacation. Once I realized they was just kids, I made them promise to call their parents the moment they could. Give them all my chocolate chip biscuits I made for Sadie. She's in the hospital, isn't she."

"Sadie?" Eric tries and fails to keep up.

"Took a terrible fall. Broke her hip in two places, didn't she just. In Arizona. Well, I had to go visit her, of course. Drove the whole way. Slept in my car. You can't trust hotels when you're a single woman on the road these days."

He sets down his tea on the doily nearest him. "When ... when did you see the newspaper article?"

"Size of a twig, our Sadie is now."

"The girls," he reminds her. When did you find out the girls were missing?"

"That paper boy of hers, I tell you. Such a lazy scrap, isn't he just."

What the hell. Might as well agree with her. "Indeed." He takes another cookie and nibbles.

"Paper fell all to pieces right there on the sidewalk. And he just runs off, not a care in the world. Leaving an old woman to pick it up by herself. Rain tomorrow."

"Ah ... ?"

"Going to rain tomorrow. Feel it in my corns." She shakes her left foot encased in a beige cotton stocking and a black, laced-up shoe. "Never wrong, am I."

"The girls?" *I'm going to drink martinis tonight until I pass out.* "When did you first see the article in the newspaper?"

"Well, they were on the first page of the third section, weren't they. Hard to recognize them, like I said, in their school pictures without all that makeup. Girls today." She waits for a response which she doesn't get. "That fellow, too. Jason. I remember his name 'cause it's the same as Sadie's boy. The one that died in Viet Nam, didn't he."

"Mrs. Armstrong. What day was that, do you recall?" He rubs wearily at his left eyelid, the one that twitches with fatigue.

The lady in question sits back stiffly in her chair, a frown on her crepe-paper features. "Of course, I remember. You think, just because I'm an old woman, I don't remember things because I do."

Save me, someone save me. He stuffs another cookie in his mouth. "I'm sure you do. I'm sure you do. I'm just trying to establish a time line so—"

"Same day that scruffy dog wandered into Sadie's backyard, chewing up all the flowers." She leans towards him conspiratorially. "Frank's mutt, wasn't it just."

"So you immediately called the police?"

"On the dog? Course not. No, just chased him out with the hose. Terrified of water."

"But after you saw the picture of the *girls* in the pap—"

"That very afternoon. I stared at that photo for, I don't know, over half an hour, I'd say. It was the eyes that give them away. Does every time. Plus I heard one of them call the other Bess. That's short for Elizabeth, you know. Well, I told the man on the phone as to how I'd picked them up in Ravenspond, didn't I, that early July 15th morning at exactly 6:15 A.M. Right in front of the park. All dolled up like fancy women. I remember 'cause I checked my clock that's taped to my dash. Always do. Then I dropped them off no more than three hours later at Jackson's Hollow just on the way into town. Give 'em all my biscuits and made 'em promise to call their parents. Northeast corner of the intersection of Highway 6 and Johnstone. Gas station and garage. Ratty old place. Been there since forever. Owned by Sam & Lovell King Bros. Sam's tall. Beer belly. Smiles too much. Needs to trim his nose hairs. Lovell isn't much better."

Eric's whole body relaxes in a wave of relief. Stretching out his long legs, he crosses them at the ankles. Cradling his head on his arms that are crooked behind his head, he breathes deeply.

You have to admit, when the old gal finally got to the point, she was letter-perfect.

CHAPTER 26: HEAVEN

Angel Court looks pretty much the same as it did the last time Bessie was in dire trouble, only this time she has Ash behind the defendant's podium to keep her company. Her grandparents sit once again on the spectator benches. Her grandma touches her shamrock broach reassuringly. Grandpa Will has another brown paper bag in the shape of a small jug in his hip pocket. Millie swats him with her elbow. And Angels Mel and Jigjag are chattering, no doubt, about one of Mel's latest screenplays.

"I feel sweaty," Ash complains, looking down at her blouse.

"You're sweaty now? Wait a few minutes. You're gonna feel like you're in a steam bath." Bessie jabs at Ash, busy examining her damp spots. "Here she comes."

Angel Boyd, magnificent in his grey uniform, moves to stand beside the judge's bench. His voice bellows like a thunder clap. "All rise. This Angel Court is now in session. The Honorable Judge Rachel presiding." Like a well-rehearsed play, which perhaps it is, Angel Rachel sweeps out once more from behind the recesses to take her place at the bench.

After the formalities are completed, the eyes of the judge bore into the defendants. She takes her sweet time before speaking. "Ashley Sophia Moreno. Bessie Millicent MacIntyre." She tilts her head sideways like a puppy. "Well. You've really outdone yourselves this time, ladies." Her soft tone takes everyone off guard. "In one foul swoop, you've managed to disrespect the most sacred laws in all of Heaven." Her glare doesn't falter. She takes a linen handkerchief to clean her reading glasses ever so meticulously. "I could send you back a couple of thousand years to a previous lifetime for a do-over." She leans forward with her cat smile. Raising her left hand in the air, she twitches her fingers in a fast, jerky rhythm while whispering some indistinguishable syllables under her breath.

In horror, Bessie and Ash gaze down to see they are dressed in Stone Age clothing, draped in decaying animal skins. Their bodies are filthy from head to toe; their hair is matted. The courtroom rings out in a united gasp of shock.

Angel Rachel calmly continues, "Or I could send you back to the Dark Ages when females were indiscriminately tortured or burned as witches." Again her fingers twitch while strange sounds emanate from her cherry-red lips.

The girls' eyes dart down to their long, bulky skirts; shawls draped over their heads and torsos. The muffled sound of distant horse hooves and the shouts of men fill the air as Bessie and Ash scramble to hide under the podium.

"But I won't." Angel Rachel's voice trills out, her fingers twitching as the girls transform back into their current attire. "This time."

Trembling all over, Ash and Bessie return with difficulty to an upright position, grasping the podium for dear life. They stare at her every move as Rachel's long fingernails, in the same bright red polish as the lipstick scratched across her thin, grim lips, fiddle with her glasses, her diamond glittering like a captured star. It seems forever before she perches them back on her nose, beginning to read silently from her notes.

Even though she's in Heaven and out of her Earthly body, Bessie can hear her own heartbeats seeming to boom like a base drum solo. Sweat is dripping inside her blue blouse and into her underwear. Her feet begin to ache in her newly-purchased-by-grandma, sensible brown flats.

Even Angels Mel and Jigjag look nervous. And despite the consequences to follow, grandpa Will takes a long swig from his paper bag. Grandma snatches it away from him, not to hide it, but to take a swig of her own.

The deep brown eyes of the unflappable Angel Boyd flicker sideways to the judge's bench. Even he, it seems, is off his game.

Suddenly, in a shock to end all shocks, something so bizarre happens, it is without precedent. Angel Rachel flies up and out of her seat like an electrocuted bat, zip-zapping back and forth, here and there across the entire ceiling. All necks in the courtroom snap backwards. Grandpa Will almost tumbles over the back of his seat.

She flies and flies, dipping and swooping like a Stealth jet in a combat zone. The crowd below her sways and wobbles, craning to follow her flight path.

Just as suddenly, Angel Rachel reverses direction and flips upside down, right in front of the defendants at their podium. Inexplicably, her flowing black gown remains in an upright position. Not a strand of her hairdo dares to wander from its ordained place.

Now she is inches away from Bessie and Ash. One upside-down face confronting two, very terrified, right-side-up ones. Eyelash to eyelash. Bessie and Ash grab each other's hands, squeezing with all their might. Still the Angel hangs there, unblinking. Minutes go by. Hours?

"Moritnlasjuitss!" the upside-down angel hisses. And two teenage defendants crumple to the floor in a dead faint.

CHAPTER 27: HEAVEN

Ash and Bessie run around in a fenced-in farm field, around and around. Where it is, Heaven only knows. Once again they're in dungarees, only this time, Ash has had the good sense to wear an old pair, several sizes too large, from the cast-off pile at Girls Dorm. Filthy head to toe, they chase frantic piglets towards a ramp leading up to a hovering cloud. Hundreds and hundreds of piglets squeal and run, squeal and run. As soon as one cloud fills with little pigs, the hatch closes, and the cloud vanishes into the afternoon sky. And another cloud appears on the horizon.

"Oh, say it isn't so." Ash wipes dirt from her cheeks with the palm of her hands.

Bessie stares at the approaching cloud, wiping the sweat from beneath her bangs. Soon full-size pigs spill out of the cloud's hatch hovering near the ground. Ash and Bessie have been assigned to herd the new arrivals towards a pen filled with fresh straw, buckets of water, and corn. Several waiting angels smile and coo, holding out treats for their returning porcine friends.

The sound of high-pitched squealing fills the air like mammoth mice on crack. And it's only Bessie and Ash's first hour. Twenty clouds later, the girls collapse on the ground, surrounded by contented pigs. One smaller one settles into Ash's armpit and goes to sleep, his head on her belly. She doesn't care. Eventually she turns her head sideways to look at Bessie. "I feel like one big giant, greasy, yucky, smelly B.L.T."

"And just think. You've only got twenty more pig retrieving sessions to go." Angel Mel materializes in a blindingly orange flowered shirt to stand at their feet.

Bessie opens her eyes to stare up at him. "Tell me I don't have a session."

"You don't have a session." He nibbles on NecNac Snaks.

"Oh, thank the Lord." Her head collapses back onto the ground.

Angel Mel reaches into the bag to dig for another chip. "Actually, you do. I just said that because you told me to."

"Oh, very funny. Oh, big ha ha."

He pulls another of his ratty screenplays from his shoulder bag and begins reading to himself. "But I can wait until you put your makeup on." He points to a corner of the field without looking up. Where his finger indicates, a spotless, up-to-the-minute bathroom and change-room appears, complete with a set of clean clothes in each girl's individual style.

Groaning, Ash pushes aside the pig, pulling Bessie up by the hand. Taking their time, the girls emerge half an hour later, all shiny and clean, wearing everything but smiles. Angel Mel and Bessie head off in one direction, Ash in another. Both girls wave to each other without turning around.

Bessie glances down at the screenplay dangling from his hand. "Your latest blockbuster?"

"Yeah, a little something I'm working on. Going to channel it to the Coen brothers. So." He jams the wad of paper into his shoulder bag. "Took care of Jason for you. He's now in rehab. Undergoing color vibration therapy with Angel Lionel."

Bessie stops in her tracks. When she speaks, her voice spills over with anger. "Well, it's about time. I hope Angel Lionel tosses him over a big, giant cliff, that's what I hope."

Angel Mel stops to look at her closely. In a low voice, unusual for him, he murmurs, "Maybe that's what happened to him. Maybe he went off a cliff."

She looks up at him, holding a stare for a long while. They both turn away to watch a crow pecking at something on the ground nearby.

"Well, good. Serves him right if he did." Bessie's fingers reach up to touch her scar. "After whatever the hell he did to me and Ash. Where're we going, anyways?"

He winks. "Patience, my little mushroom." He begins strolling again. "You'll see."

"Mel?" Bessie brushes her bangs out of her eyes. "What was that weird thing Angel Rachel spit out? Sounded like she swore at us."

Angel Mel chuckles. "Moritnlasjuitss? That's angel speak for … on second thought, no, I better not say. But it's a doozy."

CHAPTER 28: HEAVEN

In what might be loosely referred to as a children's playground, complete with swings, slides, monkey bars, and so on, Angel Mel climbs onto the seat of a teeter-totter, motioning to Bessie to climb on the other end. Despite the obvious disparity in weight, they are miraculously in balance.

Angel Mel is up in the air. "This is nice. This is nice."

Now it's Bessie's turn to be up. "Is a coma a bad way to die, Mel?"

"There is no bad death, Bessie. There's just, well, death." He's back up in the air. "Just part of life. A transition. Now, life, that's painful. Hell, life will kill ya!" He giggles at his little joke.

Some time later they find themselves side by side on skyscraper-sized swings, swooping up and up in perfect unison. "After death," Angel Mel continues, "That is, after your incarnation is over, your soul emerges from your body like a ... like a ..." On cue, a flock of Monarch butterflies flutter near them at nose height. He elaborates, "Like a beautiful butterfly emerging from a cocoon."

The angel and Bessie seem to hang suspended, high, high in the air, surrounded in exquisite butterflies. He completes his thought, "And then you fly."

Later on, they sit companionably across from each other in a huge sandbox, building a castle worthy of St. Patrick's Cathedral. Bessie taps out a Hector's Nectar cup full of packed sand to create a new turret. "But will it hurt, when I remember?"

Angel Mel scoops up sand with his paper cup. "When you remember, it will be like, like watching a movie. Matt Damon gets blown up. And then he goes to the premiere with his lovely Argentinean wife."

Bessie adds another turret, patting it down. "Like watching life stories in the Past Lives theatre."

"Exactly." Angel Mel adjusts a pillar, causing a minor crash.

"Like when Ash and I watched John Kennedy Jr. crash his plane into the Atlantic." He looks at her, smiling. "The proverbial penny drops."

Later they sit on a bench, watching toddlers play on monkey bars. Shrieks of glee blend with bursts of giggles. Angel Mel taps her shoulder to offer her some of his NecNac Snaks. "Have I ever steered you wrong, Bessie?"

She takes a chip and munches for a moment. "Well, there was that time when you tried to explain rap music to me."

He leans back in his seat, brushing crumbs from his shirt. "I thought you said crap."

The young girl turns a rarely seen earnest face to him. "Where is she, my mother? And why can't I remember how I died?"

He reaches forward to tuck a strand of her hair behind her ear, his expression tender. "Wait, I have an idea." He stands up to his full impressive height. His wings materialize and he spreads them wide. Wrapping Bessie into them, he lifts off into the clear, cloudless sky.

CHAPTER 29: EARTH

Angel Mel and Bessie reappear just outside a charming village church somewhere in the Midlands of England. Ivy covers the ancient brickwork almost completely. On a small wooden panel, decorated with a Celtic cross, the name ST. IVANS is followed by the announcement of a funeral service for one Mr. Sweeney Fiddler.

Bessie glances around at the lovely lush hedges surrounding the neighboring graveyard, where markers that look as old as the hills they stand on, scatter the neatly trimmed grass. At the stone nearest her, a small bouquet leans against the pitted marble. A scruffy dog takes a leak against another. Wild roses climb the distant rock wall where a hunched-over, elderly man in a sweater and cap watches the proceedings, leaning on a hand-whittled, walking stick.

An organ begins to play from inside. "Come on then." Angel Mel pats her shoulder and they pass through the heavy doors to take a place at the rear of the church.

A strangely long and wide coffin covered in white roses lies on a simple, wooden cart before the altar. In the front row Bessie can see the back of a slight woman and a series of skinny children ranging in age from about four to ten. A small boy, two children down from his mother, fusses. She reaches over a gloved hand to give him a swat on the ear. The rest of the seats hold what appears to be a scattering of kinfolk and friends.

At the front, the priest in his frilly robes, a frail, elderly man, is surprisingly robust in voice. "We are gathered here today to celebrate Sweeney Fiddler, whose life, although unexpectedly cut short in his prime, was filled with ..."

Bessie whispers to Angel Mel, "Filled with lots of bacon and pies by the look of his coffin."

He shushes her good-naturedly. "Pay attention."

After a weeping eulogy by the deceased's brother, also of imposing size, a rousing hymn and a series of Bible readings follow. The priest pipes up, "Let us pray."

Angel Mel gives Bessie a firm elbow poke. "Now listen up. This is why we're here." She looks up at him, confused, before turning her focus on the little man at the front, not wanting to miss the point.

The priest's voice booms in the well-known prayer, with stragglers from the congregation joining in. "The Lord is my Shepherd; I shall not want. He maketh me to lie down in green pastures. He leadeth me beside the still waters. He restoreth my soul. He leadeth me in the paths of righteousness for His name's sake."

Bessie finds herself whispering the words along with them. Angel Mel's index finger taps her shoulder insistently. "Here it comes, here it comes."

"Here comes what?"

"Listen! Listen!" His voice is filled with a rare forcefulness as the sound of the priest and his parishioners continue.

"Yea though I walk through the valley of the shadow of death ..."

Angel Mel is all business now. "See? See? That's the part they never get! It's the *shadow* of death." He's all animated, enunciating to her. "Sha-dow. Sha-dow. It's not a death. It's merely a shadow. And before you can produce a shadow, you have to have ... ?"

Bessie looks into his face, hopeful. "Ah, light?"

Angel Mel grins delightedly from ear to ear. "Light! Yes! Light! A bright, shining, glorious light! And the light is ... ?" He gazes down at her in nervous anticipation, as her features change from confusion to concentration. And finally, to comprehension.

She smiles. "God. The light is God."

He tips up her chin with his palm. "My wonderfully brilliant girl. The light is indeed God. Or Allah, Mohammed, Jehovah, Apotamkin, or Azna or whatever name you know God by." He can barely contain his pleasure. "And there is no death. There is only ..."

"The shadow of death."

He swoops her into a bear hug, almost crushing her in his enthusiasm. "The shadow of death. Not a death, only a shadow. Created by the Light of God." He pulls her back to arm's length. "Now if we hurry, we can catch that new Bette Davis movie."

He wraps her up in his wings and they vanish in a flurry of feathers.

CHAPTER 30: HEAVEN

On a balmy afternoon at Millie and Will Dodd's cottage in the valley, Ash and Bessie sit on a blanket on the lawn, playing with Peach the cat. Grandpa Will is pouring tiny glasses of his latest batch of nectarine hooch, with a whispered, "Shsh, don't tell your grandma." On a small table, a plate of Millie's brownies, still warm from the oven, emanate a sweet chocolate aroma.

Nearby Grandma is fussing with an open steamer trunk. Beside her, a pile of clothing is neatly folded, waiting to be packed.

Bessie sips on her thimbleful of the tangy alcohol. Her features reveal her distress. "But why now, grandma? Why are you going to reincarnate now?"

"Because it's time, dear." Millie gives her a sweet smile as she fingers her bright green broach, perched as always, on her left side of her chest.

"Why do you wear that silly shamrock all the time, anyways?" Bessie wonders out loud.

"This one?" Grandma says, as if there were another one. She unpins it to set it on her open palm. "I've had it, oh, well, forever. What do you see?" She hands it to her granddaughter to examine.

Bessie looks down at the silver and green stone jewelry. "Did grandpa give it to you for your wedding, or something?"

"Hush. Stare at it without blinking. Focus."

Bessie frowns for a moment before following her grandmother's instructions.

Suddenly she sees it. An aura emanates around the emerald broach. It seems to be vibrating with an energy all its own. As she continues to stare, pulsating streams of iridescent green light reach towards her. Startled, she almost drops it.

Her head pops up to look over at her grandmother who, she realizes, is observing her intently. Millie puts out her hand to retrieve her beloved jewelry. Pinning it

Bessie: Lost & Found

back on her shirt, she smiles mysteriously. "Hand me those slippers?" Millie looks towards Ash.

"These? Oh, they're so glam," Ash gushes as she holds up red-beaded, Chinese slippers, twirling them in her palm. "Where did you ever find these?"

"An Asian friend of mine made them for me. She's in Miami now, doing quite well in her next life, I hear, as a designer to the stars. Lovely gal." Millie reaches for a hand-knit sweater to admire it before tossing it into the box.

Bessie jumps up, heading out the door in the direction of the woods. Her grandparents share a look. Will grabs the plate of fresh brownies and follows her. Soon he finds her perched on a large rock, her arms hugging her legs to her chest. As he approaches, he can hear his granddaughter's gentle sobbing. Without touching her, he quietly sits on the grass beside her, handing her up a brownie. She takes it silently.

They sit there companionably for some time before Will speaks. "We'll only be gone a lifetime, sweetie. It's not as if it's forever. Why, a lifetime goes by like ..." He snaps his fingers in the air. "Like that."

Bessie looks over at him, love shining in her eyes. "It's just that I want you here with me. Selfish, I know."

He holds up the plate so she can take another brownie. "That's not selfish, that's just natural. We realize it's hard on you, sugarplum. It's just that—"

"It's your time. I know."

"When it's your turn, you'll know, too." They munch in silence, watching a squirrel chase another squirrel up and down a nearby tree.

"So what are you planning to be this time around, anyways?"

"Well ..." Will snickers. "You may not believe your old grandpa, but I've always wanted to be a policeman."

"No!" Bessie laughs. "Not you, a policeman? No, really?"

"No kidding." He pats her on the back, grinning. "A copper. A real live copper."

She looks over at him in astonishment. "Never would have guessed that one in a million years."

They both reach for the remaining brownie. Giggling, their fingers pull, breaking it nicely into half. "Maybe even ..." His old eyes twinkle. "Scotland Yard."

CHAPTER 31: EARTH

Detective Eric Pederssen pulls off the highway and parks his black BMW at the far side of a beaten-up gas station and garage. Signage, barely legible in its weathered condition, announces it as: SAM & LOVELL KING BROS. YOU WRECK 'EM, WE FIX 'EM. The humidity on this Thursday noon is so stifling, he doesn't want to leave his air-conditioning. Instead he opts to listen to some more of the opera *Carmen* before he reluctantly shuts down his engine and strolls inside the darkened garage.

"Sam or Lovell King?" He flips open his badge and dangles it from his fingers to the heavyset youth in greasy overalls.

"Nope," the lad responds before pointing towards the back of the garage. "In there."

"Thanks." Eric snaps his badge shut, heading further into the interior. He spies two men awkwardly half-standing, half-crouching to look under a Chrysler pickup which is resting on an hydraulic lift. They're so similar in statue and features, there's no question they are the brothers King he's looking for. And dead on the money, the way the old lady described them.

"Sam and Lovell King?" Eric speaks as he walks towards them, badge in hand.

"Lovell," one of them says, nose hair on display.

The other one heads towards Eric. "Sam. What can I do ya for?"

"Two teenage girls were dropped off here Saturday, July 15th. About 9:15 in the morning by an elderly woman in a 2000 light blue, Buick Le Sabre. They were hitchhiking. Wearing hooker-type get-ups. Possibly wigs. One Caucasian, one mixed heritage."

Sam King looks blank. "Don't sound familiar. Not many hookers round here abouts." He laughs. "Too bad for us."

Eric pulls out the photos. "No, they weren't hookers, just kids. Dressed like that to look older. Take a close look, please."

As the two brothers look at the images of Ash and Bessie and back again, another man in overalls, dark-skinned and sweaty, comes from the back of the shop to stand behind Eric's shoulder. 'Sure," he says, glancing at Eric. "Dressed like cheap women, only they was girls. Came in and bought some sodas. I'd just opened up." He turns to Lovell. "That was the time your mama called youse home to fix the washer."

The brothers stare at their employee until the black man erupts. "Hell, no!" His face swings around to catch Eric's eye. "Saw 'em get into Mrs. Murchie's pink convertible."

Eric believes him, whipping out his notebook. "Your name?"

"Jeremiah Gilthurst. And yeah, got a prison record. B & E's ten years back. Did my time."

"Tell me about Mrs. Murchie."

"Wild as a hair. Divorced three times. Sells some kind of cosmetics from her home. Drinks and drives. You can find her in the phone book."

The brothers exchange glances before Lovell speaks to Eric. "That all then?"

"I'll be in touch if ..." The detective takes in all three men, evidently anxious to get on with their day. "If I need to talk further." He extends his hand to Jeremiah. "You've been very helpful."

The black man shakes it with a, "Uh huh."

CHAPTER 32: HEAVEN

At the Heavenly Healing Spa, located on a high plateau in the distant mountains far away from Air Heaven Interportal airport, a young man lays face-down on a massage table in an austere white room. A sheet covers everything but his bare shoulders and head. Evidenced by the sandy-colored, sticking-up hair, it is clearly Jason Wallet.

An angel dressed in blue hospital garb, his back to the table, fiddles with dials on a large computer sitting on a nearby table. White sheers flutter on the small window revealing a starlit sky.

Angel Lionel speaks in calm tones. "You still comfortable, Jason?" A muffled *yes* emerges from the young man.

"There," the angel says. And the room fills with beams of vibrant lights in variations of yellow and orange directed at the body on the massage table. Satisfied with the result, Angel Lionel takes a seat in the single wooden chair at the rear of the room, opening up a copy of *Angel* magazine. Roy Orbison is on the cover.

"Shame about him," he speaks under his breath. "Such a hard life. Voice of an archangel." Half an hour goes by when he takes a look at his watch. Glancing over at the peaceful lad on the table, he whispers, "Mind if I leave you for a few moments? Just got to dash out and buy a welcome home gift for an elf. He's been gone in Dublin for well over a couple of hundred years. We used to spend hours gabbing. In the old days, humans could see and communicate with elves and fairies. Now they're too busy trying to be rich and famous to see what's right in front of their eyes. Anyway, be back in a flash. You relax now. Be five minutes."

Hearing no reply, he gets up to peer into the closed eyes of the young man. "Sound asleep again," he murmurs. "This treatment does wonders." Carefully he lays his magazine on the chair and tiptoes out of the room, closing the door so quietly, there is no sound.

The minute he's gone, Jason's eyes pop open. He lays perfectly still for a few seconds, testing the atmosphere for unseen dangers. Sensing none, he quickly throws off the sheet. In only his underwear, he begins to jig with the window fastener, desperate to shove up the resisting pane. Evidently it has been well secured for just such occasions. It seems Jason is not the first patient who has tried to escape the colorful energies of the Heavenly Healing Spa.

Suddenly the window gives under his powerful shove. In an instant, he's got one shoulder out when a petite, well-manicured hand grabs him by his briefs. "And where do you think you're going, young man?" Angel Rachel demands.

CHAPTER 33: HEAVEN

Outside Air Heaven Interportal airport on a warm, star-filled night, a candle-lit parade of reincarnating souls stream down the hillsides in white gowns, carrying their candles high. The long table of empty candlesticks awaits them. Soulslady has just materialized along with her empty clothes rack.

It's 3:46 A.M. and the two girls are hidden inside their little cave they created within the hedge. For once, they are unusually solemn. Bessie wipes tears from her cheeks as Ash whispers, "I'll miss them, too. They're the coolest of the cool. They're just like—"

Bessie interrupts. "There they are!"

Amongst the parade of gowned souls, Grandma Millie and Grandpa Will proudly carry their candles high. Millie spies the girls peeking out and waves wildly with her free hand. She gives Will a poke and he joins in.

Bessie's sadness is palpable as her grandparents wait next in line to put their candles into place and head towards the Soulslady. This is it. This is the last time she will see them in Heaven for God knows how long. Bessie reaches up and picks at her scar with trembling fingers. "They know what happened to us, don't they."

Ash looks over, mascara running. She puts her arm around her best friend's shoulder, giving her a squeeze.

Now Millie and Will are first in line. Bessie's grandpa steps forward, busses his wife on the cheek and blows his granddaughter a kiss. Reaching up, he takes hold of his silver thread on the crown of his head, yanking off his old image to become a glowing infant-sized aura. Millie yells out, despite the rules, "I love you, Bessie dear! You too, Ashley! See you soon. I promise." She follows her husband's lead, becoming a small rainbow of glistening light.

"See you soon? What on earth does she mean by that?" Ash frowns a little. "Maybe ..."

"She knows something. They both know." Bessie wipes more tears. "But why can't I know?"

The clock tolls three times - one, two, three - as the jet-cloud arrives. The crystal door suspended in mid-air at the rear of the airport swings open. The staircase spills out of the plane, attaching itself to the Sacred Portal.

Meanwhile outside the platform, the Head angel is handing out the individually addressed envelopes. During this process she repeats the all-important instructions, including a strong caution to the returning passengers not to lose them at all cost. Otherwise their new parents will never find them. "A fate worse than death," she warns, her voice dripping with irony.

Bessie's eyes flit from aura to aura, trying to keep track of her grandparents, but unfortunately they blend into the crowd and are lost to her. In the bushes she weeps, her head on Ash's shoulder. Too soon all the reincarnating souls have boarded, except for two who stand at the top of the staircase, waving wildly.

"Bessie, Bess. Look. Up there!" Ash pulls her friend to her feet and they step away from the protection of the bushes. Two auras wave their envelopes wildly from the plane's open door. The girls wave back, jumping up and down.

"Grandma, grandpa, I love you!" Bessie shouts.

A stern flight attendant yanks the two misbehaving souls inside the plane. The door of the aircraft closes. In silence the girls stare after the jet-cloud, overcome with emotion. "Wonder what she meant? See you soon." Bessie whispers into the warm night air.

CHAPTER 34: HEAVEN

"And for what reason, may I ask, do we owe the pleasure of your company this morning, ladies?" Angel Jigjag's smile twinkles with humor. "Delighted though we may be." His large teeth glow like ones in a toothpaste commercial.

"Oh, we just wanted to learn more about, ah …" Ash fumbles.

"Reincarnation," Bessie finishes.

"Prompted by Bessie's grandparents' decision to take their next journey, might I assume?"

Bessie grins. "Correct."

"Well, then, take a seat, ladies, and we'll get on with our lesson." He treats them to another of his glorious toothy smiles before turning back to his blackboard where he writes: SHOPPING FOR NEW PARENTS. "That should be a cinch for our part-time students since they spend so much of their time shopping at the Seventh Heaven Mall, yes?"

A buzz of titters fills the classroom. Bessie and Ash glance around at the sea of multi-cultural teenagers all looking their way. With exaggerated movements, Ash takes out a silver tube of lipstick, a tiny brush and an oval rhinestone mirror from her large pink bag, expertly applying a new layer of maroon gloss. With a quick snap of her identically marooned, manicured hand, she replaces her tools in her bag before taking her sweet time to glance from face to face with her Hollywood smile. All heads jerk down to face their notebooks. Her victory is complete.

"Now that all the drama is over, shall we begin our lesson?" Angel Jigjag points to a student in the third row. "Zygmunt? Your thoughts?"

Zygmunt jumps to his feet. "I feel choosing one's new parents should be based on what one wishes to learn in one's new life. For me, I wish to become a shaman." The serious faced young man sits down, looking pleased.

"Bor-ing," Ash whispers to Bessie.

"And how would you choose your new parents, Miss Ashley, hmmm?" Angel Jigjag begins a slow walk towards her, his gigantic sandals peeking out from under his red and yellow caftan.

"That's easy," Ash pipes up with her usual confidence. "I'd pick parents in the film business. New York or Los Angeles. That's the best place to become an actress."

As the snickers begin, Angel Jigjag interrupts them. "A noble goal, Miss Ashley. A noble goal. Many of our great personalities of the past were actors. In fact, many great politicians are indeed great actors. Winston Churchill, for one. Martin Luther King for another."

He turns to Ash's companion. "And Bessie? Your thoughts?"

"I just want to know how I died, that's all I've ever wanted to know."

Angel Jigjag considers her answer, his bearded chin resting in his palm. A sudden smile lights up his dark features. "Perhaps you may become a past-life investigator. It's very trendy these days, Angel Mel informs me."

"But why don't you guys just tell me?" Bessie insists. "You know the answer. I know you do. Why don't you just tell me?"

His kind eyes crinkle at the edges. He takes her little hands in his giant ones. Finally he speaks. "All will be revealed, my dear. When it's—"

"Time, I know." Bessie finishes. "And I've got nothing but time these days. Endless time. Especially when I'm endlessly retrieving pigs from the Earth zone."

"Well then, "Angel Jigjag suggests. "That being the case, perhaps you lovely ladies can spend a little bit more of it in the classroom? May I suggest every day? Hmmm?"

"Every *day*?" In unison, a horrified Ash and Bessie look up at him as if a hen is laying an egg on his turban.

CHAPTER 35: EARTH

Eric Pederssen strolls briskly up the driveway of a tiny, pink clapboard house. Pink and white petunias, roses, and geraniums spill from flowerbeds and from boxes under the windows. A pink Volkswagen convertible is parked by the side entrance. "Looks more like a bloody dollhouse," he comments to himself. The heat beats down as he reaches into a pocket for a tissue to wipe across his brow before he rings the doorbell.

When the woman opens it, he notices she is curvaceous, borderline plump. In her platinum hair, streaks of pink cascade into her bouffant. She holds a yappy white poodle in her arms, similarly pink-streaked. Both she and the poodle are wearing… yes, pink outfits.

"Hi, I'm Lorry-Lyn." She smiles, more than a little aware of the allure of the tall, blonde detective. "And this is Mitsy-Bitsy. Say hello, Mitsy-Bitsy." The little dog snarls at him and vice-versa before the woman stands coyly aside to allow the detective to enter.

He's almost nauseated by the sea of Pepto-Bismol pink that awaits him in the miniscule living-room. Pink walls, pink area rugs, bowls of pink flowers, pictures framed in pink seashells. Mercifully all the furniture is white. On the dining room table, visible through an archway, bright pink boxes are piled high. On the sides of them, the typeface resembling lipstick, reads: IN THE PINK BY LORRY-LYN.

"Lovell called me. You want to ask me about those girls I gave a ride to awhile back?"

"That's right, Mrs. Murchie."

"Oh, you can call me Lorry-Lyn. There hasn't been a Mr. Murchie for ages. Take a seat. You want a beer? Sit, sit."

"Water, thanks." He sits in a cutesy armchair that's way too small for him. The feeling of being in a dollhouse is greater than ever.

Lorry-Lyn returns with a glass of water filled to the brim with ice-cubes and a rum and cola for herself. Eric despises ice-cubes. He takes it, setting it on the little side table. Reaching down to the floor for his briefcase, he removes the photos of Bessie and Ashley, extending them to her.

"Oh, those are the same girls, alright." Lorry-Lyn's voice tinkles like a cheap bell. "They were such a laugh. At first they told me they were secretaries from New York." She bats her eyelashes at him. "Like I was born yesterday. Finally they admitted they were on a lark, heading out west to see Chris Lisack, you know that singer that's just like Ricky Nelson?" Closing her eyes for a moment, sipping on her cocktail, she adds, "Ooh, yummy."

Eric has the strong desire to flee. "Do you remember where you dropped them off?" He watches as the dog tap-taps in little circles over and over before choosing a spot on its own personal oval rug in the centre of another rug. As soon as it's lying down, it turns to face the detective, lips curled, a low growl in its throat.

"Oh, for sure. I was heading to my sister Joyce's house to leave her some product. I'm in the cosmetics business. Those girls were fascinated by that. My very own company, I'll have you know."

Gee, judging by the amount of paint covering every pore on your face, I couldn't have guessed. "So how far did you take them, do you remember?"

"Why, detective, of course I do. A smart businesswoman like me has to take care of all the details." She leans forward, revealing a pink bra. "The devil is in the details, isn't that what they say?"

Repulsed, he stiffens his spine, edging back into his chair. "So you last saw them …?" The dog sniffs his foot and he shoos it away.

"Took them with me to Joyce's just outside of Middlebridge. She's my business partner. Joyce loves to talk. Anyways, she had lunch ready so we ate sandwiches and drank iced tea. Except for me, of course. I just crave a glass of crisp white wine on a hot day, don't you?" Her lips are outlined in a much darker shade of pink and noticeably outside her actual lip line in a futile attempt to make them look fuller. An attempt, he mused, that resulted in a mild clown effect. She begins again, "Now where was I?"

"Your sister's house," he prompts her. One of those automatic fresheners goes on, spraying the little room with an odorous, fake lilac scent. He coughs a little before speaking. "Did you drive the girls back to the highway?"

"Well, of course. Couldn't very well leave them at my sister's now, could I?"

"And what time was that? And where did you drop them?"

She stares at him, wishing he would stop being in such a damn hurry. "About three o'clock, I'd say. We spent practically the whole day together." He doesn't respond, forcing her to continue her story. "So after me and Joyce showed them all our products ... they're amazing, detective. I've got a wonderful after-shave. I could give you a sample, if you like."

She starts to get up and he cuts her off with an abrupt, "Where did you drop the girls?"

Miffed, she sits back down again. The little dog jumps into her lap. "At the corner of River and Holsten. Walt picked them up right away."

"Walt?" Eric leans forward, all business now. "You know the person who picked them up?"

Not ready to play nice yet, the woman fiddles with her dog's fur. "Course I do. He's married to Flora." She leans in, kissing the dog on the nose. "My little Mitsy-Bitsy," she coos. Finally she looks back over at the detective. "She used to be my sister-in-law when I was with that bastard husband number two."

CHAPTER 36: HEAVEN

Bessie looks sadly at the hand-scribbled note taped to the front door of the familiar cottage: GONE FOR REINCARNATION. BACK SOON, LOVE, THE FORMER MILLIE AND WILL DODD. The cat rubs against her leg, stretching up a paw.

Ash tries the door. It's unlocked. Inside the living room everything is too neat. Spotless, in fact. Bessie wanders about, peeping into the kitchen, the bathroom, the main bedroom, and finally, the spare bedroom.

"She's scrubbed up this entire place," she grumbles. Gazing around, she spots a new quilt in soft mauves and yellows, filmy matching curtains, and a small rag-rug lovingly hand-sewn from her grandmother's old drapes. Fresh-picked wildflowers fill a small vase on an Irish lace doily draped over the bedside table. "She's expecting someone."

Bessie plunks on the bed before she spots the small envelope propped up on the pillowcase. Picking it up, she reads out loud, "Welcome, dearest daughter." Bessie can feel her heart beginning to pound in her chest. Her hands begin to sweat. Picking at the seal, she tries to open it. Not possible, it seems. Reluctantly she puts it back where she found it and goes in search of Ash.

Now they sit plopped on the comfy sofa, sipping on the last of grandma's nectarine tea. "Seems so empty," Ash says needlessly. Suddenly her voice changes to one full of excitement. "Hey, Bess, look over on the kitchen counter!"

Sure enough, in a wicker basket, a couple of packages peek out, wrapped in brightly patterned paper. The girls jump up to take a closer look.

A tiny one is labeled simply: BESSIE. The other, a larger soft package is addressed to Ashley. The girls' faces light up with anticipation. "You go first," Bessie graciously offers.

Ash rips off the paper to discover the hand-made, red beaded slippers she had so admired while Millie was packing the trunk. "Oh, she shouldn't have!" She tosses her platforms aside and pulls the wonderful slippers onto her feet. "But I'm so glad she did!" She dances around the room like a ballerina on opening night.

Slowly Bessie unwraps her tiny box, savoring the moment. And there, nestled on a layer of cotton, lies her grandmother's precious shamrock broach. As she picks it up, she notices a scrap of paper underneath in Millie's messy scrawl. She murmurs out loud, "Wear it always and think of me. It will protect you wherever you are. Love, Grandma." Carefully she pins it on her yellow tee-shirt before giving it a pat to see if she will feel Millie's energy. And sure enough, a vibration tickles her fingers. Her pale blue eyes pop open. The corners of her lips tilt upwards. "Thank you, Grandma," she whispers to the air.

CHAPTER 37: EARTH

In the MacIntyre living-room in Ravenspond, Leila sits cross-legged on the rug in her sister Bessie's Chris Lisack tee-shirt. Her brown hair, usually pulled back neatly into a ponytail or braids, hangs messily around her face. A smear of red jam sticks to her chin. Late morning sunshine pours through the window sheers, lifting them slightly on a humid summer breeze. Mouser's head is in her lap.

Sophia Moreno, in a smart champagne pantsuit, crouches down in her heels to stroke the old dog's head. She gazes across at the solemn young girl for a moment. "Where's your father?"

Leila doesn't look up. "Meeting with the detective."

"Oh yes, with Jorge, too. A good lead, I pray to God." Her hand lifts up one silky golden ear before laying it back gently against the dog's head. "When did he start acting like this?"

"He wouldn't eat his breakfast this morning. And he never does that. And he won't even touch his mouse." Leila's hand fingers the ratty rodent.

Sophia watches her for a moment, fiddling with the gold loop in her right ear. She gets up and heads for the kitchen. "I'm going to call the vet."

Along the hallway she stops to glance at a line-up of off-kilter, badly-framed photos of various family gatherings across the years. One, in particular, catches her eye. A small black and white picture taken against a stone wall has captured a moment in time - a short young man with dark hair stands stiffly in an ill-fitting suit. Beside him a grinning girl, noticeably taller in what appears to be a handmade, white dress with long-sleeves, beams from the photo. A trail of veil drifts around her short curls. In her hands, the happy bride holds a loose bouquet of wild roses. On the left side of her chest, just below her collarbone, perches a garish shamrock broach.

Sophia takes the picture off the wall for a closer look. "Strange jewelry to wear on a wedding dress. Must have been a gift. Something borrowed, something blue, something old … That's it, probably something old." She looks a little closer at the photo. "Oh, it's Will and Millie, Bessie's grandparents. They look so different at that age. So young! The kids must miss them since they've been gone, what, oh, years now. They were so much fun."

Hanging the picture back on the nail, she heads down the hallway to the kitchen, muttering under her breath. "That poor girl with her dog. Shouldn't have to be dealing with this all by herself."

CHAPTER 38: HEAVEN

In his office overlooking the formal gardens, Angel Mel hunches over his desk, pre-occupied with the screenplay he's intently scribbling notes in. Bessie slumps cross-wise in the armchair, watching out the window at the tulip garden where Jimmy Stewart and a dapper Cary Grant in an immaculate suit and tie are telling what appears to be a funny story to James Dean. Dean, in his iconic white tee-shirt and skintight black jeans, hands in his pockets, seems to be enjoying the tale.

Finally Angel Mel looks up, waving his hand at her. "Now what?"

Bessie glares at him as she fiddles with the green broach on her shirt. "When's she coming, Mel?"

"When's who coming?" He's stalling for time, knowing perfectly well what she's talking about.

She jumps to her feet, pacing back and forth in front of the window. "The cottage is all ready. For their *daughter*. Welcome, dearest *daughter*, the note said. Everything's spic and span like it never, ever, was before. Scoured and polished and swept and tidied. New bedspread. New curtains. Fresh flowers in a vase. Even the cat is brushed. I mean, come on, Mel, must be soon, right?" She leans on his desk, glaring at him, eye to eye. "Am I right? She's coming soon?"

"When it's—"

"And don't say time." She cuts him off at the pass. "If I hear that once more, I'm gonna puke. When it's time, when it's time. When there is no time in Heaven. Make up your mind, for God's sake!" She stares out the window for a moment. "And another thing you haven't explained, how will I know when she's arriving? How does everybody know when to go to the airport to wait for the next flight? Does a little bird whisper in their ear?

He turns to glance at her fondly. "Well, it works like this. They know when they're supposed to know. Not all souls in Heaven are told when their loved ones are arriving. It's decided on an individual, need-to-know basis."

"So are you going to tell me when my mother is arriving?" Her features are as stormy as a beach in hurricane season.

"You'll have to wait and see, my little mushroom. You'll have to wait and see." Spinning around, she stomps through the open door without a word of goodbye.

Angel Mel looks out the window as James Dean introduces Dennis Hopper to Jimmy Stewart and Cary Grant. Dennis, obviously a newcomer, seems blown away with awe. He shakes hands with the movie stars vigorously. Stewart smiles graciously, winking at Dean. Grant nods his head, politely engaging Dean in conversation, or so it appears.

The angel glances again at the empty doorway, shaking his head before returning to his writing. "What am I going to do with that girl? She's in such turmoil, poor little thing. First Jason arriving, then her grandparents deciding to take a hike back to Earth - just when I could really use their help the most - and now this newly dead soul on their way to the cottage." He sighs deeply, gesturing with his arms as he faces the window. "Wow, Dean and Hopper and Grant and Stewart, all at once. Wish I could eavesdrop on that conversation." He grins. "Hey, what am I saying?" And vanishes into the air.

CHAPTER 39: HEAVEN

Bessie looks over at Ash sleeping soundly in their bedroom at Girls Dorm, the latest *Angel* magazine collapsed on her lap. Shining from the cover, a middle-aged Jackie Kennedy Onassis, in her signature, over-sized black sunglasses, turtleneck, and Capri's, strolls somewhere in Paris with an unknown companion on an autumn day long ago. The copy reads: A LIFE OF WEALTH, TRAGEDY, HONOR, AND BETRAYAL: NOW PLAYING AT THE PAST LIVES THEATRE.

Deciding not to disturb her friend's rest, Bessie is soon walking briskly along the path by the edge of the cliff in the pre-dawn night, not even trying to hide her presence from Angel Rainbow Sunshine, engrossed in tuning her guitar, for all the good it will do. The St. Bernard gets up and trots over to the girl, deciding to stroll alongside.

A voice begins to destroy another hippie classic, this time Joni Mitchell's *Big Yellow Taxi*. Maybe instead of focusing on paradise and parking lots, she might consider taking some lessons, Bessie muses. But no, the happy angel is blissfully unaware of her painful performance. She addresses her comments to the dog. "How do you do it, pal? Hanging out with her, day after day after day?"

The dog looks over at Bessie with soulful eyes, continuing to trot alongside. Soon they arrive at the Sacred Telescope. Very practiced now, Bessie steps up to remove the lens cap and adjust the focus. "Please, how did I die?" She gazes with yearning up at the billions of stars, pleading for answers. The milky swirls begin to clear.

Bessie and Ash, dressed in their runaway outfits, sit in a large farm kitchen. A long wooden table dominates the room. Serving plates display meatloaf, cobs of corn, a stack of white bread, and a casserole of mashed potatoes and fresh peas. A fat dog sleeps on a mat by the screen door. A black and white cat cleans himself on the pillow of an old, painted rocking chair.

Around the table, Ash and Bessie sit on stiff wooden chairs. At one end, the tall, awkward, middle-aged man who gave them a lift, cleans his glasses with a handkerchief taken from his overalls' pocket. Over by the kitchen counter, a woman in a faded apron over a house-dress, her thin hair tied back with a scarf, pours glasses of lemonade. "You gals sure got a sense of adventure, don't they, Walt." She sits down at the other end of the table, spreading her cloth napkin on her lap.

Walt doesn't answer. Instead he begins to say grace. Ash and Bessie quickly bow their heads while he pronounces, "Lord, thank you for the meal what Flora made. And for this farm what growed the food. Amen."

Flora follows with an amen, as she picks up the plate of meatloaf to pass around.
"Eat up."

Walt takes a cob of corn carefully buttering it row by row before salt and peppering it, just so. "Sure you don't want to make a phone call to your folks? We won't charge ya."

"Course we won't." Flora agrees. 'What kind of Christian people would we be if we charge young girls for a phone call just 'cause they look like cheap hookers?"

Bessie swallows a mouthful of meatloaf without chewing. "We aren't—"

"Course you're not, dear." Flora interrupts. "You're just dressed like that on account of the filthy pictures on television. Just like that ex-sister-in-law of mine, Lorry-Lyn." She smiles knowingly, leaning conspiratorially towards Ash. "Em-tee-vee. That's what did it. Well, maybe not for Lorry-Lyn. She's too old for that. She's just a slut, plain and simple."

Bessie jumps in, desperate to change the subject. "Our parents aren't at home. They're traveling in—"

"Europe," Ash fills in quickly. "For, like, the whole summer."

"Yes, Europe. Our parents are ah, related so they travel together."

"Many trips."

"Like China."

"Hawaii."

"Brazil."

"Antarctica."

Walt and Flora look from one girl to the other, and back to each other. "Related?" Flora pipes up. "Related how?"

The girls sport matching, ingenuous smiles while Bessie takes the lead with, "We're practically sisters. We were almost raised together—" She runs her hand through her pitch-black wig.

"Sort of like twins, you might even say." Ash agrees.

Their hosts hesitate, raising their eyebrows and sharing a look. Walt announces, "Looks like rain." He picks up his fork to dig into the meatloaf.

"Sure does." Flora bites into her ear of corn.

"Good for the potatoes."

"And the peppers."

Dinner continues in silence until Flora looks directly from Bessie to Ash. "Pie?"

Startled, Bessie mumbles, "Excuse me?"

Walt shouts, "PIE. YOU WANT PIE OR NO PIE?"

The girls almost jump out of their chairs before their answers tumble over each other. "Oh sure, absolutely, yes, we love pie. Don't we, yes, pie, sure!"

One mouth-watering, fresh raspberry pie with whipped cream later, everyone sits back, full and content.

"That sure was delicious, ah … Mrs. … Flora." Bessie smiles.

"Sure was. Thanks so much. Well, we better head back into town to find a—" Ash begins to get out of her seat.

"No sense in that." Walt doctors his tea with four spoons of sugar. "You gals can share our daughter's room for the night."

"Won't she mind?" Bessie inquires politely.

"Why would she?" Walt slurps his tea before setting it down. "She's dead."

Flora sips nonchalantly on her own tea before adding, "Drugs."

Ash crumbles back down into her chair while Bessie sits immobilized, jaw slack, eyes as wide as the empty pie plate on the table.

Finally Flora sets down her cup into the saucer. "Drove the tractor into the crik last spring while she was higher than a kite in a tornado."

"Had to buy a new tractor." Walt mutters as he swings his long legs out from under the table before heading for the back door. "Come on, Poke," he calls to the sleeping dog.

They can hear him out on the porch, still talking. "That were one hell of a good tractor, too."

In Heaven Bessie sees the milky swirls returning into the lens and protests loudly to the St. Bernard, "No, no, I'm not ready. I need more!" But the lens turns dark. Reluctantly she climbs down from the Sacred Telescope and heads towards the path back to Girls Dorm.

As the faded strains of a Leonard Cohen's song fill the air, Bessie stops to listen, despite the off-key rendition by Angel Rainbow Sunshine. The images from the Sacred Telescope run across her mind - the farmhouse, the meal, the strange farmer and his wife, Flora. Their daughter killed in a tractor accident. She shivers just remembering how creepy it was listening to them talk about her death. Was it really a tragic stunt when she was high on drugs…or something else?

Suddenly she stops in her tracks on the isolated moonlit road. "I didn't have my scar yet at that farm. No scar at all." Reaching up to touch the one she now has, her eyes fill with tears. "When did I get this scar?"

CHAPTER 40: HEAVEN

Ash and Bessie cycle down the familiar road, Ash on Grandma Millie's bike, Bessie on Grandpa Will's. Stiletto platforms teeter dangerously on and off the pedals of the woman's bike as Ash attempts to steer it, or rather over-steer it, left, then right, then left. Bessie wisely slows down to ride behind her, in hopes of avoiding a crash.

On the top of the hill overlooking the valley where her grandparents' empty cottage nestles, the girls stop and look down in silence. Emotion fills Bessie's eyes. They climb back on the bikes and peddle slowly along the trail leading downwards. Halfway they stop again, reluctant to arrive.

"Ready?" Ash's voice is soft. "Maybe your mom is on her way."

"Maybe. Mel told me they don't always give you warning. Looks so forlorn, doesn't it." Moments later, Bessie's whole being lights up with joy. In the distance below them, a slender, redheaded woman walks out of the woods behind the cottage, carrying a basketful of flowers.

"Omigod!" Bessie scrambles on her bike and tears down the rough hillside, leaving her friend in the dust. "She's here!" she shouts with glee. "Mom's here!"

The woman is walking alongside the cottage. Bessie can see she is wearing coral-colored shorts with a matching, sleeveless blouse. Ropey wedgies are tied at her ankles. The cat scoots ahead of her, leading the way.

Now only about forty feet from her, Bessie slows down, almost to a stop. Her emotions are playing Russian roulette. Leaning her bike against a tree, she begins to walk as if in a trance.

The woman is stooped over, her back to Bessie, plucking a rose from Millie's glorious garden near the front edge of the little house. She is, in fact, so absorbed in her task, she hasn't realized she's being watched.

"Ouch!" the woman shouts, licking her finger.

Bessie's lips turn up at the corners. She reaches up to touch her scar. Anticipation fills her eyes as the woman, ever so slowly, turns around. And then shock hits her like a cold, cruel slap. "Aunt Fiona! What are *you* doing here?"

Fiona Dodd resembles a brassy caricature of Bessie's mother. Pretty in an over-painted, cheerful sort of way, her red hair is enhanced to an unnatural shade. She beams, doing a little jump up and down before rushing towards Bessie to wrap herself around her. Her words punch the air like a staple gun. "Well, who did you think I was? Madonna? Ha ha! Well, fancy meeting you here! Gad, what a trip, huh? Where are mom and dad, anyway? Thought they'd be here greeting me! Don't tell me, they flew the coop already! Right before I get here, those old rascals ha ha!"

Bessie tries to speak but her lips are frozen. Fiona holds her at arm's length. "Well, let me take a good look at you. Where the hell you girls been, anyway?" She stops long enough to see the irony in her words. "Hell! That's a good one ha ha! We're in Heaven, Bessie girl! We're in Heaven! What's inside?" She scampers off towards the front door.

Ash arrives to quickly put an arm around Bessie's shoulder. "Wow. Who saw *that* coming?"

"That's putting it mildly." Bessie looks towards the open cottage door. "Very mildly." Her feelings buzz like bumble bees. If her aunt is here, then where is her mother?

Minutes later, Fiona, now curled up on the sofa, gazes in amazement around the cozy dwelling while Bessie leaves to pick some fresh nectarines. Ash observes her friend's aunt in utter fascination from an armchair. "I missed you on your last whirlwind visit to Ravenspond. Where had you been living?"

"Los Angeles, honey. Los Angeles. It means, Home of Lost Angels, this guy told me."

Ash sits up in full attention. "You lived in Hollywood? I thought you were in Phoenix."

Fizz fusses with her over-glued bouffant. "That was my cover story ha ha. Actually I worked at this taco stand down on Santa Monica pier. You know, waiting for my big break. To be magically discovered, like Lana Turner was at that soda fountain."

Ash's face fills with bewilderment. "Lana who?"

Half an hour later, Bessie sets down a tray with three cups and a pot of nectar tea, freshly washed nectarines, a small jar of Grandpa Will's homemade hooch, and a bag of NecNac Snaks.

"Your aunt was living in Hollywood," Ash informs her friend. "She was, like, almost a movie star, right, Fizz?"

Bessie stares fondly at her relative. "So, how did you end up here?"

Fiona reaches for the bag of NecNac Snaks, deciding against it. "Oh hell, I don't have to worry about calories anymore, do I, girls ha ha?" She stuffs a chip in her mouth, and then another. "How did I end up here so young, you mean?" Reaching up automatically to smooth out any remembered age lines on her cheeks, she growls, "It was that Simon. That no-good, piece-of-shit, slime ball Simon. You remember Simon, Bessie?"

"That Scottish loon you brought home for Thanksgiving that one time? With the bald head and a grey ponytail?"

"Simon is an antique dealer. Has his own shop." Her eyes tear up a bit. "Maybe that's why it all happened."

Ash and Bessie look at each other. Ash pipes up eagerly, "So what happened?"

Fizz tosses back some hooch straight from the jam jar. "My brand new lemon yellow, top-loading washing machine breaks. Can you believe that? Brand new!"

"Didn't know they made yellow ones," Ash says, trying to keep the conversation going. Bessie rolls her eyes.

"They make them in all colors now. Red, blue, green, chartreuse even."

Ash glances over at Bessie who is pouring more tea. She tries, "So it broke?"

"First day! First day!" Fizz is beyond outraged. "Simon calls me a dumb, fucking bitch, can you believe that? A dumb, fucking bitch! Me! And he never swears! Never! Just because …"

"Because?" Ash can't wait.

"Because…" Fizz takes another swig. "Boy, my dad always did know how to make a good homemade whiskey."

"Because …?" Bessie repeats.

Her aunt runs her fuschia fingernails through her curls. "Just because I put that dumb carpet in my new washing machine. Listen to this one. Know what that cheapo slime ball Simon gives me for my birthday? This stupid, old, dusty carpet! Like, over five hundred years old, he tells me. I mean, who gives you a crummy, old carpet for your birthday? Anyway, it was filthy! It's Persian, he says. Persian. La dee dah."

The girls stare at her in utter fascination.

"Persian, like from Iran?" Bessie is afraid to ask. "From when it was still called Persia?"

Fizz shakes her head. "Persia, Iran, who cares? It's a washing machine for washing things. And brand new, not like that ratty, old carpet. You know, it was so worn it was thread-bare in some places. And all the colors were faded like crazy. Didn't match a damn thing in our apartment. You'd think he would have looked around our place before he chose a carpet, but no. Slime ball Simon just grabs any old thing he could find with no consideration." She turns to toss her curls in a dramatic gesture. "No consideration, whatsoever, for my carefully chosen rose and mint green decor that cost me a small fortune, let me tell you. A small fortune." She reaches over to stroke the cat, now curled up beside her. "Long story short."

"Oh, don't shorten it on our account," Bessie encourages her with a twinkle in her eyes.

"Okay, well, Simon - who knew he could be so violent - he yanks out that stupid old carpet out of my beautiful new machine like a mad man. I mean, who knew it would shrink? There were threads all over the place! He's yelling and screaming and cursing till I thought the cops were gonna come. I mean, no consideration for Mrs. Lorrie who is eighty-six and naps every afternoon who lives right across the hall. None whatsover. Who wakes up an old woman like that over some stupid rug? Well, you'll never guess what he does next. He picks me up and stuffs me head first into my brand new machine. Head first! And then ..."

"And then?" Bessie encourages her to go on.

"That rat bastard turns it on." Fizz leans back in the sofa, arms crossed behind her head. "Can you believe that?" She jumps up to walk around the cottage, admiring it. "Mom made it just like the one they used to have in Ireland. I remember seeing the pictures in her old album. The sofas, the pillows, the curtains, everything. Do you think this is actually the very same... cottage? Is that possible?"

Ash whispers to Bessie, "Was she always this nutty?"

"Well," Fizz calls from the kitchen, swigging directly from the jam jar. "So I end up in Emerge. Luckily your mother, Heather, was able to fly out and take care of me. The very same day, bless her heart. She was hoping she might find you two runaways out there at the same time. Something about Chris Lisack? Did you really run away to join his band? Wow, that is just a really cool idea! But your poor mother, she was beside herself looking for you, you can't imagine. Oh well, I guess it all worked out, didn't it? Here we all are, in mom and dad's cottage, having a great old time!"

"So you didn't recover, I take it?" Bessie tries to be comforting, although it's difficult to keep a straight face. "You passed away from your injuries?"

"Oh, hell's bells no, I was fine from that. Just a few minor cuts and bruises, no thanks to that slime ball Simon. Went home the very next day." She slugs back more whiskey.

"Oh?" The girls look at each other. Bessie pipes up, "So what happened then?"

"Well, your mother decides to stay to search for you two. We looked together everywhere. Up and down the coast from San Diego to San Francisco. Any more of this stuff?" She holds up the empty jar while Bessie jumps up in search of a replacement.

"And …?" Ash urges her on.

After pouring herself a full glass and taking a big slurp, Fizz continues, "Where was I? Oh, yeah. So a week later? Aneurism to the heart. Boom. Gone. Nothing at all to do with the stupid washing machine or that ugly old carpet." She knocks her chest dramatically before knocking back the rest of the jar. "Deader than a doornail. Ha! Whatever that means."

The three females stare at each other, soaking it all in.

"So where's the action, girls?" Fizz chirps up, just before passing out cold on the floor.

CHAPTER 41: EARTH

Rain pours down in drab sheets as the small, sad crowd huddles under umbrellas around the open grave site on a hillside in rural Pennsylvania. A sobbing Heather MacIntyre is being comforted by her husband, Art, while Sophia and Jorge Moreno stand apart. A dry-eyed Leila, in a navy blue dress, and clutching a yellow umbrella, holds herself stiffly. A stringy handful of wild flowers tied with a ribbon, droops from one hand.

A tall, middle-aged man with a bald head and greying ponytail, wearing a full-length, English raincoat, holds a large, old-fashioned umbrella with an ornately carved wooden handle.

To one side a grouping of mostly women crowd together, all around Fiona's age of thirty-six. Most likely they are high school mates, with one or two from her California life, who made the trip.

All are looking over at the officiate, a stout woman in a plain black suit, wire-rimmed glasses, and short, mousy hair, as she reads from a Bible. A solemn, color-less man who appears to be from the funeral home, holds an umbrella over her head.

A bouquet of ivory roses adorns the pale brown coffin, with a sash that reads: FIONA, WE LOVE YOU. The box perches on a metal platform surrounded by fake grass as if the large hole dug beneath it wasn't really there.

As always happens at funerals, an odd collection of strangers gawk from the distance as they stroll outside the metal fence of the graveyard, doing their Saturday chores.

The officiate reads, "Yea, though I walk through the valley of the shadow of death, I will fear no evil; For Thou art with me. Thy rod and thy staff, they comfort me."

As her voice continues with the prayer, the man in the raincoat lays an envelope on top of the coffin simply addressed to "Fee". The crowd glances at him with compassion before looking away.

"Surely goodness and mercy shall follow me all the days of my life. And I will dwell in the House of the Lord forever. Amen."

A chorus of amens follows. Art wraps his arms around his openly weeping wife as the others begin to wander awkwardly off.

Leila walks over to look at the grave stone beside where her aunt will be laid to rest. A modest stone in rose marble, it arches at the top as if to shelter the Celtic cross surrounded in roses. Underneath the words are etched: DEEPLY MISSED, ALWAYS LOVED. WILLIAM HAROLD DODD: 1917-1997. MILLICENT ROSE DODD: 1919-2000. BORN COUNTY CORK, IRELAND.

Leila carefully sets down her bouquet of mostly wild asters, periwinkles, and Queen Anne's lace - her grandmother's favorites.

CHAPTER 42: HEAVEN

In the Heavenly Healing Spa, Jason is back in the Color Vibration therapy room being zapped vigorously by beams of canary yellow, scarlet, and an intense vermillion blue.

It's not Angel Lionel who monitors him this time, but his uncle Peter, a man who resembles Jason in every way but age, right down to the strange sticking-up hair. He sits uncomfortably in the lone chair as if he's better used to standing up. His bony farm hands lay quietly in his lap, as he gazes at his nephew. "It's no use, Jason. You've got to give up this crazy obsession."

"But Uncle Pete. I—"

"No buts. Bessie has her own healing to do in Heaven, I'm sure. You need to complete your therapy. It's for your own good."

"Just one more time, that's all I ask. I just want to see her one more time."

"But is that the best thing, considering?" Peter pulls his lanky body up onto his feet encased in work boots, wandering over to lean down, hands on knees so he can look at his nephew, eye to eye. "Remember when you moved to the farm, how your father and you used to plant the corn together every spring?"

Jason turns his head to face him. "Yeah, all those seeds in the furrows."

"Covered them up with dirt. Then you watered them."

"And watered them."

Peter laughs. "And watered them some more. Even when you didn't want to. Even when it was hotter than stink outside, you watered. And what happened?"

"They grew into big plants."

"And?" Peter stretches upright, putting one hand on Jason's back.

"And then corn cobs grew. And when they were ripe, we picked them and sold them and everybody ate them."

Peter chuckles. "Yep, all us farmers sure ate corn all season long. Even made corn relish out of it. And ground up kernels for corn bread. My favorite."

"And corn tacos." Jason rolls over on his side, hunching up on one elbow. His face, as usual, is earnest. "What are you trying to say, Uncle Pete? I'm a corn stalk?"

Again, that low, warm chuckle. "No, what I'm saying is, you can't rush the corn, lad. No matter what you do, the corn seed becomes a corn cob when it's good and ready and no sooner. If you yank it out before then you ruin it."

"You're saying to wait until it's the right time with Bessie or else I'll ruin it?"

"For a kid with funny hair, you're pretty smart." His uncle treats him to an encouraging smile. "That's why you're here, to heal first. There's a whole lot of healing got to be done."

Jason looks back, lost in thought. With one hand, he rubs his creased forehead. "But I've got to make it up to her. Got to tell her how sorry I am. If only ..." He struggles to sit up, but there are restraints on his hands made of ribbons of yellow light. He slumps back down, defeated. "Got to make it right. Somehow."

His uncle reaches out to ruffle his hair. "When it's time, lad. When it's time. For now, lie back and relax. Let the lights do their job. All in good time."

Jason's eyes slowly close as he allows the healing energy to penetrate his body.

"That's a good lad, that's a good lad," Peter coos, patting the sleeve of Jason's shirt in the manner of a farmer soothing a fretful calf. "You rest now. He gets up and moves away to sit back down on the chair, shaking his head and mumbling under his breath. "You're just as stubborn as me."

Jason's eyes pop open for a moment. He grins. "Stubborner."

CHAPTER 43: HEAVEN

The truth is, it took a couple of days for Fiona Dodd to fully recover from her spectacular, nectarine whiskey-laced, over-indulgent arrival. Even though imbibing alcohol in Heaven has no physical effect, the memory of it is as potent as ever. Happily, thanks to her mother Millie's forethought who had taped homemade hangover recipes to a kitchen cupboard, Fizz made a full recovery. Now she trots alongside Bessie and Ash as they play hookie once again from Reincarnation school. "So where're we off to, gals?"

"You'll see," Bessie replies slyly.

"Just a little shopping trip," Ash adds with a giggle.

"Ooh, I love shopping. Except for rugs ha ha." Fizz is comfortably dressed in shorts and a top her mother had left in the bedroom for her. It seems Millie had thought of everything before she and Will set off on their next life adventures.

After a stroll down the country road, the trio arrives at the wonders of the Seventh Heaven Mall. Bessie leads her aunt to the Past Lives theatre at the far entrance.

"Movies, too?" Fiona stares up at the marquee.

"Real life stories," Ash explains to her. "And not just movies *about* the person, but the actual ..." She stares intently into the newcomer's face, batting her false eyelashes. "Sto-ry."

"You mean ... ?" You can almost see the wheels turning in Fizz's mind.

"Just last week we watched Marilyn Monroe sing Happy Birthday to President Kennedy." Bessie winks.

"That dress she wore?" Ash adds. "Like, sooo glam." Her eyes close so she can see it again.

Simultaneously all three look up at the marquee to see what's playing: RANGAN VADIVEL, FROM STOCK BOY TO STOCK BROKER. FLAVIA SANTAROSSA,

MISTRESS TO THE MINISTERS. And finally, MACKENZIE KERR, REVOLUTIONIZING SHEEP FARMING.

"Maybe we'll wait till next week," Bessie decides.

"I prefer slasher films, myself," Fizz remarks.

"She would have loved Edna Snerd, right, Bess?"

They stroll back to the central entrance of the mall, as Ash elaborates, "There was this nurse with a collection of hunting knives who loved to …"

Wandering down the spacious marble interior, looking this way and that, Fizz oohs and aahs over every little item.

Then, out of nowhere it seems, a movement in Ash's peripheral vision catches her eye. She hesitates, stopping to glance around to see a stocky Latin youth grinning over at her. Recognizing him as the fellow who attacked Jason in the forest when they were escaping from the Akashic Hall of Records, her eyes grow large and she quickens her step.

"*Bonita*, stop! Pretty girl, please. *Por favor*," he calls out to her.

Ash slows down to a halt, turning around again while her companions walk over to look at a display of dresses that is captivating Fizz. The young girl can't help but notice how handsome the fellow is. And he appears to have nothing more on his mind than admiring her. She begins to stroll cautiously towards him, swaying her hips ever so slightly, conscious she's being watched.

He approaches slowly so as not to frighten her, tapping her on the shoulder. "I am Miguelito." She turns around to face him as he treats her to another of his beguiling smiles. Much to her delight, he is dressed in a white shirt with the sleeves rolled up, open at the neck, long black pants, and loafers. Like a real man, not a boy.

"I just want to meet you." He speaks with an alluring Spanish accent. "I see you in the forest that time, and I think you are so very beautiful."

There's nothing like a compliment to stop a girl in her tracks. After a small hesitation, she smiles back coyly, reaching up to fluff her curls. "Jason's friend," she says.

"I try to be his friend, but he no want to have friends. Something bad happen to him. Now they take him away to Rehab. You know him?"

"Did you, like, live in Mexico?" Ash asks him. "Or Spain?"

"I come from Guadalajara before …"

"Before?"

"Before I drown in a pool at a big graduation party from the hitting of my head." His grin is sheepish this time. "How you die, then?" he inquires politely.

"So do you, like, live at the Boys Dorm?" She answers his question with another one, posing with one elegant hand on her hip.

"Yes, and it is not too far from Girls Dorm," he says softly. "Maybe I meet with you sometime. What is your name?"

"Ashley," she replies. "Ashley Sophia. My father is from Mexico, also. And yes, perhaps we can meet sometime, in the future, for a nectar latte."

"Or a movie?" Miguelito takes one of her hands. "You like the movies?"

She tilts her head. This is way too much fun. "I adore them. In my next life, I'm going to be a famous actress." She lets her hand stay there for a moment before removing it. "Well, I'll see you sometime," she finishes before trotting off towards Bessie and Fizz, glancing back over her shoulder with a little wave. "Perhaps."

"Ooh, Ashley Sophia ..." The handsome young man shakes his head, grinning. "*Que bonita.*"

Moments later, Ash, Bessie, and Fiona are running their fingers through the racks of images at the Bodysuits Boutique. To say the newcomer is blown away is an understatement. "You can just put these on and you *become* that person?" Ash and Bessie bob their heads.

Bessie whispers, "Supposed to be for investigative purposes. You know, choosing your next life."

"But we just do it to piss off the Soulslady." Ash jerks her head in the direction of the little woman in question, busily explaining her shop to a group of visitors.

"Come on, pick one," Ash urges as she grabs a bodysuit from a hanger from the Slightly Used section. "Quick, before she spots us."

Soon all three are crammed into a tiny change-room, yanking bodysuits over themselves. Three walls of the room are completely mirrored for an excellent viewing of Lucille Ball/Bessie, Desi Arnaz/Fizz, and Bobby Darrin/Ash.

"Oh, Looo-cy," coos Desi/Fizz.

"Oh, Desi," coos back Lucy/Bessie. They burst into giggles.

"Ready?" Bobby Darrin/Ash tugs them back into the shop. Once there, she performs a lively rendition of Bobby's *Splish Splash*, while her companions bee-bop to the music. Ash belts out the lyrics like a seasoned pro, swinging around her pretend microphone and doing a vigorous jive that would have made Bobby Darrin himself proud.

"Follow my lead," Lucy/Bessie whispers to her partner as they dance their way vigorously into the hall accompanied by Bobby Darrin/Ash, singing her heart out as she wiggles her hips and jumps about. To see Lucy and Desi dancing away is like catching a lost episode of their iconic television show. All that is missing is Fred and Ethel.

The crowd goes wild, cheering and clapping before the inevitable appearance on the scene of a furious Soulslady.

"Fun while it lasted." Desi/Fizz chuckles, before her ear, accompanied by the rest of her, is painfully yanked back into the boutique. "Ooww! Watch that!"

"Why on earth is everybody so damned afraid of dying?" Fiona asks of her companions as they stroll down the road away from the mall. "I mean, me included before it happened. And now, well, it's so incredible here!"

"The fear of the unknown," Bessie replies wisely.

"That's all?" Fizz is stunned by the simplicity of her answer. "That's the reason?"

"Yep, that's it." She looks at her aunt. "Angel Mel says many people on Earth are so afraid to die, they don't know how to live."

"Not us," Ash jumps in. "We weren't afraid of anything, were we, Bess. *Carpe diem*. Seize the day. That was us, at least what I can remember." She takes a moment to look back, and is rewarded by the sight of the handsome, dark-haired youth, lounging against the exterior of the movie theatre. He lifts his hand in a small wave. She waves back in a way the others can't see.

"So, how did you girls die, anyway?" Fiona looks from one to the other. "You never told me."

Both girls turn pensive. Ash leans down to pick up a scarlet flower, letting her friend do the talking for both of them. "We don't know." Bessie finally speaks up. "We just don't know."

Her aunt catches on that it's not wise to ask more questions, for now. "So, what else is on the agenda today?" Something catches her eye. "Hey, where'd all those cows come from?"

Picking up the pace, the two girls and the woman head towards a nearby field where large bovines, that weren't there a minute ago, can clearly be seen grazing on the afternoon grass. Soon the trio is leaning against the wooden fence. One black and white cow raises her head to watch them for a few minutes before returning to her meal.

"You didn't tell me? Where'd they all come from?"

A distance humming sound reaches their ears from the sky. "Watch and learn," Ash advises as the three of them turn in the direction of the hum emanating from a large cloud formation in the distinct shape of a 747. The cows in the field pay scant attention as the aircraft arrives to hover overhead.

"What the …?"

"Shsh," her niece hisses. "Just watch."

Now a large hatch slides sideways on the side of the plane. A sturdy ramp emerges slowly until it reaches the ground. In single file, cows, both dairy and beef, stroll lazily down the ramp, wander across the field, and begin to graze as if this was an everyday occurrence.

"So that's what happens to all our burgers." Fizz is jumping up and down with excitement.

Together they watch for awhile, leaning on the fence, when suddenly Ash yells, "Bessie, Bess, look over there, look, look!"

Bessie spins around. "Jason? You see Jason? Where is he? What's going on?" Her eyes are wide with fear.

"No, look!" Ash points excitedly. "At the plane."

Bessie cranes to see what the commotion is all about, just as a golden retriever trots happily down the ramp before it folds back into the plane. In his Air Heaven uniform, a large male angel shouts, "Next time, pal, wait for the Pet Flight!"

Spying Bessie, the dog runs full-tilt, tail wagging like it was motorized. A ratty-looking mouse toy hangs from his mouth. He jumps the fence in one leap to be smothered in her arms as the two of them roll and tumble like pups from the same litter.

"Oh, Mouser, I can't believe it's you. Oh, Mouser." Bessie's joy is a thrill to watch.

"She needed that," Ash quietly remarks to Fizz.

CHAPTER 44: HEAVEN

Fiona flounces away from the Sacred Telescope, eyes blazing. "The nerve. The freaking nerve of that man." Ash and Bessie share raised eyebrows as Mouser nuzzles the older woman's hip. "He's dating already."

The other two wait to hear what's next. It's going to be good, for sure.

"His business partner, Sheila." It comes out like a snarl. "Sheee-laaah. His bizzz-nezzz partner. That slime ball Simon. Couldn't wait five minutes." She stops to glance around. "How long have I been here, anyway? Never mind."

Ash decides to bravely jump in. "Maybe she's just, like, comforting him, in his time of grief."

"Grief, my butt. I saw them doing it. In their stockroom." Fiona huffs and puffs, stroking Mouser so vigorously, he moves away from her hand. "They were probably doing it before I died. Maybe they ..." Her face becomes an ugly cloud of accusation. "Knocked me off. Poisoned me."

"Pretty hard to cause an aneurism with poison, Aunt Fizz," Bessie comments diplomatically. "Although you might be able to fake one, I suppose. Wish I could ask Leila. She knows all about that stuff." The thought of her sister pulls at her heart. In many ways, she misses her more than anyone else on Earth.

"Huh. Leave it to that slime ball Simon to figure out a way." She stomps off to sit against a tree trunk, pulling a flask of her father's whiskey from her pocket and tossing some back.

"Poor Fizz, she's broken-hearted. Well, Bess, guess it's your turn to have a peek. I've already seen my mom sell a million dollar house. I'll go wait with your aunt." Ash trots off as Bessie steps up onto the pedestal to adjust the lens, waiting for the milky swirls to clear.

In a darkened bedroom on the second floor of a farm house, Bessie and Ash, in their bras and panties, perch on a double bed. Photos of a blonde girl around their age are stuck around the edges of an ornate mirror on the dresser.

Ash leans back on her arms. "Hard to believe Flora used to be Lorry-Lyn's sister-in-law. She was so much fun, showing us all those cosmetics she makes in her basement."

"Yeah. In the Pink by Lorry-Lyn." Bessie gets up to take a closer look at the pictures. "Must be their dead daughter, what's her name?"

"Jean." Ash joins her, picking up a snap of the girl in question with a handsome young man, possibly her boyfriend. "She looks very glam. Not like her parents at all."

"Do you think she really died in a tractor accident?" Bessie's voice is low.

A creaking sound in the hallway startles them. They both stand still, photos suspended in their hands. The footfalls of Poke the dog tap-tap-tap along the pine floorboards and fade away.

"This place is so creepy." Ash looks down at the pretty Jean snuggling her boyfriend at some local fair. She puts it back on the mirror, taking another one of the dead girl in a cheerleading outfit.

With no warning, the door bursts open. They almost pass out from fright. It's Flora in her nightgown. "Everything alright? You can wear Jean's pajamas. They're in the closet. She don't need 'em no more." Her voice is bitter.

The girls smile weakly, photos in their hands. Ash speaks finally, "She was a very pretty girl, your daughter."

"Fat lot of good it did her." The door closes as suddenly as it opened.

An hour later, they are lying on top of the quilt, still in their underwear as it's a very warm night. And the thought of wearing a dead girl's clothing gives them the absolute willies.

A slow rain has begun to fall outside the narrow window. "Maybe they found out she was planning to run away and they killed her and buried her on the farm someplace." Ash's eyes widen.

"I thought I saw some sort of cross in the field when we drove in."

They take each other's hands as they lie there, listening to the rain. The wind picks up. Branches of a tree swirl outside the window. Now sheets of water beat on the panes.

"Maybe they fed her body to the pigs. I read that someplace this psycho farmer dude fed human bodies to his pigs. Did you see any … pigs?"

A loud banging makes them both sit upright. Footfalls move quickly down the hall. The man shouts, "Damn that Larry!"

The girls, still upright, turn to look at each other. "Larry? Who's Larry?"

Without warning, their door flies open again. This time it's the man, Walt. His features are contorted with anger. In his arms, he cradles a shotgun.

In Heaven, Bessie's fingers tremble as she replaces the lens cap on the Sacred Telescope. Mouser leans against her, feeling her anguish.

"What did you see, honey?" Fiona touches her shoulder. "Was it bad?"

But her niece doesn't answer, instead she turns to wander away as strains of Angel Rainbow Sunshine attempting the haunting melody, *MacArthur Park,* fills the night air. Reaching and missing note after note, she moans and wails about some strange cake left out in the rain. It's almost unbearable, her destruction of the beautiful lyrics.

All three of them race to escape the singer's final screeching, "Oh ... nooooo ..."

CHAPTER 45: HEAVEN

It has been decided that Mouser will live at the cottage with Fiona and Peach the cat, as pets aren't allowed in the dorms. Although there is a Pet Haven where they are spoiled silly, Angel Mel has deemed it best for the retriever to reside with Bessie's aunt. "To keep an eye on that silly woman," he explains to Angel Rachel.

"She makes Bessie and Ashley look almost mature," his companion adds.

The two of them are strolling in the magnificent park and gardens behind Angel Mel's office. Some distance ahead of them, Humphrey Bogart is having a lively chat with Paul Newman, beer in hands, on the other side of a hedge.

"Bet they're discussing Westerns," Angel Mel remarks.

"How are the therapy sessions with Bessie going? Any progress?" Angel Rachel stops to admire some yellow peonies, touching the petals with her manicured hand.

"She's a tough nut to crack, God love her," Angel Mel admits. "But yes, she's progressing. Slowly, slowly, her memories are returning to her."

"Traumatic cases always require a great deal of patience." She looks up at him. "And a talented therapist." Her unexpected smile reveals a very attractive woman.

"Why, thank you." Angel Mel grins back, sucking in his tummy and smoothing down his Hawaiian shirt. "May I treat you to a nectarccino?" He inquires.

Angel Rachel stops, smiling up at him and taking his arm. "That would be a distinct pleasure. So, tell me, what is your latest screenplay all about?"

From behind a nearby hedge, two teenage girls roll about on the grass in fits of giggles while a retriever tries to join in the fun. In a good rendition of Angel Mel's voice, Ash mimics, "May I treat you to a nectarccino?"

Bessie chimes in with Angel Rachel's precise enunciation, "That would be a distinct pleasure. So tell me, what is your latest screenplay all about?"

"Hey, look. Let's go there." Ash gazes over to a far corner of the park where a bandstand has appeared. A small crowd of angels are lining up in a double row, facing a man with a baton whose back is to the girls. The angels wear white gowns over their street clothing and hold up song books. The man's gown is black. His hair is thick and dark and slick.

The calm is soon broken by the choir as they sing with spirit, one of the greatest hits of the fifties, *Don't Be Cruel*. By now the girls have joined a gathering of admirers who are swaying back and forth to the music. As the song finishes, the man with the baton turns around to bow to his audience. Elvis Presley, the king of rock and roll.

CHAPTER 46: EARTH

Eric Pederssen has trouble believing a single word of their story as he lounges against the counter in the farmhouse kitchen. At the table, Walt and Flora Lander sit with straight backs, facing each other. It has been established that they are, indeed, the former relatives by marriage of Lorry-Lyn Murchie, the woman Bessie and Ashley had spent an afternoon with before she dropped them off on the side of the highway. As Ms Murchie had observed, Walt had soon offered the two girls a lift. Adamantly both Walt and Flora tell the detective the girls had taken off in the middle of the night of their own volition.

"Dressed like hookers they were. Offered 'em some of Jean's clothes but they turned me down flat." Flora's arms are folded across her drooping bosom. "Not that hers were much better."

"Just asking for trouble dressed like that," Walt comments.

Eric sips his glass of lemonade, stalling for time. "So your daughter, she was about the same age when she died?" he inquires.

"Thereabouts," Flora says. "Got mixed up with a town boy." She leans across the kitchen table. "Drugs."

"She died in an accident with the tractor, I believe? Not drugs?"

"God's will," Walt mutters.

The hairs on the back of Eric's neck stand up. He glances around for any trace of Ash and Bessie. Nothing.

"More lemonade?" Flora offers.

"Ruined the tractor," the farmer adds.

"May I see the room where they spent a part of the night?" Eric asks politely.

The farm couple shares a glance, a confidence that worries him. Worries him to the bone.

Minutes later, alone in the dead girl's room, Eric plunks down on the same bedspread where Ashley and Bessie had recently been, according to the Landers. Noticing the pictures stuck along the edges of the mirror, he gets up to take a closer look.

"Nothing like the parents," he murmurs. "Better get forensics on this." He wanders over to the window, looking at the neat farm laid out below. A dog barks at a crow in a tree. Chickens run free, pecking at the hard ground. A pen of pigs is barely visible from behind the barn. A broken child's rope swing sways awkwardly in the summer breeze, dangling from a large oak.

He sits back on the bed, this time stretching out against the pillow to think. A spider spins a web around a dusty lamp fixture on the ceiling. Something tickles his ear. Propping himself up, he reaches around behind his head. A cheap blonde wig peeks out from under a pillow sham.

CHAPTER 47: HEAVEN

Souls of all ages, dressed in simple tee-shirts coordinated with loose cotton pants, wander the grounds of what is evidently a hospital. Sure enough a sign on the gate identifies it as the Heavenly Healing Spa. The gate stands by itself with no apparent fencing whatsoever. A small group is practicing Tai Chi. Another is doing yoga. A simple game of catch goes on amongst a grouping of small children. A running track is kept busy with joggers. Other souls sit cross-legged in semi-circles, listening to angels as they read from books of wisdom.

To one side, Jason sits alone on a park bench, his long arms outstretched along the wooden slats. A book lays open and face down in his lap, entitled, *The Joy of Silence.*

A bell rings. Judging by the low light, it's nearing the supper hour. Gradually the patients stream into the white stucco, minimalist-style building. Until there is only one left, apparently dozing on a bench, a book on his lap.

Jason's eyes pop open. His head bolts upright. Tossing the text, he joins the end of the line, keeping to the outside until he is about twenty feet from the entrance. With the speed of an athlete, he dashes across the hospital grounds towards the freedom that lies beyond.

In mid-leap, he leaves the manicured lawn behind him, high in the air. Victory is within his grasp when, shockingly, rows of bright lights jet up from the ground like a Vegas water display, zapping him all over his body. Jason crumbles to the ground, defeated, rubbing his arm as medical staff rush towards him.

CHAPTER 48: HEAVEN

Bessie watches from the sofa with Mouser beside her, the cat on her lap, as her aunt Fizz puts the finishing touches on Ash's make-up. They are in the Dodd cottage on a warm, late afternoon. Both young girls have been given special permission for a sleepover with Bessie's aunt for, quote unquote, "good behavior, lately", according to Angel Mel. And right now all three are focused on getting Ash ready for her first date with Miguelito.

Wearing a lavender mini with matching platforms and a stretchy top, she looks like the movie starlet she dreams of being. Her head full of tight curls has been slicked back into a sort of chignon, with ringlets dangling down beside her hula-hoop-sized earrings. Her purple eye makeup is in the exact same shade as her outfit.

Bessie, in her usual tee-shirt, cut-offs, and sneakers, stares at her best friend in awe. "You look better than Jennifer Lopez," she declares.

"A young Elizabeth Taylor even," Fiona does her one better.

"Not Nicole Richie?" No question, Ash knows who she aspires to be. She applies another layer of lip gloss, making a pouty face. "Am I glam?"

Soon they are waving her good luck as she saunters off down the road to meet up with the handsome young Latino at the Past Lives Theater.

Miguelito is there, of course, lounging beside the marquee in a crisp white shirt and tan pants. His shiny chestnut hair is combed back, displaying his wide forehead and expressive eyebrows. He stands up straight as she approaches, sauntering over and taking her hand softly in his, while they walk towards the entrance.

By the smile on her face, Ash is clearly impressed by, not just his appearance, but his gentlemanly manners.

"You are more beautiful than ever," Miguelito declares.

She notices the gold chain around his neck and asks him about it.

"It remind me of *mi madre*, my mother," he explains. "She always wear one like this."

"I miss my parents, too," she says wistfully.

"So." His large chocolate eyes gaze into hers. "You choose the movie. You know which one you like to see?"

"Oh, absolutely." Ash bats her fake lashes. "The Farrah Fawcett one." She looks up at the marquee to read out loud, "From Charlie's Angels to our own sweet angel."

"I think maybe you are my sweet angel," Miguelito whispers.

"Oh, stop," she protests, meaning the exact opposite. "Shall we?" It's her turn to take his hand.

After the film they sit at a small table in an outdoor patio, enjoying iced nectarccinos at the Stargazy Cafe. Various other patrons are enjoying their beverages, along with the soft evening air.

Miguelito gazes into Ash's eyes over the rim of his glass. "I would like to take you for dancing, but I know—"

"I have a curfew, yes. And I have a funny feeling I'm being observed." Ash looks to the far end of the patio where the outline of a petite, navy power suit can be seen behind a palm tree.

"Another time, then. Because there will be other times, yes?" The young man's face shines with hope.

Ash bats her lashes, sipping on her drink. Using her best exotic movie star accent, she replies, "Vy, of course, mah dahlink! Vy evah not?"

Soon they stroll down the road towards the cottage, holding hands and saying little. Unseen creatures scamper up and down the bark of trees. Owls hoot. A pair of eagles circle high above in the starlit sky.

"Can you tell me, Ashley, why Jason, he is so crazy?"

She loves that he calls her by her proper name. "He and Bessie were together, forever, since she was, like, eight years old. First they were just pals, you know, hanging around the farms together. They both love farms. His family took over his uncle Peter's farm, and her grandparents had the one across the road. So like—"

"So they love each other?"

Ash stops to consider the question carefully. "They loved each other like kids love each other. Innocently, you know? Then, as they got older it got, like, romantic." Her eyes go dreamy. "And they were inseparable right up to when Bessie turned thirteen. They only had eyes for each other. But then all that changed."

"Change how?" Miguelito watches a little fox at the side of the road who watches him back.

"They began fighting. Jason was always like her older brother, as well as her, ah, boyfriend, you know? Very protective."

"That I understand. I was very protective of my own little sister, Carla. It was my job to watch out for her." His eyes grow soft at the memory. "Now she no have me to watch over her."

Ash puts her arm around his shoulder and gives him a little squeeze. They stroll for a bit more. She begins again, "Well, when we got into high school, Jason was, like, two grades ahead of us. So …"

"So …" he encourages her to go on. "What happen?"

"Well, I became an instant success, of course." She stretches her neck, reaching up to touch her chignon where her irrepressible curls are bouncing free. "But Bessie, she was different. She was shy, kind of. So Jason, he … he was more protective than ever which made her—"

"Want to escape him?"

Ash grins. "Escape him, that's right. We skipped school all the time anyway, but for Bessie, it was a way to get away from Jason when she was mad at him."

"So she no love him anymore?"

Ash shakes her curls vigorously. "Oh no, she still loved him, that's what made it so complicated. One minute they were together, the next they would break up."

"What about you in high school, my beauty. You have many boyfriends?"

"Hundreds," she boasts, tilting her oval face. "Thousands, maybe." With that, she runs ahead of him, platforms and all. "Be-zillions!" she shouts over her shoulder.

Outside the cottage, they are still giggling as they stand, out of breath, facing each other, fingers entwined.

"May I kiss you, now?"

"Whah, Ah was afraid you would nevah ask," Ash in a Scarlett O'Hara voice replies, leaning in with her best pucker.

In the nearby woods, a flash of a classic navy suit disappears towards the road.

CHAPTER 49: EARTH

In the kitchen of the MacIntyre home, Eric Pederssen lays down the cheap blonde wig, discovered in the farmhouse bedroom of the late Jean Landers. The fake hair is now encased in plastic on the table. A seated Sophia and Jorge Moreno, Art and Heather Macintyre huddle stiffly.

Standing beside Eric, Leila picks up the bag, moving the hair around with her fingers before promptly supplying the answer, "Yep, that's the right blonde wig."

"Are you sure?" Eric questions her. "You must be sure. There are plenty of them around. Could have been their daughter's wig, for all that."

"See this lettering?" Leila pushes the cap of the wig so it's inside out. In blue ink, a hand-printed, "P.H." is written. "Paris Hilton. I watched Bessie write that in when they first got them. Ash put N.R. inside the other one."

No one speaks for a while. Art says, "Their daughter was about the same age when she, ah, died in an accident on the farm, is that right?"

"Any proof of that?" Jorge adds. "The accident?"

Eric takes his time answering, careful to select the right words. "She, the Lander girl, her remains were badly mangled when the police were called. It was two days after she went missing, according to the parents. The father had removed her body from the creek and lain her on the grass, washed her off, and covered her with a blanket."

Leila speaks, "So no forensic evidence could be gathered."

Eric looks at her, appreciating her quick intelligence. "You are correct."

"The tractor?" Sophia asks, her eyes filling with tears.

Eric puts the wig back into his briefcase, out of sight. "They could never say who drove it into the creek bed. Could have been anybody, I'm afraid."

Outside, the sound of a screeching cat fight rips through the air like a chainsaw.

CHAPTER 50: HEAVEN

"What d'ya mean, Angel Rainbow Sunshine has gone on vacation? To where? Vacation from what?" Bessie is stunned at Angel Mel's news. "She doesn't do anything." The two of them stand beside the Sacred Telescope on the giant cliff in the midday sun.

"Be that as it may, my little mushroom, she is gone to the Fifth Dimension Resort, according to Rachel, for a beach holiday."

"So who is in charge of the Telescope then?" They are walking towards it with no horrific misuse of hippie music to greet them.

"You won't be happy about it," Angel Mel warns her. They continue walking.

Soon Bessie can see the outline of a very large angel in a caftan. "Angel Jigjag," she mutters under her breath. The angel is question is engaged in putting up a brand new sign near the pedestal.

The replacement custodian turns to them with a sunny, toothy smile as they approach. "Good evening to you, Angel Mel and Miss Bessie. Lovely evening to observe the Milky Way, yes?" His accent is as rich as caramel.

Bessie looks at the notice: OFFICIAL ANGEL COURT PASSES REQUIRED FOR VIEWING. All around, there is evidence of a general tidying. The pedestal has been swept, the Sacred Telescope polished. Even the St. Bernard has evidently been groomed to a glossy perfection.

"Ideal conditions this night for viewing the Constellation Andromeda, you agree, yes?" Angel Jigjag suggests.

Bessie turns a puzzled face to Angel Mel. "Does he really look at, you know, stars in the Telescope?"

Angel Mel nods his head as he treats her to a silly grin. Speaking in a stage voice, he comments loudly, "Why Bessie, isn't that fortunate. Because that's exactly what we came to see. Andromeda. " He leans down to her, whispering, "Play along."

Addressing his next comments to Angel Jigjag, he expands, "I'm teaching her astronomy. Idle minds and all that."

"Why, I commend you, Mel." Angel Jigjag looks at Bessie. "Astronomy is a most noble art. A very rewarding pursuit of higher learning, indeed."

Tilting her head to one side, Bessie treats the reincarnation teacher to what she hopes comes across as a genuine smile. "I've always been very, ah, keen on the stars." A burst of inspiration comes to her. "And perhaps, I may choose astronomy as my, next, um, life's career path."

"Is that a fact. Very good progress. Very good, indeed." Angel Jigjag glances over at his colleague for confirmation. "A career in astronomy? My, my."

It's Angel Mel's turn to produce a winning smile. "Yes, well, that's why we are here this evening, Jigjag. Get her started, as it were." He pats his pockets. "I'm sorry, I was not aware of the need for passes. Perhaps this one time?"

"Why, of course, indeed." Angel Jigjag opens his giant arms in a welcoming gesture. "For the purposes of astronomical study to advance one's career choice, guided by an angel of your magnitude, I think we can overlook the new passes rule this one time." He looks from one to the other. Speaking in lower tones, he adds, "It seems there were some souls taking advantage of the good nature of our dear Angel Rainbow Sunshine. Using the Sacred Telescope at all hours without permission."

"I can't imagine." Bessie outdoes herself to appear sincerely shocked.

Angel Mel gives her the elbow. "Okay then, well, thank you, Jigjag, I see you have a book to occupy your time while Bessie and I investigate the constellations. So …" He strolls off, not too fast, not too slow, dragging his charge with him.

Soon Bessie is deftly adjusting the lens as the milky swirls clear.

The sky is pitch dark as Bessie and Ash stroll by the side of a highway. Instead of their original runaway gear they are now dressed in brightly colored Capri's, tee-shirts and flip-flops. Ash's hot pink shirt features rhinestones glued on that spell out: VEGAS BABY. *Bessie's red bob is free of the hot, uncomfortable black wig. And Ash's beautiful curls once again fly loosely, no longer crushed under brassy blonde, plastic hair. The Wallmarket bags they carry identify the origin of their new outfits.*

"Really shouldn't have used my mother's card, but we'll only be gone, what, one more day. Two tops." Ash shakes her head. "Besides, it'll be, like, months before the bill comes."

"Want a sandwich?" Bessie pulls out a couple of white bread, egg salad sandwiches still in their vendor machine plastic.

"Wish they'd had peanut butter and jam. I love peanut butter and jam."

"Strawberry, especially."

"Or grape. My mom always makes them with grape jam."

They stop talking while they eat. A look of wistfulness creeps across their features.

"Bess, where the hell are we, anyways?"

"Look, there's the little hotel I looked up. The Sun Dial."

They stop to gaze ahead at the worst excuse for a hotel they've even seen, even when you count the ones you see in the movies. The "e" and the "l" are not lit up on the neon sign so that it reads: TH SUN DIA. *The streetlight in the front yard is out. When they get closer, an enormous cement sundial with a broken arm squats on the dirt yard.*

Together they stare at the VACAN—*sign also missing letters, gathering courage.*

"Tomorrow we'll reach our destination, right?" *Ash demands.*

"We can always take a bus if we're stuck," *Bessie replies before pulling out a credit card of her own.* "My aunt Fiona's. She left it last time she visited. I tried it once just to buy a book and it worked."

"Aren't we the bad, bad girls. We could be Thelma and Louise." *Ash bursts into tired giggles before taking her partner-in-crime by the arm.* "Come on, let's check into the Sun Dia. I think 'dia' means goddess. So we can pretend we're sun goddesses."

In Heaven, as Bessie steps down from the pedestal, she remarks to Angel Mel, "Wonder if I should fess up to Fizz I used her credit card?" Her mischievous eyes seek his.

"Technically, you borrowed it, didn't you?" He grins. "I'd leave that bit out for now. Anyway, I think she's got enough on her mind, sorting out that slime ball Simon. Care to mosey?" He takes her arm and off they stroll in the warm night air.

CHAPTER 51: HEAVEN

At the Heavenly Healing Spa, all is quiet in this post-midnight hour. A chubby female angel in a nurse's uniform, with lovely Asian features, chats idly to a male nurse at the station in mid-corridor. On the counter, lays an open copy of *Angel* magazine featuring a sepia photo of the Swedish actress, Ingrid Bergman.

"She was extraordinary in *Casablanca*," the female nurse comments.

"Yes, but *Gaslight*. Ooh la la." The pale eyes of the male nurse close, as a smile plays on his handsome features. "So beautiful."

Quietly a door opens from a room at the far end of the hall. A doctor, his hands clasped around a clipboard, makes his way towards and past the Nurses Station. A tall, thin man, his shoulders hunch over with exhaustion. A large leather briefcase hangs from one shoulder. Black-rimmed glasses slide down his nose. A forgotten surgeon's cap covers his skull.

"Evening, doctor," one of the nurses greets him in passing.

He nods his head without speaking, obviously focused on the case at hand. The nurses go back to discussing Ingrid Bergman while the doctor enters the elevator.

Now he exits on the ground floor, walking swiftly towards the double glass doors to the exterior. All signs of fatigue are gone. Outside he walks in the darkness of the building, unseen, as more angel nurses stroll, enjoying the balmy evening.

"Think the crimson lights increases the flow of healing, I really do," one comments.

"Well, personally, I've noticed that when tangerine is combined with baby blue, it seems to more than double the effect when ..." her companion replies.

Leaving them to their discussion of various light treatments, the doctor walks vigorously towards the farthest end of the unseen beam fence. Once there, he crouches down behind a hedge, tearing off his doctor's uniform, skull cap, and glasses. Now that the light brown, sticking-up hair is revealed, there is no doubt as to the identity of the so-called doctor.

Yanking jeans, a black tee-shirt, and underwear from the briefcase, Jason quickly wads them up into a tiny flat bundle which he ties with a small rope. Crouching down, his hand slides between where two beams appear to originate, testing it. Quickly he shoves the bundle through to the other side, followed by one black sneaker, then another.

Now standing up to his full height, the nude, pale-skinned Jason appears supernaturally powerful in the moonlight, all lean muscle and strength. He turns himself sideways, inching his way so slowly forward he appears to be not even moving. His left foot makes it through. He tries his left shoulder. His left leg. Now the leading edge of his torso, and then buttocks.

A beam zaps him painfully. He jerks back. Getting down on the grass, he examines the sod carefully for evidence of beam positions. Miniscule clearings seem to indicate their points of origin.

He stands upright and tries again. First the left hand, left foot, left shoulder, left leg, left side of torso, left buttock. So far so good. Taking a deep calming breath, he begins to slide the rest of his body through.

Flashes of multi-color lights leap into the night sky. A screaming alarm breaks the silence. Personnel flood the grounds. And a frantic Jason grabs his bundle of clothes, tearing across the open field to the safety of the woods beyond.

CHAPTER 52: EARTH

Despite his expensive slacks and loafers, Eric Pederssen is on all fours examining what looks like a slight depression of fresh soil in the back field behind the Landers' farmhouse. Police with cadaver dogs on leashes trod this way and that, as Walt and Flora look on in dismay. A light rain is falling on this humid, cloudy morning.

"That's where I buried a coyote what got into the hen-house," Walt insists, as Eric in gloved hands carefully removes dirt, scoop by scoop.

"He always buries 'em out of respect," Flora adds. "Walt respects wild life, always has since I met him as a lad."

"Had to shoot it 'cause of the hens, but I buried it," the farmer repeats.

Eric looks up at the couple for a moment before returning to his task. Soon the remains of an animal are uncovered. The exhausted detective sits back on his heels.

"See, I told ya," Walt huffs, arms folded on his chest.

"Maybe we should tell him the other thing." Flora turns to her husband.

"Tell me what?" Eric is all ears now, energy flooding through him as he jumps up to face the couple.

"About them girls," Walt adds.

"What about the girls? We know you brought them here."

"Hell, everybody who knows anything knows that," Walt scoffs. "They knowed we give 'em a home-cooked meal and a bed to sleep in, too."

"Our dead girl, Jean's," Flora continues the story. "Even offered 'em some nighties, but they wouldn't take 'em." She looks up at her husband. "Then in the middle of the night ..."

"What time in the middle of the night?"

Walt gets angry now. "How should I know? It were the dead of night! The wind come up and the shutters start bangin' something awful."

"And then?" Eric speaks quietly.

"She had this boy-friend, Larry, a townie." Walt spits out. "Druggie. Rich boy."

Eric knows the farmer is referring to his dead daughter, Jean. He lets the silence run itself out naturally.

"He keeps saying over and over it's all our fault she's dead, and we're gonna pay for it, to anybody who will listen, especially us," Flora speaks in a halting voice. She stares over at Eric defiantly. "That's why we got the—"

"Shotgun," Walt finishes for her. "We knowed it weren't allowed under the terms of my release."

Eric, fully aware Walt has been to prison for attempted manslaughter, keeps his cards to himself.

"Not Walter's fault that damn stranger come bangin' on the door in the middle of the storm that winter. Not his fault aye-tall." Flora is adamant. "How'd we know he weren't here to hurt us? Bangin' on the door like that. Coulda woke up the dead."

"You know all this, don't ya," Walt says. "How the man kicked in the door and walks right in like he owned the place. Why'd the damn fool do that when he crashed his car up on the road? Tell me that."

"Apparently he didn't think anybody was home because you park your vehicle in your barn, and all the lights were out. Getting back to the Moreno and MacIntyre girls."

"Well, so I hears bangin' in the night, maybe it's the shutters, maybe it's that Larry boyfriend of Jean's come to carry out his threat. So I grabs my shotgun—"

"Unregistered which you are not allowed to own. Keep going, please."

Flora jumps in. "He goes to check on the girls to make sure they was alright. After all, maybe Larry knew they was here, and he were planning to take revenge that way."

Eric can feel the sweat running down the back of his new shirt. He's going to need a scotch or two after this interview is over. "What happened next?"

"Scared 'em with the shotgun, didn't I," Walt says matter-of-factly. "Didn't even get a chance to explain before they high-tail it out of here in the middle of the night. One drop-kicks me, the dark one. And the redhead, she grabs their stuff and they was gone. Just like that. In their underwears, can you imagine."

"Not even a thank-you for all we done for 'em." Flora's overlong eyebrow hairs curl down. "Ungrateful little shits."

Eric takes a deep breath, gazing from one to the other. A tiny drop of sweat rolls down his forehead into his left eye, making him blink. He takes out a linen handkerchief to rub his eye carefully. Putting it back in his pocket, he turns and walks away.

CHAPTER 53: HEAVEN

"Want to go to the Telescope?" Fiona asks Bessie and Ash, sipping on nectarade in the Dodd front garden.

"Can't," Ash replies. "You need official passes now."

"Okay, well, how about Bodysuits?" She is up for anything these days. "I'd love to try on a rock star." Passing around some cookies, she adds, "John Lennon, he's groovy."

The girls share a glance. "Groovy, Aunt Fizz?" Bessie teases. "I can't go, anyways. Got a session with Mel. You two go." She gets up. "Come on, Mouser, let's go see what wisdom the dear angel has to impart to me this time."

When they get there, Angel Mel is, as is often the case, reading out loud from one of his screenplays. Bessie watches for a moment from the open doorway, listening to him speaking in a girly, Southern twang. "Why, Sheriff Blake, I do believe you ah flirtin' with me." His voice changes to a crusty, old western one. "Flirting with danger, more like, Miss Elinora."

"Why, goodness gracious, is that you, Sheriff Blake?" Bessie sings out in her own version of a Dixie femme fatale. "As ah live and breathe."

"Not bad, Bess, not bad." Angel Mel grins. "We should run scenes together sometime." Setting his play down on his desk, he comes over to give her a hug and the dog a pat. Take a seat, take a seat."

Bessie slumps sideways across the armchair while Mouser walks around in circles on the rug a few times before settling down for an afternoon snooze. "So what's this one about? A Southern belle with psychotic tendencies?"

"Good guess." He laughs. "It seems Miss Elinora just can't resist eliminating her competition for the affections of one, Mister Frank Leamington."

"Arsenic in the mint juleps?" Bessie elaborates.

"Good one! I'm going to steal that idea, if I may. Now, let's get back to you." He takes a seat, leaning back to put his feet on his desk.

"You asked me if I remember any of my dreams. So I've been writing them down in the mornings like you suggested."

"You followed one of my suggestions? I am deeply flattered."

"Well, I only remember one. I keep having the same one."

"Hector's Nectar?" Angel Mel offers, as he opens one from the six-pack sitting on his filing cabinet.

"Sure. I'll get it." Bessie walks over and helps herself. "So this dream. It's me and Ash. We're in this weird motel, okay? Called the Sundown or something. The one I saw through the Telescope. Sometimes I can see the sign really clearly. One of those neon ones, only it has letters missing. Sun Dial, that's it. Anyways, we're inside this room that's really yucky. Dust everywhere. Bugs scurrying around in the corners. We keep the light on 'cause it's so creepy."

"What are you wearing in this dream?" He is trying to see how many details she can recall.

"Pedal-pushers. You know, Capri pants. And flip-flops. We're lying on top of the bedspread in our clothes."

"Is there a clock in the room?"

Bessie sips on her drink. "Yeah, and it's really loud. Ticka-ticka-ticka. It wheezes like it's got asthma or something."

"What time is it on the dial, can you see it?" Angel Mel's features are very serious. "Is it digital?"

Bessie's eyes are closed, the drink forgotten in her hand. "No, it's one of those old wind-up, round-faced ones. It says four thirty-three."

"Hmmm. Four thirty-three. Go on. You're both wide awake?"

"Like, totally awake. Ash is going through her wallet, counting her money, I think. It doesn't make sense. Why are we in this stupid motel?"

"Why do you think?" He tries to draw her out.

"It's just a stupid dream, that's what I think." Bessie sits up, drinking deeply. "Are dreams real?"

"Everything is real, Bessie. Everything." He looks deeply into her eyes to make sure she is taking that lesson in. "Tell me what happens after you look at the clock." He tosses his empty soda into his garbage can where it vanishes instantly.

Bessie relaxes back in the chair again, closing her eyes. "We decide to get out of there 'cause it's just too weird, so we get out of bed. Oh, I just remembered, we've got this bag with Wallmarket on it. Anyways, we grab our stuff and leave."

"Is your room on the ground floor?"

"Ground floor?" Bessie thinks for a minute. "Yeah, it is. How did you know that?"

"Oh, just that most motels are all spread out on one level, that's why." His eyes look towards the window. He must be more careful with what he says. "So, what was it like outside? Is it empty? Are there people around?"

Bessie squirms in her chair. She leans back her head, twisting her hair. "I'm not sure. Sometimes in the dream there is, and sometimes there isn't."

A long pause follows which he wisely doesn't interrupt until he says softly, "And when there is, do you know who is there?"

"Men." Her voice goes harsh. "Men. Drunk men. Three of them. They yell at us. Obscene things."

"And then …?"

"And then I wake up. Every time." Bessie jumps up from the chair, moving to look out the window. "Anyways, it's just a silly, stupid old dream."

He joins her, handing her a spare pair of binoculars before using his own. "We're in luck."

"Where?"

"Over there. By the fountain." Bessie focuses on the metal sculpture of dancing fairies spraying water where she is treated to a vision of Judy Garland, dressed up as Dorothy Gale from *The Wizard of Oz*. A small dog, no doubt Toto, runs around her red slippers.

"Mel?" Bessie puts down her binoculars for a minute. "Sometimes in the dream, I see … no, I don't see but I sense."

He takes as long as he needs to make his voice sound off-hand. "Sense what? Sense who?"

She looks out at the scene in the park before answering quietly, "Jason."

CHAPTER 54: EARTH

"I have great news." Detective Eric Pederssen looks around at the families of the missing girls. They're sitting in a room at the police station around a metal table. His face is mischievous, almost boyish, like the groomsman at a wedding who has just nailed the prettiest bridesmaid.

"The news?" Art prompts him.

Eric turns in the direction of Sophia Moreno. "Your daughter is a thief." Simultaneously they all spin their heads to look at the detective, stunned, unable to speak.

"Your daughter Ashley stole your Wallmarket card and took it with her on the run. We've just received word she used it to buy them new clothes the day after they were last seen at the farm." He lets that sink in.

"Which means they left the farm alive and unharmed," Bessie's father comments.

"Which means there will be video surveillance footage from the store," Leila pipes up brightly. "Wallmarket has the most top-of-the-line cameras everywhere, inside and out."

Eric treats her to a grin. "You watch a lot of crime shows, don't you?"

It's her turn to smile at him. "I prefer the British ones on BBC America."

"Me, too," he agrees.

"So, now we just …" Jorge runs his hand across his forehead. "Wait."

"We just wait, yes." Eric sits tall in his chair, looking down at his long, well-manicured fingers, trying not to drum them on the table.

CHAPTER 55: HEAVEN

Except for her dog, Mouser, Bessie sits alone on the cliff, dangling her legs over the edge in the night sky. She sips on a Hector's Nectar, contemplating the universe. Nearby, Angel Jigjag examines passes for the Sacred Telescope being presented to him by a middle-aged couple. By their outdoorsy appearance and apparel, one would imagine their previous lives to be that of scientists living in the outer reaches of the earth, studying wildlife or rock formations.

"They really are going to look at the stars," Bessie remarks to Mouser. "Don't know what they're missing." Taking a loud slurp, she drains her can.

She leans completely back onto the ground, feeling the bits of grass tickle her bare skin as she reaches her arms out over her head. In this position she can see nothing but the starry sky. Without pollution in Heaven, it really is a spectacular sight. The only sounds are unseen creatures scampering about in the dark, and the hoot of a distant owl. Mouser nuzzles up, putting his head on her lap.

After a while she begins to sing to herself, "Row, row, row your boat ... gently down the stream ... merrily, merrily, merrily, merrily ... life is but a dream ...."

Unbeknownst to her, in the nearby woods, Jason watches and listens. Softly to himself, he sings along to the last line, "Life is but a dream ...."

Still lying on the edge of the cliff an hour later, Bessie can feel herself being lulled into sleep, unable to pull herself back to consciousness. She can feel the dog beside her, snuggled alongside. Again, the dream returns.

She and Ash are in some sort of cheap motel room with a double bed covered in a shiny bedspread. Beside it, a gooseneck lamp sits on a small table. Near the bathroom, a tall, scratched mirror hovers over a nondescript dresser. On a coffee table that faces the bed, with veneer peeling up at the corners, a square television flashes rabbit ears.

Both girls are dressed in gaudy Capri's, tee-shirts and flip-flops. Ash is stuffing things into a big Wallmarket bag while Bessie adjusts the straps on her newly purchased backpack.

Through the dirty window, you can see it's dark. The polyester spread is smooth and shimmery, with pillows propped up at the head. Evidently they had slept on top of it. A round faced, wind-up clock says 4:33. It's so noisy, it sounds like heavy breathing, like a ticka-ticka-ticka sound. Dust is everywhere. The toilet makes a constant running noise from the open doorway of the bathroom. Everything looks sticky from neglect.

Repulsed by the grime, the girls soon exit the room and walk along the cement sidewalk under an awning towards the lighted up area outside the lobby. The buzz of Cicadas fills the air, like tiny scratches on a blackboard. As they get closer, they can hear voices. One bursts into a jeering sound; another shouts, "Fuck off, Bobby!"

The girls hesitate, looking at each other before continuing to tiptoe along the pathway.

"Well, lookee here, boys. Wha'da we got here?"

Ash and Bessie can see the outlines of three men leaning against a beat-up pickup. "Looks like two lost young chicks ha ha. Wanna screw a nice big rooster, chickadee?"

No need for consultation. Ash and Bessie spin around to dash back into their hotel room, jamming the dresser in front of the door before flopping back onto the bedspread.

When they wake up hours later, it's light outside. All the night terrors seem like silly ghost stories around a campfire. Giggling, they jump out of bed. Bessie heads to the bathroom while Ash inspects her reflection in the mirror.

Soon they are in the lobby paying their bill with Bessie's Aunt Fiona's credit card.

The woman across the counter from them volunteers, "You girls lookin' for a ride somewheres?"

"Thank you, Ma'am, but we are taking the bus, once we get back into town." Bessie is so weirdly polite, Ash's jaw drops.

"Shush," Bessie hisses. "We don't want her checking that card too close," she adds while the manager walks into the back office. Meanwhile another client approaches the desk to pay her bill. It's a woman, quite ordinary, north of forty, in a colorless suit, carrying a cheap briefcase hanging from her shoulder.

"Oh, hi, Edith. Didn't realize you were leaving this morning." The returning motel manager greets the newcomer cheerfully.

"Trying to make it to California today. A long drive across the desert so I like to get it over with," the woman says.

"California?" Ash pipes up without thinking. "Gee, we're headed there ourselves. Isn't that a coincidence."

Bessie gives her the elbow. "We're taking the bus."

Edith exchanges a quick smile with the manager before speaking. "You know, I could save you young ladies the fare if you don't mind riding in a ten-year-old Chevy without air conditioning."

The hotel manager addresses Ash and Bessie. "You'll be just fine with her. She's been a regular customer here going on twenty years, isn't that right, Edith? Sells bedspreads. Drapes, too."

"Bedspreads?"Ash makes a face at Bessie, evidently thinking of the horrid shiny thing that covered their bed last night.

The four females eye each other up. "Sure, why not?" Bessie decides out loud.

Gathering up their few belongings, they head outside into the parking lot, led by the woman only known as Edith.

"I'll bring the car around," the woman tells them as she sits her suitcase down at the entrance before heading to the parking lot at the rear of hotel. Soon she returns in a silver Chevy Impala and pulls up beside the girls. Ash climbs into the front seat, Bessie in the back, while Edith fiddles with the radio.

As they pull out of the deserted lot, Bessie spies a broken down, brown Oldsmobile sedan with a cracked windshield parked in the shade of a tree. Jason!

In Heaven, Bessie wakes up so abruptly, she almost topples over the edge of the cliff. Mouser bark-bark-barks as he tries to drag her back by her shirt.

"I'm okay, I'm okay," she reassures the anxious retriever. She rolls over to lay several feet away from the precipice. "Mel says I can't hurt myself in Heaven, anyways." Propping up on her elbow, she strokes her dog. "It was only a bad dream."

Or was it? Her thoughts tumble over each other like marbles in a jar. *What were we doing in that strange hotel? Why is Jason always in my dreams now? What's happening to me?*

"Come on, Mouser. I'll take you back to the cottage. I'm gonna sleep over. To hell with the stupid rules."

As she and the dog trot off, Jason watches from the woods. He runs his hand through his sticking-up hair. "Not yet, Bessie," he mutters to no one. "This time I'll wait 'til the time is right." A small smile skips across his solemn features before disappearing again. "Like the corn. Right, Uncle Pete?"

CHAPTER 56: HEAVEN

"I almost tumbled right off the cliff, it was so scary! Ommmmm," Bessie whispers in her lotus position on her mat across from Ash, facing her in Girls Dorm.

"I wish I could remember my dreams, ommmmm," Ash hisses back. "All I dream about now is Miguelito." She swoons. "Ommmmm."

Angel Rosmin, the new yoga instructor, stops by their mats. "You two are concentrating on your meditations, I trust?" Her voice is as soft as a tissue. "They're very healing for restless souls, are you aware of that?" She smiles kindly before she moves on.

"That new teacher looks like a movie star who forgot her makeup. So," Ash whispers. "What's your plan?"

"Haven't got one. All I know is the next flight arrives in twenty-five minutes."

Ash's eyes start to twinkle. She hunches over to fiddle with something before her hand shoots up. "Oh, Angel Rosmin, can you please …?" She calls her over.

It's clear to see by the new instructor's hesitant demeanor, this is her first teaching post. When Angel Rosmin arrives to kneel beside her, Ash complains politely, "Can you see? My earring? It's all caught up in my best shirt. May I go to my room and fix it?"

Sure enough, on the tilted head of black curls, an earring the size of a windchime is intricately caught into the threads of a very delicate material.

"Oh dear," the new angel is sympathetic. "Oh my, well, of course you may. And," She turns to look at Bessie intently meditating, "Better take your friend with you to help."

To say they're still snickering as they skip down the road, is putting it mildly.

"She's gonna be in deep doo doo, poor thing." Bessie tries to be sympathetic.

"Right up to her wing-tips," Ash agrees. "So where's Fizz? Isn't she supposed to meet us right about—?"

"Now," a cheerful voice joins the conversation from behind a tree at the side of the road. "Hi, gals! So where we off to this time?" Mouser nuzzles up to Bessie, licking her hand.

Ash shares a sly smile with Bessie. "You'll see."

Soon the trio plus a retriever are squeezed into the special hiding place in the hedge overlooking Air Heaven Interportal. Fiona's eyes are the size of fish bowls. "Oh, it's all starting to come back to me, the night I arrived. I just thought I'd taken a flight to New York City to catch *Mama Mia*."

"How long did it take you to realize you were in the after life, Aunt Fizz?" Bessie gives Ash an elbow.

"Well, to tell you the truth, I thought I'd made my big break, and I was in some big splashy Broadway production. Some sort of weird musical about Heaven or something. All these angels everywhere! So when I first got off the plane, I just skipped down the stairs, and dashed through the Sacred Portal with a big whooshing sound. Then I danced all over the platform until this huge angel - he was sooo handsome - grabbed me by both hands. Well, I thought he was there to dance with me in my big number, so I burst into that song, like Julie Andrews in the *Sound of Music*." Fiona stands up to demonstrate. She throws her arms wide and her head back. "The hills are alive … "

By now, both younger girls are rolling about, their arms wrapped around their bellies, giggling to beat the band.

"Danced that poor angel all over the place, I did. And right out the floral archway and up the hillside. Hey, how come you weren't here to greet me?"

Bessie replies, "Mel didn't notify me for some stupid reason."

Below them, loved ones who have passed on before, are gathering around outside the exit to greet the new arrivals, chatting excitedly amongst themselves. Ground crew angels check manifests, fiddle with their uniforms, and look somewhat bored, as they have done this same routine forever.

The golden bell solemnly tolls seven times. An approaching jet-cloud materializes in the sky, beginning to make its final descent. All stop what they're doing to look skyward, including the threesome and a dog hidden in the hedge. Fiona's jaw flies open like a trap-door in a wind storm.

The newly deceased begin to drift down the staircase from the plane's open hatch, through the Sacred Portal and onto the platform. Their families, who must wait outside the floral arch, watch as angels approach each returning soul to give them words of comfort, guidance, or whatever is required in each individual situation. After healing rosy hugs that restore them to their pre-death radiance, the new arrivals slip through the flowered arch into the arms of their loved ones.

It is a sight that never ceases to render both Ash and Bessie speechless. It has, however, the opposite effect on Bessie's relative. "Oh-look-over-there…I-think-I-see-a … isn't-that-the-Queen-of … he-reminds-me-of-a-famous-movie … oh-those-poor-boys-they-must-have-been-in-a-war … I-oh-look-is-that-really-isn't-that … she is-just-the-sweetest …"

The other two amuse themselves by making faces at each other. Eventually they sneak off to join the milling crowd, as Bessie gives a low whistle for Mouser to follow.

An oblivious Fiona continues her flabbergasted monologue as she trips along behind them. "And-look-over-there-she's … that's-a-famous-soap opera-star … name-is-oh-but …"

Keeping careful to stay clear of any suspiciously over-observant angels - they seem to have lucked out this evening with no sign of Angels Mel or Rachel - the group mingle into the joyous chaos in front of the airport entrance.

Nearby, three female Air Heaven attendants appear to be waiting for companions, the handles of their flight bags dangling from their fingertips.

"I always wonder if that would have been a good career for me?" Bessie says out loud. "You remember my goal, to see every square inch of the world."

"You mean, like, instead of becoming an astronomer?" Ash teases. "According to Angel Jigjag, you are now officially his raving success story."

Bessie grins before her thoughts jump elsewhere, as the group of flight attendants, now numbering five, head along a path leading upwards on the far hillside from the airport.

Ash turns her head to face her. "Hey, Bess, ever wonder where they live?"

Bessie's tone becomes conspiratorial. "You thinking what I'm thinking?"

She addresses her aunt beside her, "Fizz, I know you're not hearing a word I'm saying, but we're just going to trail after these … Aunt Fizz?" The aunt in question seems to have disappeared herself, skipping down closer to the airport to get a better peek.

Following the flight attendants is rather easier than Bessie and Ash might have thought, as the little group is closely engaged in sharing their recent adventures. Keeping to the sides of the path, with their heads down and covered with scarves they now carry everywhere since their trip to the Hall of the Akashic Records,

Bessie and Ash, Mouser trotting close behind, trail the flight crew all the way over the next hillside. Once on the crest, they stare in awe at the scene below.

In the muted distance, nestled in the next valley, lies a glorious, bustling city! Connecting the top of the hill to the metropolis, the girls observe a boarding platform for open-air gondolas on cables, sort of like at a ski resort. The air-born carriages rhythmically ascend and descend the hillside, apparently at no charge, as folks are hopping on and off.

Bursting with excitement, Bessie and Ash scramble to hop on the one behind the gondola holding the flight attendants. The view is indescribably breathtaking. On misty, rolling verdant hills, various forms of wildlife like mountain goats, rabbits, deer, horses, elephants, giraffes, llamas, and peacocks wander freely and in apparent friendship. From the occasional small plateau, the odd cabin pokes out. In the skies, eagles and crows and parrots and all sorts of birds circle and fly.

The girls are unable to speak. Instead, they gaze here and there and everywhere, taking it all in. As they approach the distant valley below, a murmur of hustle and bustle reaches them.

"Omigod, Bess, it's a … it's a …" Words are stuck on Ash's lips like glue. "A real … live … city!"

"All this time we never knew it existed, right over this hill."

"They probably have, like, designer stores and everything!" Ash gazes dreamily at the glorious collection of skyscrapers below them. 'Why didn't the angels ever tell us?" She answers her own question quickly, "Dah."

The high rise buildings are separated by countless parks and gardens. Flower baskets seem to sprout from every affordable spot. Awnings of little bistros nestle among the tall structures with open-air tables on the sidewalks. Despite the congestion, there is absolutely no dust, no litter, and no pollution from the vehicles driving up and down the streets.

After Bessie and Ash disembark at the lower gondola station, they quickly blend into streams of souls strolling along the paved streets of the city. Others are catching little open air buses, again with no fare needed. Glancing up at the gleaming buildings, a mix of modern glass and steel, side-by-side with old-style brick and mortar, it's difficult to remember they're supposed to be hot on the heels of the Air Heaven personnel. Three of the crew head one direction, waving goodbye to the other two walking away in another.

"Oh wow, we're looking into, like, a famous designer!" Ash exclaims, staring into the store windows at a display of high-end shoes. "Now I know for sure I'm in Heaven."

Bessie reads the name of the store out loud. "Angelitos Heavenly Footwear."

"And omigod, look at all that bling." Now Ash is transfixed by the hallowed interiors of the store next door to Angelitos called Seraphim, Jewelry to the Stars.

"Quick. We're losing them." Bessie drags her awed pal by the arm. "We can come back later. C'mon, Mouser. We've got to hop on that next bus." Trailing the flight attendants, first by public transit, and peering into every floor, and then on foot, through a crowded intersection, the girls follow at a discreet distance. Eventually they end up walking along a side street of modest, brick apartment buildings exquisitely ornate with wrought iron balconies trailing geraniums and ivy.

Ash gives Bessie the elbow. "They're turning into that one." Sure enough, the uniformed angels climb up the steps, disappearing into a corner building.

"Let's wait until it gets dark," Bessie advises.

"And then what?"

"And then we'll figure out what to do."

They don't have long until evening cloaks the city in soft, velvety shades highlighted with streetlights at every corner. The rush of the day dies down as the city dwellers drift home, or out to dine at the countless bistros and patios alive with guitars, flutes, violins, and singers from every culture.

After a small meal of nectar-dogs and Hector's Nectar from a street vendor, Bessie and Ash take up seats on a park bench across the street from the apartments, while Mouser enjoys his portion of the food. Not long after, they are treated to a view of the very same flight attendants, now in party gear, heading out on the town.

"Isn't that a metal staircase running up the side?" Bessie wonders out loud. "Maybe we could just take a peek."

Soon they are skipping up the steps, careful to stay close to the darkened ivy-covered brickwork. In no time they are standing on a tiny metal balcony, staring into a bachelor apartment where three single beds are lined up in a row. Draped across the beds, Air Heaven uniforms are carelessly tossed.

"Hmmm, wonder if this window is locked?" Ash slips her long fingers under the framework of the half-opened pane. She turns to grin. "Nope."

Bessie speaks to Mouser. "Stay here." Immediately he lies down. Reaching down to give him a pat, she smirks at Ash. "After you, my dear."

Checking to see if anyone is watching, Bessie first, and then Ash, pry the window open just wide enough to roll inside like two tadpoles.

"Do we dare?" Bessie's eyes are fixated on the messy uniforms cast aside on the bedspreads.

"When have we ever not dared?" Ash giggles. And before you can say Angel Rachel, one small redhead, the other a tall and thin brunette with masses of black curls, accompanied by a large golden dog, race down the outside stairwell. Over the girls' shoulders hang awkward, hobo-like bundles wrapped in sheets. Quickly they blend into the milling night crowd.

CHAPTER 57: EARTH

In silence the Morenos and the MacIntyres stare at grainy footage from the Wallmarket video surveillance, around a table at the police station. Eric Pederssen lets the images speak for themselves, as a pair of giggly teenagers pay for a shopping cart of clothes, chocolate bars, and a 6-pack of orange soda. On the police station table, a manila file folder lies open with an enlarged photo of a credit card receipt, scrawled with the signature - Sopia Moreno.

"I can't believe she spelled my name wrong," Ash's mother comments.

The family members keep gazing at the tape as the girls exit the store into the parking lot. Ash teeters on her platform shoes, chatting excitedly to her pal.

"No one was seen with them or following them, and they didn't get into a vehicle. We can only assume they were on foot, presumably heading into town. We've spoken to the cashier. She remembered them because they were talking in weird accents. Said they had told her they were hairdressers on tour with a band. She asked them what band, and both their faces went blank before the redhead piped up, Chris Lisack."

"Did they say where they were headed?" Heather inquires as she reaches for her husband's hand.

"Touring North America before Europe, apparently. Anyone want some coffee?" Eric stands up. They all nod yes. He heads into the outer office accompanied by Leila.

The little group continues to stare at the screen although it's turned off.

"At least we can thank the good Lord they're alive and well," Art remarks. "Because when Bess gets home, I'm going to kill her."

CHAPTER 58: HEAVEN

With the stolen uniforms now safely stowed in Grandma Millie's trunk, a wound-up-like-a-top Fiona goes on and on about how they deserted her at the airport, and what were they thinking to leave her on her own like that. Lucky for her she had managed to retrace her steps back to the cottage before any of the angels took notice. Listening with sheepish grins, Ash and Bessie relax with glasses of nectar tea.

"Do you suppose we'll get caught?" Ash whispers, stroking the cat on the sofa.

"Eventually," Bessie replies with a grin. "But before we do …" She lets her thought dangle, while her mind fills with delectable possibilities.

"I saw this man walk off the Air Heaven flight?" Fiona finally settles on the rocking chair. "He was carrying his own head. Like it had been blown off in a conflict somewhere. And this other one? A lady about forty, I'd say. Well, she was trying to explain to this angel how she'd changed her mind, and didn't really want to be in Heaven yet. She didn't mean to have taken an overdose. It was all an act to impress this jerk who was ignoring her, and she got the dosage all wrong, and could they let her go back now, please. Know what the angel said?"

"No, what did the angel say?" Bessie gives Ash a side glance.

Fizz nibbles on a chip from a bag of NecNac Snaks before answering. She leans forward. "Better luck next time."

CHAPTER 59: HEAVEN

"Well, I think it's time for your next astronomy lesson, don't you?" Angel Mel winks as he and Bessie stare out the window of his office with binoculars. "We don't want you to get behind." He reaches into his pocket to bring out two small pieces of cardboard. "See? I've got the official passes this time. Oh, look."

Both of them follow a newcomer entering the park. The portly gentleman sports an over-sized, powder blue shirt, shorts, sandals, and a billow of blonde curls on his chubby head.

A guffaw of laugher can be seen but not heard on the jolly features of the new guy. It appears he is telling a tale to a petite Audrey Hepburn. Audrey, forever fashionable in a tiny black shift, her hair classically upswept, a choker of pearls around her elegant neck, tilts her head back in reaction to some amusing comment, no doubt.

"John Candy, my hero!" Angel Mel exclaims. "Did you ever see *Planes, Trains and Automobiles?*' Funniest movie ever made, I swear."

"You swear, Mel?" Bessie teases. "Angels swear? My, my. What is this world coming to?"

"Very funny. Okay, wake up, Mouser. We've got places to go. Lessons to learn."

Hearing his name, the retriever lifts his head from the armchair where he has been chewing on a pile of paper held together with two brass fasteners. Fortunately for him, the angel doesn't seem to notice, as the three of them head out the door.

Awhile later, after a leisurely stroll along the cliff, Angel Mel and Bessie greet an enthusiastic Angel Jigjag, busy waving goodbye to visitors departing from the Sacred Telescope. "You're just in time," he proclaims to the newcomers. "Apparently there is a most excellent sighting of a new planet, as yet unnamed." He pats Bessie on the arm. "Perhaps a star will be named after our reborn astronomer in her next incarnation." Mouser barks as if in agreement. "You see? Even your pet agrees."

"Actually, me and Mel, I mean, Angel Mel and I, we were just discussing my future, weren't we?" She looks up blandly at her therapist. "And I was telling him I've got my sights set on an astrophysics program at the Space Science Lab in the University of California-Berkeley, didn't I, Angel Mel?"

The eyes of the angel in question pop open in surprise. As they walk away he admits, "You're good."

"I know," Bessie agrees. "I know." Soon she mounts the pedestal, removing the lens to peer in. "Maybe this time I'll find out how I died, finally."

Empathy shines from the angel's eyes. "You take your time, astrophysicist MacIntyre. You take your time." He coaxes the dog with a tennis ball he produces from his pocket. "You and me will go play a game or two of catch, shall we?"

The milky swirls of the Sacred Telescope lens begin to clear.

Bessie and Ash are in a vehicle, a ten-year-old, nondescript, silver Chevy. Ash sits in the front passenger seat, yakking away to a middle-aged woman. The woman is on the plain side, her thinning hair etched in grey, her glasses too heavy for her small face. She's dressed in a cheap pantsuit that's too small for her flabby body. As she talks, she has the habit of tapping the brake every couple of minutes so that the car jerks continuously. Bessie sits in the back seat with their bags, looking out the rear window. There's no one else on the road. "Must have imagined it," she mutters to herself. "Paranoid. Jason couldn't possibly have trailed us all this way."

Eventually they settle into a companionable silence, as the woman drives mile after hot, dusty mile. Both girls drift off to sleep, having not gotten any the night before.

Bessie wakes up, slumped across the Wallmarket bag, momentarily disoriented. Glancing in the front seat, she sees the woman, Edith. Ash is snoozing, her head lolling back. Bessie can hear the driver humming something. Outside the window, it's flat without hardly any vegetation or signs of life. Occasionally they pass a rundown convenience store or gas station. Her eyes drift closed again.

The hard brake of the Chevy jerks both girls awake. Startled, they look around, and glance at each other before staring at the woman busy turning off the car.

Edith smiles cheerfully. "Here we are," she announces.

"Here we are where?" Ash looks out the window.

"I'm treating you gals to a late breakfast." She hops out to head for a makeshift outdoor taco stand and tables.

Ash and Bessie share a shrug. "Free food," Ash says. "Why not?"

While boisterous children hop about, a young Latino couple happily serves them up paper plates brimming with fried eggs on corn tortillas smothered in a spicy tomato chili sauce. Sides of refried beans and sliced avocado decorate the edges. Digging in hungrily, the girls polish off every bite, washing it down with thick, black coffee.

"Señora, these are the best huevos rancheros I've ever tasted," Ash calls out to the woman, smiling. "Even better than my papa's, and his are very good."

"Gracias, gracias." The woman's smile reaches up and fills her beautiful almond eyes.

After the three of them take a bathroom break, Edith pays for their meal. They all climb into their same positions in the Chevy. Now back on the road, the older woman begins conversationally, "So, you girls fornicators?"

"No, we're not foreign, actually, we're American." Ash pipes up. "Although our parents are traveling in Europe and Antarctica."

"I mean, are you girls on the game? Do you boink the boys?"

"And what game would that be, Edith?" Ash is ever so polite, not to mention confused.

Edith's foot taps the brake several times. "'Cause I can set you up with businessmen on the road. I'd do it myself, but I'm too old for it now. Did it for years."

"Yes, we heard you are a traveling salesman. Saleswoman," Ash corrects herself.

Bessie squeezes her friend's shoulder. "Pssst, Ash, Ash. Pay attention. She's talking about prostitutes."

"As a matter of fact, I called ahead while you were eating, and set you up at this nice hotel here on the right." Edith swerves her car into a parking lot just ahead. "There are your first two customers."

Slack-jawed, Bessie and Ash spin their heads to stare at two, fat, greasy-looking, middle-aged men standing in the parking lot of a cheap hotel, grinning and waving. One of them makes an obscene gesture with his hands. The other one is waving a box of condoms as if they were a welcome gift.

The vehicle comes to a screeching halt, feet away from the men. Edith reaches over, pointing at the passenger door. "Get out," she commands, her voice curdling with aggression."Now!"

In Heaven, as Bessie jumps back in shock, Angel Mel tries to lighten the situation by commenting, "So did you see that new planet or sun or star or whatever Jigjag was going on about?" He snaps the tab on a Hector's Nectar he pulls from his pocket. Reaching in for another soda for Bessie, he is only too aware of the change in her demeanor.

She's gone all white. Her eyes stare into space with a glassy look. Her bottom lip trembles as her fingers reach up to touch her scar. Listlessly she leans down to pat Mouser.

"Bessie, dear, are you alright?" Angel Mel hands her the drink. She takes it without acknowledgement. "Remember, nothing can hurt you here in Heaven, nothing at all."

Slowly they begin to walk away in silence. After awhile she stops to turn to him, "It's all just a dream, right? Life is but a dream and all that. Those things I saw ..." She doesn't elaborate and she knows she doesn't have to.

"Come on," he says, "Let's go find some nectar cones. I'm in the mood for strawberry with chocolate sprinkles. How about you?"

Gently he leads her along the path as Jason lopes off into the darkness of the woods.

CHAPTER 60: EARTH

In her front yard Sophia Moreno waters her garden. Shades of yellows and purple blooms, mixed with white for contrast, dominate the well-cared-for roses, geraniums, petunias, and peonies. Her head turns to the sound of a car entering her driveway. Before Eric Pederssen turns off the engine of his black BMW, she can hear strains of Rossini's opera *Eduardo e Cristina*. Quickly she goes over to the outdoor tap to turn off the water, dropping the hose on the ground.

Eric swings his long legs from his car, leaning back in for a moment to pick up his briefcase before striding over to where Sophia stands in front of the garage.

"You have news? Jorge isn't home right now, but I can call him. He and Art have gone off somewhere, but Heather's inside." Together they head into the spacious living-room where Bessie's mother sips iced tea on a plush cream sofa. She jumps up to greet them.

"Lady called in from a hotel, The Sun Dial. Happened to hear the missing teens report on the radio. Says the girls we're looking for, spent a night there. Businesswoman named Edith Van Heflin gave them a ride in the morning. She's a bedspread sales person, apparently. Well known to the hotel manager. We're tracking her down now." Eric glances from mother to mother. "Unfortunately the address she gave at the hotel does not exist. I have her photo in my case." He takes a seat, opening it up and pulling out a snapshot of Edith from her phony driver's license.

Heather collapses back onto the sofa before giving Eric a weak smile. "Well, that's some progress, anyway, isn't it, Sophia?"

Ash's mother adds, "And they're safer with a woman, I should think." She runs her red nails through her mess of dark waves. Her eyes are rimmed with shadows. "You agree, detective?"

Eric doesn't respond. Heather sighs, her glass of iced tea suspended in her hand, her lips parted. Her eyes bore into those of the policeman standing stiffly in the entranceway.

"We've alerted law enforcement in the area. Their circumstances don't fit the requirements for an Amber Alert as they ran away willingly. And we have no reason to suspect ..." he hesitates, not wanting to frighten them any more than they are. He almost chokes on his next words. "Foul play."

CHAPTER 61: HEAVEN

"How do I look?" Ash models an ill-fitting, Air Heaven uniform. The open trunk in the spare room of the Dodd cottage is being rifled through by Mouser and Peach, while Bessie yanks on the other outfit. Together the girls stare into the free-standing, wicker mirror. Ash's sleeves are miles too short. Bessie's skirt is way too long.

"Let's switch. Give me that, Mouser." Bessie snatches a perky blue cap from the dog.

"Yeah, sure, okay." Ash yanks off her blazer. Ten minutes later, they stare at themselves again, this time looking much more presentable.

"I wish I was taller," Bessie whines a little.

"I wish I had boobs." Ash tugs at her uniform, trying to get it to perk out.

"We better scoot before Fizz gets back from the Mall." She whistles to the dog. "Sorry, Mouser, but you're going to have to stay this time."

They just manage to disappear behind the cottage into the woods before Grandma Millie's bicycle rounds the corner, the basket overflowing with purchases. The rider is singing some silly love song at the top of her lungs. Evidently the shopping spree went well, and she has forgotten all about that slime ball Simon, at least for the moment.

Early in the pre-dawn hours at Air Heaven Interportal, personnel are readying for the next returning flight. Reincarnating souls in their white gowns, holding their lighted candles up high, are tense with excitement, when the Soulslady from Bodysuits Boutique appears with her racks of hangers. Off to one side of the airport, two flight attendants in ill-fitting uniforms try to look preoccupied.

"Attention, please," calls out the head angel. "Departure is at 4:00 A.M. on the button, no delays. Form two lines now to place your candles in the holders, then immediately go to the Soulslady to hand in your last incarnation body suit. Ready?"

The souls drift towards the long table of candlesticks. Soon the surface is glowing with light.

"Attendants, in your positions, please." Head angel directs the airport personnel who are lounging about in small groups, chatting.

"What's our plan?" Ash looks around her.

"As usual, we don't have one. Let's just mingle."

Following the lead of the others, they stroll alongside the reincarnating souls, smiling brightly, but moving on before they are asked any questions. Another flight attendant looks at them curiously in their odd, rumpled uniforms, but says nothing. Most likely she knows first-hand what it's like to rush to a flight after a late night out.

Now in an orderly fashion, the souls are busy tugging off their bodysuits by the silver threads atop their heads. They hand them over to the Soulslady, who efficiently hangs them on her rack before she moves on to the next one.

Head angel, with her box of envelopes, begins to hand them out, admonishing passengers not to lose them on the flight, whatever they do. This is their passport to their new lives. Without them, they will drift endlessly in the Earth vibration until they are rescued by some kind angel or psychic. "But sometimes," she warns, "That can take centuries, so hang onto them for dear life."

"I wonder if that's what psychics do? Rescue lost souls." Ash is unusually philosophic. "Like, spiritual medium type people. Is that what gypsies are?"

"Someone's watching. Turn around."

Ash peeks over. "Oh no, Soulslady. Heading right at us."

Sure enough, the clerk from Bodysuits Boutique is marching smartly towards two very young flight attendants, her eyebrows lowered, her mouth in a thin line.

Just as the imposters are about to round the corner of the platform, the jet-cloud forms above the airport, and the hatch opens to allow the staircase to spill out. The magnificent golden bell, suspended in the tower, begins to sway.

Glowing auras drift through the flowered archway, across the platform, through the Sacred Portal, and up the staircase to disappear within the plane. Flight attendants are shepherding them along the way with hand signals, as Bessie and Ash mimicking their actions, blend into the commotion.

"Come on," Bessie urges as she walks rapidly through the archway onto the platform.

"Not so fast, you horrid, little missies." The voice of the dreaded Soulslady smacks the air like a broken guitar string. Her thin arms reach out to grab both girls by their uniform sleeves as they attempt to wiggle away. She's surprisingly strong for such a tiny angel, but then again, she's an angel.

"Your jacket. Ditch your jacket." Bessie hisses in a panic.

"What?" Ash looks about, confused.

Bessie wriggles out of her jacket just in time to make a dash across the platform, through the Sacred Portal, up the staircase, and onto the entrance to the plane. She spins around, assuming Ash is right behind her. Sadly, she sees her pal being led away by two strong male angels while Soulslady looks on, arms crossed. Once again, as luck would have it, or maybe it's fate, Ash misses the flight.

Slipping onto the plane, Bessie tries to slow down her pace as she walks down the aisle, pretending to check for envelopes.

"Helen, is that you?" A blonde male attendant calls after her. "Helen, wait up. Haven't seen you since the Second World War."

Reluctantly, Bessie turns around to face him.

"Oh, sorry. My mistake. You working the galley?"

"Ah, think so, ah, just finished flight school, and ah …" Bessie tries on her version of a winning smile as she reaches up to adjust her cap that's sliding off her head.

He chuckles. "Your first flight. That's why you forgot your jacket, I guess. Follow me, darlin', I'll put you to work."

It's easier than she would have thought to blend in with the rest of the crew. Most of them are busy with their own chores, and don't have time to pay attention to the young redhead in the messy uniform who forgot her jacket, her makeup, and her manicure.

Jarrod, for that is his name, keeps her busy, offering passengers NecNac Snaks, Hector's Nectar, pillows, and mostly encouraging smiles.

"Can't believe they gave you such a ghastly, ill-fitting uniform. What's happening to standards these days? Used to be, back in the day, I'm talking Cleopatra, my dear, we were inspected before every single flight, top to toe. Now, they're just tossing new graduates onto the flight schedule with barely a proper training program, let alone the …" Jarrod tugs at Bessie's sleeve, making a face. "What, they don't bother with tailors anymore? You should complain, you really should."

Fortuitously, Bessie is in no need of response, as Jarrod can't seem to stop talking about the state of Air Heaven Interportal these days, the governing board, the training courses. He can go on and on apparently.

Given that he has such an engaging personality, Bessie is tempted to confide in her new friend. Wisely, however, she asks him about his travels instead. "So, you've been doing this a long time," she inquires.

"Oh, gads, forever!" Jarrod slaps her on the shoulder, bursting into giggles. "For-ev-er. Well, since the fifteenth century, anyway. I was going to put in for a transfer to another dimension, but thought, I mean, I know these routes like the back of my hand." He pats her shoulder. "Why rock the proverbial boat, right?"

Intrigued, Bessie can't help but ask. "So, so there are other dimensions other than Earth?"

He shrieks, "Oh my, you really are an ingénue, darlin'. Well, of course, there are other dimensions. Countless numbers of them. Earth is only the Third Dimension, sweetheart."

"So that's why the bell tolls three times?" Bessie is thrilled to learn all this new information. Angel Mel has never mentioned anything about other dimensions.

He winks. "Bravo. You catch on quick. You're going to do just fine." His attention goes to his watch. "Oh gads, we're landing soon. Quick, collect up all those empty glasses, would you, dear?" He rushes off in quick little steps to direct the other attendants to their chores.

Just as they are about to land, he whispers in her ear, "Don't forget, the return is in twenty minutes sharp. That would be 4:20 PM Earth-time. They will *kill* you if you miss your flight. I did that once, eons ago, when I had my first date with Mohammad." He giggles as he points to the co-pilot who is visible through the open cockpit door, a heavy-set angel with greying temples. "Isn't he just divine?"

CHAPTER 62: EARTH

Bessie glances around her at the shuffling body of auras on the Earth Portal platform as they greet their Guardian angels for this incarnation, handing over their white envelopes. Taking herself off to a crowded corner, she turns to face outward, whispering, "Home," which reverberates in the atmosphere. "Ommm-ommm-ommm-ommm …"

Landing on her front lawn in the middle of the night, she sees a black BMW zip into the driveway. A tall, fit, fair-haired man in an expensive suit jumps from the vehicle at the same time the front door is thrown open by Art MacIntyre in his old housecoat.

"I'm heading for the airport right now, Art," the blonde man yells while standing beside his open car door. "Police have tracked down the woman, Edith Van Heflin. I'm interviewing her this morning. She claims the girls got out of her car soon after she gave them a ride, saying they had decided to take the bus instead. However, we have no evidence to suggest they were ever at the bus station. She's being held at her home until I arrive."

Heather MacIntyre has joined her husband at the doorway, her pretty features crisscrossed with tension. Putting his arm around her, Art yells back, "I'll pass the word on to the Morenos."

A bewildered Bessie stares from one adult to the other, not knowing what to make of it or what to do. Torn between wanting to be with her family and finding out what they're talking about, on impulse, she jumps into the back seat of the BMW. The blonde man hops back into the driver's seat, backs up, and makes a violent U-turn before heading out of the maple-treed suburban cul de sac and onto a highway, unaware he has a wide-eyed passenger gazing out the back seat window.

The blonde man turns his stereo on full-blast to something Bessie recognizes as operatic. She listens as he mutters to himself about this woman he is flying halfway across the country to meet at the crack of dawn. Staring at the back of his close-cut, flaxen hair and the little blonde hairs on the back of his hands on the wheel, she feels like she should know him. Or maybe, she senses that he knows her, which seems ridiculous but nevertheless, true. As he drives well over the speed limit on the empty nighttime highway, she stares at the briefcase on the passenger seat in front of her, wondering what's in it. And worries what's going to happen now that's she is certainly going to miss her return flight in less than twenty minutes.

An hour and a half later, they stroll through a small local airport before he checks in for his flight. He takes a seat in the waiting area and opens his briefcase. Sitting close beside him, Bessie is astonished to see photos of herself and Ashley - school photos, plus the glamorous head shots they had made several years before, along with some family pictures and even some of Jason. Before long she figures out he is the lead detective looking for them. Frustrated at her inability to communicate with him, she is forced to sit and wait.

Soon they are boarding their plane with a scattering of sleepy passengers. After a few minutes, the detective takes an aisle seat, leaving Bessie the window seat beside him, in her rumpled Air Heaven uniform. During the two and a half hour flight, Eric listens to music through headphones, his eyes closed, hands resting on his briefcase. Staring out the window at nothing but sky, Bessie's thoughts race. What is she about to discover? What will happen when she doesn't make her return flight?

When they arrive, Eric emerges from the small airport with long, purposeful strides, taking the first taxi in line for the half-hour ride to his destination.

The sun has barely risen as the detective walks up the sidewalk alongside a modest, one-story home. The siding, although faded, is clean, and the flowerbeds are weeded and healthy. He rings the door bell, swinging his briefcase back and forth, as Bessie watches on, beside him.

A policeman in uniform opens the door. They enter directly into a small living-room decorated in surprisingly tasteful, and what appears to be, expensive antique furniture. A middle-aged woman with thin brown hair sits in an armchair, smoking a cigarette in her housecoat, the ash tray held in her lap.

Bessie is shocked beyond belief. It's the woman she had seen in the Sacred Telescope! The one who had thrown them out of her car after she had bought them a Mexican breakfast. And dumped them at the rundown hotel parking lot, where those creepy old men were standing, waiting. In desperation, Bessie bangs on the detective's shoulder to no avail.

Eric takes a seat on the sofa, facing the woman, not wasting any time. "Edith Van Heflin?" he inquires politely. She nods her head. "My name is Eric Pederssen from the police department in Ravenspond, Pennsylvania. I just want to ask you a few questions, if I may. This is strictly voluntary on your part. You are not a suspect in any way. We simply need your assistance in trying to locate two runaway teenage girls who left their homes in the early morning of July 15th. We appreciate any help you can offer us as to their current whereabouts. Do you understand?" He looks over at the female policewoman who is standing by the door, listening. She appears nervous, perhaps just out of the Police Academy. Her shiny dark hair is pulled back into a knot at the base of her neck. She looks at him, revealing unusual green eyes.

Edith butts out her cigarette, setting her ash tray onto a nearby coffee table. "Already told these officers here, I gave those girls a lift from the Sun Dial motel to some restaurant near the bus station. They said they were headed to California to find work as waitresses."

Bessie pipes up, "We never told you that. You're a liar!"

"They also told me they were twenty-one. And from Boston, or maybe it was Canada."

"We didn't say any of that. You're a liar, Edith!" Bessie's fury can hardly be contained. "She's lying!" she yells at Eric. Realizing no one can hear her, she gives up.

"So you dropped them off in town at a restaurant?"

Edith's eyes jump around. She digs into the pocket of her housecoat for another cigarette. "One of them, I think it was the redhead, changed her mind and said they wanted to stick around town for awhile before they headed west. Maybe pick up a job there for a bit."

"It's a very small town. What part of town did you drop them off at, Ms Van Heflin?"

"Some restaurant. Italian, I think. They wanted to try there first, I think they said. Wasn't listening too closely as I was in a hurry to get to my next hotel appointment. I'm a sales rep in the hotel business. A well-established sales rep, you can ask anybody." She glares at the detective, daring him to challenge her reputation.

"Yet you showed up for your appointment three hours late that day." Eric's pale blue eyes are riveted to her every nuance. "And the only Italian restaurant in town is closed for renovations. Would you like to try again?"

Edith's mouth opens then shuts again, lost for words.

"This is a lovely home," Eric comments, as if he's being a friendly new neighbor. "That solid walnut chiffonier ..." He gets up to run his fingers along the elegant Victorian sideboard. "A genuine Waring and Gillows, if I'm not mistaken."

"Inherited money from my aunt," Edith explains quickly. Too quickly.

Eric's eyes reveal it hasn't escaped him. "So this aunt, she was from around here, was she?"

Edith takes one drag after another. "No, from Seattle. Used the money to buy myself some treats. Got that one from Maine." She stubs out her cigarette. "I work hard. I deserve treats."

"You are such a liar, Edith." Bessie is furious. "You make your money from selling girls to creepy, filthy, disgusting men. You're a ..." She searches for the right word. "You're a pimp, a crazy, lying pimp."

"The problem is, Ms Van Heflin, we've already checked the story you gave the officer, and the young girls in question did not arrive at the closed-for-repairs, Italian restaurant. Nor at any of the three open restaurants in town. Nor were they seen strolling the sidewalks, or purchasing items in any of the stores. And ..." He crouches down to stare directly into Edith's face. "The home address you gave at the hotel was false. Why is that?"

"Yeah, why is that?" Bessie repeats. "Tell him, Edith, why is that?"

The woman doesn't answer. Eric stands up again, turning his back on her to go and speak with the two police officers.

"Tell the truth, Edith. Tell the truth." Bessie glares at the woman, now smoking another cigarette, her head lolling back on her chair. Running over to the detective, Bessie tries to shake his shoulder. "Make her tell you the truth, please!"

It's to no avail. Eric doesn't hear her. And the woman doesn't budge. Finally Eric nods to the attending policewoman, and with no final words to Edith, heads to the front door and back into his waiting cab. Bessie tags along on his flight home, but learns no further information from the detective as he sleeps the entire way.

Realizing again her return flight left hours ago, Bessie decides she must return to Earth Portal and, at least, try and find out when the next plane departs. "I'm in deep this time," she says softly, staring at the tall, blonde detective as he heads for the exit. "So long, Eric Pederssen. Our fate is in good hands, whatever it is." Closing her eyes, she whispers, "Earth Portal" which echoes into "tal-tal-tal-tal ..."

In the same moment, Bessie finds herself standing on the Earth Portal platform, facing a tiny flight schedule board suspended in air. Quickly she runs her eyes down the list of departing flights until they land on one which is glowing in neon yellow.

"Leaving in five minutes!" A grin emerges on her tense features. "Just got time to pop home."

Closing her eyes again, she focuses on the sound of "home", filling the platform with the sound of "ommmm". When she reopens them, she's thrilled to find herself in her family kitchen where her dad, mom, and sister Leila are seated for lunch.

Lunch? How is that possible? It was early morning when they flew back. "Oh, time zones on Earth," she says under her breath. "Earth has time zones."

Glancing down at the plate in the centre of the table, she murmurs, "Egg salad sandwiches, my fave." She quickly takes a seat at her empty place, gazing around from one family member to the other, love shining on her features.

"Lee, put down your book while you eat," her mother who is just returning from the counter, admonishes her younger daughter.

Leila's head lifts, and her eyes dart around the table. She seems to be sniffing the air, like a scent dog. With delight, Bessie realizes that once again, her little sister can sense her presence! Their bond is alive and well!

She watches the familiar tableau in fascination as her mother offers around a plate of treats. "Anybody for cupcakes?" Leila is too distracted to respond. Art reaches for a chocolate sprinkle. "Thanks, dear. Well, we should be hearing from Eric anytime now. See what he found out from that Edith woman."

"They're probably just having a lark, like the Wallets say." Heather's smile is unconvincing as she nibbles on her cupcake's vanilla icing. "Besides, they've got Jason looking out for them."

Bessie can feel a shiver up her spine at the mention of his name. She glances at her watch. Time to go. Leila turns to stare at the "empty" chair, directly into her sister's tear-filled eyes.

CHAPTER 63: HEAVEN

"Miss, Miss." An elderly gent on the Newly Dead flight persistently calls out to the young flight attendant in the ill-fitting uniform. Bessie scrambles to distribute NecNac Snaks, while directing passengers to their seats, as well as trying to calm her own nerves along with theirs. "Can you tell me, will my Susie be there to meet me?" He pleads, "She died forty-two years ago. Miss? Miss?"

She stops long enough in the aisle to assure the upset passenger that, yes, indeed, his beloved Susie will be outside Air Heaven Interportal waiting for him, along with all his other predeceased family members. She rushes away as he cries out again, "But Miss, how will she recognize me? I'm an old man now!"

Spinning around, she gives him a quick smile. "You will become ageless and she will be ageless. And you'll know each other just like before, okay?"

"You were a no-show on your return last night. That's not going to sit well on your report. What in the world were you thinking of, missing a flight like that?" Jarrod brushes past Bessie. "Fortunately for you, I'm on this one, too."

"I ... lost track of time ... I was just so overwhelmed with ... report?" Bessie is taken off-guard. "What report?"

"I have to write up a report after every flight. Them's the rules, sweetie. Although I do understand. I've missed a few myself. Especially when I first met Mohammad. Gads, we were always late there for awhile. What's your name anyway? I don't even know your real ..." He peeks at her name badge on her blouse. "Clotilde."

"Clo-what? Excuse me?" Bessie is totally confused. She tries to read her tag upside-down.

"Your name-tag. I could have just looked at your name-tag, Clotilde. That's French, isn't it?"

Bessie smiles beguilingly at Jarrod. "*Oui.*" As soon as he disappears towards the galley, she tries again to read her tag upside-down. "Clo-who? Clo-tilly? Clue-hildy?"

CHAPTER 64: HEAVEN

Back at the Dodd cottage, Mouser jumps all over Bessie as she wiggles out of her stolen uniform in the spare bedroom. From outside the door, she can hear Ash greeting Fiona unnecessarily loudly to alert her of her aunt's arrival. Big surprise, she was out shopping at the Mall again. Ash adds, "And what treasures did you find this time, Fizz? Something for lunch, I hope. We're starved."

'I've brought a guest,' Fiona's voice pipes up.

"Hello, Miss Ashley. And where might your lovely co-conspirator in crime be this time?"

"Angel Mel!" Bessie stuffs the uniform into the trunk, slamming it shut and grabbing her denim shorts and tee-shirt from the dresser. She changes in a flash before bursting into the living-room. "Oh, hi, Mel." She is all smiles. "Fancy meeting you here."

"Yes, fancy that. Meeting you here, a day after our missed session." His lips twitch at the corners. "What an amazing co-inky-dink, as you young folks say."

"So," Bessie offers.

"So," Angel Mel counter-offers.

Half an hour later, two figures sit on top of a stone wall. One appears from the back to be a young teenage girl with bobbed red hair. The other is large and bald, wearing an Hawaiian shirt, dangling an Air Heaven uniform minus a jacket on a hanger over one shoulder. A dog snoozes beside them on the warm stone, blissfully unaware of the crisis at hand.

"First of all, I need to tell you, Jason has escaped." The angel speaks first.

"Jason? How?" The shoulders on the young girl stiffen. The dog's head pops up in concern.

"We're monitoring him, don't worry. We have him under surveillance at all times."

"Like you do me and Ashley?"

"Not very amusing, considering your current circumstances." He bops her on her head with his free palm. "You are in a heap of trouble, my little mushroom. A heap of trouble. What am I supposed to do with you?"

"Take me to the Sacred Telescope?" Bessie is forever hopeful.

"Not today. I've got to think about this situation." He hops down from the stone wall. "Why don't you do the same?" He wanders off down the hillside path, leaving her and Mouser to their own devices. Turning around for a moment, his face holds no expression as he adds, "Clotilde."

Bessie hugs her dog, muttering. "This feels weird. The calm before the storm, no doubt. And this time, it's gonna be a doozie."

CHAPTER 65: HEAVEN

Several days have passed and still no sign of Angel Mel. No sightings of the dreaded Angel Rachel. No visits from the Soulslady. Ash and Bessie attend Reincarnation School without fail, listening to lesson after lesson under the joyful guidance of Angel Jigjag - Finding your soul mate. Discovering your moral compass. Make peace not war.

"Blah blah blah blah blah," Ash whispers to Bessie in the back row.

"I wish they would just punish me and get it over with."

"Hey, I'm going to get it, too. And I never even got to go to the Earth dimension. Like, talk about unfair."

In another part of Heaven, other discussions are taking place, the participants namely, Angels Mel and Rachel. Together they stroll through the magnificent parks behind his office.

"She's a unique case," Angel Rachel remarks. "Impervious to discipline. Has no effect on her whatsoever. Even pig duty didn't do the trick. Whenever she's sees an opportunity for a new adventure, off she goes."

"Most ones her age are scared to death of you," jokes Angel Mel. "And many of the older ones, too."

Rachel flashes her feline smile. "And that's just the way I like it, Mel."

"Oh, I know you do." He grins back. "I know you do."

CHAPTER 66: HEAVEN

"This Angel Court is now in session." Angel Boyd's voice booms through the small room. "Judge Angel Rachel presiding." She sweeps out in her usual grand fashion from behind the bench. In the spectator seats, Fiona fidgets with her necklace. Angel Mel chats to Angel Lionel. Soulslady, in an unbecoming brown suit, scowls beside a waving Jarrod, out of his Air Heaven uniform.

Behind the defendants' podium, an anxious Ash and Bessie stand side by side. Bessie's fingers reach up to touch her scar before resting on her shamrock broach for a moment. Ash busies herself applying a final layer of lip gloss.

Angel Rachel takes her seat, adjusting her glasses to read from papers she picks up from her desk. When she speaks, her voice is almost conversational. "Although technically, Miss Ashley Moreno did not, in fact, travel on the sacred Air Heaven Interportal flight in question, she did, however, engage in the crime of theft. And if she had not been spotted by our very attentive Soulslady from Bodysuits Boutique, she would have been on the flight ..." She snaps her fingers. "Like that. Therefore I consider these two cases as equal in weight and severity. Do you understand me?"

A murmur of "Yes, Judge Angel Rachel, yes, Judge Angel Rachel," follows.

Angel Rachel tilts her head and smiles as if she's at a gathering of close friends. "Listen up. This time I'm going to give you girls what you really want."

Everyone's eyes pop open in surprise. This is not good. This can't be good. Bessie feels her skin go prickly. Ash bites her lower lip.

The judge grins some more. "You gals love adventure? I'll give you an adventure."

CHAPTER 67: EARTH

"She is a procurer, I'm afraid to say. That is, she lures teenage girls into prostitution. Occasionally males." Eric Pederssen's face is grey with fatigue. He was hoping to give these good families better news. "Often against their will."

The Moreno and MacIntyre parents lean together for support. Art speaks for the group, "Tell us everything you know. Please, Eric, don't hold back."

Eric paces around the MacIntyre kitchen, wondering how best to present the next piece of information he's received. "She is known to have lured teenage girls, and sometimes boys, into prostitution for as far back as twenty years." He takes a breath. "Seven of them have disappeared, and they, or their remains, have never been found." He pauses. "There is some speculation her victims may have been transported south of the border."

"To Mexico." Jorge Moreno chokes out the words. "I'm from Mexico. And my baby may have been ..." He's unable to finish his thought.

Sophia takes her husband's head in both her palms. "We must not give up hope. We must not give up hope. They may still be just having some summer fun." She shakes his head. "Listen to me, Jorge, listen to me. They are smart girls. Very smart. They would not let this, this ... this woman, take advantage of them. And they are together. They do everything together. They are very smart."

Heather collapses in sobs onto Art's shoulder. It's just too much for her to bear. From the shelter of the doorway, Leila watches and listens, having been banned from this particular meeting with the detective this afternoon. She turns around and disappears.

CHAPTER 68: HEAVEN

The room is the size of a gymnasium. Hundreds of winged angels in tai-chi pants, jackets, and belts stand in row after row, facing the front stage where a magnificent angel, eight feet in height, glowing copper skin, and wearing a gown of deep blue, commands the attention of everyone in the room. This includes two very bewildered teenage girls, huddling together, apart from him. They alone, wear jeans, tee-shirts, and running shoes.

"Greetings, new angels. I am Grand Angel Gibran. I am the Commander-in-Chief of the Seventh Seal Flight Academy. On our program this semester, we have a very special assignment." He turns to nod at Bessie and Ash. "We have two human souls who have expressed a desire to fly. Isn't that wonderful, fellow angels?"

A murmur of surprise and assent vibrates through the crowd. On the stage, it's hard to tell whose eyes are rounder, Bessie's or Ash's.

"So although only angels have wings, and humans are humans and never angels, we have made a rare exception on the request of Angel Rachel, and special-ordered these. Ta-da." He dramatically sweeps from behind his back, two pair of detachable gossamer wings made of pink netting and sprinkled with sequins. "Aren't they pretty?" He asks of his enthralled audience. He walks over to hand one set to Bessie and one to Ash.

The girls stand dumbstruck, unable to react, other than to clutch the wings in front of them like bouquets in a wedding party. A loud cheer envelopes the room. It seems to go on forever, until Grand Angel Gibran's voice booms once more. "New angels, please, follow your instructors to your designated areas. And may Angel Rocco please come forward at this time."

As the rest of the newly-minted angels disperse in an orderly fashion, a broad-chested, middle-aged angel about four-foot-nine soaking wet, pops onto the stage like an overweight garden gnome.

Angel Gibran wastes no time making the introductions before he leaves. "Bessie Macintyre and Ashley Moreno, meet your most excellent flight instructor, Angel Rocco. Good luck. And enjoy your time with us at the Academy."

The gnome tilts his head to look up at them. "So you gals wanna fly, do ya? Show Rocco what ya got." He speaks like no angel they have ever met before. His face is almost round. Longish dark brown hair bushes out from the sides of his noticeably bald head. Black-rimmed glasses perch on his nubby nose.

Ash takes the lead. "There seems to be some sort of, ah, mistake. That is, we, ah, don't really, actually, like, want to, you know, have, like … wings. We, ah, just, like, ah, wanted to fly, like, you know, book a flight on an airplane type of flight, ha ha."

"Ha ha on you." Angel Rocco's grin is pure leprechaun. "Attach."

"Excuse me?" Bessie finally finds her voice. "Attach?"

"Attach your wings. Time's a-wastin'. And Rocco don't like that." He speaks like one of Angel Mel's gangsters in his bad screenplays. Angel Rocco jumps off the stage, signaling to them to follow. "When you're ready."

Hastily Bessie and Ash help each other into the fragile wings that attach with a slim harness fastened by Velcro to their backs and shoulders.

"And whatever you do, don't touch the buttons in front," Angel Rocco yells as both girls glance down to see four, over-sized, primary-colored buttons across their bellies. "Follow me."

Outside in the fresh air, he commands them to climb the staircase leading up to a wooden platform twenty feet off the ground. "After you, ladies."

Now they stand shakily on the top level, listening to the angel's next instructions. "Okay, now about your four buttons. Very important. Look but don't touch. The red button means go. The green button means stop. The yellow button means reverse. And my favorite …" His evil grin creases his features. "The blue button. That means panic."

Bessie and Ash gawk at their buttons, gawk at each other, gawk again at their buttons.

"Press the red button now!" He yells like they're going into battle, and maybe they are. "I said today not tomorrow!"

Frantically Bessie and Ash look down to try and press the right buttons. As soon as their fingers touch the red circles, the hapless pair is launched high into the atmosphere, zooming back and forth, up and down, left and right, full speed ahead. They appear and disappear into clouds before almost dive-bombing the field below, making a fast turn just before crashing. Back up into the clouds they zoom around in circles, back and forth and upside-down. Over and over. Over and over. Over and over.

Desperate to control their flight patterns, their fingers punch wildly at their buttons, unable to find them at such topsy-turvy speeds.

Meanwhile, on the ground, a calm Angel Rocco ignores the hysterical chaos above. And on closer observation, he appears to be manipulating some sort of miniature panel in his fingers. A remote control device, perhaps?

Around the edge of the flight academy, two angels are rolling about on the grass, so convulsed with laughter they can't stand up. The huge bald one wears an oversized Hawaiian shirt. The other is still in her judge's robes.

CHAPTER 69: EARTH

In a nondescript garage, men in white jumpsuits, gloves, and paper masks go over a ten-year-old Chevrolet Impala with a fine-tooth comb, while a tall, blonde man observes. All four doors are open, floor mats are pulled out, and the glove compartment gapes open.

One of the men in overalls walks over to the detective. "No evidence so far, sir, of any foul play. We found hair samples though, one from a natural redhead, one from a brunette, likely enhanced with a do-it-yourself black dye job, and I'm guessing non-Caucasian. In the lab we can match them to the hair brushes supplied by their parents. And a lip gloss." He hands over a shiny pink tube encased in a plastic bag.

"We'll test it for fingerprints, but it seems pretty obvious this is most likely Ashley Moreno's." Eric's voice is flat. "I'll run it past Leila Macintyre, she would know. So far, Leila appears to be our leading expert in this case."

"Got something." Another man in a jumpsuit walks over, holding a piece of paper in the air. Handing it to the detective, he remarks, "Looks like a receipt in Spanish."

Eric holds it up to his eyes. "Hotel Toro de Oro. Can't make out the date or the town but the lab will sort that out. For two rooms, one night. Thanks, Jim. I'm on it." Carefully he inserts the hotel bill into a clear bag and seals it. Taking his briefcase from his shoulder, he lays the receipt in a manila folder.

"Wait." Another man stands beside the open trunk. Eric rushes over along with the others. Together they stare into the trunk of Edith's Chevy where the investigator had removed the spare tire and cover. A young girl's bag made of brightly colored cloth with a blue drawstring is exposed. Eric puts gloves back on to remove it. Judging by the dust and grime, it seems it has been there for some time. Carefully he opens the strings which are threatening to break at any time. Inside he finds various items of a young girl's life - a tee-shirt, a cheap plastic bag of makeup, a bra and panties. Digging around deeper, he pulls out a small purple wallet. He removes two five-dollar bills, and a photograph of a young Asian girl around fourteen, and various sundry forms of identification like a membership to a middle school tumbling club in Tempe, Arizona. Another photo of a smiling young lad about the same age slips out. Her boyfriend? Her library card identifies her as Sue Li Wong.

Rushing over to his BMW, Eric climbs in to use his phone. The other personnel huddle around the open door, waiting to hear.

It doesn't take long before he steps out again into the blazing sunshine to announce, "Sue Li Wong's remains were discovered three years ago in a shallow grave in Jalisco, Mexico."

CHAPTER 70: HEAVEN

"Holy moly, Mel, you could have killed me. Both of us." To say Bessie is furious with her therapist is an understatement. They are sitting on the teeter-totter in the amusement park. Like before, it tilts up and down with no regard to their differences in height and weight. He gives her an amused stare until the irony of her comment sinks in.

"Okay, okay, I get the drift. I know me and Ash, we're no longer able to get killed, but still. You scared the life out of me."

He stares again, smiling. "Or you might say," he goes on, "You scared me half to death."

Now it's Bessie's turn to grin. She gets into the game. "You scared the living daylights out of me."

"You scared the beejesus out of me." Angel Mel one ups her. "Whatever that one means."

"You scared the shit out of me." It's Bessie's turn. "Although that one actually makes sense. When you're scared, you really can soil your pants. Like, you scared the piss out of me. I remember from way back when, I fell off a swing when Ash gave me a big push and I wet my pants. Wait a minute, how come I can remember that, but I can't remember how I died? That doesn't make any sense. I can remember soaking my pants but I—"

"Let's stick to the less graphic, colloquial expressions, shall we? Like, you scared me silly. Ooh, I just love that one." He takes his little notebook and pen out of his pocket to write it down. "You scared me silly. What on earth does that mean?"

"What does 'living daylights' mean?" Bessie leans back on her seat looking at the sky. She's way up in the air while Angel Mel is on the ground. "Talk about silly. How silly is this teeter-totter? So, Mel, have we fulfilled our punishment for stealing the uniforms? Poor Ash, every time we try to get on a flight, she either loses a shoe or gets caught." His frown causes her to hastily add, "Not that we're ever planning to take another reincarnation flight. Ever, ever again."

Now Angel Mel is up in the air looking sternly down at her, as sternly as he can, that is. "Not unless you want to spend some more time with my fine friend, Angel Rocco."

"Rocco the Wacko. Who dreamed up that little stunt, anyways? Was it you or Angel Rachel?"

Angel Mel's mischievous giggle is infectious. Even Jason, listening behind the nearby stand of trees, begins to smile. And Angel Lionel, some distance behind the wayward youth, seems to have a twinkle on his solemn features.

CHAPTER 71: HEAVEN

By the luck of the Irish, you might say, or perhaps it is their gift of the gab, Fiona Dodd has managed to wrangle a pass to the Sacred Telescope from Angel Jigjag. She, too, it seems, has expressed a desire to learn more about the magnificent constellations, being a newcomer and all that. And since her niece is pursuing her goal of reincarnating as an astronomer, it only seems fitting that, as her closest relative in Heaven, blah blah blah.

"Now I can find out what that scumbag Simon is really up to, damn his hide," she spits out as she, Bessie, and Ash, accompanied by Mouser, make their way towards the pedestal. Soon she is gazing into the lens, talking to the girls as she adjusts the focus. "There he is, the rat." Suddenly her tone changes completely. "Oh my, oh my. He's sobbing over a picture of me. It's in that beautiful silver frame. I remember that frame. Oh, that's so sweet. He's hugging it to his chest, aw. He misses me, aw, he's such a sweetie."

Her tone abruptly changes again. "Now he's taking the photo out of the frame and, what's he doing? Simon, what are you doing? He's putting, he's putting that bitch Sheila's picture into *my* frame! That bastard! That scumbag, ratfink, cheating, English bastard. He's putting my picture into his dresser drawer. Ooh, wait till I get my hands on him, I'm gonna wring his little neck. I'm gonna ..."

Bessie and Ash can barely contain their snickers over Fiona's tirade. Even if they are temporarily banned from the Sacred Telescope until further notice, this was well worth the trip.

"Gotta go," Ash announces. "Meeting Miguelito in half an hour."

"Your dreamboat, as Grandma Millie would say." Bessie teases her. "Your hottie. Your current flame. Your eye candy."

Ash's eyes go all misty. "Oh, he's dreamy alright. We think we're going to, like, try and reincarnate together when it's time. And go to Hollywood. I'll be the famous actress and he'll be my manager." She bats her fake lashes. "And my lover, naturally."

"Go before I toss up my NecNacs." Bessie gives her a little push. Watching her best friend skip along the path, her mind drifts off to other thoughts. "They're having so much light-hearted fun, those two. Silly and romantic... making little plans together... He adores her just the way she is... flaws and all. And she adores him just the way he is... flaws and all. Maybe that's the secret - loving the flaws. Wish Jason and I had been like that."

Unbeknownst to her, he listens to her words from the protection of the forest. "I wish that, too," he whispers under his breath.

CHAPTER 72: EARTH

Eric Pederssen stands beside his BMW in a dirt patch alongside a highway in the middle of nowhere. It's so hot, sweat drips down inside his dress shirt. He stretches up his long body, arching his back. His aviator sunglasses slide down his nose, slick with moisture.

In front of him, two dirty picnic tables are littered with empty plastic cups and a discarded tower of paper plates and plastic utensils. On the ground, a huge spider tiptoes along a half-empty roll of paper towels. Near the table, a pair of taco-smeared plates are providing a delicious lunch for a horde of ants. He spies a torn scrap of paper - a card of some sort. Looking at the writing on it, he recognizes "*Feliz Cumpleaños*"- Happy Birthday. Nearby a partially burned candle is stuck with icing.

"Fuck," he mutters. "Fuck fuck fuck. They've gone." Taking out a handkerchief from his breast pocket, he wipes his face, as if he could wipe off the stress in the same motion.

He yanks his phone from his pocket. "The Latinos are long gone. No way to back up Edith's story she bought them breakfast here. Time to check up on the boy-friend, Jason Wallet again. Call his parents, see if they're heard from him yet."

Jamming the phone back into his pant's pocket, he walks over to one of the picnic tables. In one violent motion, he heaves it in the air as if it is as light as a cardboard box, tossing it on its side.

CHAPTER 73: HEAVEN

In her bed in Girls Dorm, Bessie appears to be in a deep sleep. By the twitching of her eyelids, it seems she is dreaming about something.

She is in the backseat of an old Chevy. The woman named Edith is driving. Ash dozes in the front passenger seat. Without warning, the woman swerves into a parking lot just ahead. Two greasy-looking, middle-aged men stand in the driveway, grinning and waving. One of them makes an obscene gesture, while the other dangles a box of condoms from his hand.

Edith reaches over to push the passenger door open as she yells, "Get out."

"Run!" Bessie screams as both girls grab their things and scramble out of the vehicle. "Run!" Bessie repeats, "Never mind them!" Ash takes off in bare feet, clutching her shoes to her chest.

They run and run and run and run some more. It feels like they've been running for hours, when Bessie spots a discarded refrigerator on its side, a ways back from the highway. Soon they are lying flat on the ground, peeking out from behind it.

"How long should we wait?" Ash eyes some beetles, busy chewing on a dead something just out of reach. "'Til we see her car disappear," Bessie replies. "She'll think we got another ride."

It doesn't take more than half an hour till the dusty old Chevy, with a very pissed off Edith, jerks down the road, evidently tapping the brake with a fury.

Waiting for another ten minutes to make sure she doesn't turn around, the girls jump up and brush themselves off. Eventually they begin to walk along the side of the highway, trying to laugh about the terrifying encounter with Edith.

"When she said fornicators, you thought she said foreigners." Bessie bursts into giggles. "Our parents are traveling in Europe and Antarctica, you said." She can hardly get the words out.

"It's hot." Ash stares at the endless sky. "Got to change shoes." She pulls out the flip-flops from the Wallmarket bag.

"Let's play a game," Bessie suggests. "Spot the fairy."

"Spot the what?" Ash lets out a comfortable sigh as she begins to walk again. "That's better."

"Fairies. We used to play this on road trips with my grandparents. Look, there's one over there." She points to a clump of spindly vegetation.

"Where?"

"Peeking her little head out from under that bush. Look, there's another one."

They pass the time, spotting imaginary fairies, trying to ignore their predicament.

"Hey, my grandma believed in the wee folk. She swore she could see them in her garden in Ireland before they immigrated. She said they paint the flowers, that's where they get their color from."

"So, like, do you believe in them, too?" Ash looks ahead at the endless, empty highway.

"Sure, why not? Fairies, elves, gnomes. Maybe not unicorns. What is a unicorn, anyways? Like some kind of lamb or a goat or … ?"

"Hear that?" Ash breaks into her friend's wandering thoughts. The sound of an unhealthy engine approaches and slows down. In the back of a pickup, so old it almost looks like a cart, about fifteen, brown-skinned, small men and women are impossibly squished in. One of them plays a guitar. The rest are singing to their hearts' content.

Beckoning to the girls in invitation, the front seat passenger leans out his open window with a big, gold-toothy grin to say, "Come join the fun. We no harm you, we are Guatemalan. We sing, we dance."

Bessie looks over at Ash who is looking back at her. Giggling with the absurdity of their day, Bessie makes the call. "Oh, what the hay. Can't be any crazier than crazy Edith, right?"

She and Ash climb in the back and settle in amongst them. The people seem friendly and jolly, and are dressed in dirt-stained, working clothes, as if they have been in fields. Maybe they are migrant workers?

One of them, a woman, strums an old guitar as they sing some Spanish song. She and Ash join in, even though they have no clue of the lyrics. It all seems very merry.

Ash pipes up, "Okay, now we'll teach you a song." She says it again in halting Spanish. "One we learned at camp, right, Bess?" Taking the lead, she bursts into a rousing chorus of, "Row, row, row your boat, gently down the stream … "

Bessie jumps into the round, "Row, row, row your boat, gently down the stream … "

Ash continues, "Merrily, merrily, merrily, merrily … "

Now Bessie, "Merrily, merrily, merrily, merrily … "

Together they sing at the top of their young lungs, "Life is ... but a ... dream."

Their new friends listen, smiling politely until Bessie prompts them, "Now your turn. You try it."

The guitarist begins to search for a chord. Shyly at first, the Guatemalans add their voices to the ones of their hitchhiking companions. "Row, row, row your boat ... gently down the stream ... " But because they have no ideas of the actual words, it comes out as, "Ra, ra, ra you ba ... henly dun aseem ... "

"Merrily, merrily, merrily, merrily," Bessie and Ash lead them.

"Menly, menly, menly, menly," they sing with gusto.

"Life is but a dream." The girls finish with a flourish.

"Lika buta bean." The entire group burst into raucous laughter as the truck putt-putts down the highway.

Funny how she doesn't have a scar on her—

In her darkened bedroom at Girls Dorm, Bessie jerks violently into a sitting position, a gasp flying from her lips. Her eyes pop open wide. She reaches up with trembling fingers to touch the bird-like ridge on her forehead. Glancing over at Ash's bed, she notices it's empty. A sob catches in her throat. "What happened to us? Will I ever know?"

CHAPTER 74: HEAVEN

That morning, Bessie shares with Ash her weird dream as they get ready for their day. They're alone, being late as usual. Their room-mates have already dressed and gone, their beds perfectly made up, their dressers tidy.

"That's the same goofy song we learned at camp." Ash leans in closer to the mirror in order to line her eyes with smoky lilac. "We were singing that here in Heaven on our way to the airport that one time. Funny how a song you learned in childhood can, like, stick in your head, but we don't know how we died. I don't get it." She glances around to look at her friend. "You, okay?"

"Yeah." Bessie rubs her eyes wearily. "Guess so." After attaching the shamrock broach to her tee-shirt, she flops on her back on her unmade bed, staring at the ceiling. Her fingers pick at her scar. "At least I get to go to the Telescope again today. With Mel, for my astronomy lesson."

"Lucky you. I've got to wait another week since I missed my curfew last night." Her smile is beguiling. "But it was worth every minute."

"So this new dream," Angel Mel begins the conversation, looking out his office window into the park with his binoculars. "Did it frighten you? Look, there's George Burns and Gracie Allen. Well, I'll be a star-struck angel."

Bessie gives him a sideways look before glancing out the window for herself through his spare pair. "That's the weird thing. After the scary part with Edith and those awful men, it was a very happy dream, riding around in the back of that old truck with those fun people, but then I woke up terrified. That song."

"What song? Gracie's making him laugh, see? And George, he's smoking that big fat cigar."

"Oh, that stupid round we used to sing at camp. Row, row, row your boat. Me and Ash, we were teaching it to them. Then I woke up with this awful feeling in my gut, wondering when I got this scar." She puts down the binoculars to turn to the angel. "When did I get this scar?"

He takes one hand to ruffle her hair. "You'll know, when it's—"

"Time, I know. How long have I been here now?"

"They're walking towards Jack Benny. Wow, today sure is a gold mine for star gazing. How long do you think you've been here?"

She takes the bait. "Two weeks. Three years. Five minutes, I don't know."

Angel Mel doesn't hesitate. "What's the big difference? I'll be right back." Suddenly he races towards the door. "Got to find Rachel. She'll just die when I tell her who is out there now!" Mouser lifts his head from the armchair where he's enjoying a nap.

"What the ...?" Bessie focuses her binoculars on the little paths lacing through the gardens until she sees what Angel Mel had seen. "Three of the Golden Girls. Grandma used to love to watch them. Let's see, Dorothy, Blanche, and who's the older one? Sophia. Hey, that's Ash's mother's name, Sophia. Cool." As she watches out the window, she catches sight of an excited Hawaiian-shirted angel dragging a petite, female angel in a power suit by the hand towards the famous trio from Miami.

CHAPTER 75: EARTH

"Thank you for seeing me today on such short notice." In a rural area just outside downtown Ravenspond, Eric Pederssen takes a seat at the table in a plain farmhouse kitchen, laid out with coffee cups and homemade brownies. Outside the window, fields of corn wave in a strong breeze. A middle-aged couple, both tall and rangy, stand together at the door. A boy and a girl, close in age, around four and five, sneak looks at the strange man, from a hallway behind the kitchen.

Opening the screen door, the man calls to his young children, telling them to go out and play. Without a peep, they skip outside.

"Well behaved," Eric remarks.

"We do our best," the woman replies with a small smile, picking up the coffee pot to pour them each a cup. "Help yourself to cream and sugar. So, what's this you want to know about our Jason? Thought we told you everything we knew."

"I just want to know a little more about his relationship with Bessie. I know they were …" Quickly he corrects himself. "I know they *are* very fond of each other." He drinks his coffee black.

"Fond?" The man laughs, seeming not to notice Eric's gaffe. "They're crazy about each other. Ever since we moved here when Peter died, that's my older brother, he had a heart attack, those two have been stuck together like glue."

"But …" His wife breaks in. "Don't forget, Bri, how they started having those fights once they got older." She leans towards Eric. "Jason is very protective of her, is all. She's a bit of a daredevil, if you know what I mean, especially when she hangs around with that Moreno girl. I'm not saying they do anything really bad. Just regular kid stuff. Sweet girls, really. Both of them."

Eric helps himself to a brownie. "So you still think he's been trailing them around since they ran away, making sure they're okay? When's the last time you heard from him?"

Jason's mother gets up to let the cat in. While she's there, she looks to check that her younger children are within sight. "Just keeping an eye on them, that's all. Called what, last Sunday? From a pay phone. Forgot to take his cell." She sits back down. "Says not to worry about any of them. He's got it all under control, right, Bri?"

"You see, he wants to be the hero," Brian Wallet explains. "Impress her, if you know what I mean. Thinks that'll win her love back for good. They've been on the outs a lot lately. His mother here told him we need him home on the farm soon, but to take his time and have fun, just not for too long."

"He works very hard, detective," she elaborates. "There's a lot to do on a place like this. He's such a good son, always helping out, wonderful to his little brother and sister." She gets up to refill the tiny creamer. "Besides, he's almost grown. Seventeen last March. We never have any worries with Jason. Hope our young ones will be just like him."

Her husband agrees. "They'll be home soon. Right as rain, you just watch. Did much the same myself as a young lad. Running around the countryside, seeing the world before I settled down, didn't I, Janie?" He gives her a wink before turning back to the detective. "No harm in that, is there?"

Eric looks at them kindly, lying through his teeth. "I'm sure they're fine."

CHAPTER 76: HEAVEN

"Evening, Angel Jigjag," Angel Mel greets his colleague with warmth, perched on a colorful mat near the Sacred Telescope. "We're back for another look at the constellations. What was it I heard about a new Milky Way?" He gives Bessie a nudge.

"Yes, I'm very excited to see it tonight. Discovered by an angel, wasn't it?" Bessie plays along. Mouser barks as if he's all excited about the new find, as well.

Angel Jigjag puts an embroidered marker carefully in his giant hardcover book before turning to the newcomers. "Indeed. By one of the new angels, too, fresh out of the flight academy. Angel Jing Feng."

Angel Mel hands over Bessie's pass. "Well, we're off for another astronomy exploration. Practice for her next incarnation."

Angel Jigjag's face beams with pleasure. "Marvelous. Bravo, my dear, bravo." He reopens his book as they trot off towards the Sacred Telescope.

It's not long before the milky swirls are clearing and Bessie leans in to gaze into the lens. "Please, I need to know how I died," she begs quietly. "No matter how bad it is, I need to know."

Bessie and Ash stand in the packed dirt driveway of a nondescript diner set back from the road. A single gas pump is off to one side. The sign, hand-painted above the door, announces it as: MAVIS & JIM DEW DROP INN. *A transport truck, a couple of sedans, and a well-used, red Ford pickup with a tarpaulin in the bed are parked here and there. The girls turn and wave to the old truck loaded down with Guatemalan migrant workers, as it drives off down the highway. Strains of the guitar and their Spanish singing voices faintly reach their ears.*

"They were so much fun. Especially after the lovely Edith," Ash remarks. "This day started off so terrible, and now it's great. I'm starving."

"So let's do drop in to see Mavis and Jim."

Inside, the diner is *Retro Fifties*, only in this case, it's for real. It seems nobody got around to updating it, except for the appliances. The floor is tiled in black and white. The booths lining the side wall display old pictures cut out of magazines that appear to be of vintage Florida. In each one, chunky salt and pepper shakers huddle with squeeze bottles of ketchup and mustard around a metal napkin holder. A small vase displays plastic flowers of unknown origin on a turquoise and yellow Formica tabletop.

Ash and Bessie gingerly pile into a booth near the front before glancing around. At the counter, a woman, plump as a pudding and presumably Mavis, pours coffee for an elderly man. Beside him, a clear plastic dome displays slices of various pies. He points to the apple one on the second shelf. The woman lifts off the dome to slide the pie onto a plate, setting it in front of him with a fork. She moves down the counter with her pot of coffee where a woman reads a newspaper.

"Wow, Bess, that guy over there, he is sooo hot." Ash, facing the rear wall, indicates with a tilt of her head, a young man in tight black jeans and a white tee-shirt, using the pay phone attached to the back wall. "He's, like, Zac Frontenac hot."

Bessie takes a quick peek over her shoulder. The young man is around a baby-faced twenty-two or -three, lean and muscled. A lock of his dirty, sun-streaked hair keeps falling in his eyes as he talks and listens. Noticing the girls' attention, he treats them to a lazy smile.

Quickly Ash and Bessie jerk back around, embarrassed to be caught, as Mavis approaches with plastic-covered menus. "Nice day."

Bessie orders for both of them. "We'll have two coffees and two ChocOnut bars, please."

"Interesting choice." Mavis smiles as she saunters back towards the counter with her menus.

A man opens the screen door, waving a twenty dollar bill. "Just took fifteen dollars worth of gas, Mavis. Nobody around."

She goes over to take the money from him. "That Jim. Stay for a coffee?"

"Sure, why not. No big rush." The man takes a seat at the counter. Mavis pours him a cup of coffee, setting down his five-dollar change. Without asking, she serves him a slice of blueberry pie, evidently his favorite.

Tittering like the school girls they are, Bessie and Ash nibble on their candy bars while stealing glances at the young man at the back.

Without warning, Zac Frontenac-hot is now leaning over the end of their table, his fingers splayed on the Formica. "You ladies from around here?" His eyes are an intense blue framed by long, dark lashes.

Ash almost swallows the rest of her ChocOnut bar whole. "No, we're from, ah … New York City. Like, in New York."

"We're secretaries on vacation," Bessie elaborates.

"Well, ain't that a kick." His chuckle is more like a cat's purr. He stands up straight. *"Well, you all have yourselves a nice little vacation, ladies."* When he walks, he seems to glide in slow motion over to the counter where he slides onto a stool.

Mavis pours him a large cola. *"So what are you up to today?"*

"Thought I'd take a ride into town," he replies. *"Too nice a day just to hang around here, don't you think?"*

Ash is buzzing like a bumble bee. *"Bess, we want to go into the town, too. Why don't we, we could … I mean, after, like … catch the bus. We … "* She jumps up from the booth and flits over to the counter beside the guy. *"As it happens,"* she begins nervously. *"My friend and I are traveling there, also. We're just wait—"*

He winks at Mavis. *"You want to ride in with me then? In my big, old truck?"* Glancing out the window, he indicates where the red Ford pickup is parked.

Ash follows his gaze before turning to look over towards Bessie. She makes a silly, pleading face. Chuckling, Bessie nods yes, as Mavis shakes her head with a small smile. She's obviously familiar with this young man's action.

"Sure, that would be, like, very gracious of you." Ash turns to bat her eyelashes at the mysterious, hot guy.

He slips off his stool, grinning at Mavis. *"Just gotta make a couple more calls first. Be back in a flash."*

Ash bounces back to their booth to gather up her things. Leaning across the table, she whispers, *"He's, like so, so … "*

"Like, totally hot?" Bessie teases. *"Like, totally Zac Frontenac-hot?"*

The screen door creaks.

In walks Jason.

In Heaven, Bessie jumps back from the Sacred Telescope as if she's been bitten by a snake. "Jason again!" She takes off in a full run into the night, Mouser chasing after her. She shouts back over her shoulder, "It's always him! Always!"

Angel Mel watches her figure disappear, concern filling his eyes. "My dear sweet, funny little mushroom," he whispers under his breath. "I wish I could take it all away."

Slowly he begins to stroll back along the cliff until he finds what he's looking for. A giant oak stump is soon covered with his generous butt. Taking a tattered screenplay from his briefcase, he begins to read out loud. "Darlene pleads with Todd for mercy. If you leave me I will die of a broken heart, I beg you, don't go! We were always meant to be together! Always and forever! No, that sounds too melodramatic.

Better change that. Where's my pen?" He searches through his pockets until he finds what he's looking for, and scribbles in the margins.

Within the shadows of the forest, a lanky young man with sticking-up hair canters across the ground in the direction that Bessie has just taken. His features are stricken with deep emotion. He stops finally, tears running down his cheeks. "I'm so sorry, Bessie. I'm so very sorry."

CHAPTER 77: HEAVEN

"Wake up, sleepy heads." Angel Mel ruffles Bessie's hair as he stands between hers and Ash's twin beds in their room in Girls Dorm. He turns to do the same to Ash, snoring lightly behind her pink, quilted eye mask. "Up and at 'em. Let's go."

They both sit up at the same time, astonished, no doubt, to see the blazing cerise and lime green Hawaiian shirt in their room, and so early at that.

"Wha ... wha ...?" Ash pulls off her sleeping accessory.

"What the hell?" Bessie rubs her eyes.

"Careful, no cussing in the presence of an angel, please. Hurry up, now. No dilly-dallying. Put on your best fancy duds. I'll wait for you in the office." He disappears into thin air.

Looking over at each other to make sure it isn't a dream, the girls reluctantly climb out of their beds. "Must be a trick." Bessie yawns. "Has to be a trick."

Excited by the idea of dressing up, regardless, Ash is soon yanking outfits from their mutual closet, tossing things onto her bed.

Not long after, two mini-skirted teenagers, one in purple platforms, one in running shoes, peek into the office where Angel Mel is chatting up a giggling Angel Coretta. He turns to see. "Why, aren't we a sight for angel eyes!"

Angel Coretta agrees. "Very sophisticated, I must say."

Jumping from his seat, he waves a quick goodbye to his fellow angel. As the trio exits the front door into the early morning sunshine, he gallantly takes the arm of each one. "Ladies?" In a twinkling, all three vanish from sight.

—

When they reappear, the girls discover to their intense delight, they are in the heart of the very same glorious, bustling city, where they had trailed after the Air Heaven flight crew, not to mention, stealing their uniforms. Now they sit in an outdoor bistro with Nectaccinos and a plate of feather-light croissants awaiting their morning dining pleasure. A small crystal vase on the white linen tablecloth holds a single, delicate, pastel orchid.

"This is, like, so totally …" Ash gives up trying to make sense.

"Totally, like, awesome?" Angel Mel teases. "Well, you ain't seen nuttin' yet, my beauties. Croissant?" He picks up the plate of delectable delights. Eagerly the girls help themselves, exclaiming with pleasure.

"These are heavenly!" Bessie speaks with her mouth full.

"Why of course, they are." Angel Mel's eyes twinkle. "Where do you think we are, LaLa Land?"

Finally satiated, everyone leans back in their tiny wrought iron chairs to look around at the mesmerizing buzz and bustle of the strolling crowd passing by, intent on the business of their day. A scruffy dog sleeps on the sidewalk, blissfully unaware of the footfalls all around him. Small birds nibble on crumbs under the tables. Horns honk from streets thick with traffic but no pollution. After all, vehicles run on vibrational energy here.

"So what's the hook, Mel?" Ash inquires ever so politely. "I mean, like, I'm loving every second of this, don't get me wrong, totally love being back in the city again but … ?" She leaves her thought unfinished.

"Must there be a hook?" Angel Mel's eyes are full of amusement. "Relax, gal friends, no hook. Just thought you two have been behaving so well lately, you deserved a little treat."

"Treat, no trick?" Bessie grins, her chin propped in her palm. Her shamrock broach pinned to her yellow tee-shirt sparkles in the brilliant sunshine.

"Treat, no trick," Angel Mel confirms. "So, ready for the next bit?"

"Choose one pair of whatever your hearts' desire." Angel Mel has one arm around the shoulder of each girl as they gaze in wonder at the endless shoes perched delicately on glass shelves. The store clerk, immaculately turned out in black slacks and a skin-tight black shirt, grins indulgently. His sleeked-back hair enhances his exotic features and perfect teeth.

Bessie scampers over towards the amazing collection of running shoes unlike any she has ever seen before, with sparkles and cut-outs and small heels and peep-toes and … It goes on and on.

Ash is instantly drawn to the rows of exquisite stilettos, so delicate they seem impossible to even hold in your hand, let alone put on your feet. Her sighs pour from her lips as she stands as if before an altar.

The clerk shares a conspiratorial glance with Angel Mel before he speaks. "And a see-cond pair, on dee house," the salesman declares in a thick French accent. "For dees pretty yon ladies." Ash grasps at Bessie's shoulder to avoid fainting.

Some time later, they are strolling along a wide boulevard edged in perfectly spaced Japanese maples. "So what's the name of this gorgeous city, Mel?" Ash rebalances the two shoe boxes squashed into a clear bag, dangling over one arm along with her giant, sparkly handbag.

"You don't know?" Angel Mel glances down at her.

"We could hardly ask," Bessie returns. "As we weren't exactly supposed to be here in the first place, as you recall."

"Ah yes, your little investigative mission, trailing after Air Heaven flight attendants. I remember it well." He chuckles. "Stealing their uniforms so you could stow away onboard a forbidden reincarnation flight to Earth. Tsk. Tsk. Tsk."

"One of us, anyway." Ash pouts. "I never seem to make it for some stupid reason."

"It's those silly shoes of yours, I keep telling you." Bessie leans around the angel in between them. "Should wear runners like me."

"No petty disagreements today, my sweets. Today is all about pure devil-may-care pleasure."

Bessie tugs on his colorful sleeve, grinning up at him. "Devil may care, Mel?"

He stops to look into her eyes. "Indeed, my little mushroom. Devil-may-care pleasure. Speaking of which ..." The threesome vanishes into thin air.

Now they stand in a little group on a pure marble floor gazing up at colossal sculptures and statues, so astonishing, and of such flawless beauty and wonder, Bessie and Ash are unable to blink, let alone speak. Each display is more magnificent than the one before, as Angel Mel leads them gently from one to another. There is not a sound in the entire gallery, save for the soft shuffle of footfalls, and a quiet murmuring of oohs and ahs from the hundred or so souls who are soaking up this divine pleasure.

Angel Mel explains, "You see, when artists reincarnate to the Earth dimension, they unconsciously try and recreate these glorious works of Heavenly art."

"This is where their inspiration comes from?" Bessie is thrilled with this tidbit of new information.

"Exactly. They are 'inspired'. Which, of course, means 'in spirit'. Like we are right now, in spirit form." Angel Mel smiles benignly.

"Wow, Mel," Ash pipes up. "I'm speechless. Totally speechless."

"She said speechlessly." Smiling at her fondly, he eventually beckons them to exit, whispering, "You must always leave some treasures unexplored for another visit."

Now the trio is seated in a very chi-chi restaurant many floors above ground level, the windows open to the balmy air. A crisp waitress pours a bottle of sparkling Nectarrino into three crystal glasses, as the angel and his charges pour over the embossed ivory menus. Outside the window, skyscrapers twinkle in the afternoon sunshine.

It takes a while before Bessie excitedly announces, "We're moving! Ash, we're turning around in a slow circle. The view keeps changing! Look!"

Sure enough, the scene of skyscrapers has become one of a mammoth, art deco legislative building of some sort. Awhile later, the view evolves into a lush, spacious park laced with pathways, and filled with souls enjoying it. Still later, a river fills their windows, where open-air boats carry sightseers up and down.

"Oh Mel, could we take a ride later?" Ash pleads. "Pretty please?"

Now leaning back in the wooden bench seats of the flat-bottomed boat, Angel Mel and the girls gaze from one side of the waterway to the other where a motley collection of artists display their work, or are busy making quick sketches of intrigued tourists. Jugglers juggle, magicians do magic tricks, singers sing. There is just no end of things to gawk at as the boat slowly putt-putts along.

"Bess, look at all those beautiful necklaces." Ash points to a small stand on the left bank where colorful jewelry drips from multiple hooks.

Angel Mel reaches into his pocket and hands a brightly colored necklace to each of the girls. "Got these while you were busy eyeballing the boys."

Mumbling their thank you's, Bessie and Ash quickly put them around their necks. Soon they are distracted by a troupe of trapeze performers on the right bank, transforming themselves into an elaborate, mind-bending sculpture as a crowd gathers.

"How can they do that?" Ash's mouth falls open.

"That's impossible," Bessie declares.

Angel Mel looks from one girl to the other. It would seem this day is everything he wanted it to be.

"What's the name of this city again?" Ash asks while she continues to stare.

"Celestia," he replies simply. "Didn't you guess?"

—

"Ash? Ash?" Bessie reaches over to slap at her friend's hand dangling out of her bed. "Wake up."

"What'd I miss? What'd I miss?" Ash sits up, still wearing her mask.

"I was just having this amazing dream," Bessie explains. "We went on this incredible trip to the city of Celestia with Angel Mel."

Ash pulls off her mask. "I had the same dream. Bess?" She glances over at her friend's bed. They stare at each other for a moment before Ash babbles, "Is that possible to … to have the same dream?"

Sitting up simultaneously, they peek around where their room-mates are, as always, sound asleep.

"Look-look-look! Over there, on the chair." Ash jumps out of bed followed by a stunned Bessie. Piled high on the little seat, a stack of elegant shopping bags lean against each other. While Ash pulls out a pair of jewel-encrusted stilettos, Bessie notices a glittery string of purple beads around her friend's neck over her nightgown. Her fingers leap to her throat, where, sure enough, she discovers turquoise beads around her own.

CHAPTER 78: EARTH

His condo is Scandinavian masculine, all black leather, glass, and chrome. Eric Pederssen lounges on a single chair in the open concept living area. His long legs are stretched out on the foot-rest. A glass of single malt scotch dangles from his right hand.

Above the gas fireplace, a modest, flat screen television is filled with the face of a local news reporter, with a bleached bob and heavy eye makeup. She is showing pictures of Bessie MacIntyre, Ashley Moreno, and Jason Wallet. A hotline number flashes beneath. "If anyone has seen any of these three teenagers, please call in to the number below, or the Ravenspond Police Department," her voice says. "All three disappeared from Ravenspond on July 15th. They are apparent runaways." Her lips smile. "Having a bit of a summer adventure, I expect. I remember when I took off one July."

"Stupid bitch." Eric is disgusted. No one is taking this seriously.

A Siamese cat strolls into the room, climbing onto his lap and falling asleep. Eric's free hand absently strokes the beautiful creature.

The reporter continues. "Several phone calls have been received by the young man to his parents saying they are alright. However, both girls appear to have left their cell phone chargers at home. They have been known to have run away previously. If you have any information regarding these teens, please call. We turn now to the fire that broke out last night in a local clothing store. Arson is suspected."

Eric angrily picks up the remote on the small glass table beside his chair to switch off the television. Turning to look out his high-rise, floor-to-ceiling window at the twinkling skyline, he takes a large gulp of his scotch.

CHAPTER 79: HEAVEN

"You'll never guess," Ash whispers across to Bessie beside her in the next seat in rein-carnation class. "Angel Rainbow Sunshine is back from her vacation."

"Thank the Lord," Bessie whispers back.

"We thank the Lord every moment of all our lives and in-between, don't we, students?" Angel Jigjag appears from nowhere to tower between their desks. His chunky teeth are gleaming white as he smiles broadly. An affirming murmur floats through the classroom.

"And how are your astronomy lessons going, Miss Bessie?" he inquires politely. "You are learning the basic intricacies of celestial navigation, I trust?"

She smiles up at the angel, false enthusiasm for her new-found calling beaming from every pore. "Oh yes, Angel Jigjag. I am so very grateful that I am fortunate to get such a head start, as it were, on my next incarnation." She looks around the classroom, daring the other students to contradict her.

From their sulky expressions, it is obvious how little they believe her. Ash quickly hides her face behind a book as a small snickering sound trickles out from behind the pages.

———

"So where does an angel go on vacation, I wonder?" Fiona asks of either Ash or Bessie who are lounging in the Dodd cottage living-room later on that afternoon, sipping on nectar tea. Mouser climbs up on the sofa between the girls, laying his head on Bessie's lap.

"The Fifth Dimension beach resort, wherever that is. Apparently she was suffer-ing from on-the-job fatigue." This statement from Bessie causes both young girls to burst into giggles.

"She suffered from an overdose of off-key-itis," Ash adds, causing them to laugh some more.

"She got whiplash from a broken guitar string." Bessie can barely get the words out.

Fiona sets down a plate of cookies and a small jug of Grandpa Will's homemade hooch. "This is the last of it, I'm afraid. I'll have to wait till he returns for more, or learn to make my own." She helps herself to the whiskey, adding a pinch to her tea. "So, does this mean we can go back to the Telescope tonight?"

Ash's eyes turn dreamy. "Not me, I have a date."

Bessie imitates her voice. "With Miguelito. He's, like, sooo totally awesome."

Her friend slaps her on the arm, causing Bessie to jump up and dance around the room in a chorus of, "Miguelito, Miguelito, Miguelito …"

—

The stars seem to twinkle even more brightly than ever this clear, warm night as Bessie, her aunt Fizz, and Mouser make their way casually along the cliff. Sure enough, they begin to hear the strains of an horrific rendition of the Bob Dylan classic anthem, *Don't Think Twice, It's Alright.*

It seems her time off at the beach resort did little to improve her finger to guitar coordination or her ability to sing in tune.

Bessie whispers to her aunt, "Poor Bob Dylan. Imagine having your lovely lyrics destroyed by an angel."

The St. Bernard trots up to greet Mouser in a friendly fashion, happy to have some company other than the singer. Together they make their way to the Sacred Telescope unnoticed.

"You go first, Aunt Fizz." Her niece smiles. "See what that slime ball Simon is up to this time." As her aunt eagerly steps up onto the pedestal to remove the lens cap and peer in, Bessie glances around at the forest beyond.

Is that a branch playing a trick on me? Is someone watching me again? She keeps her eyes glued on the spot until finally an exquisite deer with antlers raised, makes its way into the moonlight. Laughing off her fears, Bessie waits her turn as she listens to the mutterings of Fiona, going on about you won't believe what that creep bastard Simon is up to now.

"Okay, your turn." Fizz stomps off the pedestal, "If I could get my hands on him, I swear, I'd roll him down Mount Everest in one of his damn stupid carpets."

Smiling, Bessie steps up, adjusts the lens, and peers in as the milky swirls disappear.

She and Ash are in the Mavis & Jim Dew Drop Inn diner. Ash is over at the counter, one hand propped on her hip, as she chats coyly to a young man in black jeans and a white tee-shirt. Bessie, facing the door, is gathering up her things as the screen door opens. And Jason walks in.

Dropping her stuff on the table, Bessie stomps over to confront him. "You've been trailing after us all the way from Ravenspond, haven't you? I knew it!" Her eyes burn with anger. "Quit following me. I mean it."

He reaches out to touch her. She yanks her hand away. "Let me go."

Gazing steadily into hers, he speaks softly and with determination. "I'll never let you go, Bessie. I'll never let you go."

She jabs her finger in his face. He doesn't flinch. "You're so, you're so ... "

Ash pipes up from the counter, smiling at Zac Frontenac-hot. "Immature?"

Bessie fires off, "And I'm not."

Undeterred Jason adds, "You're just fifteen, Bessie."

"Fifteen and one month," she hisses.

Again he tries to touch her. She slaps his hand. "Go home. Go home and milk a cow or something."

His pale eyes fill with sadness and an indescribable longing. "But it's my job to protect you."

Bessie spins around to head back to the booth. "Well, you're fired, so go home." Grabbing the rest of their things, she rushes over to Ash, dropping cash on the counter for Mavis. She yanks her friend by the arm towards the door. As she passes Jason on their way out, she yells once more, "Go home, Jason. I mean it."

The screen door slams behind them like a bullet as Zac Frontenac-hot saunters towards the rear of the diner to use the pay phone. The elderly man chats with Mavis, examining her chipped nail polish.

Oblivious of the strangers who are observing him curiously, Jason goes over to the window to watch Bessie and Ash through the faded café curtains. The girls are yakking a mile a minute beside a red truck, their hands flailing in the air.

To no one, Jason mutters, "I'll never let you go, Bessie."

In Heaven, the milky swirls fill the lens as a visibly upset Bessie climbs back down from the Sacred Telescope. Her aunt is still blathering on, "You'll never guess what that slime ball Simon was up to this time. He's moved that partner of his - she looks like a horse, I swear, like an old nag past her prime - she wears, get this, she wears wire-rimmed glasses like some senior citizen or something, and she doesn't even dye the grey in her hair. For the life of me, I can't figure out the attraction, I mean, after having me!" Fizz stops in her tracks to illustrate her obvious assets to her niece. "After all *this*, how could he sleep with that old ..."

The litany goes on and on, anger flowing into fury; indignation melding into threats of destruction to all parties involved in this terrible betrayal of her trust... and on and on.

Fizz makes a face. "She must be rich. Money up the ying-yang, I bet." Dramatically she stretches up her neck, reaching her nose skyward. "Inherited it from some rich uncle, no doubt. Reeled that slime ball Simon in like a red snapper." She stops for a moment to catch her breath. "Hope she robs him blind. And takes all those damn stupid carpets with her ha ha." She glares meaningfully at the girls. "When I think of all the time I wasted on that pony-tailed slime ball, when I could have been a star! Well, it's just too ..."

Bessie stares off into the darkened woods, oblivious to both the whining of her aunt and the wailings of Sister Rainbow Sunshine.

Wait, is that shadow over there moving?

CHAPTER 80: EARTH

Heather MacIntyre and Sophia Moreno sit side by side on a wooden bench in Ravenspond's town park where their daughters' belongings were found in the grocery cart of a homeless woman, what seems like a lifetime ago.

"There she is." Heather motions to a tall, outdoorsy woman approaching in shorts and a sleeveless blouse.

"Can't stay long," Jason's mother says as she takes a seat at one end. "The kids are a handful when it's just their father at home. They know how to get around him." Her smile is tentative. "So what did you want to see me about?"

Heather takes the lead. "Oh, just to compare notes, Jane. Nothing specific, really. It's just that we all know our kids better than the police do."

They get distracted for a few minutes as a young collie pup, dragging his owner-less leash, runs in circles. A laughing toddler chases the dog. From nearby, a harried mother, with a sleeping baby in a stroller, yells out, "Brucie, you get back here right this very minute!"

The youngster ignores her as he and the pup go round and round. A teenage boy calls out, "Ruffy, come here, boy, Ruff!" He trots over to his dog. Idly he picks up the leash before yanking his pet in another direction.

The young child stops running, all disappointed. He takes off in tears towards his mother. She picks him up and comforts him. "Never mind, my sweetheart. One day daddy will get you and your sister your very own doggy when you're big enough."

All three women on the bench smile. Heather's voice is soft. "Reminds me of our two at that age, doesn't it, Sophia? Chasing poor Mouser around all the time."

"Oh, they were a pair alright," Sophia agrees. "Always getting into mischief of one sort or another. I remember that first time when they splashed us in that kiddy pool, the little devils. Remember that day?"

"It was Bessie's third birthday. She got the swing-set and the puppy."

"So, so you think they're okay, don't you?" Jane Wallet breaks into their reverie. "I mean, Jason is looking after them, I'm sure. He's such a responsible boy."

The other two look over at her, holding her purse too tightly in her lap. Jason's mother continues, "I know he and Bessie were on the outs for the past few months, growing pains I call it, but my lad loves her with all his heart. You know, he's planning on them marrying one day, did you know that?"

Sophia, who is closest, reaches over to pat the tall woman's hand. "They've been a pair ever since they first met, haven't they? Nice boy. Real nice boy."

"I'm sure they're alright." Jane turns to look at them. "I phoned that detective, just before I came to meet you. Told him my son called today right after lunch, it was. Said he'd lost the girls for awhile, but found them again. He called from some gas station halfway across the country, way the heck from here. They were in the back of some old truck of migrant workers, singing apparently. Said they looked like they were having a whale of a good time."

For the first time in ages, Heather and Sophia break into hopeful smiles.

CHAPTER 81: HEAVEN

Bessie sits on the edge of the cliff, dangling her legs over the edge, the Sacred Telescope a small distance away. There appears to be a line-up for it tonight, something about a strange triple rainbow in the night sky. She's all alone except for Mouser, snuggled in beside her.

About a hundred yards away from her, a man with longish hair, glasses and a guitar sits down, also dangling his legs over the edge. He doesn't notice her, occupied in tuning his instrument. When he begins to sing, Bessie is mesmerized with the lonely beauty of it.

In a tender, soulful melody, his voice fills with a love song to the glory of nature - nights in the forest, mountains in springtime, and walks in the rain.

Bessie leans back and lies on the ground, cradling her head in her bent arms, as the exquisite music fills the air.

The haunting voice is almost worshipful about storms in deserts and sleepy blue oceans. How they fill up his soul.

Unaware of Jason hidden in the shadows, Bessie begins to sing along to the well-known song. She remembers it so strongly. It's one of her mother's favorites. Often on a summer evening when her daughters were asleep, and her husband was watching TV, Heather would turn on her little CD player on the picnic table in the backyard. With a glass of wine in her hand, she would sing along to the tunes, not knowing Bessie was lying in her bed accompanying her as the soothing sounds drifted in her window above. Bessie's eyes tear up at the memory and she snuggles into Mouser for comfort.

Jason joins in, ever so softly, his eyes filling with tears. In halting, wistful notes, he lets the lyrics carry him away to another time in another life when love was young and full of hope.

The man with the guitar continues his song, calling to his sweetheart to stay with him, sharing in love forever.

Totally unaware of each other, all three are lost in their own thoughts, as they sing along to the guitar.

Eventually the musician puts his instrument down beside him to gaze into the wondrous starlit sky. His blonde-streaked hair is tousled. His round, wire-rimmed glasses frame boyish features. He glances over to discover Bessie watching him and he waves. His smile is pure John Denver.

She waves back before turning her attention skyward. All three of them crane their necks to gaze at the streak of a falling star.

CHAPTER 82: EARTH

Eric Pederssen's green Mazda, rented at the airport an hour before, screeches to a halt on the dusty, packed dirt driveway of the Mavis & Jim Dew Drop Inn. The opera *Don Giovanni* plays full blast on his stereo. He listens to it for a few more minutes before switching it off, almost reluctant to go in. Reaching for his briefcase on the passenger seat, he opens it to pull out the various photos of the missing teenagers - Bessie Macintyre, Ashley Moreno, and Jason Wallet. Stuffing a small notepad into his jacket pocket, he opens the door to stretch out his cramped limbs and get out.

On his way in, he glances curiously at the brown, junkyard Oldsmobile sedan parked alongside the diner, almost out of sight. He goes over to look inside, trying the door handle. It's unlocked. A knapsack in the backseat reveals male clothing - a pair of jeans, some tee-shirts, underwear, and minimal toiletries. He spots a photo and picks it up. It's Jason and Bessie obviously taken a few years ago. They are standing, grinning ear-to-ear, in a barn beside a newly born calf. No need to worry about fingerprints on the vehicle. He slips the picture into a plastic bag, walking over and tossing it into his rental car.

The screen door creaks open. A plump woman behind the counter turns to look at him, a coffee pot in hand, as she pours for a customer seated on a stool in front of her.

Eric takes a seat further down.

"Coffee?" Mavis says automatically and he nods his head yes. The brew is surprisingly good in this rural, nowhere place. Gazing around, he notices only one other person, a young man in tight black jeans and a white tee-shirt, chatting on the phone attached to the back wall. The man hangs up, shouting a see-you-later-Mavis as he saunters past behind Eric's back, inches away, on his way out the door.

"See ya, Terry," the woman says without looking up while she lifts the dome from the slices of pie to serve an elderly man reading the newspaper.

Eric waits. After all, there's no reason to rush her. Or alert her. He orders a slice of blueberry pie. It's wonderfully fresh and tasty which he communicates to the woman.

She treats the stranger to a sunny smile. "Make 'em all myself. Even picked the berries for that one. Rest of the fruit comes from my daughter's farm down the road."

Eric pulls out his bag of photographs. "These three teenagers were in here very recently. You remember them?" He lays them carefully on the counter like a poker hand, facing towards her.

"Two coffees and two ChocOnut bars. Sure, I do." The stranger's puzzled face prompts her to add, "That's what they ordered, the two girls. Said they were secretaries on vacation from New York City." Her laugh is throaty from cigarettes. "And the lad there, with the funny hair, he comes in after, had an argument of some sort with the redheaded girl. Both girls, they left with Terry."

Eric's spine stiffens as if he had been struck with lightening. The little hairs on the back of his neck stand up. "Terry? The young man who was just here?"

"Yeah, that Terry. Give 'em a lift into town. Said they wanted to catch the bus to California. Never saw the other one leave, that young man." She points to Jason's photo. He left his car here and everything. We're going to have it towed tomorrow."

"No. Don't." Eric's voice is sharp. "I'll have it picked up within the hour. Please do not go near it, or let anyone else go near it."

Mavis' face turns cloudy. "Something wrong?"

"These teens have run away from Ravenspond, Pennsylvania." He softens his voice. "Just having a bit of fun in the summer, most likely. But their parents are concerned. They took a ride with Terry?"

"Terry Blacksmith. He's a good kid. Family's been around hereabouts for, oh, at least a couple o' generations. He's my second cousin's son. You don't have to worry none 'bout him."

The elderly man at the counter lifts his head from his newspaper. "Tell him, Mavis."

Eric's ears perk up. "Tell me what?"

The woman is reluctant. "Well, I guess I should. Terry, he was in a bit of trouble awhile back. But ..." Her eyes bore into Eric's. "He's straightened himself up. Used to hang around with my daughter and her friends sometimes, so I know him pretty good."

"What kind of trouble?" Eric is going to find out, one way or another.

Mavis picks up a cloth to wipe down the countertop, stalling for time. "Oh, you know, a bit of this and that."

The man jumps in. "Armed robbery. And there was something about a young tourist girl."

Mavis grows angry now. "That were only a rumor, Ed, and you shouldn't be spreading gossip."

By the look of her face, Eric sees he's not going to get any more from her. He puts a ten-dollar bill on the counter and stands up. "We'll pick up the abandoned car within an hour. Thank you for your time and your information."

As he passes the old man, the gentleman swings around on his stool to speak under his breath. "Two summers ago last August. Name was Penny Marshall."

"Thanks," Eric mutters, heading out the screen door. In the driveway, he dials his phone. "Need a tow for a suspicious vehicle right away. Like now."

CHAPTER 83: HEAVEN

Two men of similar height and build walk along a path in the woods. By the back of their sticking-up hair, Jason is one of them, his uncle Peter the other.

It's a lovely quiet dawn, barely light out. Birds are twittering and small creatures scamper here and there. They find a log to sit on. Peter passes his nephew a Hector's Nectar before he opens his own.

"Got to stop blaming yourself, Jas," he says. "What's done is done and you can't undo it."

"I know that. Only too well." There's a catch in the young man's voice. "If only I could. Live it all over again, maybe it would have—"

"Hush, now, lad. You will find your peace with it when it's—"

"Time, I know, Uncle Pete. So the angels keep telling me."

They don't speak for awhile, content to soak up the awe-inspiring view. The older man takes a bag of cookies from his pocket, nudging Jason's arm, holding out the little container. "Home-made," he says. "Made them myself last night."

"Thanks." Jason takes one and begins to nibble.

"At some point you're going to have to tell me what happened."

Jason's eyes fill with pain. "But just not yet. I'm not ready yet."

His uncle puts an arm around him as unbidden sobs escape the younger man's lips. Leaning his head on Peter's shoulder, Jason weeps and weeps, and weeps some more.

CHAPTER 84: EARTH

Eric Pederssen rubs his eyes, glancing up at the clock on the police station wall. It reads 2:33 A.M. On the desktop of the computer resting on the table he sits at, a grainy photo of Penny Marshall smiles out at him. He sips his cold tea before returning to the task at hand.

Penny Marshall from Atlanta, Georgia, was thirteen years old when she went camping with her younger brother and her parents about two miles south of the Mavis & Jim's Dew Drop Inn at a well-known campground. According to the report, she went for a walk by herself one evening, telling her parents she just wanted to go to a nearby shop to get herself some gum. Her mother later said she wondered why Penny was all dolled up, wearing her best shorts and lipstick. She had questioned her daughter, but she had just given her a stare and said she was bored. Her mother had shrugged it off as the behavior of a young teenager on the verge of womanhood. It was still light out when the girl set off. The rest of the family was busy watching a movie on their DVD player.

By midnight, when she hadn't returned, her parents went searching for her on foot for about an hour, then drove around in a three-mile radius. The next day, they called the police. As the young girl by her parents' admission had left voluntarily, nothing could or would be done for a minimum of forty-eight hours.

By then, Penny's family was frantic. She had not contacted anyone by cell phone which was highly unusual. Finally the police agreed to look for her.

The search was extensive. Within a week, troopers from all over the state came to assist law enforcement, along with volunteers from the nearby communities. They searched every field, every creek and river, every hotel room, every restaurant, every empty shack - anywhere a young lost girl might go for shelter. Nothing. Not even a sighting.

It wasn't until two weeks later she was discovered, wandering about ten miles away up in the surrounding hillsides, in dense bush — dehydrated, incoherent, and with her clothes dirty and torn. A medical examination indicated she had had sexual intercourse, likely against her will; it was impossible to determine after this amount of time had passed. Her brother revealed that Penny had been flirting with an older guy who hung around the little store sometimes. His description matched that of a local fellow, Terry Blacksmith. Although Terry had been brought in for questioning, no evidence, other than Penny's fingerprints in his truck, was found. He explained he had given the teenage girl several rides a few weeks previously when she had been staying at the campground. She had a crush on him, the young man had told the police. He had looked at them with a smile. Yeah, so he had flirted with her a bit, just for laughs, he had expanded with a chuckle. A bit of harmless summer fun. Surely the police were familiar with harmless summer fun? Penny herself refused to talk. As her parents declined to press charges, the matter was dropped.

CHAPTER 85: HEAVEN

"Let's do something different this time," Ash suggests as she and Bessie stand outside an accessory shop in the Seventh Heaven mall, waiting for Fiona to make up her mind between two scarves.

"Like what?" Bessie munches on a chip from her bag of NecNac Snaks.

"I don't know, like, maybe let's pick unknowns."

"Instead of famous people?"

"Why not? Here she comes." A happy Fiona approaches, wearing a new tie-dyed, green and gold scarf draped around her neck.

"Am I glam, gal friends?" She twirls the ends in the air with her fingers.

"You're movie star glam," Ash agrees. "Let's go bug the Soulslady."

Soon they're in Bodysuits Boutique, drifting back and forth among the endless images of now reincarnated souls. The sales clerk eyes them sourly from the other side of her store, surrounded by a group of newcomers, eager to learn the true meaning of her merchandise.

"We're picking from the great unknowns today," Bessie informs her aunt.

"How is that fun?" Fiona is not remotely impressed. "How can you imitate someone you've never even heard of?"

"I guess we'll find out. Here's one." Ash holds up the bodysuit of a young lady, possibly from New York or Chicago, circa 1920s, judging by her mode of dress.

Bessie finds one remarkably similar, striking them both as rather fun. Fiona, meanwhile, decides against choosing an unknown body image, reaching for Greta Garbo instead. A role, she insists, she was born to play.

Quickly they disappear into the tiny change-room, only to reappear ten minutes later, transformed into two flappers, and one of the most remarkable movie beauties of all time.

"Ah vant to be alun." Fiona/Garbo drags on her unlit cigarette. Dressed in a black tight-fitting suit with matching cloche hat, she sashays into the showroom in a sort of slow waltz, closely followed by two pretty but garish, young women. Their hairstyles are wavy and bobbed, their lips scarlet, and their eyes lined in smoky makeup. They flounce in, wearing low-waisted mini-dresses, doing a lively jive, holding hands and giggling.

It's not long before Soulslady makes her presence known. Her anger is volcanic. "How dare you?" She shouts at the young pair. "How dare you make fun of them?"

Bessie and Ash ignore her, as usual, for awhile until they hear, "Have you any idea of who they were?"

Deflated somewhat, the flappers slow down their dance. The scrawny woman gets between them, shaking her finger from one face to the other. "You're wearing Felicity Marrs and Rhonda Fairweather."

"And who might they be?" Ash tosses over her shoulder.

"Victims!" Soulslady shouts.

"Victims of what?" Bessie takes the bait. "Loud music?"

Ash contributes, "Too many rum cocktails?"

"Too many foxtrots?" Bessie heaps on the pile of possibilities.

"Harassment from sales ladies?"

The elderly clerk's voice turns into a growl. "Victims. Of violence."

This stops the girls dead in their tracks. Their features fill with unknown dread.

"How … how did they die?" Bessie reaches up to touch her scar, her fingers trembling.

Soulslady's eyes dart from one flapper to the other. "It's not my place to tell you that. All I can say is, these poor girls never had a chance. Cut down horribly in the prime of their young lives."

Bessie can feel a lump in her throat. Her stomach turns queasy. Her limbs feel wobbly. Words slip out of her mouth. "I … ah, I don't know how I died."

Soulslady doesn't relent. "Then you shouldn't make fun of others who died, and died …" She leans in for effect and spits out, "Tragically."

Without being asked, Bessie and Ash rush to the change-room to remove their bodysuits. A solemn Fiona/Garbo watches for a moment before following them.

Somehow this game has lost its sparkle.

As the three of them somberly exit the boutique, Soulslady hisses at Bessie as she passes by, "Never, never take a ride from a handsome stranger."

CHAPTER 86: HEAVEN

A restless Bessie slumps sideways across Angel Mel's armchair in his office. Her bright blue running shoes, one of his generous gifts from the city of Celestia, jerk up and down, up and down. The angel stares out the window with his binoculars while Mouser observes. "Rachel tells me she spotted Paul Newman the other day telling jokes to Steve McQueen. Cool, don't you think? Two of the hottest stars Hollywood has ever seen?"

Bessie doesn't answer. Her thoughts are elsewhere. "What happened to Felicity Marrs and Rhonda Fairweather?"

"You know about them?" He doesn't turn around. "How did you hear about poor Felicity and Rhonda?"

"Bodysuits Boutique. We tried them on. Soulslady went ballistic."

He puts down his binoculars to look at her. "I shouldn't wonder. She doesn't allow anyone to make light of tragic deaths. Especially when ..." He stops himself.

"Especially when what?" She never misses a beat.

"Hey, Bessie, there's Johnny Carson, the king of talk show hosts. That's no easy feat, my girl. I mean, it looks easy, but it's probably the most difficult job of all, dealing with all those inflated egos, and insecurities, and over-indulgent personali—"

"Especially when what?" Bessie insists, getting up to go over to the window, picking up the spare binoculars from the desk on her way.

"He's greeting someone. Oh, wow, that's his old sidekick, Ed McMahon. Well, I'll be a monkey's uncle."

Bessie can't resist. "Chimpanzee or gorilla?"

He sucks in his belly. "Think I'm more of a debonair, chimp-about-town type. They're walking towards someone. Look, Ed's gesturing over there, towards the hedge."

"Where?" Bessie's binoculars dart back and forth. "Oh, yeah, I see him. It's that Welsh guy. Used to be married to Liz Taylor."

"Richard Burton? 'The' Richard Burton? Get out." Angel Mel's enthusiasm is infectious. "Last week I saw Sir Lawrence Olivier."

"Who's he?"

"Only the most incredible British actor of all time, my little mushroom. Mostly Shakespearean plays, but I adore him in Alfred Hitchcock's *Rebecca*. Did you know he was married to Vivien Leigh?"

"*Gone with the Wind*?"

"Good girl. You know your old movies."

"Got a good teacher."

In the foreground of their view, a hulking Richard Burton sways back and forth, a bottle in his hand. Bessie comments, "Looks sauced."

"Most likely is. Or rather, he feels like he is. Alcohol has no effect in Heaven, you do realize. It's only the memory of it that makes him feel drunk."

"I know. Grandma explained that to me about grandpa."

"Your whiskey swilling auntie doesn't realize that yet, though, does she?"

"Nope. She still gets hangovers ha ha."

"A source of great amusement to you, no doubt."

It seems the fate of Felicity and Rhonda is forgotten. For now.

CHAPTER 87: EARTH

"Lee-Lee?" The overhead light in Leila Macintyre's bedroom blinks on. Through the window, dawn is just breaking.

"Mom?" The young girl sits up in bed, rubbing her eyes. An open copy of P.T. Mitchell's *A Zest for Death* lies on her pillow. "What's up? They find Bessie and Ash?"

"Nooo ..." Her mother's voice is coy. "But someone found this."

A whimpering sound brings Leila to full attention as her father plops a plump, black and white puppy on the bedspread. "Her name is Mutt," he chuckles. "But you can call her whatever you want."

"Where did you get her?" Leila looks up at them for a moment where they are standing in her doorway, leaning on each other.

"Ash's mom," Heather says. "Apparently it was found wandering last night near one of her empty houses. Very hungry and no tags."

Quickly the girl picks up the wiggly, soft body and hugs it in her arms. "Oh, how sweet! Can I keep her? Maybe I'll call you Miss Marple," she tells the dog. "After Agatha Christie's detective." Miss Marple gives a little bark-bark-bark before taking a pee on the quilt.

"Whoa." Art jumps up to retrieve the dog. "Miss Marple needs a little walk."

It's the first time the three of them have laughed together since Bessie and Ash went missing.

CHAPTER 88: HEAVEN

As Bessie strolls up the pathway to the Dodd family cottage, Mouser bounds out the open door to greet her. She crouches down to wrap her arms around his silky fur, feeling tears welling in her eyes. "I had another bad dream last night, Mouser," she explains. Finally she stands up. Together they head towards the garden where Fiona weeds the roses.

"You're becoming very domestic," Bessie teases, sticking her nose into a fragrant bloom. "Grandma would be so proud."

"I know. Maybe in my next life I'll be a gardener." Peach the cat rubs against her ankles. "Like a reality-star gardener, of course." She poses, one gloved hand on a hip, the other tilting back her straw hat. "What's up?"

"Oh, had a bad dream again last night."

"You've been having those a lot, lately." She holds a bloom to her nose, her eyes closed, lost in the fragrance.

"It's this guy. He's handsome in a baby-face sort of way. With intense blue eyes. Very muscled. His face is all smiley and flirty, then it twists and turns all hideous and evil. And I wake up in a panic."

Fiona's smile vanishes from her features as if she's been slapped. She can feel a cold sweat break out on her neck. "I think you should tell Angel Mel. Right away."

"You think he's … ?"

"Oh, I'm probably over-reacting as usual. Likely just a bad dream, like you said." She picks up her shears and chops vigorously at the poor rose bush.

CHAPTER 89: EARTH

There are no niceties this time when Eric Pederssen stands in front of the counter at the Mavis & Jim Dew Drop Inn. No welcoming cups of coffee, no offers of pie. "Where is he?" His voice is flat.

Mavis turns to look at a huge man busting out of his plaid shirt, standing at the cash about ten feet away. "Haven't seen him. Ask Jim if you don't believe me. Where's Terry?" she shouts too loudly.

"Left town," Jim mutters. "Said something about maybe a job coming up in Colorado."

"Left town after you warned him I was looking for him." No one looks at Eric, not even the scattering of customers. "Two girls are missing, most likely in extreme danger, and you warn him off."

Mavis turns away to the coffee pot. Jim picks up his plate of pie to take over to an empty booth. Glaring around the diner, Eric holds up photos of Bessie, Ashley, and Jason he takes from his briefcase. "Anyone who has any information about these missing teens, call the police hotline. At once. You don't have to give your name or number." Without asking, he takes out clear tape and sticks the photos to the window.

No one speaks until finally the detective heads for the exit. "Thank you for all your cooperation." His voice drips sarcasm as he slams out the screen door.

Mavis and Jim share a look, but say nothing. She comes out from behind the counter to watch the rental car, with the detective in it, scream out of the driveway in a cloud of dust. Quickly she heads for the pay phone at the back of the diner.

CHAPTER 90: HEAVEN

"Now I'm more afraid of this guy with the blue eyes than I am of Jason." Bessie is full of frustration as she strolls beside Angel Mel and Mouser along the cliff on their way to the Sacred Telescope. "I don't care anymore how awful it was when I died. I just want to know the truth. Get it over with."

"Good evening, Angel Rainbow Sunshine." Angel Mel is ever so polite to the singing angel as they stop for a brief chat. "And how was your vacation on the coast?"

"Oh, just heavenly, Angel Mel." She beams with delight as she attempts to tune her guitar. "Learned a whole bunch of new songs, too. Want to hear some?"

He quickens his step, taking Bessie by the elbow. She whistles to Mouser sniffing noses with the St. Bernard. Angel Mel adds, "Another time, perhaps. I'm sure they are quite delightful." Whispering into Bessie's ear, he urges, "Let's get the hell out of here on the double." Over his shoulder he calls out, "See you later. Good luck with your new repertoire."

Soon they approach the Sacred Telescope. As Bessie unscrews the lens cap, she can't resist. "Tsk, tsk, Mel. You used the 'h' word?"

"It's only an expression," he puffs. "And whatever you do, for God's sakes, don't repeat that to Angel Rachel."

Bessie chuckles under her breath as the milky swirls begin to clear.

Outside in the parking lot of the Mavis & Jim Dew Drop Inn, Bessie and Ash are hanging alongside the red pickup. Bessie is yakking a mile a minute, still pissed off that Jason has shown up out of the blue. Finally she takes a deep breath before adding, "Should we call our parents before we leave?"

Ash shakes her head. "Maybe after we get there. The bus trip won't take long. We're in so much hot water now anyways."

Bessie giggles. "We'll be grounded for the entire year. I need to use the bathroom before we take off." They head inside.

Moments later Jason rushes out. Climbing into his vehicle, he turns on the ignition, but it won't start. He tries and tries. It's as dead as a junker in a scrap yard which is where it should have been long ago. Looking about in desperation, he sees no one else around. Running full-tilt, he jumps into the bed of the red truck, pulling the tarpaulin over him. His head peeks out for a minute before disappearing again under the tarp. And moments before Zac Frontenac-hot emerges from the diner.

The alluring stranger climbs into the driver's seat, leaning over to open the passenger door, as the tee-heeing of teenage girls drifts from the screen door. Ash climbs in with some difficulty in her platforms with a push from Bessie who deftly hops in after her.

"Name's Harry," Terry lies easily, putting the truck into gear. "Harry Mercer. And you are?"

As the vehicle moseys down the dusty road, one of his front seat passenger babbles, "I'm Ash and she's Bessie. We're secretaries—"

"From New York on vacation. Yeah, you told me. So, you like living in the city that never sleeps?"

"The what?" Ash is confused until Bessie hisses in her ear. "He means New York."

Her smile is bright. "Oh yes, we adore living there. We share an apartment … downtown. And we work at the same … company."

He drives one-handed. The index finger on his right hand is lightly stained with nicotine. An odd silver ring with a skull in the centre almost covers his little finger. His knuckles are bony and his nails cut straight across. A small scar, like a slash of a knife, runs across from his thumb to his wrist. He realizes Ash is staring at it apprehensively, and he turns to look at her with a steady gaze. "Mind if I smoke?"

"Not at all," Ash replies. "We don't mind, do we, Bess. We're used to smokers at our … office."

"No, I guess I don't mind." Bessie leans back into her seat. She stares out the window at the scruffy scenery. It's as if the trees and bushes have given up trying to grow, waiting to collapse back down onto the dry dirt.

He lights up some weird smelling cigarette. "So what kind of office do you pretty ladies work in?" he inquires politely, blowing smoke out his open window.

Ash's eyes go wide before inspiration hits her. "A travel office. Agency, I mean. That's why we like to travel." She wrinkles up her nose from the smoky odor.

"Travel agents. My, my, my." He grins at Ash for a minute.

"What kind of cigarette is that, anyways? Bessie turns to ask him. "Smells pretty strong."

"It's imported from France. That's what they all smoke over there," he replies, taking a big drag. They ride along the highway for awhile without conversation. The man they know as Harry fiddles with the old radio until he finds a clear station. Some gravel-voiced country and western singer starts bellowing on about being stuck in prison for playing with guns and killing someone - just to watch them die.

Bessie turns to watch the driver out of the corner of her eye. There's something about him that's just not right. Is it his voice? His eyes? She can feel a vibration coming from him that doesn't match the man she's looking at. Is she imagining it? Probably. She turns to gaze out the window.

For some inexplicable reason, Harry bursts into gales of laughter. Ash and Bessie look over at him, frowning in confusion.

Seeing their anxiety, he quickly explains with a smile. "Had a buddy who used to sing that song to attract women. Thought he sounded really good. Only every time he sang it, the girls, they just high-tailed it and run away. Thought he sounded just like Johnny, but he had a voice like a lawn-mower." He laughs some more.

Ash shrugs her shoulders, glancing at Bessie. She raises her eyebrows before turning to look out the window.

Without warning, Harry spins the wheel onto a rough road heading uphill.

"Is this a short cut?" There's no mistaking the fear in Ash's voice now.

In Heaven, Angel Mel catches Bessie as she trips and falls backwards in her rush to get away from the Sacred Telescope. He sinks to the ground to cradle her in his great arms, rocking her back and forth. "Almost time," he whispers to himself.

They remain there until her eyes open. Quickly she pulls herself away into an upright yoga position, legs crossed in front of her. "So," she says, trying to regain her dignity, watching Mouser and the St. Bernard run, stop and sniff. Run, stop and sniff. "So it's him then, he's the one, not Jason?"

"It's not for me to say. It's for you to uncover, my dear. But ..." He jumps to his feet, surprisingly agile for such a large angel. He grins. "Meanwhile, while you're doing you're uncovering thing, what do you say to you and me, just the two of us, taking in a movie at the Past Lives Theatre tonight? You know, hang out, as you young folks say."

Bessie grins back. "Sure, who's playing?"

He pulls her up by her hand. "Oh, you know, the usual. A tragic movie star, a soldier in the Middle East, a miracle worker, a politician, a queen. The usual riff-raff."

She giggles as he keeps on rambling on about the possibilities. "You don't have a clue what's playing tonight, do you, Mel?"

His eyes twinkle. "So is that a date?"

"Might as well," she responds. "Ash is out anyway with Miguelito the magical."

"Well, don't hold back on your enthusiasm."

"How's this? I would be most delighted to accompany you this evening."

"That's better."

CHAPTER 91: EARTH

It's late in the evening when Eric Pederssen climbs into his BMW in the airport parking lot outside Ravenspond. He checks his phone messages before dialing the police station. "Any calls, Derek?" He starts his car, driving with one hand around and around the parking lot levels until he reaches the exit, handing the fare-taker his ticket plus a twenty dollar bill. "Keep the change," Eric tells him, much to the young man's surprise. "But I need a receipt, just for the actual amount."

As the smiling fellow hands it to him, Eric listens intently to his phone. "What time did this call come in?"

He pulls out onto the ramp road towards the freeway. "That's right after I left the diner. Did he give a name?" Seeing a gas station, he pulls off to finish his call, cutting the engine and taking out his notepad. He repeats his phone message out loud, "No name but he says he spoke to me at the diner and his voice sounds like an older person. I remember him. He's the old guy who filled me in on the background of this bastard. And his connection to Penny Marshall."

He scribbles furiously for about five minutes. "Derek, you're an angel, I swear." Tossing his phone onto the passenger side, he lets out a whoop. "Thank you whoever-you-are for giving a shit! And the best break I've had since this fucking nightmare case began!"

He reaches over to his stereo, turning it up full blast to Puccini's *La Bohème* before screaming out of the gas station.

CHAPTER 92: HEAVEN

"I prefer the hot pink myself." Fiona lounges on the Dodd cottage sofa, sipping on a Hector's Nectar which she has doctored up with a little whiskey. It seems she has discovered her father's handwritten recipe pinned to the inside of a drawer in his dresser.

"Powder blue, I say the blue." Bessie stands in the open kitchen area as they stare at Ash twirling in her new sparkling high heels from Celestia, in one outfit after another. "What's so important about this date anyways?"

"We're going to this romantic outdoor Spanish bistro where they have, like, a single red rose on a white linen table cloth and—"

"You're going to dance under the stars listening to the strains of a lone violin. Pardon me while I puke." Bessie mimes putting a finger down her throat. "You guys are getting so icky."

"No, we're not icky at all." Ash stops in her dance to pose like a supermodel. "We're getting engaged."

"Engaged?" Fiona gives Bessie a look. "But you're only fifteen!"

"In Heaven we're ageless, right, Bess?" Ash readjusts her pose. "Besides, there is no time here, as Angel Mel keeps saying."

"So you're getting engaged so when you reincarnate you—"

Ash cuts her off. "We'll already be sworn to each other. Isn't that, like, so romantic?"

Bessie grabs her Hector's Nectar. "If you say so, but do you really want to be tied to someone right off the bat? I mean, just look at what happened to me and Jas ..." She drops her thought like a hot potato. Draining her drink in a single gulp, she bolts to the door closely followed by Mouser. "Almost forgot, Fizz. Meeting up with Mel. Going to the movies. Have fun, you two, whatever." She disappears down the hillside as the two others watch in silence.

"Will she ever find out what really happened to her?" Fiona addresses the air more than her companion.

Ash gives her a blank look.

———

Angel Mel watches Bessie approach, her second pair of new running shoes from Celestia - these ones in neon lemon - shining in the twilight. When she closes the gap between them on the road, he says, "Thought we might stroll the rest of the way to the mall together, being as it's such a lovely evening."

Her fingers fiddle with her shamrock broach. "So what are we going to see, have you decided? Some old movie star from the olden days? Please don't let it be in black and white."

He takes her hand. "It's a surprise."

They stroll without speaking, content to soak in the balmy evening atmosphere. There's no one else around except an unseen young man with sticking-up hair lurking in the woods.

Now they enter the bustling parking lot outside the Seventh Heaven mall. Vehicles of various shapes and sizes come and go. Couples chatter and giggle. An old man is having a serious conversation with a woman of his own vintage. Perhaps his wife from his former life?

Bessie turns to head to the far end of the mall where the movie theatre entrance is located, but Angel Mel stops her. "Ours is a midnight special. Come on, let's pass the time window-shopping while we wait."

Bessie looks up at him curiously before complying. "Let me guess. We're going to Bodysuits Boutique?"

"Not exactly." He smiles. "At least not in the way you rascals do. Poor woman."

He guides her around to the back of the mall where the rear entrance of Bodysuits is situated. "Here we are," he says triumphantly. "You're going to get a behind-the-scenes look."

As they approach, the back door swings wide open. Just outside of it, Soulslady materializes out of thin air with her endless rack of new images from a recent rein-carnation flight. Two angelic assistants also appear in crisp, white outfits. Without hesitation, the three of them begin to gently carry six body images at the time over their arms, disappearing into the store. They repeat this operation over and over again until the rack is empty.

"But how do they fit them all into that tiny little shop?" Bessie's eyes are glued to the back door, still ajar. "What do they do with the ones already in there?"

"You see how little you know, my little mushroom?" Angel Mel pats her head. "Watch and learn." He heads towards the entrance, taking her by the elbow. "Shall we?" For no reason at all, he reaches up his left hand and shakes it all about. Bessie eyes him curiously, but she is too caught up with the goings on to ask.

A curious procession of an angel in a gaudy shirt, a redheaded girl in glowing sneakers, and a golden retriever enter Bodysuits Boutique seemingly unnoticed. Angel Mel explains, "I just doused us with disappearing dust."

"Ah, so that's what the weird hand thing was all about. So they can't see us?"

"Not at all. Well, they could if they were paying attention. But they're not."

She grins up at him. "Cool."

As the invisible trespassers observe, Soulslady and her assistants move so swiftly they seem to be in speeded-up time. You can see them here, see them there, but you can't see them move from here to there. The existing bodysuits on the racks lift off their hangers by themselves and drift up into the air, making room for the new ones. At the same time, Bessie notices to her great astonishment, another room is forming within the store before her very eyes. The old body images float through a newly created entranceway into the next room and settle on endless rows of empty hangers.

Dashing through to take a closer look, Bessie soon realizes that, behind that room, exists another room, and another, and another, in an endless chain of chambers. She runs through them, chased by a barking Mouser who is thoroughly enjoying this new game, until finally she slows down.

Angel Mel appears beside her. "So now you see why the shop looks so tiny on the outside?"

"But but ..." Her mouth refuses to form words. "But how ...?"

"We're in Heaven, silly. There are many dimensions here. Endless dimensions. These rooms just keep rotating around and around."

"So that's why we never seem to see the same bodysuits twice." Bessie finally finds her voice.

"The proverbial penny drops." He takes her hand and they are instantly transported into the interior hallway of the mall. Now back to their visible selves, they peer into the windows of the little shop. Nothing appears out of the ordinary. Astonishingly, it's business as usual. Soulslady chats to a middle-aged, portly gentleman. Several teenagers make a mess of the Used & Abused section, much to the diminutive clerk's irritation. The angelic assistants in their white gowns and the endless rooms are nowhere to be seen.

Angel Mel checks his watch. "Let's go get some snacks before the film starts." He leads Bessie across the corridor to the candy store full of open bins of colorful treats. "I just adore jelly beans, don't you?" It takes him forever to make up his mind.

"Just pick some, for heaven's sake," Bessie snaps, rolling her eyes.

"My, my, Little Miss Temper Tantrum, this evening." Angel Mel smiles at the salesman as he points to the cinnamon, the lemon, the watermelon, and the mocha-mocha. "I'll have a large bag of these four mixed together and two Hector's Nectars, please. Now Bessie, my patient companion, what will you have?"

She points to the caramel corn, giving him a smirk. "Lots of that, please."

Soon they are back outside in the balmy night air. The parking lot is empty of shoppers. A light breeze sways the fronds of the palms alongside the lot. The duo munch and stroll towards the movie theatre at the far end, trailed by the retriever.

Now reaching their destination, they stare up at the marquee. There is only one movie playing: THE LIFE AND TIMES OF BESSIE MILLICENT MACINTYRE.

CHAPTER 93: EARTH

Eric Pederssen doesn't waste a moment, climbing up the exterior fire escape two steps at a time. Below him in the moonlight of the deserted side street, a police car lies in wait, lights off. Walking swiftly towards the front of the four-storey, rundown apartment building, a uniformed officer enters. Several more scurry around outside the building, weapons drawn.

Flattening himself against the wall above the fire escape behind a back door on the fourth floor, Eric waits. It's three A.M. in the morning, the time most people are asleep. At least that's the plan. He can hear his breathing, in and out, in and out, every muscle coiled and ready. A drunk wanders along the street below, oblivious, singing some pub song to himself and laughing at his own cleverness in the dark.

From the wrought iron landing where Eric stands, he hears through the open window, the officer hammer on the front door of the apartment, yelling, "Police! Open up." A scrambling follows. Things tumble to the floor. A woman hollers, "What the flaming hell? Who's there?" A dog begins barking.

The door leading to the fire escape flies open and a man in nothing but his white cotton briefs dashes outside. In a flash, his head is slammed into the brick wall by two fair skinned fists. In fact, it hits the exterior wall so hard, it lolls to one side, as if he's about to pass out.

"Terrance Blacksmith, you are under arrest in connection to the disappearance and suspicion of foul play in the matter of Bessie MacIntyre and Ashley Moreno, you son of a bitch."

CHAPTER 94: HEAVEN

Bessie's jaw falls open and her eyes fill with fear as she stares up at the marquee announcing the single film of her life now playing at the Past Lives Theatre outside the Seventh Heaven Mall. Frantically she looks at the other two marquees, but they are empty. "Mel, I don't think I'm …"

Gently he crouches down in front of her before taking both her hands in his. "It will be alright, sweet girl, I promise you." Mouser snuggles in. "Besides, you have us with you, all the way."

"Think I need more time to—"

"Remember what I told you? It's only a movie. Like when Matt Damon gets blown up by terrorists or …"

"But that's just a movie-movie. This is a real life movie. This is *my* movie."

He tilts her chin to look directly into her eyes. "What's the big difference?"

She turns away, her trembling fingers reaching for her scar. "I know, I keep saying I want the truth. But now … maybe it's better that I never know."

"Everyone knows eventually, Bessie. And now it's time for you to know." He can hear her sudden intake of air as she stares at the starlit sky.

"You sure I'm ready, Mel?" She strokes her dog. "I have a knack for bluffing, as you know. Maybe I need to look into the Telescope a few more times or—"

"I wouldn't say you were ready if you weren't, Bessie. Trust me on this."

She wipes a tear from her cheek and gives him a weak smile. "Okay," she says finally. "Okay."

CHAPTER 95: EARTH

If there is only one word to describe Terry Blacksmith, it would be insolent. Those baby blue eyes fringed in long dark lashes dare the detective to make just one little mistake. Like throw the cup of coffee in his face. Give him a punch. Smash his fingers. Anything Terry can use to take control. From his smiling expression, the suspect appears to have no fear, none whatsoever. He looks around, aware that others are watching behind the two-way mirror. Chuckling, he waves at them. Police stations are evidently very familiar territory.

Eric does everything in his considerable power to maintain his calm exterior. Fortunately he's very good at it. "You dropped the two girls off near the bus station, you say, yet they never got on a bus. Nor were they seen by anyone at the bus station or on the surveillance footage from the bus station, inside and outside."

"Like I told you in the cruiser, officer, I dropped them off about a block or so before the station. I waved goodbye, they waved back. Hey, what would a guy like me want with a couple of teenies?"

"A teenie like Penny Marshall?" Eric's voice is flat.

For a micro moment, shock wipes the smile from Terry's features before it returns. "Aw, that was some kind of mistake. She was chasing me all over the darn place that summer, that little pixie. Why, you like 'em young, detective?"

Every muscle in Eric's body goes rigid. "We were talking about you, Mr. Blacksmith. Your preference for young ladies."

"Oh ho ho." The suspect bursts into guffaws. "That Penny, she wasn't what I would refer to as a lady." He winks towards the two-way glass. "She knew a trick or two. And what she didn't know, she was very eager to be taught, if you get my drift."

Remember your yoga breathing. Breathe from your abdomen. Breathe in, breathe out. Eric lets the silence drag on.

Terry slouches back in his seat, reaching for the cigarettes he's been allowed to smoke. He lights up an imported French Gitoine. "So these girls, you can't find them now, is that correct?" Tapping a fingernail, he points to the two photos on the table in front of him. "This one's Bessie, this one's Ashley, right? On our journey to the ..." He leans forward. "Bus station, they chattered on as to how they were secretaries from New York on vacation."

"At fifteen years of age?"

"Gosh, these young ladies are only fifteen? Why, they told me they were twenty-one." He shakes his head as if he and Eric were best buddies in a bar.

"Where did you go after you dropped them off at the ... bus station?"

"Oh, just around. Just general messing around. Summertime, you know. All the girls are prancing around in hardly nothing at all. You notice that?" He blows a perfect smoke ring. "I love summer."

The detective begins to doodle an airplane on a small writing pad. *Patience, Eric, patience. This guy loves to talk. Let him talk.* "That's a very small town. That couldn't have taken very long. So what did you do after that?"

Stubbing out his cigarette, Terry scoffs. "Oh well, a little this, a little that. Ran into my old gal buddy, Fran. We had a few beers. Woops, I guess I shouldn't admit to imbibing in alcohol, should I, officer, on account of I was driving a vehicle at the time."

Eric doesn't react. "And does Fran have a last name, Mr. Blacksmith?"

The young man chuckles easily. "You can call me Terry. I don't mind. Let's see now, Fran's last name. She's changed it a couple of times, Franny has. She has a thing for getting married at the drop of a hat. So, to tell you the honest truth, I'm not exactly sure what her name is now."

What I would give to smash your arrogant, pretty boy face right this very second. "Perhaps you can enlighten us as to where to find this Fran person."

"Oh, that's easy. She's always around the Lost Dog Tavern. That is, when she's in town. You see, she's not from around here." He shrugs with one hand in the air, palm upwards. "Nobody really knows where Fran comes from. That's the mystery. Do you like mysteries, officer?"

Breathe in. Breathe out.

CHAPTER 96: HEAVEN

It seems weird to her, walking through the empty lobby of the Past Lives Theatre. There's not a soul around, not even the usual popcorn lady. Bessie walks reluctantly as she holds tightly onto Angel Mel's hand, Mouser following closely behind. Too soon they are at the entrance to the theatre itself. The doors swing open of their own volition.

They begin to stroll down the navy carpet between all the endless, empty seats. In the middle of the theatre, Bessie hears an odd, creaking-popping sound and cranes her head to look.

Three seats have flopped down into position, dead centre of the middle row. Angel Mel smiles at her encouragingly and they make their way towards them. Mouser climbs onto the far one. Bessie takes the middle and Angel Mel on the other side of her. She lifts the arm rest so the anxious dog can lay his head on her lap.

With no fanfare, the crimson velvet curtains at the front of the stage swing open. The screen remains pitch dark while the following words appear, one by one: THE LIFE AND TIMES OF BESSIE MILLICENT MACINTYRE.

Bessie squeezes the angel's hand tightly. A sweet, giggling sound emanates from the screen as the scene lightens.

In a hospital room, a very young Heather MacIntyre lies in a frilly, powder blue robe in bed. Her husband, Art, with a full head of dark brown hair, sits on her starched, white bedspread. In his hands, he holds a ridiculously large bouquet of pink roses. A small, plain bassinet stands to the right of the bed. As the scene widens, a newborn baby with tufts of strawberry hair giggles and gurgles. Something or someone is making her laugh on this her first day on Earth.

The scene widens even further to include a middle-aged couple peering into the bassinet. The woman is noticeably taller than the man. He wears a dark suit and is reaching down to tickle the baby's nose.

"Oh, Will, will you look at her lovely smile." The woman wears baggy slacks and a plaid shirt. Her hair is curly and copper red, cascading onto her shoulders. On her generous bosom, a garish shamrock broach is pinned off-kilter. "Isn't she just the most darling little peach?"

Bessie, leaning into Angel Mel in the theatre, is filled with an overwhelming sense of wonder and joy. Her eyes pop wide and tears trickle down her cheeks. "Grandpa Will and Grandma Millie." She touches the shamrock pinned to her tee-shirt. "But how can this be?"

Angel Mel squeezes her hand. "She told you it was a magic broach, remember?"

CHAPTER 97: EARTH

An ashtray overflows with cigarette butts as Terry adds another one. "I know you don't need my fingerprints, officer, because you already have them on file, don't you now?" His smile is pure choir boy. "On account of that little incident with Penny Marshall. Oh, and that armed robbery I was mistakenly identified for."

Eric doesn't bother to answer the obvious. Although it is hour three of the interrogation, the detective looks as crisp as he did when it started. Only the bluish tone under his eyes gives him away. "One more time, Mr. Blacksmith. Tell me exactly where you dropped the girls off."

"Eric, may I call you Eric?"

"No." His voice could cut glass.

"Alright, officer, if you must, I will explain that detail one last time. I dropped the two girls off about one or two blocks south of the bus station." He pats his shirt pocket for his cigarette pack, pulling it out. It's empty. "Shit."

"Why didn't you drop them off right at the bus station?"

"Can you get me some more cigarettes?"

"No. Why didn't you drop them off at the bus station?"

Terry looks as if he's having to deal with a slow learning child. "They said something about wanting to buy some supplies for the trip. Magazines and girly stuff."

"So you dropped them off in front of a store? What store?"

Terry leans forward, both elbows on the table. "Okay, I'll be honest with you now. I wasn't really paying a whole lot of attention. On account of there was this babe. She was wearing practically nothing, sashaying down the sidewalk. I was totally captivated."

"You were captivated."

"I was. Practically swooning. Little teeny short-shorts and a bikini top. Black and white polka dots. Don't you just love summer?"

"So you don't know exactly where you dropped off your two passengers."

"I don't. Sorry." He runs one hand through his messy hair and treats everyone, in and out of the room, to an aw-shucks grin. "Good luck with finding those young ladies, though. As it doesn't appear you have any reason to keep me here, I assume I am free to go now?"

As Terry pushes back his chair, Eric's voice cuts through the air like a saber. "Sit. Down."

CHAPTER 98: HEAVEN

In the Past Lives Theatre, Bessie can feel herself relax into her seat as she gets caught up in the exquisite reliving of her younger years. Angel Mel turns towards her to share a smile. "Oh look, now the scene is changing to winter. You look about what, four now."

Bessie's attention is drawn back to the screen to the sound of her Grandma Millie's voice. And something else. The cry of another baby?

Her grandmother sits in a rocking chair, cuddling a blonde infant in her arms. On a footstool facing her, Grandpa Will dangles a teddy bear. Millie leans down to kiss the child's forehead. "Do you know you are named after your great-grandmother Leila in Ireland?"

In the cozy living-room, Art and Heather share the sofa. A much slimmer Jorge Moreno leans back in a comfy chair, with his wife, Sophia, perched on the arm. Bessie and Ash sit on a rug in the centre of the room, playing with their own babies, or rather their new, life-sized baby dolls.

"My new baby's name is Ashley," Bessie announces proudly.

"And my new baby's name is Ashley, too," Ash follows.

"You can't name your baby Ashley. My baby's name is Ashley." Bessie whacks her best friend's shoulder with her doll's head. "And anyways, that's your name."

Ash bangs Bessie back with her own doll. "Ashley, Ashley, Ashley."

The adults grin as they sip their Sunday afternoon cocktails. Outside the bay window, chunky snowflakes fall in a windless, grey sky. Art pipes up, "Why don't you both make up brand new names for your babies? Names that no one has ever heard of before. That way, no other baby will ever have the same name as your baby."

Heather laughs. "And we thought this was such a good idea, giving them their own infants to take care of."

The girls stop battering each other with their new dolls. Bessie speaks first, "I'm going to name my baby … Repicnac."

"Hmmm," Grandma Millie tries to say with a straight face. "Repicnac. What a lovely name."

"And it's a brand new name," Sophia adds diplomatically. "Nobody has ever had a name like Rep …" She can't say it. Instead she smothers her giggles with her hand.

"And my baby's name is …" All eyes are on Ash. Cocktail glasses are held suspended in mid-air. Not even the real baby in her grandmother's arms makes a sound.

Finally Ash speaks. "Woknok."

The room fills with hilarity. Noticing her young daughter's woeful expression, Sophia quickly begins to clap her hands. The others follow suit. "Welcome, Woknok. Very pretty name, sweetheart. Very pretty."

Bessie-in-the-theatre tugs on Angel Mel's shirt, her voice merry. "And our dolls were always called that, Mel. Repicnac and Woknok. Can you imagine?"

He ruffles her hair. "Only you two could have come up with those names." *If only he could stop the film.*

CHAPTER 99: EARTH

Eric Pederssen has left the interrogation room to confer with his fellow detectives. In particular he directs his comments to Leonora Cavish, the Chief of detectives who has just flown in from Ravenspond. More than anyone in the station, he trusts implicitly in her razor sharp intelligence. No one, except the two of them, is aware that they meet outside of work to listen to opera, among other pleasures.

"He's a slick piece of work," Leonora comments as they stare through the two-way window where Terry is pulling a cigarette from a regular American pack that has been brought in for him. "He hasn't asked for a lawyer yet. That's highly unusual."

"He's so arrogant he thinks asking for a lawyer would show weakness."

"We don't really have any evidence to hold him at this time, I'm afraid."

Eric stares at Leonora's flaxen bob. "I'm afraid, too."

She turns to look at him before staring back at Terry. "We'll get this little punk bastard, don't you worry." At the sound of a gruff male voice, Leonora turns to face a thin, middle-aged police officer who is in charge of this station.

They listen attentively as he speaks. "Okay, we're going to set Mr. Blacksmith free under 24-hour surveillance. And I mean surveillance. I want to know what kind of toothpaste he uses in the morning. Jeremy ..." He turns toward a stout, young man with glasses. "Find this Fran or Frances person. Veronica ..." He addresses a plain, olive-skinned woman. "I want to know everything about the female, Dallas Convey, who was in the apartment with him when he was arrested. Plus, his family, his associates, known and unknown. Eric ..." His eyes are no-nonsense. "Where is Terry's red pickup truck?"

CHAPTER 100: HEAVEN

Bessie reaches for more caramel corn only to realize it's all gone. Staring at the empty bag in the darkened theatre, a smile begins to play around the corners of her mouth as the container slowly refills to the brim all by itself, one kernel at a time. Giggling, she turns to Angel Mel. "Cool."

"Why, thank you. Well, would you take a boo at the two of you rascals." They turn their attention back to the screen as the sound of pelting rain fills the theatre.

Two young girls, who appear to be around the age of six, scamper down a wet sidewalk, holding hands. They wear the same style of raincoats with matching hats and rain boots, Ash in pink, Bessie in yellow. Their giggles are the only sounds that rise above the pounding of the spring shower. A young retriever races around them, dashing here and there. On a nearby front porch, three women and a man huddle, watching and laughing. Bessie recognizes her mother and Ash's, along with Grandma Millie and Grandpa Will.

Every time they come to a puddle, the little girls jump in with both feet, splashing the dog. The dog bolts, returning almost immediately.

"You see that, Mouser? That's you as a young pup." Bessie-in-the-theatre hugs him close. "We used to love to run in the rain." She turns to Angel Mel. "My grandma bought us those outfits from a catalogue. She was always doing neat stuff like that." She leans back to enjoy the show.

In the pouring rain, Bessie's unsuspecting father, appears from two homes down from his own. He's on foot, his head buried under a big black umbrella. Two little girls in raincoats share a conspiratorial glance before they hide behind an oak tree on the neighboring lawn. Just as Art approaches his own home, they fly through the air to land in a puddle right in front of him.

"You little devils," Art yells. "I'm going to get you for that!" The girls scream and run as Bessie's father chases them around and around the yard until all three of them fall down, laughing.

Bessie-in-the-theatre giggles, too. "Oh, I remember that day. Daddy had been out visiting his friend George who lived down the street. George was in a wheelchair so Dad always made sure he was okay if there was a storm or anything." She strokes Mouser as he watches her intently. "After we finally got up, we all went inside and had hot chocolate and oatmeal cookies." She turns to Angel Mel. "Thank you for this."

His eyes are soft. "You're very welcome, my dear."

If only every scene could be like this one.

CHAPTER 101: EARTH

Two days after the briefing at the police station, Eric drives aimlessly around the back streets of the small rural town in his latest rental car, a gold Ford Focus. It's somewhere between three and four in the morning. The usual pathetic human beings wander in the night - the homeless, the stoned, the lost, the hookers, and the seekers of hookers. He misses Leonora like crazy and wishes she was still with him, but she had to return right away to Ravenspond. Tragically, the bodies of a young black couple had been discovered behind a dumpster not far from the town park where Bessie and Ash had stashed their clothes beneath the wooden seat in the gazebo that early, steamy July morning.

Where in the hell is that damn red truck? Eric had questioned Terry again yesterday, this time at the home of his cousin, Cindy-Ann. It was less a home and more like a rundown shack, to be correct, with broken glass in the grimy windows, a step missing on the front porch, and weeds growing like they owned the place. Maybe they did.

Terry had sauntered outside Cindy-Ann's house as cool as a cucumber. Despite his poverty-line living quarters, his white tee-shirt was Clorox clean, and his black jeans ironed with a crease.

"Morning, detective," he had greeted Eric as he climbed out of his car. "Looks like rain." Terry gazed up at the sky for a moment. "Something I can help you with?"

Eric had cut to the chase. "Where's your red Ford pickup." It wasn't a question.

"Hmmm, now that's a puzzle." Terry had rubbed his chin with his hand. "You see, I lent it to this friend of mine, Dolby. He tells me he has this great interview in Las Vegas for a job, but like that ..." He snapped his fingers. "Doesn't his car go bust."

Eric's voice dripped sarcasm. "So being the wonderful friend that you are, naturally you gave him your vehicle to use."

"Correct. Sorry I forgot to ask him where he was staying or when he'll be back." His smile had beamed wide as he reached out to put an arm around his scrawny, washed-out cousin who had just wandered out the front door, looking like she needed a bath a week ago. "Isn't that right, Cindy-Ann?"

When Cindy-Ann had smiled, the detective could see the rot in her front teeth. She was probably only about nineteen, but looked twenty years older. Her thin hair hung in greasy strings. Her blouse was miles too large. Her cut-off jeans were tied in a knot with a man's tie. In her thin fingers, a cigarette dangled. Small scabs dotted her face and arms. Crystal meth was her god of choice; that fact was only too tragically obvious.

As Eric took out his notebook and pen, Terry had cheerfully offered up the information he knew he was going to be asked. "Dolby Campbell. Real name is Dolbert. Lives on Rural Route #4 in the white wood house with the chicken coop right beside it. Can't miss it because it's the only new house around. Sorry, don't have Dolby's phone number. We just hook up in town from time to time."

Eric had glanced from one cousin to the other. Without another word, the detective had climbed back into his gold car and driven off.

Now, as he cruises around in the middle of the night a day later, unable to sleep in his hotel, even though he had upgraded the room assigned to him to a better one, he watches a probable drug deal go down on an unlit corner. A man in a black hoodie stands too close to another man in a black hoodie. *Why do they always wear black hoodies? Do they really think they're in disguise?*

His CD ends and he slows down to insert another. Johannes Brahms *Lullaby for Cello and Piano* by Leandro. Music to soothe a troubled spirit.

We're coming to get you, Terrance Blacksmith. And when we do, we're going to wipe that smirk off your face so hard, you'll need surgery to get it back.

CHAPTER 102: HEAVEN

Angel Mel glances over at Bessie who seems content to munch absent-mindedly on her caramel popcorn in the Past Lives Theatre. Occasionally she feeds a kernel to the dog who chews it noisily. Seeing his companion is still enjoying the film of her life, the angel turns his attention back to the screen.

"Okay, now keep your feet and knees together. Now bend over … keep your head between your arms … tuck it in … That's not right, watch me." An eleven-year-old Jason in swimming trunks is demonstrating how to dive to his nine-year-old companion, Bessie. She is on the end of a wooden diving board, awkwardly standing with her arms over her head. A retriever dog runs up and down the board, barking. On the grass next to the pond, Jason demonstrates.

Bessie watches, assumes the position and attempts a dive. Instead she belly flops, coming back up sputtering and shouting. The dog goes crazy, running back and forth along the banks as Jason giggles, arms wound around his skinny waist.

Bessie pulls herself back on the bank, shouting, "That's not funny!" to the boy who flops down beside her.

"Can't help it," he sputters through laughter. "You just went … " He arcs one hand and bounces it against his other one, making a loud noise. "Splat!"

She punches him in the arm and he falls back, still giggling as the dog licks his face. Bessie jumps up to leave. He pulls her back with his hand. "Oh, come on, it's only your first dive."

She glares down at him as he attempts to prevent the dog's licks until she herself, bursts out laughing, falling backwards beside him.

In the theatre, Bessie bursts into giggles, too, watching them on the screen. "This isn't so bad, Mel. This is, actually, kind of cool. I forgot how much fun we used to have, me and Jas, at the farm."

"Ready for more?" He gazes carefully at her, squeezing her hand a little.

"Sure," she pipes up. "Why not?"

They both turn back to the screen, munching away on their treats.

"One-two-three … together. One-two-three … together. Not like that!" A twelve-year-old Bessie shouts in irritation at a fourteen-year-old Jason. They are in his barn, and through the open door, the weather appears to be mild, perhaps early spring.

She is attempting to teach him the basic waltz. Mouser dozes on a bale of hay, one eye open to a chicken that has wandered in. "Again, one-two-three … together, one-two-three … together. Oh, forget it." She stomps over to plunk herself beside the dog.

A gawky Jason stares at Bessie for awhile, then turns to head out, muttering under his breath, "Nothing I do seems to please you these days. Nothing at all."

As soon as he's gone, the young girl's remorse floods her serious features. "I'm so stupid. What's the matter with me, anyways?" She jumps up to run after him yelling, "Jas, I'm sorry. Jas, where are you?"

She finds him heading across the back field, a pail in one hand, a saucer in the other. Stopping for a moment, she can't help but admire his long, strong physique. His back and shoulders are those of a man now. His jeans above his rubber boots show off his lean butt. And as always, his hair sticks up in any direction it wants to.

She chases after him, lunging onto his back, knocking him to the ground where they wrestle like pups. Only they aren't pups anymore. Lying on the damp spring dirt, facing each other from inches away, Bessie stares into his pale eyes that turn down at the corners, fringed with eyelashes of no color. "I'm sorry," she says, kissing him softly.

"I know," he replies, kissing her back. Scrambling upright, he leans down and tugs her up beside him. "Make yourself useful. Go feed the wild kittens out behind the potting shed." He hands her the saucer and the pail of milk, or what's left of it.

"Kittens?" She fairly bursts with excitement. "Little baby kittens?"

"All kittens are babies, you silly." His voice is warm and teasing as they stroll together towards the small building in the far corner of the field.

Bessie-in-the-theatre wipes a tear from her eye. "One minute we were so close, the next we were fighting like cats and dogs."

Angel Mel decides to elaborate, "One minute he was your buddy, the next he was your boyfriend?"

Bessie grins. "You nailed it. As usual."

"I'll take that as a compliment. Do you want to have an intermission? That can be arranged."

She thinks about it for a moment. "No, let's keep going. So far so good."

So far so good. Ah, my sweet, brave girl.

CHAPTER 103: EARTH

This time when the MacIntyre and Moreno families sit around the table in the Ravenspond police station, Brian and Jane Wallet are also present. Chief of Detectives Leonora Cavish wastes no time. "We have a suspect." She sets down the enlarged photo of Terry Blacksmith.

"He looks just like Zac Frontenac." Sophia Moreno picks it up to examine it closer. "Ashley has a magazine about him. He's one of those young Hollywood movie stars," she explains as they watch her.

"Have any of your children ever mentioned this Terry person? Has Jason ever said anything in his previous phone calls? I know you haven't heard from him since he called from the gas station." Leonora pushes her wandering hair behind one ear. "No? Nothing about meeting this young guy, that he was going to go somewhere with him? Anything at all? Be sure, please. It's very important."

The Wallets look at each other, searching their memories, trying and failing to find a connection to the Terry person. Reluctantly, they shake their heads. "Sorry."

"He has a record?" Art MacIntyre looks up at the detective standing beside him in her charcoal pant suit. "What for?"

Leonora pushes her black-rimmed glasses back onto the bridge of her nose. "Armed robbery. Assault. Arrested for kidnapping and ..." Her voice quivers slightly. "Possible rape of a thirteen-year-old girl, but he was never charged."

Sophia's cry of anguish speaks for all of them. Quickly Jorge puts his arm around her as she collapses into his shoulder.

In the outer room, Leila lifts her head from her book while she sits waiting on a metal chair. The stout policeman in uniform gets up to offer her a chocolate from the open box on his desk.

The young girl looks at him for a moment before answering, "No, thank you." As he walks away, she buries her head in her book, biting her lip until it bleeds.

CHAPTER 104: HEAVEN

The melancholic voice of Chris Lisack fills the Past Lives theatre as Bessie and Angel Mel stare at the screen, mesmerized. Chris moans and groans in that moody, distinctive voice of his about the usual love betrayed, love lost, and hope extinguished. It's the kind of song that can make a person burst into tears on the sunniest of days.

Angel Mel gives Bessie a pat on the shoulder as they stare at the screen.

In the front seat of an old, brown, Oldsmobile sedan, a stiff-backed, fifteen-year-old Bessie sits beside a seventeen-year-old Jason. Out the open window, the hot summer morning is heavy with the buzz of mosquitoes, moths, and birds from the fields surrounding the dirt road where they are parked. They are on a rise of land in an empty field beyond which cows are grazing. The door of an abandoned barn gapes open. Plants are growing on the sagging roof where a row of crows perch, watching the world go by.

"So you're breaking up with me. Forever this time." Jason's voice drips tension. "You feel suffocated and you want to see the world."

"You're planning out my whole life for me!" Bessie explodes. "You're talking about building a house for us right in this very field. I'm only fifteen. I want to see the world, every square inch of it!"

"This was the parcel of my uncle Peter's land he left to me. He always said when we used to visit him before he died, this was the perfect spot for a man to put down his roots." His head jerks to stare out the side window, away from the field where his dream home stands proudly in his mind. Unable to endure the physical closeness a second longer, he pushes out the door and jumps out to stand in the early dawn, his long, bony arms wrapped around his middle.

In the vehicle, Bessie's eyes fill with tears as she watches him. "I can't do this anymore, Jas, I just can't." Slowly she climbs out her side of the car to stand apart from him, her childhood companion, dear to her heart, all the way from an outdoor skating rink at the tender age of eight until this moment.

He doesn't acknowledge her presence when, after minutes have passed, suddenly he rushes over, shaking her by both shoulders, hard. "I want to just kill you!" he shouts in her face. "I wish you were dead!"

On the stereo from the sedan, Chris Lisack's voice gasps one last time about the end of love before it mercifully dips and fades into silence.

CHAPTER 105: EARTH

"We caught up to your pal Dolby in Las Vegas." Eric Pederssen pulls up a chair across from Terry Blacksmith in the interrogation room, located only four miles from the Mavis & Jim Dew Drop Inn.

"Oh yeah? What did he have to say?" If Terry is surprised they found him so quickly, he doesn't let on.

"Says you would loan out your mother or your girl-friend for a gang bang before you would loan anybody your red pickup."

Terry leans back in his chair, laughing out loud. "Dolby said that? Son of a bitch." He goes to take a cigarette.

Eric slams his hand down hard on the blue Gitoine box. "Where's your truck?"

"Hey, you messed up my smokes." Terry glares at him. "You owe me a new pack. And they're hard to find. Imported from France. And very expensive, if you don't mind."

"Where's your truck?" Eric's hand stays put. "We can sit here all day. Where's your truck?"

Minutes go by with no reaction from either man. Terry glances over at the two-way glass, no doubt wondering who his audience is today. Finally he stares directly at Eric, mumbling under his breath, "Okay, here's what happened. I'm embarrassed about it and pissed off, that's the only reason I didn't tell you straight off."

"Tell me what?" Eric is in no mood for games.

"Got stolen."

"Stolen by whom? When and where?"

CHAPTER 106: HEAVEN

"We got along just fine until ..." Betsy munches on her caramel corn, leaning back in her seat in the Past Lives theatre.

"Until you hit puberty?" Angel Mel's voice is warm as he picks out a watermelon jelly bean and pops it in his mouth. "And, in fact, Jason being two years older than you, he got there first."

"You're pretty smart for an angel in a flowered shirt," she teases him.

"Careful, toots. I'm rather fond of these."

"As if I haven't noticed. So what's next?" She rubs her free hand on Mouser's coat.

"It's going to be like you're seeing this next part of the movie for the second time for a bit." He sips on his Hector's Nectar. "And that's because you did."

"Through the forbidden Telescope?"

"Not to mention the most sacred, gold computer in the extremely forbidden Hall of Akashic Records, my little mushroom." He gives her a playful poke. "Ready?"

"Ready, Eddie."

The now familiar scenes begin to flash on the screen before her eyes...

After the fight with Jason that morning, a furious Bessie lounges in her bedroom with Ash and Leila. Ashley is painting her sister's toe nails. Bessie snatches up every photo she ever had of him, tearing them into little shreds. Both Ash and her sister tease her about her on-off boyfriend, and Bessie tells them it's so over. He's such a know-it-all. And besides, she's got a brilliant idea for what they're going to do come morning.

The following dawn, Bessie sneaks out of her home to meet up with Ashley. After changing from their regular clothes into what they consider 'grown-up' gear in the park, and putting on the Nicole and Paris wigs, Ash paints their faces with over-the-top makeup. Quickly they stash their gear under a seat in the gazebo before heading out to the highway to hitch-hike. After all, they will only be gone for a few days, tops.

It doesn't take long until an elderly woman in a baby blue Buick gives them a ride and homemade cookies, to boot. Unbeknownst to them, Jason follows at a distance in his junk-yard Oldsmobile.

Three hours later, the old woman drops them off across the street from the rundown Sam & Lowell King Bros garage. They go inside. A nice black man shows them where the pop machine is before they head back to the highway.

Before long, a hot pink Volkswagen convertible beeps its horn at them. A blonde woman waves them over. In no time, they are sailing along the highway with the chatty Lorry-Lyn who intriguingly makes and sells her own brand of cosmetics, In the Pink by Lorry-Lyn. She takes them to her sister Joyce's home in Middlebridge. Joyce is her business partner, she explains. After lunch and sampling all the overly perfumed products, Lorry-Lyn takes them back to the highway. She is greatly surprised to recognize the non-descript sedan that has pulled over and offering the girls a ride. "He's okay," she yells across the road to them. "That's my ex-brother in law, Walt. Hi, Walt."

The tall man who speaks little takes them to his farmhouse twenty miles away where his wife, Flora, serves them a wonderful meal. They explain to the girls that their own daughter, Jean, had died in a tragic accident - a combination of drugs and driving the tractor into the creek. Since it's getting late, they offer the girls the use of their daughter's bedroom for the night. They gratefully accept.

It's eerie for Ash and Bessie, being in a dead girl's room. While they look at the deceased Jean's photos stuck to her mirror, the farmer's wife pops her head in to say they can wear her daughter's pajamas if they care to. They decline. In the middle of the night, it becomes even creepier with the wind howling and shutters banging. Without warning, the farmer pushes open their bedroom door. He's carrying a shotgun. In a mad panic, the girls scramble for their belongings, taking off in the storm in nothing but their underwear.

They find shelter in an abandoned barn at the neighboring farm for the rest of the night. By morning, when the sun comes out, it all seems like a giant laugh. A local fellow gives them a lift into town, dropping them off in front of Wallmarket. A smirking Ash holds up her mother's store card. Merrily, the girls skip their way inside.

Not long after, they are back on the road looking for their next ride, wearing brand-new Capri's, tee-shirts, and flip-flops.

The day goes by in a series of non-eventful rides. The girls gaze out the windows of various vehicles, taking in the new countryside.

By night-time, they are strolling along a highway, munching on egg-salad sandwiches from a vending machine. Ash wonders out loud where the hell they could be. Bessie explains *that right up ahead is a small hotel, The Sun Dial, she had looked up earlier on. When they get there, some of the neon letters are missing so that the sign spells:* TH SUN DIA.

Inside their room, which they have paid for with Bessie's aunt Fiona's credit card that she had left behind at the MacIntyre home on a recent visit, they are horrified by the grime and neglect. The toilet makes a constant running noise, unseen insects scurry, and the ugly, wind-up clock makes a wheezing ticka-ticka sound.

Unable to sleep, they decide to make a run for it in the middle of the night. But once they exit the room and begin walking along the sidewalk towards the lobby, they encounter three drunken men who make their lewd desires known. Do the young chicks want to screw a nice big rooster? Terrified, they race back to their room, jamming the dresser in front of the door.

In the morning, the hotel manager introduces them to another guest, Edith. She is a forty-plus, traveling saleswoman who sells drapes and bedspreads for commercial use. Since she is heading west, perhaps Edith would give the girls a ride?

A woman seems safe enough, so they decide to take her up on the offer. For a moment Bessie thinks she sees a glimpse of Jason, but later decides it was only her imagination.

The driver, Edith, appears ordinary enough. Exhausted from their night before, the girls doze off in the hot sunshine pouring in the windows of the old Chevy. They wake up to a lovely surprise. It seems the traveling saleswoman is treating them to a delectable Mexican breakfast at an outdoor makeshift restaurant she knows.

Now back in the car after their meal, the woman begins an odd conversation. She asks them if they are fornicators. Confused, Ash explains that, no, they are not foreign, but their parents are traveling in foreign countries. Bessie clues her friend in - Edith is asking her if she is sexually active.

Suddenly the car pulls into a parking lot of a cheap roadside motel and comes to a screeching halt. Edith's face contorts with aggression, as she reaches over to push the passenger door open, yelling at them to get out. Two fat, greasy-looking men stand in the driveway. One of them is making a sexual gesture. The other holds up a box of condoms.

"Run!" Bessie orders as they scramble to grab their belongings and get out of the vehicle. They run until they can run no further. One of them spots an abandoned refrigerator lying on its side. Quickly they crouch down to hide behind it until they see a furious Edith and her Chevy pass by, jerking the brake all the way.

Relieved at their narrow escape, they burst into hysterical giggles. This really is an adventure, to say the least. To pass the time, they play a game of spot the fairies, an old amusement taught to Bessie by her grandparents on road trips.

After awhile they hear the sound of an unhealthy engine. A pickup slows down alongside them, loaded down with Guatemalan migrant workers. In the bed of the truck, fifteen or so men and women sing songs while one plays a guitar. The man in the passenger seat leans out, smiling, to invite Bessie and Ash to hop aboard.

Why not, they wonder. After the near-disastrous experience with Edith, what else could possibly go wrong today? Laughing, they climb into the back of the truck and join in the fun. Soon Bessie and Ash teach them an old camp song they know, "Row, row, row your boat." Their hosts' Spanish version of the song is hilarious, to say the least.

Some hours later, the Guatemalans drop them off at Mavis & Jim Dew Drop Inn, a diner off the side of the highway. While enjoying a fine meal of ChocOnut bars and coffee, Ash spots an alluring young man using the phone at the back of the restaurant. In his tight black jeans, white tee-shirt, and tousled blonde-streaked hair, he looks very much like the hot, young Hollywood actor, Zac Frontenac. Ash is enthralled, especially when she over-hears him say he's heading into town. Begging for Bessie's approval, she saunters over to hint they are heading that way, too. Grinning at Mavis, the young man offers the giggling girls a lift.

While they gather up their things, the last thing Bessie expects to happen, happens. Jason walks in the door, much to her intense embarrassment and fury. Mortified, she yells at him to go home and milk the cows. Leave her alone and quit following them. As they stomp off outside, yakking a mile a minute, Jason watches them from the window, his eyes filled with sadness.

When the girls come back inside the diner to use the bathroom, Jason takes the opportunity to exit. But when he turns on the ignition in his rickety sedan, it won't start. Frantic, he spies the tarpaulin in the bed of the red truck. In a flash, he jumps in the back, while no one is looking. He looks around for a moment before yanking the tarp over his head.

Soon Ash and Bessie exit the diner with the handsome stranger. The young man gets in the driver's seat, Ash sits in the middle, and Bessie at the passenger door. They cruise along the highway, chatting to each other easily. He tells them his name is Harry Mercer. They explain they're from New York on vacation. They work in a travel agency and are seeing the world as part of their job. He turns on the stereo, playing some country and western, singing along with a tune about being in Folsom prison, a rather unsettling choice.

When he turns off the main highway with no warning onto a side road, Bessie and Ash begin to feel very nervous. "Is this a short cut?" Ash asks the man she knows as Harry, unable to disguise the anxiety in her voice.

In the theatre, Betsy moves in close to Angel Mel, her fear rising along with Ash's on the screen. The angel puts his arm around her, giving her a little squeeze. "Be brave. I know you're brave. Look at the way you defy Angel Rachel!"

"Yeah, but this is …"

"Real? Were you going to say real? Because being here with me and Mouser watching a movie is very real, don't you think? Every bit as real as anything on a movie screen, right?"

She gives him a weak smile. "You're right, as always."

"Well, not always, but I try."

CHAPTER 107: EARTH

"So you were giving some twelve-year-old kid a lift and got out to urinate somewhere against a tree, leaving your keys in the ignition. And this boy stole your truck, that's what you're telling me." Eric Pederssen's voice drips with acid.

Terry leans forward defensively. "Hey, my cousin Cindy-Ann, I taught her to drive when she was ten."

"I bet you taught your cousin Cindy-Ann a lot of things," Eric can't resist saying, although it's not relevant to the case. "I bet you even taught her how to smoke crack."

The young man's jaw tightens, but he says nothing.

"So where on the road were you when this underage boy made off with your vehicle?" The detective never takes his gaze from the face across from him.

Terry's eyes open wide as he looks towards the two-way glass. "How should I know? I wasn't exactly following a map."

Eric jumps on his words. "You weren't exactly following a map because, in fact, you knew exactly where you were going. Because you grew up here and you know every inch of this terrain." He leans forward, his hands on the table, palms down. "And that means, Mr. Blacksmith, you were heading somewhere very specific with ... not a twelve-year-old boy, but two teenage girls, namely Bessie MacIntyre and Ashley Moreno."

Terry fumbles for another cigarette, obviously stalling for time.

"I repeat, where was that very specific place, Mr. Blacksmith?"

CHAPTER 108: HEAVEN

A fearful Bessie in the Past Lives theatre jumps out of her seat, starting to run up the aisle to the exit, trailed by a barking Mouser. Close behind, Angel Mel reaches out to grab her shoulder gently. "The movie's almost over, I promise."

"I … I don't think …. I just can't watch anymore, Mel. I've got this terrible feeling … he … something …"

"Whatever it is, it's already happened, right?"

Bessie stops moving. "I suppose so."

"Matt Damon jumps out of a burning building—"

She grins, wiping away a tear. "And then he goes to the premiere with his beautiful wife or his best pal, Ben Affleck. It's only a movie. Okay, I get it." She turns and follows him back to her seat.

He hugs her for a moment before they sit back down. "It's just harder when it's your own movie. I get that, too." Soon they settle back into their seats. Angel Mel hands her a fresh bag of popcorn and a Hector's Nectar.

The red pickup cruises along a winding dirt road, heading up a sloping hillside. In the driver's seat, the guy who looks like Zac Frontenac drives with one hand, smoking a smelly, French cigarette with the other. His car keys display a pair of dice on a small chain.

"Harry, where are we going, anyways?" Bessie's voice trembles slightly. "Thought we were going right to the bus station."

"Oh, it's such a nice day, don't you want to see the countryside a bit before you go? Besides, I checked the schedule. Your bus doesn't leave for another few hours."

Ash speaks while looking at her friend. "You checked that before we left?"

"Well, yeah, course I did. Didn't want you to miss your important bus, did I?"

Bessie lets out a long breath. "So is this on the way?"

Harry takes his eyes from the road to smile enigmatically at his passengers. "We're almost there."

Without warning, he turns sharply onto a rough dirt road. Hardly a road, it's more like a trail. Bessie and Ash stare wide-eyed out the windows of the truck as the man they know as Harry Mercer steers up the rock-strewn path.

"You see?" He smiles broadly as he suddenly halts and turns off the engine. "Isn't she a beauty?"

In a small clearing, squats a one-room, wood-beamed cabin. Harry jumps out gleefully to run towards the door which he kicks open with a single bang.

Still inside the truck, Ash and Bessie huddle together, unsure of what to do. "We might as well get out." Ash decides finally. "We can always run away."

"And there are two of us and one of him," Bessie adds to bolster their confidence. "Come on." They scramble out and slowly head towards the open doorway just as Harry appears, grinning ear to ear.

"Man, I haven't seen this place in years! Sorry, ladies, for the spider webs and such." He's got an old cloth in his hand he's using to brush them away. "This is an old buddy of mine's cabin. He's long gone now. Come in. Make yourselves comfy."

Reluctantly the girls enter. Gazing around their surroundings, they see an old, single metal bed with a woolen blanket on it, full of holes.

Ash gives Bessie a poke. "Look. On the bed." On the quilt, a young girl's cheap blue purse gapes open. The metal hinges are rusted, and the plastic is fuzzy with grime.

Harry notices what has caught their attention and pipes up, "Oh, that old thing. My sister's girl left that there ages ago." He goes over, picks it up and tosses it in a garbage bin. Bessie feels a shiver go up her back.

In the kitchen area, the bare minimum of pots and pans hang from hooks above the counter. Mismatched dishes, mugs, and glasses sit in small stacks on a shelf beside the sink. In a box, a few knives, spoons, and forks lay in rows.

"Sit, sit!" Harry insists, brushing off two wooden chairs and setting them side by side. As Ash and Bessie slowly take seats, he heads into the kitchen, opening one cupboard after another. "Old Ray used to come up here to hunt, but mostly it was to get away from that mouthy bitch of a wife of his, Candy. Christ, that woman could talk your damn ear off. Well, lookee here!" He swings around to display his find - a dusty bottle of Mountain Jack whisky. "We got ourselves some hooch, little ladies."

Ash stands up. "We, ah, we don't actually drink, Harry. But thanks. I think we'd like to, ah, like, take a walk instead." Bessie quickly rises from her chair.

"*Sit your asses. Down.*" *His features turn dark and threatening. Once they do as he tells them, his face becomes all sunny again. "Now, that's better."*

When he turns his back to them, a terrified Ash and Bessie stare at the open door, thinking the same thing. Their muscles tense, ready to spring.

In a flash, Harry spins around. Before they can reach the opening, he flies to the door, slamming it shut with his foot. In his hands, he plays with a coil of rope.

In the Past Lives theatre in Heaven, Bessie lets out a chilling scream. Angel Mel wraps her in his arms. She clings to him. Mouser jumps out of his seat, running up and down the aisles, barking in distress.

CHAPTER 109: EARTH

In the interrogation room, Eric Pederssen the Spider knows he has Terrance Blacksmith the Fly cornered, right where he wants him. "I'll ask you again. Where is that specific place you were heading with the missing under-age girls?"

The handsome, baby-faced young man looks stony now. His fingers, brown with nicotine, play with the Gitoine pack. He decides to reply, finally. "I just wanted to show them the countryside since they had a couple hours to kill before their bus."

His use of the phrase "to kill" sends a chill down the detective's spine. "What time was their bus?"

"Forget the exact time now. Four or five, something like that."

"A bus to where?" Eric picks up something from his briefcase and lays it on the table. "Here is a copy of the local bus schedule. I'd like you to tell me what bus you were taking them to?"

Terry picks it up, still looking at the detective. "They said they were heading to San Francisco to see some singer, Chris Lisack. Yeah, that was it."

"Show me on that schedule where there was a bus leaving on the afternoon in question for San Francisco. Or for California, for that matter."

Still not looking at the brochure in his hands, Terry takes a deep breath but says nothing.

"Besides the fact that no call was made to the bus station from the diner that entire day." Eric feeds him more rope with which to hang himself. "And all your calls were made from the pay phone, as you apparently don't own a cell phone."

Terry sucks in his left cheek for a moment, an old nervous habit. He stretches up his neck from his tight, black tee-shirt. His Adam's apple pulsates. As he goes to pick up his cigarettes, Eric slides the pack out of reach.

The young man's eyes dart over to the two-way glass before he seems to come to some sort of decision. "Look, man," he says in a pleasant voice. "It was a nice day. The girls wanted to go for a ride. I just thought I'd swing by the cab ..."

The spider springs. "Bin?" He finishes the word for him. "You wanted to swing by the ca-bin? What ca-bin was that exactly?"

Terry's eyes squeeze half-closed to mere slits while beads of sweat break out on his tanned forehead. This time his voice is dead quiet. "I want to see a lawyer."

As the detective exits the room, the suspect, back to his belligerent persona, reaches over to snatch his cigarettes. He pulls one out, lights up, and blows a perfect smoke ring in the direction of the two-way mirror.

CHAPTER 110: HEAVEN

In the Past Lives theatre, Bessie's scream subsides into sobs as she stares through her tears at the screen. Angel Mel has his arm tightly around her while holding both her hands in one of his large ones.

The eyes of Bessie and Ash are saucer-wide with terror. Their hands are tied behind their backs, their feet at the ankles. Their bodies are secured at their waists to the chairs. Across their mouths, strips of duct tape are crudely stuck.

Harry is going through their bags. Suddenly he stands up, wearing the brunette Nicole Ritchie wig. "How do I look, ladies?" He prances about with a tall glass of whiskey in his hand. "Am I dashing?"

Now he heads back to the kitchen before pulling up another chair with one hand to sit directly in front of the terrified girls. Grinning, he pulls a large hunting knife from behind his back and lays it on his lap. "Sorry about the duct tape, ladies, but nothing bugs me more than the holler of a woman. My mama used to holler something crazy."

In the darkened theatre, Mouser begins to bark uncontrollably. He runs towards the front of the theatre as if he could attack the screen and stop what's happening on it.

Bessie buries her head in Angel Mel's great chest as he rocks her back and forth.

CHAPTER 111: EARTH

Eric Pederssen sits in his rental car outside the local police station. It's pouring rain in the late afternoon. Even the crashing percussion of Beethoven's *Fifth Symphony* playing full-blast doesn't wipe out his malaise. Reaching into the glove compartment, he removes a small silver flask.

As he takes a swig, he watches out the window. *Am I ever going to know what happened to those poor girls? How many victims has this bastard kidnapped all together, that smirking, psycho, son-of-a-bitch?* Eric takes another long drink. *How much longer can I stand this job, chasing the Terry Blacksmiths of the world? Most of them getting away with murder, day after day. The statistics were appalling. I wonder what Leonora is doing now? What's she wearing? Maybe she and I could...*

A sleek silver Audi pulling into the police station parking lot interrupts his thoughts. A black umbrella emerges first, followed by a stumpy man in an expensive suit. Terry's lawyer, no doubt.

Another vehicle, this time a rusty Suzuki truck, screeches to a halt. Terry's cousin, Cindy-Ann, jumps out the passenger door and runs towards the entrance in a nylon dress, flip-flops, and a magazine held over her thin hair.

"And so it begins," Eric mutters to no one. He takes another swig before sliding the flask back under a pile of papers in the glove compartment. Wearily he turns around to reach for the flimsy, drugstore umbrella lying on the back seat. But when he gets out of his car, he forgets to use it, walking instead the twenty feet or so to the door in the pouring rain.

CHAPTER 112: HEAVEN

"Take a deep breath," Angel Mel advises. "Take a long, deep breath. You're a strong girl, Bessie. And pretty soon you're going to feel so much better." Sitting beside her in the Past Lives theatre in Heaven, the angel reaches over to hug her in his great arms.

She looks up at him. "When it's all going to be over?"

"Hey, only the movie will be over. You'll still be here. And me. And Mouser. Don't forget that. You're here now, right?"

She lets out a big sigh. "I guess so."

"Guess so?" He tilts his head. "You guess you're here right now?"

"Okay, I know so. How's that?"

"Better. Much better."

"If I eat any more popcorn, I'm going to toss my cookies." She sets down her almost full container on the other side of Mouser.

"You mean you're going to toss your popcorn, don't you?"

"Oh, ha ha. Big ha ha." She smirks up at the angel.

"I aim to please."

With that, they turn their attention back to the screen where Bessie's life on Earth is relentlessly unfolding.

Harry heads back to the kitchen area to fetch a large metal pot. Bessie and Ash can barely turn their heads enough to see each other. Their eyes are black with fear. Ash's mascara runs creeklets down her cheeks and over the duct tape. Holding the pot by the handle from one hand, the knife in the other, Harry returns to his chair, facing them from inches away. His blue-jeaned knees touch Bessie's bare right knee and Ash's left.

"Now, ladies," he begins conversationally. "We can do this the easy way. Or the hard way." He runs the tip of the knife under Bessie's chin, then Ash's, as they struggle in vain to

avoid the sharp metal. "So which of you is going to prove your love for me first?" His eyes are like glass as he calmly flicks the knife from one nose to the other.

In a singsong voice, he whispers, "Eeny, meeny, miny, moe. Catch a girlie by her toe. If she hollers …" He stops to giggle. "Well, hell, you can't holler with that tape on there. Sorry about that, but you never know when some damn tourist is going to wander too close to your cave." His breath reeks of whiskey and cigarettes. Sweat stains ring his underarms. "Where was I? Oh yeah, eenie, meeny, miny, moe."

Suddenly, in her struggle to free herself, Bessie's head jerks forward. The blade gleams as it moves like lightening in his hand to strike her just above her left eye. "Don't ever do that again." His voice is freezer cold. "Or you'll really piss me off."

In the theatre Bessie's voice cries out in remembered pain as her trembling hand reaches up to touch the scar on the left side of her forehead. In the shape of a small bird.

CHAPTER 113: EARTH

Someone hands Eric Pederssen a paper towel to dry his face as he heads towards the interrogation room. Terry slouches beside his stubby lawyer, a John D. Fanshawe, according to his business card.

Where in the hell did he get the funds to hire a fancy lawyer? Someone in the outer room catches his eye as she emerges from the washroom. *Ah yes, Cindy-Ann, the meth addict. The one most likely to know where Terry hides his drug dealing stash.*

A tap on his shoulder makes him spin around. A policewoman in uniform hands him a slip of paper as she murmurs, "Here are all the shacks in the near proximity. He mentioned going up to a cabin, so we have highlighted the ones in the surrounding hills. There are eight. However ..." The lines around her eyes wrinkle. "Two of them are directly connected to Mr. Blacksmith in some way. One belongs to the father of his friend, Dolbert Campbell. One is owned by his relative by marriage, Jim Saunders of Mavis & Jim Dew Drop Inn."

"Good work, Helen." Eric's voice is encouraging. "Very good work."

"There are some other abandoned ones in the hills, but they've been there for years. We're trying to track down information on them, as well. So far nobody seems to know much about them. They're used for hunting, broken into by vagrants, and by anyone who claims them first."

"I'll ask for a search team on every last one of them," Eric tells her before he hurries off towards the Police Chief's office and shuts the door.

CHAPTER 114: HEAVEN

"At least you know, sweetheart, where you got the scar." In the Past Lives Theatre, as they turn away from the screen for a moment, Angel Mel's voice is filled with gentle love. "At least you know. And it doesn't hurt any more, does it?"

Bessie's hand returns from the scar to the shamrock broach which she clutches tightly. "No, it doesn't."

"And that's a good thing, right? Repeat after me."

"Yes, Mel, that's a good thing." Her voice is a pretty good imitation of his.

"In your next life, you should be an impersonator."

"Oh, Angel Rachel would love that idea."

"You'd be surprised. She's much more fun that you and your sidekick, Ashley, think."

They share a look. Bessie mocks. "Angel Rachel? Fun? Really?"

He nods his head. "Would I, an angel, lie to you? Yes, really. Now let's not miss this next bit." He gives her hand a squeeze.

Standing so close to the girls tied in the chairs they can smell his cigarette breath, Harry speaks in that singsong voice again, which is more unnerving than his cold, menacing one. He is explaining that he prefers water with his whiskey, as he swings his metal pot back and forth. "Just going to fill up this baby in the creek. Be back in a flash, don't worry your pretty little heads." With a wide grin he moves slowly towards the doorway, looking back at them the whole time. "No funny business, ladies." Satisfied they can't possibly escape, he disappears.

Blood trickles down Bessie's forehead into her left eye and she squeezes it shut. Realizing she can jump around a bit in her chair, she does. Ash follows suit.

The pain in Bessie's forehead is excruciating, but fear far outweighs the pain. They try and hop their chairs about some more. The minutes seem to be crawling by multiplied by a thousand with the sheer terror of Harry's imminent return, and what new torture that return will bring. In desperation, they hop and hop, hop and hop, in a frenzy to somehow free themselves, at least one of them. Suddenly Ash's chair lands on a piece of wood and she crashes over backwards, smashing her head on the floorboards and instantly going unconscious.

CHAPTER 115: EARTH

The Morenos, the MacIntyres, and the Wallets are gathered in the MacIntyre living-room in Ravenspond, huddled together for comfort as they await word. The female Chief of Detectives has assured them they will be informed the moment there is any news.

In the kitchen, Leila has the Wallet youngsters busily engaged in coloring pictures on expensive paper she has torn from her art pad. At the counter she makes peanut butter and strawberry jam sandwiches cut into four wedges. Miss Marple, the pup, happily chews on a child's sneaker under the table.

"No crusts," the Wallet girl announces. "We don't like crusts." The child whose name is Marie seems to speak for both of them.

"Okay, no crusts," Leila replies, taking up a small knife to slice off the offending brown edges of the white bread sandwiches, slicing her finger in the process. "Ouch!" Quickly she sucks her bleeding finger as the knife clangs onto the tile floor.

In the living-room, Heather twists her head around on the sofa where she sits squished in between her husband and Jorge Moreno. Hearing the commotion in the kitchen, she gets up to investigate. The others look at her for a moment before returning to stare at the collection of phones on the coffee table scattered amongst the hastily made and untouched snacks.

On entering the kitchen, Heather's eyes are drawn to the droplets of blood on the yellow tiles. And the flash of a blade lying nearby. She gasps for air like a drowning victim.

CHAPTER 116: EARTH

Eric Pederssen can't believe he's drinking the dreadful police station coffee, a habit he has refused so far in his career to pick up. Search parties have been organized, he has just been informed, and police cars are zooming up the hillsides. It's getting late, and due to the rain and cloud cover, they may have to resume in the morning.

Policewoman Helen Farr is standing by with the checklist of cabins ready to cross them off, one by one. Terry Blacksmith is being held without bail for twenty-four hours which is the best the judge can do without corroborating evidence. Currently they are checking for unpaid parking tickets or any other minor offences with which to hold him longer.

Terry gives Eric a sullen stare as he is being walked to the rear of the station and into a holding cell. His features are neither belligerent nor defeatist. Whatever Terry knows, it appears he feels confident they won't get him for it. And maybe they won't.

His emaciated and long suffering cousin awaits her ride by the police station door. Someone has given her a towel to dry off with and a blanket, as she was drenched to the skin when she arrived. And given the condition of her meth-addicted body, she would feel the cold faster than anyone. Cindy-Ann smokes one cigarette after another, menthols, judging by the ghastly odor that drifts occasionally in Eric's direction.

His phone rings and he pulls it out of his jacket pocket. He checks the number first. It's Leonora back in Ravenspond. No, he tells her, nothing yet. The search cars have just left to go to every cabin on the list, starting with Terry's uncle Jim. She's aware of the weather conditions they are facing. He asks about the families, knowing they are gathered together for strength. She tells him about Leila, how she's being the parent of them all, making sandwiches and entertaining the young children. Eric smiles, remarking he thinks she'll make a great detective one day. Or a writer of detective fiction, Leonora counters. They both know they are making chit-chat to ease the stress they are all feeling.

Wait, he tells her. Something is happening here. I'll call you right back. Swiftly he walks over to Helen Farr who is taking down a message on the phone. She hangs up and turns to him, as he leans over her desk. "That was the police car calling from Jim Saunders' cabin, the uncle by marriage. They've gone over it with a fine-toothed comb. No evidence anyone has been there in recent months."

"Seven left," Eric says and walks away to call Leonora back.

CHAPTER 117: HEAVEN

Huddled in her seat in the Past Lives Theatre, Bessie's head is buried in Angel Mel's chest, her hands over her ears, as if she could stop what is happening on the screen.

"I know how hard this is on you, sweet girl, but I promise you, there is a surprise plot twist in store for you."

She glares up at him with shock through her tears. "A surprise twist? This is the worst kind of death. The worst! And you talk like this is just one of your silly screenplays! How can you be so ... so lah-dee-dah about my cruel fate?"

He hugs her tight. "Hush, now. There is a good kind of surprise coming soon. Cross my heart. Please, for me, just take a look."

She can't comprehend how that can possibly be true after what she's learned, but decides to humor him, anyway.

Bessie struggles against the ropes pinning her to her chair. In vain, she tries to help an unconscious Ashley, lying limp, twisted and restrained, backwards on the floor. What can she do? What must she do?

A sudden knocking on the window catches her attention. She jumps her chair around enough to look. The face of Jason with a finger to his lips is the last thing she expects to see.

He looks around him in all directions before his face abruptly disappears. Moments later, he dashes through the open door. Swiftly he unties Bessie and rips off the duct-tape with a "Sorry sorry" knowing it hurts, but has to be done.

Turning his attention to Ashley, he unties her slumped body before lifting her gently and carrying her from the cabin, making a mad dash towards the red truck. Neither he nor Bessie notice Ashley's pink sandal as it slips from her foot, tumbling to the ground.

Bessie scrambles inside the vehicle first to assist Jason as he folds Ashley into the passenger seat. She whispers, "But how are we going to ... ?"

Jason jangles the keys with the two dice on it. "Found these in the ignition. Quick, close the door but quietly." He's all business and in charge.

As Harry emerges from the back of his cabin, swinging a full pot of water, he sees his truck disappearing down the dirt trail in a cloud of dust. Stunned, he screams at the sky, "What in the flaming, mother-fucking hell?"

Something catches his attention on the ground. He leans down to pick up a glitzy pink sandal. With the strength of a professional baseball player, he tosses it through the air where it crashes against the side of the cabin.

"Omigod, Mel, we escaped that bastard!" Bessie's voice in the theatre is filled with stunned relief. She leaps out of her seat, a movement that causes Mouser to follow suit.

"See? You see?" Angel Mel jumps in. "You never know what's right around the bend. Like I keep telling you, never assume … because …"

Bessie loves this one. "You make an ass of you and me."

"That's right, sweet girl, that's absolutely right. Now let's watch and see what happens next. Because you just never know."

CHAPTER 118: EARTH

"Damn this god-awful weather," Eric Pederssen tells policewoman Helen as they stare out the window of the station at sheets of rain. "And now it's almost dark."

The chunky little woman bites her bottom lip. "They're doing the best they can, sir."

"Oh, I know. Didn't mean to sound so cross. Sorry. It's just that we're that close now to nailing this bastard."

"We'll get him, sir. We'll get him."

A uniformed policeman rushes over. "Another report is coming in, sir."

The three of them head over to the speaker phone on the nearby desk, leaning down to hear better. A rattling of static emerges before a male voice announces, "Helen, are you there?"

"Yes, Frank, where are you?"

"Up west of the Fourth Concession Road, thirty-five minutes out of town."

"What'd you find?"

"We've cleared another two cabins. One has a hippie living in it full-time by the name of Sam Malachy, of no known address. Says he hasn't seen anybody for months. The other one, close to his, burnt down July First weekend, he tells us."

"Nice work. Can you keep searching in this storm? How are the roads up there?"

"Two of them are not drivable until dawn. The rest we can get to."

"You'll be rewarded in Heaven," Helen says, glancing over at the weary detective from Ravenspond, before she disconnects.

CHAPTER 119: HEAVEN

"Need a stretch?" Angel Mel stands up in the aisle of the Past Lives theatre, raising his arms over his head.

"Sure, why not?" Bessie joins him, twisting her torso left and right to get out the kinks. Mouser decides to climb out of his seat as well, running up and down the empty theatre.

"Ready to find out what happens next?" The angel in the Hawaiian shirt gives her an encouraging wink, sitting back in his seat.

"Guess so," Bessie is tentative. "Mouser," she calls the dog. "Movie time."

The truck careens around the bends of the road at a dangerous but necessary speed. No one speaks. From the glove compartment, a polka-dot bandana has evidently been retrieved which Bessie wears tied across her forehead. Seated in the middle, her arm around the still unconscious girl's shoulders, she looks over to see her dear friend is beginning to wake up. Ash's eyelids flicker open. Her lolling head lifts and slumps back against the seat.

Sneaking a glance at Jason, Bessie can see the fury in his features. The muscles in his arms and hands are as tightly coiled as a panther about to strike. She puts a finger gently on his wrist for a moment, but he doesn't respond.

An unholy scream unnerves them both as Ash stares wildly around her, her mouth gaping wide in terror. Jason almost loses control of the truck as he pulls off to the side and into a small grove, jerking on the hand brake. Running around to the passenger side, he yanks open the door. Together he and Bessie help the hysterical girl out of the truck and lay her gently on the grass.

Bessie lies down and wraps herself around the sobbing girl, cradling her like a child, as Jason sits down on the other side, stroking Ash's hair. It seems like her cries will never subside.

CHAPTER 120: EARTH

In the MacIntyre home, the Wallet children are sleeping soundly in the master bedroom. Leila has joined the adults huddling in the living-room. Everyone is dozing, collapsed onto each other, either on the sofa, or in one of the two armchairs. Or in Art's case, stretched out on the carpet with Miss Marple, the puppy.

Only Leila is wide awake, reading from her novel, *Appointment with the Devil*. Within reach, beside her on a small table, rests the home phone. She stares at it from time to time, unable to be absorbed in her book for more than a few pages at a time.

Suddenly it rings. All the adults in the room spring to an upright position. Quickly the young girl answers. "Yes, Detective Pederssen," she says. "It's Leila." She smiles for a moment at something Eric asks her. "Reading an Arabelle Smythe," she says. "But it's not very good. I guessed who did it from a third of the way through. Yes, everybody is here. I'll tell them what you say, word for word." She looks around at the anxious faces.

Their eyes are glued to the young girl as she listens intently. Her father begins to get up from the floor. Leila motions to him to stay put.

"There's a bad storm out there," she tells the room. "But they've managed to get to every cabin but two." She listens to the voice on the phone before adding, "And they will be setting off again at first light." She tunes into Eric for another few minutes. "Okay, I'll tell them. Bye." Hanging up the phone, she looks from one adult to another. "He says to tell you only another couple of hours, tops."

Another couple of hours might as well be another couple of years.

CHAPTER 121: HEAVEN

In the Past Lives Theatre, Angel Mel glances over at Bessie, calmer now that she has seen evidence on the screen that she and Ash actually escaped from the terrible cabin and that psychotic Harry, thanks to the sudden arrival of Jason. "Ready for the next scene, toots?"

She gives him a tentative smile, petting Mouser now back in his seat with his head in her lap. "Sure, okay."

Holding hands, Bessie and Angel Mel turn their eyes back to the screen.

The three of them - Bessie, Jason, and Ash - are still resting in the grove off the side of the road; the red truck not far away. Calm seems to have descended on the group. Pulling herself up to a standing position, Ash wanders off, carrying her one remaining shoe. "I'll look for some water."

"What's she going to put it in, I wonder?" Bessie grins at her disappearing figure.

Reaching over, Jason gently removes the bandana from Bessie's forehead. "Let's get a good look at this." He peers at the ugly gash before heading back into the bed of the truck for a few minutes, emerging from the tarp with a beaten-up box. "At least that creep was prepared," he says as he removes a first-aid kit. "Sit here." He motions to a large rock.

Bessie does as he requests while he gets down on his knees in front of her. Taking a cleansing pad from its packaging, he expertly cleans the wound.

"You'd make a great doctor," she teases, "If you weren't so damn stubborn about being a farmer."

He stops in his task for a moment to gaze intently into her eyes. "Maybe I shouldn't be so decided about everything. Maybe ... " He takes out a bottle of iodine and a square of sterile cloth. "This is going to hurt."

"Ooow," Bessie gasps as the red liquid touches her skin. "You're not kidding, it hurts."

"Okay, that part's over." He turns away to retrieve some antibiotic cream and squeezes the tube across the wound.

She can feel his breath on her face, he's so close to her. Reaching up her hand, she touches his cheek with one finger. "I'm so sorry for all of this."

"If I hadn't of been so pig-headed, talking about our future and building our house, and planning out your whole life for you when you're only … " He suspends a bandage in the air, "Only fifteen, maybe you wouldn't have wanted to run away like that. Hold still." He applies the cloth strip across her injury.

"Oh, I would have run away, anyways. Me and Ash, we're like gypsies." She reaches over to tug his hand. "Come here."

They crumble down to lay side by side on their backs, still holding hands, looking up at the blue sky. "This was all my idea, going to see Chris Lisack in concert." She adds, "Not because we had that fight. Well, maybe a little."

"Well, I've made a decision. I'm also going to go traveling, before I settle into the rest of my life." He turns his head to look at her. "Maybe with you and maybe on my own."

"And see every square inch of the whole world?" Her eyes are soft. "You mean it?"

"Yeah, I do. The farm will still be there when I get back."

"Or medical school."

He grins. "Or medical school. Or veterinary school. Or … "

"Law school."

"Never law school. Too much bullshit for me. But maybe … forestry."

"You could be a teacher. You'd be a wonderful teacher."

"Hmmm, teacher. Spent a lot of my life teaching you." It's his turn to tease. He turns on his side towards her. "How to milk cows. How to drive a tractor. How to do a swan dive in the pond."

"How to skate backwards." Bessie rolls over to face him also. "How to drive a motor boat."

"How to build a kite. Wait here." He gets up and wanders out of sight while Bessie lies on her back, facing the sky. Her hand goes up to touch the bandage, the wound obviously aching. Closing her eyes, she whispers, "I do love you, Jason."

Soon he returns, a grin on his face, his hands full of colorful wildflowers. Plopping back down beside her, he tickles her nose with a bloom before kissing her gently.

Her eyes pop open. "I'll never leave you like that again." Her voice trembles with emotion as a tear trickles down her cheek. "I promise."

He draws her to him. "Until next time," he whispers. "Until next time."

CHAPTER 122: EARTH

Clearly out of place in his tailored slacks and pin-striped shirt unbuttoned at the neck, Eric Pederssen sits in a booth by a grimy window in the local tavern. Outside, rain pelts the neon sign: THE LOST DOG. Willy Nelson drones on the jukebox, something about somebody always being on his mind. A mismatched couple lean against each other, wandering aimlessly around the dance floor, too drunk to do much else.

The barmaid is too long in the tooth to be wearing a low-cut, skin-tight top and short skirt, Eric muses. Her wrinkled, sun-damaged skin bulges at the neckline as she leans over to see if he wants another scotch. Her pierced earrings look like they're about to slice right through her earlobes, the holes looking more like slits. The fat under her upper arms wobbles as she sets down a bowl of peanuts.

"Refill?" She says, looking at him with bored curiosity. "You're not from around here."

"Sure." Eric ignores her other remark.

She waits a few minutes, hoping for more information. After all, he's the only available man in the joint, other than the rowdy group at the bar arguing loudly over some sporting event.

Eric nibbles on stale peanuts, looking out into the bleak night sky. A Chris Lisack tune begins to play and he is reminded of the posters in Bessie's bedroom. And then of Bessie herself, somewhere out there in this awful night.

CHAPTER 123: HEAVEN

"Hey, I know that song," Bessie in the Past Lives theatre is surprised to hear the beginnings of that old childhood round, "Row, row, row your boat," coming from the movie screen. "Ash and I even sing it here sometimes in Heaven."

"Of course you do. Because you used to sing it on Earth. A song you learned at camp."

Bessie looks over at the angel, pleased. "You know all about me, don't you?"

"I'm an angel," he boasts playfully. "Of course I do. Let's listen in, shall we?"

They both turn back to watch the screen.

Jason, Ash, and Bessie are back in the red truck, heading down the road at dusk. The sky is rosy with a sinking summer sun. They giggle as they sing the round, the tension broken from this long, traumatic day.

"Row, row, row your boat," Bessie pipes up. "Gently down the stream ... "

Ash begins her round. "Row, row, row your boat ... gently down the stream ... "

Now Jason's turn, "Row, row, row your boat ... gently down the stream ... "

They can hardly get out the next line; laughter filling the air. First Bessie: "Merrily, merrily, merrily, merrily...

Then Ash: "Merrily, merrily, merrily, merrily ... "

And finally Jason: "Merrily, merrily, merrily, merrily ... "

It's a while before their giggles subside enough for Bessie to get out the last line, "Life is ... but a ... dream."

Ash belts at the top of her lungs, "Life is ... but a ... dream."

When it's his turn, Jason's voice turns into a whisper. "Life is ... but a ... dream."

As Angel Mel's eyes fill with emotion, he watches Bessie as she sings wistfully along with the film. Her voice is full of longing, "Life is ... but a ... dream ...." She turns to look up at him. "Is that really true, Mel? I remember Ash and I thinking this one time, when we were singing that song on our way to the airport..." She stops, realizing it was a prohibited, middle-of-the-night walk, then continues. "If life is but a dream then reality must be Heaven? Is that just an expression? Or is it... the way it is?"

Instead of answering, he tosses a jellybean in her direction. "What do you think, my little mushroom?"

CHAPTER 124: EARTH

Outside the windows of the MacIntyre home, early morning light pours in. Adults wander about with cups of coffee. A child cries. A small dog barks and runs in circles. In the kitchen, Heather makes toast and sets it on plates where it remains uneaten. A young Ethan Wallet sits at the table, slurping a glass of orange juice. Finally Marie stops whining and reaches for a slice, demanding the lady put some jam on it for her.

"Say please," her brother tells her. "Say please or I'm telling on you."

Heather picks up the toast to spread a generous amount of jam on it, and hands it back to the little girl. Marie smiles sheepishly before saying, "Thank you."

Only Leila remains beside the phone in the living-room, willing it to ring. When it does, she almost jumps in fright, tossing her book from her lap to jump to her feet. The doorway to the kitchen fills with adults squished together as she answers it.

There's no chat about murder mysteries this time. Leila listens for a few minutes before turning to face them. "They've found the right cabin. Outside was one of Ash's shoes."

Unable to face the sobbing Sophia Moreno, the young girl turns away as she listens intently to the voice of the detective. "Yes, I understand. Yes, I will tell them. Goodbye." Hanging up, she turns around again. "He wants you to know he's very hopeful they will be found very soon." Seeing the dread on their faces, she quickly adds, "Alive. Found alive. And ..."

Her parents crowd around her. Miss Marple begins barking. "And what?" Art demands. "And what?"

"He thinks Jason is with them."

Everyone's faces brighten. "Jason?" Brian Wallet almost smiles. "He's with them?"

"He thinks so," Leila cautions them. "They found a cotton handkerchief at the site with a J embroidered on it."

Jason's mother jumps in. "Oh, my goodness. That would be Jason's alright. He doesn't like the paper ones, you see. I sew them for him. Old fashioned, I know, but—"

"A forensic team is heading to the cabin right now." Leila explains to them as if they were the children. "They will test everything for DNA."

"Still, they'll be safe if Jason is with them," Jorge speaks with conviction, hugging his wife. "Safe."

"And they'll be home soon," Art adds, "Real soon."

CHAPTER 125: HEAVEN

"Mel, I'm so confused now." Bessie squirms in her seat at the Past Lives Theatre. "Jason isn't a bad guy, after all. He saved us ... from a fate worse than death." Her fingers play with her shamrock broach.

"I hate that expression, a fate worse than death. Death is a very pleasant transition from one dimension to another."

"Like the butterfly leaving the cocoon." Bessie relaxes back into her chair, petting Mouser who has raised his head. "But ... if we escaped, then why are we ..."

"Shsh," he hushes her. "We're going to miss the most important part."

The sound of the truck's engine draws their eyes back to the screen.

The horizon is crimson now as the sun begins its descent below a distant hill. "Where are we, anyways?" Bessie stares around. "It all looks the same."

"We're not in that cabin," Ash declares. "And other than that, who cares? Hey, I'm starving." She pops open the glove compartment. "ChocOnut bars." Pulling out three of the miniature-sized bars, she reaches over to hand one to Jason, then Bessie, keeping one for herself.

Quietly Jason says, "We're on our way home, that's where we are." He pats Bessie's hand for a moment.

A half a mile ahead, a magnificent buck emerges from the shadows of a wood to munch on grass on the side of the road.

"Yuck. This tastes stale," Ash complains. "But soon we'll be eating tacos."

"And hotdogs and fries," Bessie pipes up from the middle.

"And lemon meringue pie," Jason adds. "Homemade."

The buck lifts his head, his antlers glorious in the evening light, sniffing the air.

"Macaroni and cheese." Ash stares out the window. "With ketchup."

"Apple pie," Jason says as he maneuvers the truck around a long curve. "With cheddar."

"No, with ice-cream," Bessie counters him. "My pie is gonna have ice-cream."

The buck ambles out into the middle of the road, moments before the stolen red pickup appears around the bend.

"JASON!" Bessie screams as he slams on the brakes. Without knowing she's doing it, her hand grasps onto the steering wheel, yanking it away from him.

Out of control now, the truck careens crazily back and forth across the road, before flying over the edge of the cliff. Horrific screams echo in the sweet, summer sunset sky.

Now safely across the road, the buck begins to chew on more grass.

All that can be seen in the stillness of the evening are the wildflowers Jason picked for Bessie less half an hour before, floating in the air like butterflies.

CHAPTER 126: EARTH

Outside the MacIntyre home, a police cruiser drives quietly into the driveway. Judging by the light, morning is in full swing. A light rain drizzles on neglected plants.

Leila peeks out the living-room curtains, the only one aware of the event. The others are busy freshening up, amusing the Wallet children, cleaning up dishes, drinking cold coffee, and whatever mundane occupations they can think of to keep themselves mindless.

The young girl opens the door before Leonora has a chance to ring it. The look on the detective's face is grim. She pushes a strand of hair from her face.

Art stops feeding treats to Miss Marple. Heather takes her hands out of the dish water. Sophia gets up from the sofa, a hair brush dangling from one hand. Jorge looks up from his Spanish magazine. Jane Wallet yanks a tee-shirt over her son's head before standing. Her husband, Brian, appears on the stairs in a bathrobe, rubbing wet hair with a towel.

They gather to huddle in the living-room, awaiting whatever news the woman detective has brought them. Husbands and wives hold hands. Even the toddlers are still. Only the puppy runs around their feet.

Leila notices that the policewoman's jacket is buttoned improperly. Her usually immaculately brushed bob is lank. Her chiseled features are bare of make-up. Her pale eyes look from one to the other, as if begging them for forgiveness, for what she is about to say.

"Detective?" Art prompts her.

Finally she speaks. "We've found them."

CHAPTER 127: HEAVEN

In the Past Lives theatre, Bessie's sobs are smothered in the great chest of Angel Mel. "There, there," he says, "There, there."

Mouser moans from his own seat, upset with all the emotion he can hear but not understand. He nuzzles up to the weeping girl as best he can, shoving his nose under her arm and wiggling it.

"But you know, my sweet, the story doesn't end there."

Bessie lifts her head. "It *doesn't*? That's not possible!"

"Oh, but the best part is yet to come." His smile is enigmatic. "I know this has been a very painful movie to watch, but you have to trust me, dear girl. Please just trust me."

Eventually Bessie gains the courage to look back at the screen.

It's moonlight. The sound of trickling water is inexplicably pleasing. Bessie lies in a shallow riverbed. She's on her back, her limbs splayed outwards. Away from her about sixty feet, crushed and broken, the red truck is tossed upside down like an empty fast-food container. There's no sign of Jason or Ash anywhere.

As water splashes her body, a paler, incandescent version of herself drifts from the top of her head to stand beside her physical self, gazing around the river bed with a bewildered look.

Her spirit body reacts to a voice that is speaking to her in gentle tones, saying, "Bessie, what on Earth am I going to do with you?"

Her spirit eyelids flicker open. Above her, a huge, bald personage floats in the air, wearing a loud Hawaiian shirt. He extends a hand to her spirit body. She gazes at him, unsure for a moment.

He smiles and whispers, "Come." Her spirit body looks around at the carnage one last time. She reaches up and takes his huge hand. Wrapping her in his giant wings, they take flight.

In the theatre Bessie leaps out of her seat. "*You*? You're my guardian angel?"

"Well, dah." Angel Mel grins. "Took you long enough."

"And we really did ... come home. Home to Heaven!"

"Oh, we're not finished yet." His smile is mischievous. "Come with me." He pulls her out of her seat as the curtains close in the darkened theatre. "Mouser," he calls to the dog. "You, too."

The trio makes their way from the lobby and into the parking lot outside.

To her intense surprise, Bessie sees a small gathering, evidently waiting for them. Ash leans on Miguelito, Aunt Fizz stands with Jason and his uncle Peter. Angel Jigjag in his colorful caftan chats to Angel Rachel in one of her smart power suits. And Angel Rainbow Sunshine, mercifully, is not playing the guitar slung around her neck. Her St. Bernard saunters over for a greet-and-sniff with Mouser.

Holding tightly onto Angel Mel's hand, Bessie strolls hesitantly towards them. First she puts her arms around Ash, hugging her close and rocking her back and forth. Releasing her, she moves to fall into Jason's open arms.

Tears flow down his lean face as he whispers, "I'm so sorry, Bessie. I'm so very sorry. It was all my fault."

She pulls back from him. "*Your* fault? I'm the one who grabbed the wheel!"

"It was no one's fault," Angel Rachel intervenes. "It was one of life's unexpected mysteries."

Bessie moves towards her aunt's embrace. "Like Aunt Fizz having an aneurism."

"Exactly."

Bessie stands back to gaze from one to the other. "And now we're all here together in Heaven. And nothing can ever keep us apart again."

Her joy transforms into confusion as she turns to look at Angel Mel. "But how come, Ash and I, we didn't know how we died when everybody else here does?"

Inexplicably Ash turns away to clear her throat. Bessie stares at her best friend, wondering what is going on. No one else offers an explanation, watching her too kindly for some strange reason. Not even Angel Mel comes to her aid.

Slowly the truth dawns on her. Rushing over to shake Ash by the shoulders, she shouts, "You knew! You knew all along about the accident, didn't you? You knew everything!"

Sheepishly Ash looks at her dearest friend. "Well, ah, maybe, like, ah …"

"Spit it out." Bessie's eyes are flashing. "You knew and—"

"Okay, yes, I knew all along. I just pretended I didn't know. I was being an … actress."

Angel Mel jumps in. "And a very good one, I might add."

Ash can't keep the pride from her voice. "You never guessed, Bess. Like, not even once."

"But why?" Bessie's bewilderment is palpable. "Why would you do that?"

"I wanted to stay with you." Ash's voice is soft. "And Angel Mel said I could. As long as … as long as, like … I didn't spill the beans."

Jason moves to wrap his arms around Bessie as she repeats, "Stay with me?"

"She'll make a wonderful actress in her next life, won't she, my little mushroom," Angel Mel says firmly. "She did this all for you. Remember all those times you returned to the Earth dimension?" He continues with a nod, "But Ash never quite managed to go with you? That's because she couldn't. That was part of our agreement."

Ash's teary eyes stare intently into Bessie's. "I just wanted to be with you for as long as I could. Forgive me?"

"Forgive you?" As Bessie looks around, still held in Jason's arms, she can sense she's the only one who doesn't comprehend the situation.

"Bessie, please don't ever forget me, promise me." Jason's voice trembles with pain. "I will love you, forever and always."

She stares up into his pale eyes, confused all over again. "I promise. But why would I ever forget you?"

He pulls her tightly into his chest, cradling the back of her hair in his hand. With his other one, he strokes her back. She can feel his sobs shaking his body.

Pulling back a little, she tries to soothe him. "Jas, it's okay. We're back together now. I'm here. Stop looking so sad. Everything is fine now. Hush." She gives him a soft kiss. "We can go for long walks. And watch the cows recycle. And catch movies. And be together like we were always meant to be."

Mouser begins to make an odd moaning sound. Fiona leans down to cuddle him.

A very faint voice reaches her ears, calling her name, over and over. "Bessie … Bessie … Bessie …" It's familiar somehow but she can't quite recognize it. The voice grows stronger. "Bessie … Bessie … Bessie …"

Miguelito moves quickly to wrap his arms around Ash and squeeze her as she begins to weep.

Bessie can feel herself floating, drifting upwards and away from Jason's arms. His uncle Peter moves to grab the sobbing Jason just before he crumbles to the ground.

Bessie continues to float as she listens to the lovely voice, calling her, over and over. And then it hits her. Whose voice it is.

Her sister, Leila....

CHAPTER 128: EARTH

Bessie's spirit body reappears, floating on a ceiling in a white room, staring downwards. Beneath her, she can see her own face sleeping on a pillow, a bandage on her forehead over her left eye. Her sister Leila holds her hand, pleading, "Bessie ... Bessie ..."

Now Bessie's spirit body is drawn by a powerful energy towards her physical version. It re-enters through the top of her head and disappears from sight to become one.

Bessie's eyes pop open. Realizing she's lying down in a bed, she looks around, bewildered. Leila still holds her hand, a fistful of wildflowers dangling in her other one.

"Bessie," Leila calls her. "You're awake! She's awake." Her grinning face darts around the room. Bessie's eyes follow suit.

Her mother sobs into the shoulder of Art before rushing over. "Oh, my darling girl, we thought we had lost you forever!" Heather can hardly get the words out.

"Well, aren't you a sight for sore eyes! Weren't sure you would make it out of that operation. And then you went into a coma." Her dad busses her cheek. "Now here you are!"

Bessie stares into her father's eyes, inches away. "But where's Ash? Where's Jason? They were here just ... just a second ago ...."

Her father's pleading eyes look over at his wife, now sitting on the hospital bed.

"They didn't make it, honey." Heather's voice is stronger now. She knows what she says must last her daughter's lifetime. "Ash ... she died instantly. No pain, the detective assured us." Holding both of Bessie's hands, she continues, "Jason lingered for quite awhile. Eventually he succumbed to his injuries." She takes her daughter in her arms as Bessie weeps on her bosom like a small child. "When they found you, they thought you were gone, too, but they got you breathing again in the ambulance.

They didn't think you would make it, but here you are." She pulls back to look deeply into her daughter's weeping eyes. Heather's smile is wide and filled with joy. "Thank the good Lord."

"Look what I found for you, Bess." Leila takes something from her pocket. It's Grandma Millie's shamrock broach. Carefully she pins it on her sister's hospital gown.

In the doorway a nurse pops her head in. "Okay, everyone, Bessie needs her rest now." The hefty black woman in green scrubs marches in, picking up the small bouquet of wildflowers tied with a string from the spread. Opening up the bedside table, she takes out a slim glass vase. "Always keep a spare one in here, just for occasions like this." Her voice is rich and cheerful as she heads to the bathroom.

Bessie can hear the tap running. Soon the nurse returns to set the vase on the table. "There," she announces, giving the visitors the eye. "Now scoot."

Art, Heather, and Leila are evidently familiar with the woman and know better than to cross her. With big smiles on their faces, they send air kisses to the patient and disappear from the room ahead of the nurse. "Have a nice snooze, honey." The woman's voice softens. "You've been through a huge ordeal."

The door closes quietly. Bessie lies back on her pillow, fingering the gaudy shamrock pinned to her gown. It seems to glow with an energy all of its own.

Suddenly the door pops opens again and her father's grinning face appears. "Remember your mother's cousin, John, in Ireland? And his nutcase wife, Maureen? They visited us about three years back? Well, you won't believe it, but after fifteen years of a childless marriage, they've got themselves a set of fraternal twins! A boy and a girl. Most rambunctious kids you ever saw, he says."

The door closes only to open again. Snickering, Art adds, "Says he reminds them of his uncle Will and aunt Millie. Isn't that the craziest thing you ever heard of in your whole life? Okay, have a nice nap, sweetie." His face disappears.

Bessie, all alone now, looks around her. Was she dreaming? All that weird stuff about angels and flights to Heaven and Angel Court and a shop with body images in a mall? Being with Jason and Ash even though…

A whirring sound reaches her ears. She turns her head to stare at the bedside table where delicate blooms of buttercups, daisies, black-eyed Susan's, and Queen Anne's lace are waving wildly in the air, all by themselves.

She stares at them for the longest time, listening to the odd whirring sound. The flowers dip and dance as if a strong breeze were in the room. Yet the air around them is perfectly still.

A hazy memory fills her mind. It is of an Angel Serena, on the Earth Portal, trying to coax the last remaining reincarnating soul to be brave enough to live his new life. Slowly her eyelids close…

The words of the little aura tumble out around his sobs. "I … I … I've changed my mind. I … . I … don't want to be re … reborn. I want to … to stay in Heaven."

The angel crouches down to his level. "Sweet one, I know you love Heaven. Goodness, everyone does. What's not to like? But now it's time for you to live a little. Experience a brand new adventure. Learn new things. Expand your horizons." Stroking his head ever so gently, she continues, "I am Angel Serena, your guardian angel. And I promise you, I will stay with you every moment of your new life." She holds him back so he could look up into her smiling face. "I will be your little piece of Heaven on Earth."

The sniffling stops for a moment. "You … you promise? You'll stay with me? All the way?"

"Every precious moment." She gives him an encouraging smile. "But after you're born, you won't be able to see me like you can right now. But I'll still be there. Always. Promise. Cross my heart." She hugs him to her chest. "Hush now, little one, and I'll show you a special surprise. Close your eyes tight. Really, really tight. No peeking."

Angel Serena rises to her full impressive height. Her wings materialize in a glory of radiance. "Keep your peepers closed, remember."

"I promise."

The angel flutters her wings vigorously. A whirring sound fills the air. "Can you feel that? That little breeze?"

Suddenly the aura jumps up and down. "I can feel it, I can feel it!"

Serena grins, still fluttering. "So now, listen carefully. Whenever you need me, in your whole life, you just have to close your eyes … " She flaps her wings even stronger for effect. "And you will feel that little breeze. And you will know that I am with you." For a few more moments she continues to flutter in silence. "Now open your eyes."

The aura gazes up at her in awe as the wing motion continues.

"You see? That little breeze you feel? It's me!" So whenever you feel that sensation and there's no wind around, you will know in your heart of hearts, that it's me. And I, your guardian angel, am with you. Always. Every step, every breath."

Bessie's eyes pop open. Realizing she is still in her hospital bed, she stares at the wildflowers moving of their own accord, around and around. At last, she lays her head back down on the pillow, closing her eyes. Tears trickle down her cheeks as, emotional but accepting, her lips form the words, "Angel Mel."

~ **THE END** ~

AUTHOR'S BIOGRAPHY

Jody Overend is the author of *UpHill*, a middle-aged romantic comedy published by Eirelander Publishing, U.S.A. You can visit her website at: jodyoverend.com or on Facebook. To learn more about *Bessie: Lost & Found*, be sure and drop by Bessie's own Facebook page, coming soon.

And if you're wondering if there will be a sequel to Bessie's tale, well, you'll just have to wait and see ...

AFTERWARD: A MESSAGE FROM THE OTHER SIDE

Souls' dreams are never lost; they always come true. It may take many, many years, but you always get what you want. Never lose your dreams. Never.

Every soul can have Heaven on Earth if they stay positive and trust. There are no bad things in your life – only learning lessons. We can all have that if we trust what we receive from our loved ones on the Other Side. They have never left us. They are just in another world we call Heaven.

I passed away from my Earthly life in 1902. This year, 2012, my dream came true.

Julie Ré alds (via Joanne Sicard)

ACKNOWLEDGEMENTS:

Goldie Hawn

Clark Gable

Frank Sinatra

John Kennedy Jr.

Carolyn Bessette Kennedy

Janis Joplin

John Belushi

Uday and Gusay Hussein

Kathryn Hepburn

Spencer Tracy

Alfred Hitchcock

Carole Lombard

Cary Grant

Clint Eastwood

Kevin Kostner

Harry Potter

Humphrey Bogart

Ingrid Bergman

Nancy Drew

Lady Diana

Dodi Al Fayed

Honda

Ford Focus

Kurt Cobain

Madonna

Singer sewing machine

Internet Explorer

Google

Lauren Bessette

Jayne Mansfield

Nicole Richie

Paris Hilton

Johnny Cash

June Carter Cash

Gucci

Louis Vuitton

American Tourister

Bruce Willis

Grace Kelly

John Wayne

Honda Civic

Hiawatha

Marlene Dietrich

Ricky Nelson

Buick Le Sabre

Ford

Oldsmobile

Chevrolet

Reece Witherspoon

Matt Damon

Richard Burton

Roy Orbison

Winston Churchill

Martin Luther King Jr.

Volkswagen

Jimmy Stewart

Dennis Hopper

Jackie Kennedy Onassis

Lana Turner

Lucille Ball

Desi Arnaz

Bobby Darin

President Kennedy

Paul Newman

Elvis Presley

Lindsay Lohan

Elizabeth Taylor

Farrah Fawcett

Scarlett O'Hara

Vivien Leigh

John Lennon

Judy Garland

Dorothy Gale

John Candy

Julie Andrews

Audrey Hepburn

BMW

iPod

Waring and Gallows

George Burns

Gracie Allen

Jack Benny

Coen brothers

John Denver

Greta Garbo

Steve McQueen

Johnny Carson

Rock Hudson

Ed McMahon

Sir Lawrence Olivier

Miss Marple

Agatha Christie

Chevrolet Impala

Ford

Suzuki

Songs/Music:

"San Francisco (Be sure to wear some Flowers in your Hair)" by
 Scott McKenzie performed by the Mamas and the Papas

"Mercedes Benz" by Janis Joplin. Michael McClure, Bob Neuwirth

"New York, New York" by Leonard Bernstein. Betty Comden,
 Adolph Green, performed by Frank Sinatra

"Close to You" by The Carpenters

"The Wayward Wind" by Gogi Grant performed by Patsy Cline

"Carmen" opera by Georges Bizet

"Big Yellow Taxi" by Joni Mitchell

"So Long Marianne" by Leonard Cohen

"Splish Splash" by Bobby Darin

"Don't be Cruel" by Otis Blackwell performed by Elvis Presley

"MacArthur Park" by Jimmy Webb

"Eduardo y Cristina" opera by Rossini

"Don't Cry for me Argentina" by Andrew Lloyd Webber

"Don't Think Twice, It's Alright" by Bob Dylan

"You Fill up my Senses" by John Denver

"Folsom Prison Blues" by Johnny Cash

"La Bohème" opera by Puccini

"Lullaby for Cello and Piano" by Johannes Brahms

"Someone's Crying" by Chris Isaak

"Beethoven's Fifth Symphony" by Beethoven

"Always on my mind" by Johnny Christopher, Mark James, Wayne Carson, performed by Willie Nelson

Films and Television:
Psycho
Waterworld
Seinfeld
Gone with the Wind
The Sound of Music
Planes, Trains, and Automobiles
The Golden Girls
Rebecca
Mama Mia
Casablanca
Gaslight

CPSIA information can be obtained at www.ICGtesting.com
Printed in the USA
LVOW13s0123210214

374569LV00001B/19/P